The

Dallas Women's Gu...

to Gold-Digging with Pri...

The

Dallas
Women's Guide

to Gold-Digging with Pride

A NOVEL

J. C. Conklin

BALLANTINE BOOKS
NEW YORK

Published in the United States by Ballantine Books,
an imprint of The Random House Publishing Group,
a division of Random House, Inc., New York.

BALLANTINE and colophon are registered trademarks
of Random House, Inc.

ISBN 978-0-345-49294-4

LIBRARY OF CONGRESS CATALOGING-IN-PUBLICATION DATA

Conklin, J. C. (Jennifer Beth)
The Dallas women's guide to gold-digging with pride /
by J. C. Conklin.
p.   cm
ISBN-13: 978-0-345-49294-4
ISBN-10: 0-345-49294-3
ISBN-13: 978-0-345-49295-1
1. Mate selection—Fiction.   2. Rich people—Fiction.
3. Dallas (Tex.)—Fiction   I. Title.

PS3603.O534D35 2007
813'.6—dc22   2006036133

Printed in the United States of America on acid-free paper

www.ballantinebooks.com

2 4 6 8 9 7 5 3 1

First Edition

Book design by Katie Shaw

*This book is dedicated to Kim Ross, who insists
like many Texans that he is sixth generation Texan
(I'm pretty sure he's fourth generation), reaffirming Texans'
genetic predisposition to exaggeration. Thank you for
reading my drafts and zealously promoting my work
to every friend, colleague, and stranger met!*

Acknowledgments

Many thanks to friends who didn't laugh when I said I was writing a novel. I can't express my appreciation for my agent, Kathy Anderson, who encouraged me through years of drafts. Thank you to all the wonderful people at Ballantine: Allison Dickens, Jill Schwartzman, Libby McGuire, and Nancy Miller. Your creativity and patience were crucial. Thanks to fate, which laughed at me when I said I'd never live in Texas. Thanks to my son, Columbus, for being my son.

This is it, where my life took a ninety-degree turn toward shallow, drove as fast as it could toward mediocrity, and swerved away a second before I became another statistic. There are 257 trophy wives in the greater Dallas area.

The
Dallas
Women's Guide
to Gold-Digging with Pride

Chapter One

Never Directly Engage a Man You're Interested In

My face isn't tingly. In fact, everything feels quite normal, which isn't normal, considering I just paid six hundred dollars for several shots of Botox, a deadly toxin, to be injected into my crow's-feet—my infant crow's-feet that I didn't even notice until my friend Aimee pointed them out to me at lunch a month ago. I immediately became obsessed with them. Every time I looked into the mirror they seemed to be furrowing deeper and longer into my face. Soon I'd be looking like Barbara Bush on a bad day.

Aimee is my age, twenty-nine, but she shows no signs of age because she's done all the procedures—Botox, microderm, the blue face peel. Her skin looks airbrushed. She is unnaturally smooth. It's like she has never smiled, frowned, or had contact with the sun.

"I'm not supposed to try to squint or lie down for six hours, right?" I ask Aimee as I brush my fingers over my temples, feeling where the needles went in. I wonder what will happen if I squeeze the holes like a zit. Will deadly toxic puss shoot out and hit my mirror?

"That's right, honey. You don't want toxic mold spreading around."

Aimee pushes down my hands, then sips her chocolate martini and scans the room. We're at Beaux Nash. In Dallas, this place is a gold mine. It's brimming with trial lawyers, lobbyists, oil execs, techie sellouts (when the selling was good), and other men of leisure, meaning men with a net worth of ten million dollars or more.

It's not as sexy as it sounds. For one thing, the place smells like old men, cigars, and shoe polish. A massive mahogany bar and green leather booths crowd the room. A huge glass vat of soaking pineapples with a spout overwhelms the bar. How much demand is there for pineapple juice at a place like Beaux Nash anyway? Yes, I'll have a twenty-year-old Scotch and a side of pineapple juice? The best part of the place, aside from the rich men, is the fresh potato chips, right out of the fryer. It's impossible to resist wolfing down a whole basket of them, especially if you've been caught in the open on one of those Nazi-like no-carb diets.

We are husband-hunting. If you're a Northerner by birth, like me, this is something you don't quite understand about the South—people get married early and often, and for women it's still quite acceptable to husband-hunt as a profession. Most of the Southern women I know spent twenty thousand dollars on their debutante dresses (Vera Wangs and Escadas), vowing to wear them again when they walk down the aisle. But they never do, of course. By the time the wedding comes around, they say the dresses are old-fashioned and out-of-date, come to think of it, like most of their marriages after a couple of years.

The point is, in high school they were already unabashedly planning the perfect wedding, calculating it would happen in three to five years. In high school, I was convinced I'd never get hitched. I held on to that belief through college and for several years afterward. But the longer you're in the South, the ideas of marriage and regular churchgoing don't seem so abhorrent, more like benign details that give the South its quaint character the same way floral wallpaper, Laura Ashley pink duvet covers, and rusty water faucets give atmosphere to local bed-and-breakfasts. Here, in the land of conspicuous consumption, marriage isn't considered a life-long commitment. It's the ultimate accessory. Your husband is someone whose name you can slip into conversations. He's a reliable date, gift-giver, and someday car-pool-sharer. He's not really your companion, because most married people I know have dinner with a collection of their same-sex friends. Men eat together at steak houses. Women lunch at sushi spots. A husband is like a Hermès bag or a Chanel coat, a good investment that will mature over time. If he no longer fits, you can trade up to a more luxurious model.

There is no shame—and some would say there is honor—in divorcing once, twice, three, or more times. There are starter marriages. Children unions. Second-house-in-Aspen matrimonies. Private-plane collaborations. Many women view multiple marriages as promotions to better stations in life. One particularly ambitious woman divorced her politician husband because he was a Democrat in the Texas state legislature and couldn't afford to send her abroad. A week after the papers were signed, she walked down the aisle with a beer king in front of four hundred "friends." She was born-again, financially. Two years of well-placed political contributions later—Republican, of course—and, voilà, she's an ambassador to some island republic under our protection.

I'm not shy about wanting money. I have my needs like every other woman. But I'd like my marriage to have a little love in it. God willing, I'll be walking down the aisle with a man who has a sizable bank account and also my heart. That's what Aimee has promised me, at least.

By day I'm a professional girl—a reporter for the *Wall Street Journal*—and by night I'm a husband-hunter or, at least, I intend to become one. I'm fed up with the ramen-eating artist who can't work a real job because he must think about creating. I'm sick of the relationship-phobic professional who is great for the first month, then turns aloof and weird. He gets angry at you because you assume he's your steady Friday-night date and rebels against cuddling. I'm disgusted with the emotional vampire, the guy who leeches on to your own reserves and demands that you validate his whole existence. *Yes, you are a great writer/lawyer/politician, and*

great in bed and very, very funny. This kind of man is never generous in return, neither emotionally nor materially. I should add that
invariably in all these involvements there is some incident of cheating; one of them drunkenly kissed my friend at a party; another accidentally slept with an old girlfriend; still another became more of
a partner with a male friend—in the Vermont sense of the word
than a beer buddy. I'm exhausted from the relationships I've en-
dured, so I've decided to try it Aimee's way.

I met Aimee four years ago as a fledging reporter. My first story
for the *Wall Street Journal* was about a lunatic-fringe Fort Worth
judge who threw an obese man in jail because he couldn't lose
weight, the same judge who made an adulterer plant a sign in his
front yard listing his indiscretions. Who knew that ear kissing was
a punishable crime? Aimee provided a lot of backstory on the
judge, like his habit of wearing women's garter belts under his
robes.

We met on the steps of the courthouse as I was chasing after one
of the judge's law clerks. The scrawny guy was more frightened of
the press than moving cars. He ran from me right into traffic.
Luckily he was nimble and avoided a head-on collision. As I
watched the law clerk scurry away, Aimee walked up to me and invited me to lunch. Over an Asian chicken salad she loaded me up
with tantalizing details about the judge with a fondness for the
garter belts. In full disclosure, the judge had dumped a friend of
Aimee's a year ago so she had motivation to spill the beans. During lunch, something clicked. We recognized some sort of similar-
ity—a hard thing to imagine given how different we looked and
talked. We started having regular weekly meals, which evolved
into daily phone conversations and ran into happy hour drinks.

Aimee is a paralegal extraordinaire, and she looks like a Miss
America beauty contestant, one of those tall women who appears
to have never grown inner thighs. Aimee lipoed hers out. She has
long blond hair (bleached, with extensions, of course—we're in
Dallas after all) and a perpetual fake tan. A sign of her skill is her
natural look, even with all the work she's had done.

A picture of me: I'm five feet four inches tall; occasionally I say
five-five. When I lived in New York, I thought this was average

height. In Texas, they grow people big. Most women are five feet seven at a bare minimum. I wear heels to compensate. I don't weigh that much, 110 pounds. I do possess my original thighs and spider veins, though I'm thinking more and more that my genetics are a bad fashion statement that I should make over. I must admit I was geek chic in the Northeast. I wore as a badge of honor the fact that I had never used an eyelash curler or lip liner and had no idea if I possessed blue or yellow undertones in my skin. I never got hit on at a bar and was never a recipient of a double take from a man on the subway. I thought that my practiced careless appearance telegraphed that I was smart—she must have a brain if she's that plain. But now I think it just said: wannabe librarian.

After I met Aimee, I decided I'd indulge in some of the feminine things that I ran away from in New York—makeup, regular waxings, and formfitting clothes—because I secretly wanted to be hit on and appreciated for my appearance. It felt like a sin or a sign of weakness to admit that to my friends in New York. Now I highlight my hair to a dark blond and submit myself to weekly manicures. I am still proud to own pale, freckle-free skin, though. I run from the sun.

I was sent to Dallas by the *Journal* because I am young and have no clout. I cover retail—JCPenney, Wal-Mart, etc. It isn't bad if you have an enduring affection for two-dollar flip-flops, polyester-blend clothing, and cubic zirconia. Did I mention that I get all the irregular T-shirts I want? This is the first time I have ever lived below the Mason-Dixon Line. My mother, ever the Jewish liberal, thinks I won't be able to find a good bagel, let alone a good man here. She's worried about my eggs rotting before I have a child but she is happy I started waxing.

There was and still is some culture shock. I'm still getting my sea legs with the whole woman thing. In New York, men never opened a door for me or insisted that I get on and off the elevator first. They never talked about marriage as if it was a good thing. They didn't carry the heavy groceries. They thought that women should pay for dinner, movies, and their own clothes. The South does have its advantages in this sense. And its disadvantages. In New York, I'm Jennifer Barton; here I'm Jenny, because people either add a "y" to your name or a "Bob" as in "Billy Bob" or "Joe Bob." Or, they shorten it to initials. I guess I got the better end of the naming stick. My middle initial is "R," so I could've been stuck with the worst nickname in Texas: J.R.

Then there's my boss, Carol Becker. She hates me. She spells mentor s-a-r-c-a-s-m. She hates her age (forty-seven), her lumpy body, and anyone younger than she is. She even hates that she'd have to exercise to be thin. At lunch, she devours Lean Cuisine microwave meals (the implication of multiple meals is intentional). By three o'clock, she's popping Hershey's Kisses like Courtney Love slams down painkillers. She wears matching oversize cotton T-shirts and long skirts with horrible little prints of cherries, carrots, happy witches, or something else totally incongruent for a woman who can't speak a civil word until her second cup of coffee. She sharpened her careerist pencil at the *Journal* when editors thought that allowing women into the pressroom was nothing more than a libidinal distraction, increasing adultery and lowering professional standards. She holds a bit of a grudge against the younger females who don't appreciate her pioneering efforts to overcome misogyny. She's bitter, just a little bitter. She also resents that I'm taking charge of my love life.

Whenever I leave work before six o'clock, she always manages to mutter, "Not putting in a full day, huh?" Or, if I wear a knee-length skirt, she quips, "Don't you want your sources to respect you?"

Aimee says I should get away from Carol as soon as possible because she's the kind of woman who will wear my looks away with stress, jealousy, and hatred. "She's a free radical brought to life," Aimee said.

She nudges me and rolls her eyes to the left of the bar. I wait a few seconds before I glance in the direction of Baylor Jones, a trial lawyer known for his wavy dark hair (does he dye it?) and his client list, which has included Enron's most wanted. He has the money and shoulders to wear Armani and the charm of a *"truh suthun genulmun."* He's sitting with two other men in suits and tightly knotted Brioni ties.

"See the guy next to Baylor? He's my target," Aimee says.

Aimee is cunning enough to be a lawyer herself. She was accepted into Stanford law school, but thought it would use up too many of her peak appearance years. Instead, she got hitched. But her then-husband didn't stop dating other women during their marriage, including several of her former sorority sisters. After he passed along gonorrhea, he tried to explain it to her by saying there are the girls you marry—the cute, smart ones like Aimee—and the others you had fun with. Aimee laughed in his face and took the house, a lovely 1930s Frank Lloyd Wright adaptation with open rooms and beautiful wood floors. That's where I live now.

After the divorce, Aimee got smart. She decided she was going to treat marriage like a business investment because she says, "Next time I'm gonna get something more out of it than a broken heart and a disease." She wants to marry rich and performs the due diligence to ensure that she will. So many people in Dallas are credit rich but cash poor. They lease cars, rent houses, and expense dinners. Instead of being stuck with a huge credit card load and a guy that's not all he said he was financially, Aimee does intensive research on every potential target. She always Googles before she oogles. It helps that she is a paralegal for a high-powered divorce attorney—free access to Lexus Nexus, financial databases, and, when necessary, guys who collect information. If her target is an officer of a public company, she reads SEC documents. She phones secretaries, maid services, and car dealerships, posing as an American Express representative, to find out more information about their liquid assets and how they use them. She doesn't move in for the kill unless her target is worth more than ten million dollars net, meaning, minus all debts and liens. She has elevated gold-digging to a science. She is a man-hunting entrepreneur.

Aimee makes a beeline for Baylor now, since he is sitting next to her target. One thing Aimee has taught me is never to act too eager with men. They like the mystery and to feel like they're chasing you. Hence her decision to greet Baylor rather than her target.

They do the North Dallas hug: breasts at forty-five degrees, kiss the cheek, pat the back, the shoulder, squeeze the arm, and maybe more. I still haven't gotten used to the idea that it's an officially sanctioned grope.

From across the bar, I can tell that Aimee and Baylor's conversation is going well. She's leaning in with semi-casual touching and her laughter is less forced than usual. She hand-signals me to join them as Baylor pulls up two chairs.

Husband-hunters have their own secret sign language:

- A short, wavy motion with the eyes slightly askance means, *Drive on by.*

- A two-handed catch-a-watermelon gesture means, *Get your ass over here and rescue me.*

- A one-handed bend-the-knuckles and waggle-the-wrist means, *Check this out.*

I'd hoped for a quick drink, a basket of hot potato chips, and a night at home recovering from the Botox, but this turn of events means at least a few hours of drinking and trying to be charming when my face is frozen, and I am acutely aware of needle holes in my temples. I know that I'm supposed to be into this game, but not tonight. Nevertheless, I grab my glass of red wine and head over.

"We were just talking about the Mavericks' new power forward," Aimee fakes.

Forward is what Aimee is. The first thing she reads in the morning paper is the sports page and not because she likes basketball. She harvests small talk like minnows in a net. I'm actually a better faker at this than she is. I'm one of two women in a bureau of twenty reporters. The other woman is the previously mentioned perimenopausal poster child whom others would call "editor." I read about sports mainly so that I can bond with my co-workers, which I tell myself is much more legitimate than trying to connect with self-important nouveau-riche Italian suits.

"Johnson's going to help them out on the boards. He cleans the glass like Windex. But he has to work on his jump hook because they need some more scoring in the low post," I say.

Aimee's target, all Zegna and receding hairline, is silent. Not a sports fan. Try a new tactic, I think.

"The NASDAQ was a roller coaster today," Aimee volunteers, a little more convincingly.

Bingo. Receding Hairline's face lights up and jiggles the small waddle of skin under his chin. This is promising (his interest, not his chin waddle). If you're marrying for money, it's good that money is your guy's main interest. Aimee and Receding—his name turns out to be Rance Cox, which Aimee already knew, of course—begin talking conspiratorially. The third man excuses himself. I never catch his name but it would be a safe guess that it consists of initials: J.T., T.C., or J.D. It's axiomatic that in groupings of three or more men in Texas, at least one of their first names will be initials.

Baylor leans over to me.

"Love connection. I mean, money connection," he says slanting his eyes toward Aimee and Rance.

"That's cynical," I counter playfully. *I know, I know, I'm a hypocrite,* I think to myself. But in the deepest part of my heart, I still believe that it's wrong to assume the best chance for women to support themselves is to marry rich, even though women make only seventy-two cents for every dollar that men make. And there are how many female CEOs?

Look at me. I'm a financial reporter and my only asset is my 401(k). I haven't scraped together enough money for a new car because of my clothing addiction, so I tool around in a seven-year-old Honda Civic. Can I help it if I want to step up the financial ladder?

Baylor pours me a glass of Margaux, a French red that typically costs five hundred dollars a bottle. It's velvet-coated heaven. When wine geeks talk about "oak undertones" and "fruity accents," they're not faking. Until I had my first upscale merlot (more than five dollars a glass), I thought all that stuff was a crock of elitist snobbery. Now I've tasted the difference, and it's hard to go back to what I can afford, the wine equivalent of Hawaiian Punch.

"So what are you working on? Any big cases?" I ask, feeling my way into small talk.

"Not at the moment. I'm helping my family with some work," he says. "I read your article in the paper. The one about people who live in their Winnebagos in the Wal-Mart parking lots. It reminded me of my cousins in Oklahoma. It was a cute little story."

Little story? I think. "Oh, really, you have cousins in Oklahoma?"

"Oh, yeah. High Bubba co-efficient. Indexed by the size of their dooleys divided by the number of dogs they own."

"Dooleys? Is that Okie for trailers?" I ask.

"Not exactly. Oklahoman," Baylor smiles. "Have you ever noticed that when a tornado hits a trailer park up there, which is about every other week in the spring, the victims interviewed on television are all obese women in muumuus saying stuff like, *Hit waz just like a frait trayn.*"

I laugh, rolling with it. It's sort of true. I saw a woman in a muumuu in the news just this morning with a crushed trailer in the background. Baylor is cute. He's a fifth-generation Texan but I can't tell if he's being a Southern gentleman or actually likes me. That's the trouble with Texas men.

There are few kinds of discrimination that Texans enjoy more than ridiculing their neighbors in Oklahoma, probably because many of them are only a few degrees of separation away from the Panhandle, and that's too close for comfort. Baylor's Oklahoma accent thickens into syrup. *"Dew yew know thuh three biggest lies an Okie tells? One: The bass boat is payyud fur. Two: I wun this buckle in uh rodeo. Three: I wuz only helping that sheep through thuh fence."* He gets serious. "Of course, I don't mean to say that your article was a joke. I really did like it." Baylor cracks a grin. "I'll read it again, if I ever get homesick."

"Thanks, I think," I say, laughing again, doing the hair flip, and lightly touching his knee. "What about you? What work are you doing for your family?"

"Nothing exciting. Just helping out on title stuff and other legalese when I can. Makes family holidays run a lot smoother," he says.

Aimee and Rance wrap up their conversation with an exchange of phone numbers and a tentative date for dinner. I am reminded again that Southern women are relentless. Why can't those of us from the more civilized Northern regions network so shamelessly? Too much angst?

"Nice meeting you—I mean seeing you again, Baylor," I stumble.

"Nice being seen," he says, and helps me away from the table. Rance nods and stands. He awkwardly grabs Aimee's elbow and leads the way, guiding Aimee through the crowd like an untrained Labrador.

This is only the second time I've really talked to Baylor. The first time was at a fund-raiser for a political candidate Aimee was scoping out as husband material. He didn't pass go. While his family had a fortune from their insurance company, the aspiring congressman didn't have more than two million to his name. An important Aimee rule: If it's family money, forget it. You'll spend the best years of your life playing handmaiden to a mother-in-law you'll probably detest and who most likely won't die until she reaches triple digits. Add on to the family money fiasco the fact that Aimee would have to wear the bad suits of a politician's wife and she decided he wasn't the one.

When the politico approached Aimee at the event, she was very aloof. Baylor was beside him, and did his best to keep the conversation going while Aimee sent verbal and nonverbal signals that she wasn't interested. The politico tried move after move to change her mind. Baylor glided over the awkwardness of the moment with the finesse of a skilled con man with a background in hostage negotiations. He actually listened to people and played off of them. He said things slowly with the confidence that everyone who heard him speak would listen to every word. He's known Aimee for years from parties and mutual friends so he had the know-how to handle a high-maintenance diva routine. I was impressed.

I'd seen him at parties since then but hadn't talked to him. He always looked busy. He didn't scan the room when he was talking to people. He seemed to be exactly where he wanted to be all the time.

As we exit, Baylor's and Rance's cars are waiting by the curb, twin Mercedes SL black sedans side by side.

"Was there a two-for-one deal?" I say. Baylor laughs.

People in Texas are big on cars. *Car translation:*

- Mercedes—respected, rich.

- Lexus—an up-and-comer on the wealthy landscape.

- Honda—Are you the help, dear?

"You should see our planes," Rance says.

They have planes. Matching planes. I can see what Aimee is thinking.

The parking valet drives up in Aimee's sixty-month-lease silver Lexus. Doors are opened for us. We get in and wave good-bye.

"I think Rance owns his plane outright and Baylor leases his with a group of friends," she says as we drive away in her respectable, financed car.

I must look incredulous.

"Honey, in Texas planes aren't a luxury. They're a necessity. Chicago is closer than El Paso. You can't fly Southwest to Lufkin, or anywhere else behind the pine curtain. Try getting to Corpus Christi, or some godforsaken place in West Texas, on the same day."

I catch the slip in diction. Aimee hails from some godforsaken town behind the pine curtain herself, the Texas version of a double-wide-trailer-park-laden highway exit. She trained like a heavyweight champion to remove all traces of her polyester, macramé potholder, and Cheez Whiz background, but sometimes when she drinks she reverts to "ain't" and "fixin' to." "So how did it go?" I ask.

Aimee beams. "I got the hoe in my hand," she says.

Translation: The hoe in the hand refers to a saying: "The time to kill a snake is when you have the hoe in your hand."

"He has the assets," she says. "He's more interesting than dry wallpaper. His breath doesn't smell like coffee and cigarettes. Oh, and he has a house in St. Barth's and a penthouse in New York City."

"I thought New York was too cold for you."

"Not if I have a big fur coat to keep me warm. Don't worry, I'll be generous. I'll get you a rabbit's foot or something."

Aimee might be Southern, but she's as sarcastic as any Yankee I've ever met.

"What'd you and Baylor get all cozy about?" Aimee asks me.

"Nothing. He said he's doing a little work for his family—titles and stuff," I say.

"You know what that means?"

"That he's working for his family," I say as I check out my Botox face in the car mirror.

"No, darling. It means that he is gonna take over his family operations real soon."

"That's good, right?" I say.

Aimee lets out a deep breath. "Darling, this is the best piece of advice you'll ever receive from me—stay away from that man."

I don't say anything in response. The tone of Aimee's voice warns one not to wade further into the topic. I've never heard the stern don't-touch-that voice from her before.

Aimee pulls into the driveway. She smiles to herself.

"It's gonna be nice to move into a five-thousand-footer. Rance's house is at least that. I mean, when we're married, of course," she says as she gets out of the car.

I think Texas women may have one thing right. You shouldn't live with a man before you marry him. If you do, you have to be on your best behavior all the time, the deal isn't closed yet, and who knows when it will be? You know what they say: Why buy the cow if you can get the milk for free? If the situation drags on for a few years, no wedding date in sight, even the most laid-back woman starts to get pissed off. So then you break up, and you wind up in another live-in relationship that breaks up, and the cycle begins again. It's a retail transaction that never closes.

Once inside, we decide to have dinner and try to eat healthy. We cut up spinach salads with broiled chicken and just a splash of dressing. Aimee brings her salad into the living room and turns on her laptop. She accesses a database from her law firm that will search for criminal records, financial problems (collection notices, etc.), and articles. She puts in Rance Cox.

"I thought you already did that," I say as I sit next to her on the couch.

"I need to memorize it," she says as she scans the screen.

"Why?"

"Because to be his soul mate I have to love what he loves," she says.

"I thought he just had to love you. I didn't know soul mate was a requirement to this."

"A soul mate doesn't get asked to sign a prenup because she'll be with him forever," she says as she scrapes the last bit of lettuce from her bowl. I finished my salad minutes ago and am still starving.

I walk back into the kitchen in search of something else to eat. Unfortunately, Aimee did a food purge recently. She threw away all ready-to-eat sweets and junk food. I find honey and maple syrup, grab two spoons, and sit back down on the couch. I hand Aimee a spoonful of maple syrup. She puts it in her mouth and savors the sweet taste. I do the same.

"I think I'll have to break into his house," she says.

I choke a little. "Do you usually?" I ask.

It wouldn't look good for me to be caught breaking into houses. I'm betting it would end my career as a reporter.

"Yeah, I'll bribe the cleaning staff to let me look around for an hour. It's a good way to get a better feel for what a guy likes," Aimee says as she takes another spoonful of syrup.

"Will I have to break into a guy's place?"

"Depends on the guy. We should make cookies," she says.

"At least cookie dough," I say.

She whips up chocolate chip cookie batter in minutes. She doesn't even need the recipe. We use our maple syrup spoons and eat dough right from the bowl. There's something nice about living with a friend; I always have the same warm feeling I get when I go home for the holidays and stay with my family. There's no worry about who will cook, who will wash the dishes, or who's hungry for sugar. And I can wear sweats, socks, and a big ugly sweater.

Chapter Two

There's More to a Relationship than Physical Attraction

I should back it up a little bit. Explain what pushed me over the edge into husband-hunting. What was the final straw or series of ever-increasing ego-razing straws?

The truth is, when I first got to town and highlighted my hair, I dated like a drug addict in a free pharmacy. But eventually I settled down for two years with Rafe Halprin, also a journalist. Rafe writes about crime at the *Dallas Morning News*. I met him at a Super Wal-Mart break-in. Both of us were discreetly ducking under the police tape to get some exclusive quotes from the investigators. He elbowed me. I tripped him. I have more cleavage, so I got the good quotes. I borrowed his pen when mine ran out of ink and slipped him my phone number rolled up in his pen cap.

He's cute in a college boy, irresponsible way. And our relationship was good in that college, irresponsible way, too. He would buy me a Coke if I had a migraine, we'd eat lobster dinners in front of the television, and he'd make me laugh at my type A traits, such as competing against middle-aged frat boys in yoga class. But those were his three best qualities. He also believed in always going Dutch, playing touch football with the guys every single Saturday and Sunday, and never getting married. And his scalp smelled like cabbage. Worst of all was his habit of staying out until three a.m. without inviting me.

The night everything started to come into focus, Aimee was holding my hair and preaching all the commandments of her belief system as I was puking from the flu.

"Men only do what's necessary to sleep with you, so women should only be with the kind of men—that is, rich men—who can enable women to pursue satisfaction in other parts of their lives. In the first part of a relationship they do everything for you because they haven't figured out what they can get away with yet. But slowly their kindnesses peel away like so many exfoliated skin cells. They gradually morph into Rafe. And where is Rafe now? That's right, he's in the other room watching football while you're barfing your brains out," she said as she wiped a cool, wet washcloth over my face and handed me a ginger ale to rinse my mouth.

"Most women are looking for men who will be their mothers—take care of them when they're sick, eat dinner with them while they watch cheesy movies."

"Rafe brought me McDonald's before you came," I said feebly.

"Sure, it took five minutes of his time and guaranteed that you'd sleep with him when you felt better. And look, you're throwing it up."

She had a point.

Just then, Rafe poked his head into the room and pointed to a *Sports Illustrated* on the floor. Aimee threw it at him, he mumbled thanks, and closed the door.

That would've been the end of it. I would've forgotten about what Aimee said and continued in my somewhat satisfying relationship if it hadn't been for a little piece of fabric, luxurious fabric.

A week after the flu, I was washing our clothes in the laundry room of our apartment complex—I was living with Rafe in what had been his place. I was in the process of folding a pair of jeans when I found a pair of hand-embroidered slate blue silk underwear with the brand name C. Gilson stitched in the back. These were expensive. They were made out of the kind of silk that is so delicate and plush you don't understand how it stays together. They were definitely not mine.

I pocketed the underwear and asked people around our apartment complex about who they might belong to. I started with the young attractive women and as their strange looks and denials of underwear ownership increased, I grew desperate. In the elevator, I cornered the fifty-eight-year-old bank manager who lived the floor above Rafe and me.

"I know this is a strange question, but you aren't missing any underwear, are you?"

She looked at me like I was a pervert and took a small step away from me. I rushed back into the conversation.

"I was doing my laundry the other day and I found some underwear that wasn't mine," I said as I pulled the underwear out of my bag to show her.

"You carry it with you?" she asked as she took another step away from me. I looked at my hand holding the lustrous slate silk. I could see how from her point of view this was obsessive, bordering on crazy, behavior. But she didn't understand that I needed some sort of rational explanation for the appearance of this underwear in my laundry because the alternative didn't bode well for my current relationship.

"I'm just trying to figure out whose they are," I said by way of lame explanation.

"I would've left them in the laundry room," she said as the elevator opened to my floor. I debated riding up to the next floor with her but stopped myself. This was a dead end.

My detective routine didn't stop with her or the rest of the residents of my building. I proceeded to ask any friend who could have remotely been responsible for leaving underwear in Rafe's and my apartment. By remotely, I mean anyone who lived within a mile radius of us or tangentially knew anyone who had been to a party at our place. Rafe's embarrassment grew with each inquiry. "They're just underwear, drop it," he whined. Most of my friends were polite enough to quickly and earnestly answer no. A couple of people gave me looks that expressed the enormous amount of pity they felt for my cluelessness. When I pulled the underwear out while we were sitting at a restaurant patio in full daylight, Aimee just said, "Oh, honey, why don't you come live with me?"

It wasn't until I decided to run home for a quick lunch that everything became clear to me. I was walking up to my apartment building when I saw a woman so skeletally thin I couldn't tell from a perspective point of view if she was enormously tall or devoid of flesh. Her clothes hung off her in the supermodel, heroin-addict way. Her hair was long and blond, of course. Her skin sparkled, golden like fried chicken. She dropped her lipstick on the sidewalk and bent over from the waist in one slow movement to pick it up. I watched the graceful arch of her body, basically re-creating a yoga pose, as her fingers swooped to the sidewalk and her hair fluttered around her face like fringe on a theater curtain. That's when I saw a petal pink silk with taupe embroidery stick out from her jeans. It looked so familiar. I instinctively reached in my purse and grabbed the underwear I had been carting around for the last few days. I pulled it out, looked at it, and looked at her petal pink variety.

"They're the same," I mumbled as I stood still, examining her and trying to figure out the connection between her, the underwear, and Rafe. She's not a person one would meet on the police beat, at the newspaper, or playing touch football in the park. She looked up with emotionless almond eyes at me, my frozen body, and the underwear I clutched in my hand. She smiled in a conspiratorial way, walked over to me, and took the underwear out of my hand.

"Thanks," she said as she walked by me.

"What's going on here?" I asked softly.

She turned around and said, "I think you can figure that out."

I had never been completely numb or physically paralyzed before then. I couldn't move for the few seconds I could hear her heels click on the sidewalk. When I was capable of walking again I raced up to my apartment. My heart was beating like it was dipped in caffeine, while everything moved so slowly in those few moments as I waited for the elevator, took it up to my apartment, and fiddled for my keys. By the time I unlocked the door and walked in, I felt for sure Rafe would be gone but there he was. He lay naked in our bed. He seemed startled.

I stood in the hallway by the front door staring at him. Our apartment basically consisted of a long hallway that branched into the living room, kitchen, and bathroom but ended right in the bedroom. From the front door, the bed was all you saw. I didn't want to take a step farther in his direction. I anchored myself by the front door and kitchen.

"I found out whose underwear it was," I said.

He grabbed a pair of shorts and a T-shirt and walked toward me into the kitchen.

"What are you talking about?" he asked as he reached past me and into the refrigerator for the orange juice.

"The woman, on the sidewalk. She took the underwear and said thanks," I said.

"What? You gave some woman the pair of underwear you've been obsessing about?" he asked and looked at me like he thought I lacked a basic sanity chip.

Ever the reporter, I thought I needed more proof. I needed an airtight case before I could get an admission of guilt. Isn't that always the way it is with men? Unless you have actual pictures of them having sex, an e-mail in which they said they had sex, or some other kind of physical evidence, they'll deny it until the bloody end, making you feel absolutely crazy.

I walked past him into the bedroom, looking for more tangible proof of sex. The bed was tangled and unmade—no big surprise if Rafe was home. It smelled like sex or it could be gross guy smell. The signs were ambiguous. Rafe followed me into the room.

"Why are you home?" I asked.

"I didn't feel good. I came home to sleep," he said.

I would've dropped it right then and thought I was crazy, except I saw K-Y jelly seeping out of a tube on the bedside table. I looked at Rafe and saw the fear and guilt in his eyes. I knew I wasn't crazy. I pulled a suitcase out of the closet and started packing. Rafe circled around me. He talked fast.

"It's not what it looks like. We can work this out. I love you. Let's get engaged," he spewed out.

I countered. "Why would you want to be with me if you're sleeping with someone else? You're bringing up marriage now? How can you possibly love me? Is the sex that bad with me?" I asked.

"It's not about the sex," he said as he tried to pull my suitcase out of my hands.

Any time a guy says it's not about the sex, it's about the sex and his desire to have it with anyone he wants.

That morning, around, oh, 2:59 a.m., I finished packing my clothes, arguing the finer legal points of cheating, and left.

Rafe was shocked. He thought I'd stay through strange underwear and K-Y-soaked sheets. He didn't notice that we weren't in love, that we barely looked at each other, that we never kissed anymore, that he hugged his friends more than he did me. We had mapped out our respective sides of the bed, met each other's parents without bloodshed, and purchased a set of white dishes with thin blue lines around the rims that we both liked. Pretty soon we had gone halfsies on a Whirlpool dishwasher. Wasn't this commitment? he argued. Weren't we inextricably moving toward something greater as the months and years unraveled before us?

I understand that to Rafe commitment was part of the middle age that he so feared. He expected a woman to nag and cajole him into it as all of his friends' wives did. One woman withheld sex until a ring was offered. Another bought the ring herself, wrapped it up, and put it under the tree. She made sure his parents were around when she unwrapped it and said yes. He never knew what hit him. If marriage is the ultimate downer to most men, as Rafe assured me it was, then I'm going to get smarter about whom I nag or trick into it, I thought as I rode the elevator down to my car.

You know there is something to be said for a real committed relationship in which you can assume that your significant other will whip up chicken soup when you're sick, uncork a bottle of champagne for your birthday, and want to spend Friday nights with you. I've never had that kind of relationship. I don't really believe they exist. None of my friends has one. No one I even remotely know has one. The first time I was consciously aware of the fairy-tale nature of a real committed relationship was a week before I stood in this elevator. When I laid in bed with the flu, I made a mental list of all my friends who have good relationships. There were none. Most of them confessed—with words soaked in resignation—that they had settled because "this was the best I found." The ones who wouldn't unburden themselves to me were enmeshed in dramas so extreme that they deserved a term worse than *co-dependent*. Sure, there was passion and great sex, but there was also hatred, mistrust, and vindictiveness. Not the best foundation.

At one point in the relationship I really loved Rafe, and I think he loved me. What happened to it? I didn't even notice it slipping away. As I packed my car up and drove away, I thought to myself: *Be a businesswoman about your love life.*

Aimee had harped on me for months about how Rafe is "beyond loser." She indicted him for being more interested in reading the morning paper than having sex with me. She scorned him for refusing to pick me up from the airport because it was out of the way. She condemned him for complaining when I asked for help with the grocery bags. Maybe, she said, he didn't like me that much.

Now Aimee yelped in happiness when I showed up on her doorstep in the wee hours of the morning. She said nothing else about Rafe except "Thank God you're finally here." I moved in with her the very same day and that's when my true education began: Botox, liposuction, plastic surgery, lip enlargement, hair extensions, HGH shots, fake tans, color contacts, all manner of breast enhancements, perfectly matching outfits, bleach, makeup application on a drag queen scale, weight lifting, Kegel exercises, yoga, running, the ladies-who-lunch diet (staple: Don't eat), the working women's diet (don't eat carbohydrates). I decided to follow Aimee's mantra: Plan, strategize, conquer. Make the smart decision. She promptly gave me a reading list. If I'm really going to be a husband-hunter, she said, I'd have to plow through *Valley of the Dolls, Kama Sutra, The Taming of the Shrew, Madame Bovary, The Art of War, Hollywood Wives,* and *Men Are from Mars, Women Are from Venus.*

Other things I should consider to better my chances of marrying rich: an etiquette course, a wine appreciation course, a real estate license, more stilettos, being less aggressive, lying about my age, getting a tattoo removed (this is the Bible Belt), studying a useless language (anything other than Spanish), going to church, joining Junior League, buying better running clothes, and getting a personal stylist.

You can see why trophy wives don't work. They're too busy.

If all the drama I had experienced that week with the underwear and Rafe wasn't enough to put me firmly in Aimee's corner of husband-hunting, my mother cinched the deal.

A couple of days after I moved out of the apartment, I reluctantly called my mother to tell her about my change of address and Rafe.

"So does this mean it's over for good?" my mother asked. She liked Rafe. Plus, in her mind I was too old to start, develop, and close another relationship before my biological clock stopped.

"Yeah, I think cheating is pretty much a deal breaker," I said.

"You know your sister is trying to have a baby. She's taking Clomid," my mother said. My sister is three years older than I am and from what my mother just said is having enough trouble getting pregnant that she's taking fertility drugs. My mother says fertility problems are genetic. This doesn't mean good things for my future in motherhood.

"I think I'll be all right," I said with less conviction than necessary to get my mother to stop harping.

"Your eggs are rotting," my mother moaned. "I have this feeling that your ovaries are just shriveling up as we speak. I think Rafe was your last chance."

"Women can have kids in their forties," I countered.

"Those women are freaks," my mother said in a depressed voice. She sighed. I knew she was calculating her chances of being a grandmother. I felt the guilt as well as my competitive nature rising. I wanted to have what other women my age had. Why couldn't I?

"Maybe Rafe isn't so bad," my mother suggested.

I could feel the rage in me starting to build. I'm an attractive, smart woman. Why should I have to settle and why would my own mother suggest it? This is a screwed-up society.

"I'll be married by the end of the year," I said with confidence.

"To Rafe?" my mother asked, her voice brightening.

"God, I hope not," I said.

"Then to whom?" she asked.

"Don't worry. I have a plan. Start looking for a dress," I said with a conviction I felt in every pore of my body.

That's what cinched it. That's when I decided absolutely and without hesitation to listen to everything Aimee said.

Chapter Three

When You Break into a House,
Have Plenty of Twenties

A month later and I am sitting in the passenger's seat of Aimee's car. We're parked on the street a block away from Rance's house. Aimee squints at his driveway. She holds her cell phone tightly in her hand. We've been here ten minutes when a shiny Mercedes pulls out. Seconds later her cell phone rings.

"Yeah, okay," she says, then starts the car and turns into the long brick driveway. The cedar gate swings closed behind us. She parks in front of a large stucco house with a tile roof.

"Nice," I say.

Aimee gets out of the car, slips a servant a bunch of cash, and waves for me to follow. I get out of the car and sprint toward the front door.

"We're not doing a covert operation. You can walk normally," Aimee says as she heads toward the stairs. I follow her. Once she gets to the landing she ducks her head into each room as she glides down the hallway.

"What are you doing?" I ask as I bump into her when she stops to examine a guest bedroom.

"I'm looking for the master bedroom," she says.

"I'm pretty sure this isn't it," I say as I shove her, prompting her to walk down the hall again.

"I'm trying to get an idea of his taste in general," she says.

"You said we only have an hour," I whine. I'm already nervous about breaking into the place. I don't want to cut it close and get caught by Rance. After the meeting at Beaux Nash, they've had a couple of dates and he sure appears to be attracted to Aimee, but breaking in won't endear her to him. They're not at the "it's so cute that you're stalking me" stage of their relationship. I'm not sure where that stage fits. Is it in between obsession and addiction?

Aimee struts to the end of the hallway where a large master bedroom is situated. We walk in together. The moment I enter I feel like a midget. Massive mahogany furniture dominates every inch of the place. A king-size bed stands three feet off the ground and has bedposts that stretch almost to the ceiling. The headboard gleams with polish and ornate carvings of cherubs and flowers. The nightstands are the width of a shopping cart. The dresser spans one whole wall while the armoire takes up another. There's so much mahogany in here, it feels like a wood-paneled room.

"You have to change this if you marry him," I say as Aimee dives under the bed.

"Men always use too much wood," she says from under the dust ruffle, "to pun an unfortunate side effect of Viagra."

She comes up for air holding a box. She places the box on the bed. It's large, the length and width of my entire arm. Aimee opens it up. Inside are hundreds of G. I. Joe figures.

"Think he's going to take over a toy factory?" I ask, half joking.

"He's such a nerd," she says as she examines the figures. She gets out her digital camera and takes pictures—group shots and individual photos of the toys. Some of the figures have names written on the bottom in marker: Jeb, Stonewall, Lee. He must be a huge Civil War buff. I bet he reenacts the big battles like Antietam. Aimee carefully puts the box back under the bed.

She walks over to his dresser and opens the drawers. She inspects his underwear and scribbles down what size and kind he buys in a notebook, Burberry boxer shorts, medium. She inventories all his clothes and toiletries this way. She finds his briefcase next to the armoire. She is gleeful. She skips over to the bed with it and sits down.

"Why are you so excited about that?" I ask as I sit down next to her.

"Are you kidding? This gives me key and crucial items to make small talk with," she says as she lays the papers out on the bed and takes more pictures. "I'm finding out what companies he's studying. I can casually drop the name of one of these companies into conversation and he'll think I'm amazing."

I walk around the room while Aimee performs a photo session with paper. I open a drawer of his nightstand and find a high school yearbook photo that looks like it was cut directly out of the book. The girl in the picture is cute. She's dressed in a short skirt and little shirt.

"Look at this," I say as I show it to Aimee.

"Cheerleader. Bet she didn't give Rance the time of day in high school," Aimee says as she puts the papers back into Rance's briefcase.

"What do you think this is for?" I ask as I point to a bottle of lotion right next to the picture.

"What do you think? Poor guy is too embarrassed to buy K-Y in the store. He makes do with lotion. I bet he's never had sex," she says as she puts the briefcase back in its place next to the armoire. She scans the room one more time before heading toward his closet. I follow.

Aimee quickly feels inside every jacket and pants pocket. When she finds a piece of paper with a number scrawled on it, she takes it.

"I can understand taking the ones with the girls' names, but why the ones with guys' names?" I say, bewildered.

"I need to know who his circle is. Nothing would be worse than to insult someone who's his friend," she says as she starts looking through his shoes.

"Now what are you looking for?" I ask.

"Orthopedic devices, odor eaters, anything else that gives me insight into who he is," she says as she reaches behind the clothes.

"What are you doing? Method husband-hunting?" I ask. She

ignores me and feels along the wall for a couple of feet. She pulls out a box of DVDs, CDs, and books. Every one of them is by Tony Robbins, the motivational speaker.

"Now we know how Rance does it. This is why he's rich," I say and giggle.

"You laugh but I bet this did help him a lot," Aimee says as she flips through the box. She's ready to inventory the whole thing when Albert, the servant she originally bribed, runs into the closet.

"He's back," Albert screeches.

"It's only been a half an hour," I say.

"He was supposed to be playing golf. I don't know what happened. I'm gonna be so fired," Albert whines.

"We have to get out of here. We can't be caught," I say in full panic mode. I charge toward the closet door but Albert clotheslines me.

"He's already in the house. You have to hide. I'll come get you when he's gone," he says.

"What about our car? Didn't he see our car?"

"I told him one of the help got a new car, so he thinks your car is the chef's," Albert says. "I'm going to have to bribe him."

Albert holds out his hand and Aimee places a few more twenties in his palm.

Just about everyone in Dallas who isn't a millionaire drives a Lexus.

Aimee scans the closet. She walks over to the shoe rack and feels all over it like she's giving it a massage.

"We can hide behind here," she says as she crawls behind the rack. I follow. There's about two feet of room between it and the wall. We lie down next to each other and stretch out along its six feet of length. It's a good thing Rance has a thing for shoes.

"How long do you think we'll be here?" I whisper as Albert walks out of the room.

"Not long. He probably forgot something and is coming home to get it. He'll head back to the golf course real soon," she whispers.

We fall into silence. Minutes pass. An hour has gone by, maybe more. I'm starting to get hungry, thirsty, and in need of a bathroom. I'm also getting crampy and claustrophobic.

"The servant forgot about us. Let's go," I say as I try to crawl out. Aimee grabs my arm and pulls me back.

"We can't take that chance," she says.

"I need to go to the bathroom," I plead.

"Hold it," she says and elbows me to keep quiet. We both can hear footsteps. Someone has walked into the room. The footsteps walk over to the dresser. A drawer is opened. Shoes clunk to the floor. Some kind of clothing is removed. Someone is whistling the song from *Snow White,* the one the dwarves sing. That can only be Rance.

I can hear footsteps headed toward us. The closet door opens. The whistling is right above us. He can't see us, can he? I am preparing a reasonable explanation as to why Aimee and I would be behind the shoe rack.

- There's a surprise party for him and we got the wrong date.

- We're part of a scavenger hunt that requires we hide in someone's closet.

- Aimee really, really loves you. It's a cross between obsession and addiction.

There's a rustling sound behind the clothes. Rance pulls out the Tony Robbins box, the last thing I saw before my captivity behind a shoe rack.

"I have the power within me," Rance mutters and keeps muttering like a mantra. He gets louder and louder until he is shouting and, from what little I can see, stretches his arms up to the sky like an overdramatic superhero.

"What's he need the power for?" I ask Aimee. This time she puts her hand over my mouth.

She intently watches Rance. I wonder if she'll do a similar superhero move with him on their next date as a way to show soulmate status. I would pay to see it.

"I am the god of my domain!" Rance yells and then hoots. Albert rushes in. "Sir, don't you have a dinner tonight? I don't want you to be late." He tries to usher Rance out of the closet.

"Join me," Rance says and clasps hands with Albert and then raises their arms in the air.

"I have the power within me!" Rance yells while Albert sort of whispers.

"Come on, together, louder this time," Rance commands. This time Albert yells it but there's not much enthusiasm behind it. It doesn't matter to Rance who walks into his bedroom. "I need pants," Rance calls and Albert rushes back into the closet to retrieve some.

"I have the power within me," I whisper.

"Shut it," Albert says as he grabs some clothing and closes the door.

A few minutes pass and Aimee exhales deeply. I giggle. She giggles, too, despite her best efforts not to.

"That's quite a stud you have there," I say.

"At least he's just a dork and not some sexual deviant," she says as she climbs out of our hiding place.

"What are you doing?" I ask.

"I heard the door close and the front gate open," she says as Albert opens the closet door. He looks like he's about to launch into a huge speech. Aimee hands him more money. He instantly closes his mouth.

We walk out of the closet.

"Good choice on the pants," I say as we walk down the hallway to the stairs and our car.

When we get in Aimee yells with conviction, "I have the power within me!"

"That's good," I say, impressed by her ability to throw herself into something so utterly not her.

"I am a master-class husband-hunter," she says as she pulls away. "Now we have to get you up to speed. I'm working on who to set you up with."

"Great, what's the next step with Rance?" I ask.

"More dates to show how perfect I am for him," she says as she dials his cell phone.

"Rance. Hi, I'm so glad I reached you. I'm in desperate need of your advice. Well, I'm looking at investing in a couple of tech companies, Om and TelActive. You know them? Well, great. Of course. It's not too much trouble," Aimee says. I can only hear her end of the conversation and it sounds like crime does pay.

Aimee hangs up.

"What'd he say?" I ask.

"He wants to meet me in half an hour at Beaux Nash. He's real into TelActive. He was s-o-o-o excited when I said their name," Aimee says.

"Do you even know what the company does?" I ask.

"Improves voice recognition software," she answers, "and they're privately held and are looking for investors."

"You got all of that from scanning a few pieces of paper. You're a lot smarter than people give you credit for."

"I know," she says as she reapplies lip gloss at the light.

Chapter Four

The Dark Side of Husband-Hunting

Even though I already knew a lot of Aimee's other friends in a social sense, I didn't know them in the husband-hunter arena. With these women there's a big difference in the conversation they'll have over a drink with a Yankee acquaintance and a woman they know shares the same goals they do.

Aimee planned to welcome me into the fold with cocktails a few weeks after I moved in with her, but her friend Natalie called with an all-out emergency that required more privacy than a bar could provide and more time than a two a.m. last call.

Aimee convened a sleepover. No female emergency is viable without Oreos, S'mores, chocolate, gummy bears, Cheetos, fried chicken, and chili cheese Fritos, for starters. Then you ramp up the feel good with hard alcohol, gay porn, romantic comedies, *US Weekly,* sleeping bags, feather pillows to put under the sleeping bags, and baggy pajamas. Always have an extra pair ready for the woman who hasn't succumbed to the idea of getting comfortable.

Aimee instructed me to get the grocery store provisions, which I thought I'd do on my way back from working out. Frankly I was happy to be asked to do something that I know how to perform competently, or, at least, I thought I could perform competently.

Dallas has a whole different standard for grocery shopping. Let me explain. I do yoga, the hot kind. Afterward, I look like I wrapped myself in cellophane and stewed in a sauna for hours—eau de locker room and dripping. The night of the sleepover I calculated the time it would take to go home from yoga, shower, dry my hair, and look acceptable: two hours—there's not enough time. I know a tenet to running errands in Dallas is to be impeccably dressed and groomed, no matter what. But I thought if I stopped at your basic grocery store—a normal one, not Whole Foods—no one with a net worth less than half a million should be there. So I am walking down the sports drink aisle looking to pick up a couple of good hangover electrolyte-filled drinks. My basket is full of whipped lard, trans-fatty acids, and fake flavorings with multiple syllables. Naturally I run into Baylor.

"You look like someone I used to know, only she was cleaner and ate better," he says. "Is this a suicide attempt or just a cry for help?"

"It's an effort to get in touch with my feminine side," I say.

"Is your feminine side sweaty and fat?" he asks.

"I don't know. Is your male side a sugar addict with a taste for thick red meat?" I ask, eyeing his cart. He has root beer, vanilla ice cream, thick red steaks, and asparagus—a very manly grilling-appropriate dinner.

"Yes, it is. I can show you why these are classic foods."

Was that a grin and a wink?

"Can't tonight, I have this female-bonding-junk-food-gay-porn thing going on," I say.

He visibly stumbles at the gay porn. I like getting him off balance.

"How about Monday?" he asks.

"Monday."

I bounce off to the checkout line. My emotional high is lowered as Aimee's words and tone of voice come back to me: "Stay away from that man." She was so emphatic and she's not the emphatic type. She has a voice like honey even as she's telling you she killed your cat and you look like hell. It can't be that bad, I think, as I pay for my junk food and leave. He's too cute for it to be that bad. Maybe I'll sniff around and see what others think of Baylor at the sleepover.

I look back into the store as I walk through the parking lot and see him talking to the elderly checkout woman. He has Southern charm written all over his body. You know the kind of guy who asks how you're doing and means it.

Aimee and I spend the rest of the evening girl-proofing our home. We hide vibrators, the Retin-A and all other wrinkle creams, and any other indicators that we're worried about weight, age, or sex. We spread out the sleeping bags, soft pillows, and junk food.

"This is just like a sorority, isn't it?" Aimee says.

"I wouldn't know. I've never had the privilege of living with a bunch of self-important cheerleaders who dress and talk alike."

"Well, excuse me. I forgot you aren't normal. You were into the faux-lesbian, nonconformist, Dead Head, drug-induced living in a four-bedroom hovel thing with twenty people."

"Sororities aren't the norm anyplace outside of the South," I retort. I keep forgetting that these women take their group living seriously.

"Yeah, yeah, yeah, and women should be treated as equals. Keep telling me your fairy tales," she says.

I ignore her and think over our invitation list.

- Lizzy Hunt, a soon-to-be bride, who is trying to lose another twenty or so pounds before her wedding, which is a month away. She says she's only drinking Diet Coke. Right. That's like saying five more minutes, and meaning it, when you hit the snooze alarm. I've hung out with her a lot in the past couple of years and have established a pretty good friendship.

- Cindy Trammel is a viper of a woman. She scares me. She has the ability to turn anything you've said into an insult, just in the way she repeats it back to you. It's uncanny. She's also a husband-hunting expert. She's already tucked away a couple of nice settlements.

- Natalie Gibbons, a junior lawyer at Akin & Gump and in active pursuit of—more like obsessed with—a society oil man named Bradford Goodnight. She and Aimee pledged to the same sorority. She is the woman in crisis—the reason we're having this shindig—something that Bradford did.

- Tommy Sue, at Lizzy's request. She has no gag reflex. Lizzy pled her case over the phone: "She needs friends. She broke up with her boyfriend a month ago and he got all the friends." She seems sweet. I just hope she doesn't use the toilet as a vomitorium.

"I hope there's no blood drawn tonight," I say.

"That's what alcohol is for," Aimee says as she arranges cocktail glasses on a silver tray.

We have about two gallons of vodka. Aimee says vodka is to drinks what flour is to baked goods—the glue. She's made a half dozen different kinds of cocktails. The glasses on the tray hold every color liquid imaginable.

"Are you going to give me any hint as to what crisis we're dealing with?" I ask Aimee for the zillionth time.

"That's for Natalie to explain."

The doorbell rings. Aimee grabs the cocktail tray and throws open the door. Cindy stumbles inside. Aimee hands her a drink. Cindy takes a dainty sip.

"Now, I know you can fit a lot more than that down your throat," Aimee says. They toast each other and down the contents of both their glasses.

"What's going on with your outfit?" Aimee asks. Dressed in white silk men's pajamas and cashmere socks, Aimee exemplifies sleepover chic.

Cindy looks at her pressed tweed Chanel jacket in bewilderment.

"Honey, tweed is not standard-issue sleepover gear. Go change," she says and shoos Cindy into the bathroom.

"But I don't . . ." Cindy stammers.

"I have an extra pair of pajamas in there," Aimee says, waving Cindy away. "You'd think the girl'd never been to a slumber party."

I give it to her—sorority life taught her how to manipulate high-maintenance women into submission. Cindy complied with Aimee's every command without so much as an eye roll.

I met Cindy a couple of years ago when I was having drinks with Aimee. I can attest to the fact that she doesn't take suggestions from other women all that well. The night I met her, Cindy almost slapped our waitress when the poor girl suggested she try a chili-infused mojito. Cindy was insulted the waitress inferred that she didn't know what she wanted. Cindy verbally insulted the woman to such a degree that the waitress asked a fellow employee to take over our table.

"You need to change," Aimee says to me, too. I jump up and slip into a pair of green cotton pajama bottoms with a camisole top and robe to match.

By the time I walk back into the living room, Lizzy and Tommy Sue are ensconced on the couch. They're both wearing terry-cloth robes. Tommy Sue sips a cosmopolitan. Lizzy sticks with her Diet Coke. Aimee did convince her to put some rum in it.

Natalie arrives decked out in Prada as if the outfit were plucked in its entirety from the look book—you know, those books of runway models that high-end stores carry. Aimee hands her a drink and is about to give her the same treatment that she just gave Cindy and me when Natalie interrupts.

"Oh, honey, I brought Versace," she says and pads off to the bathroom. She doesn't act like a woman in full crisis. She seems like a woman who enjoyed a nice day of shopping.

Cindy, dressed in a gray version of Aimee's pajamas, double-fists a couple of cocktails. "I always sleep in the nude," she says to explain why she seems so shaken by the whole pajamas thing.

"Always?" Lizzy asks.

"I don't own pajamas."

"A robe?"

"Not even a robe," Cindy says.

"That's not a real good environment for kids," Tommy Sue says earnestly.

"It's a good thing I don't have any."

Natalie saunters into the room in a long, chiffon, psychedelic-print nightgown with matching robe. Most people don't dress up that much for their weddings.

"Beautiful," Tommy Sue gasps as she walks up to Natalie and feels the fabric.

"It's nothing. From last year's collection," Natalie says.

There's a knock at the door. I look around the room. Everyone is here unless Aimee invited someone else at the last minute. Aimee walks over and opens the door. She says hello, doesn't let the person in, and turns her head to me. "You have a visitor." I cautiously walk over to the door. I have a visitor? Who even knows I live here?

It's Rafe. He holds a cardboard box with an odd assortment of stuff in his hands. Aimee makes way for me to stand directly in front of the doorway.

"Hi," I say with the intonation of a question.

"I found more of your stuff," he says and holds up the box. There's a large foam hand from a baseball game, a spider plant, a bottle of shampoo, and dish towels.

"You can keep them," I say.

He peers over my shoulder and sees the pack of women sitting in the living room. They stare hard at him.

"Could I talk to you for a minute, over there a little?" He motions toward his brand-new Honda parked in the driveway.

I'm about to answer when Cindy grabs my shoulder and says to Rafe, "Honey, it was nice of you to drop by but we're doing a little private party right now. If you could come back after you stop being an ass, that'd be great." She pulls me in the house and closes the door.

"Darling, there's a reason you broke up with him. There's no need to prolong it," she says to me as she guides me back toward the couch.

"I haven't been. He calls me a lot," I say.

"Don't pick up the phone," Cindy says.

"That's the miracle of caller ID," Natalie says.

I have been screening Rafe's calls but it's gotten more difficult. He's been leaving these messages that sound like he's crying or on the verge of it. The last one involved our cat plaintively meowing. I do miss our cat.

"Never go back to an old boyfriend. He's gonna think that he can treat you ten times worse than the first time because you came back," Cindy says.

Throughout the banter, Aimee stealthily refills everyone's glasses. We're all on a three-cocktail high. Natalie has been watching us carefully. She waits until we're lulled into a sense of comfort or maybe a condition in which we won't remember everything the next morning.

"I found out something about Bradford," she stutters.

The group quiets down. Everyone, even me, knows that Bradford is her last chance in Dallas. Natalie has dated most of the eligible "good" men in the city already and if they weren't willing to seal the deal the first time, the second time isn't going to do it. Aimee explained to me that if Bradford doesn't work out, Natalie will have to move to Atlanta or Houston for at least two years. If she's still single after two years she might have a chance again in Dallas, but it would be an uphill battle. Natalie made the unfortunate mistake of enjoying herself in her twenties and going a little wild in her hometown. The smart women leave that behavior in Las Vegas or Mexico.

"What is it, honey?" Lizzy asks with genuine concern.

Natalie looks into her drink and takes a couple of deep breaths, "Bradford's been on a lot of business trips lately. Strange ones to Wisconsin and North Dakota. I was curious. I broke into his e-mail."

"How'd you do that?" Tommy Sue interrupted.

"I bribed his secretary," Natalie says dismissively. "I opened up this folder in his e-mail titled 'Bouncing Bundle,' and there were all these messages from pregnant women. He's having sex with freaking pregnant women from all over the country. I can't believe he has a thing for fat women."

"Pregnant women, there's a difference," Aimee says contemplatively.

"Big, fat pregnant women. I don't understand. He gave me that Hermès scarf. You don't give Hermès unless you feel something. I don't look pregnant do I?" Natalie asks as she scans her skeletal frame.

"Maybe it's some kind of special charity," Lizzy offers up.

"He wrote to one woman in Boulder that he was looking forward to caressing her magnificently sumptuous belly," Natalie moans.

"I hope my husband treats me like that when I'm pregnant," Tommy Sue croons.

"The problem is Bradford isn't this woman's husband," Cindy says.

"How did you get into his e-mail again?" I ask. I'm in shock over an apparent new trend of pregnancy fetish and the blatant disregard for privacy.

"I asked his secretary, but if that didn't work I would've called the server and changed his pass code," Natalie says matter-of-factly. "What should I do? He's real rich and cute—you don't get that often, you know, rich and cute."

"I know. And didn't he just start spending the night? I don't think you should say anything. There are worse things than having a husband who likes pregnant women. They can't stay pregnant forever," Cindy says.

"You have to focus on closing the deal," Aimee says.

"You think he's the father of all those babies?" Tommy Sue asks.

"I don't think so. They're all married. And one woman, he hadn't even met her yet," Natalie responds.

"Online dating is amazing," Tommy Sue says.

"More like online perv-hunting," Cindy retorts.

"We have to get you a plan to close the deal," Aimee says.

"You're lucky. You know what your man's strange is. Now you have to look like what he wants," Cindy says.

"She should get pregnant?" Tommy Sue asks.

"Ideally. In the meantime, she can gain a little weight, stuff her bra," Cindy says.

I am amazed. This may be the length I have to go to, to land a man. Natalie is beautiful, smart, and funny, though I don't know if she realizes she's being funny when she is. Unfortunately, women's biology, and oftentimes our economics, make us much more aware of marriage earlier than men. A man can decide to get married for the first time at forty-two years old and have children with no problem. A woman the same age would have to enlist a team of fertility experts with less than a 50 percent chance of success.

Natalie stuffs her face with Fritos. She's already hard at work gaining weight. A look of ecstasy mixed with disgust crosses her face—years of convincing herself that food is bad battles with the fact that the food is delicious.

Feeling an intense desire to change the subject and wanting to use my new status as an insider to full advantage, I decide to take a poll to see how many of us have had plastic surgery.

"So, it's that truth-telling part of the evening," I announce. An immediate silence befalls the room and everyone gives me a diabolical look. "How many of us have come under the knife for cosmetic purposes?" I ask.

Ever so slowly, everyone but Lizzy raises their hand.

"Lizzy is the only purist," Cindy says.

"Actually, I've been thinking of getting liposuction. I don't think my thighs are going to shrink into my wedding dress. But it's so against my beliefs, I'm putting it off as long as possible."

"Good girl," Aimee says, a little sarcastically.

Natalie has had everything worked on. She's gone under the knife for breasts, nose, chin, and cheeks, and she's even been known to correct the surgeon's pronunciation of procedures and anatomy. She doesn't look remotely like her high school yearbook picture anymore; in fact, she looks a lot like the captain of the cheerleaders.

Aimee has even more expertise than Natalie. She went through three breast surgeries before she got the right look. She put it all on her credit card and keeps transferring to low-interest cards until she pays it all off. We're talking thirty thousand dollars or more.

"Implants have to go under the muscle. If the doctor doesn't put them under the muscle they look like two pieces of plastic sitting on your chest," Aimee says and takes a sip of her martini. "And if you breast-feed you'll have to get them redone. They sag."

"Can you breast-feed after getting implants?" I ask.

"If you have a good doctor. But if you have a reduction, forget about it," Aimee says.

"What about mine? What do you think?" Tommy Sue says as she stands up and pushes out her chest.

Aimee circles her. Then she walks up and squeezes her breasts.

"From the front they're pretty good. But from the side they're too round."

"I know. I was thinking about getting the tear-shaped ones."

"They're hip right now."

"Do you have them?" Tommy Sue asks.

"No, I have classic silicone."

"God, I'm so jealous. Silicone is the best," Tommy Sue says.

"Look at these," Aimee says and unbuttons her top, exposing the most beautiful and unnatural breasts I've ever seen. Even at sixteen, mine didn't look close to those.

"You have to give me the name of your doctor. I'd like to try those out," Tommy Sue says.

We move from men to surgery to men seamlessly. It feels like we're comparing recipes. Just add a dash of silicone and a GPS tracking system to your boyfriend's car, wait six months, and you'll be married.

Natalie, not surprisingly, is on the cutting edge of paranoia when it comes to the opposite sex. She already told us she tapped into her boyfriend's e-mail. She also figured out all his voice mail codes (work, home, and cell), arranged for an extra copy of his credit card bills to be mailed to her house each month, and has copies of everything on his key chain. I'm pretty cynical about men and fidelity, but Natalie is hard to keep up with. After what we've seen tonight, she also has good reason to be worried.

"How do you get away with all that?" Tommy Sue cries.

"Well, he doesn't know anything I do," Natalie says.

"That's my problem. I'm too obvious. One of my boyfriends caught me going through his wallet. That ended it," Tommy Sue says tearfully.

"Don't you think it's a bit obsessive?" I ask Natalie.

"No, I know what I want and I have to be deviously aggressive to get it. Y'all have seen the proof of that tonight," Natalie says.

"If I'm not one step ahead of even his subconscious thoughts, I don't stand a chance. I have to steer him toward the conclusion that I'm the one and marriage is the answer."

"I paid Rance's help to let me into his house when he was away," Aimee says as she rearranges junk food on the coffee table.

"Why?" Tommy Sue asks.

"For him to fall in love with me, he has to think we have a special connection. I had to go through his things to find out what we could connect on," Aimee says.

"What'd you find?" Lizzy asks.

"He loves G. I. Joe, tech companies, and Tony Robbins," Aimee replies.

"And now you love those things," Cindy says.

"Absolutely. I've been trying to improve my knowledge of military history," Aimee says. "I went on a date with him last night to talk about tech companies. He was eating out of the palm of my hand."

"I understand what you were trying to do, but aren't there laws against stalking?" Lizzy asks.

"Ends and means, darlin'. All these other she-wolves are stalking my man. Why can't I? Of course, I have to take a different approach now," Natalie says as she stuffs an Oreo in her mouth.

Giggles erupt around the living room.

"You're so lucky. You can eat whatever you want," Tommy Sue says miserably.

"Honey, are you sure he's worthy of such high-level surveillance?" Lizzy asks.

"Yes, and I'm going to make damn sure this rolls out. I'm not leaving anything to chance or human nature. . . ." Natalie trails off. "Love is a first-place prize masquerading as a feeling."

Aimee agrees. "It's not the emotion. The emotion fades. It's how you want your life to look when you're thirty, forty. What your kids' lives will be like. You can't wonder all the time if he's going to cheat. You have to accept that he will."

"Would you marry someone you're not attracted to?" I ask. Unlike my peers this evening, I admit to requiring some measurable and sustainable level of animal and intellectual attraction to the person I'm supposed to be sleeping with for the rest of my life.

"Yes, without question, if the other things are there," Aimee says.

"Friendship matters," Lizzy volunteers and collapses onto the sofa. Too much Diet Coke mixed with rum?

"Money, money, and kindness," Tommy Sue says.

"Attraction, chemistry, it all fades," Natalie says.

Lizzy is uncomfortably silent. She is the piggy bank jackpot. She's a millionaire herself, thanks to oil, and is getting married in a couple of months to J. T. (Hoss) Christenson. The wedding will be one of those grand Southern events at which you wear big hats and declare what religion of rich you are—Methodist or Baptist? Methodist is blue blood: small, older houses on big lots with horse stables. Baptist is big: big cars, big houses, big diamonds, big attitude, and big tacky. Lizzy is a Baptist, either by birthright or accident. Needless to say, it's the best kind of wedding to attend. I believe I heard that the bar at the reception will be an ice sculpture of Bevo, the University of Texas mascot, a longhorn steer.

Anyway, she's worth at least twenty million dollars and she's marrying a man who is attractive, charming, and doesn't have a penny to his name. She even jokes about her fiancé marrying her for her money. But it's a different thing when you're inadvertently assaulted with the truth.

"I think Hoss is attracted to me," Lizzy almost squeaks.

"Of course he is. They all talk big. But none of them would marry someone they're not in love with," I say.

"I love him," Lizzy says.

"That's just horrible. Love is the most wonderful and heartbreaking thing you can imagine," Aimee says. "It brings you so far up that you realize you're happy just cutting vegetables. When it ends, you can't sleep, eat, or concentrate. You watch a lot of bad TV and lose weight."

Her first husband burned her bad.

"Maybe that's what I need now," Lizzy says as she scoops up a handful of Fritos.

"Losing weight or daytime television?" Tommy Sue probes. She honestly doesn't know the answer.

Right on cue, there is a knock at the door. Popeye's fried chicken, mashed potatoes, and biscuits have arrived.

"Gay porn time," Aimee announces, rubbing the DVD between her legs to rhythmic pelvic gyrations. She slides in the DVD and pours another round of martinis as we transition from the sublimely painful to the utterly ridiculous. Why gay porn? More men, less analysis of how you should look, and the production value is so much better.

Aimee spreads a gingham picnic blanket on the floor. She places the chicken on a large china serving dish, the mashed potatoes in a crystal bowl, the gravy in a ceramic gravy boat, and the biscuits in a wicker basket.

"You can eat trashy food as long as it's in elegance," she says.

When she finally gives the okay to start eating, we circle the blanket and descend upon the food like wolves.

"Don't hog the gravy. Give it here," Cindy orders.

"Butter, we need more butter. I'm working on my pregnancy pouch," Natalie calls to Aimee. When Aimee doesn't move, Natalie gets up and takes a whole stick out of the refrigerator and puts it on her plate. She uses half of it on a biscuit and her mashed potatoes.

The room is full of the sounds of gay porn and chewing. We are all lulled into that stupefying contentment of having our basic desires met. Dallas women basically deny themselves the feeling of being full or satiated most of their lives so they can be five pounds underweight and fit into all their clothes. When they get to cut loose, watch out. They make up for all the times they said no to bread at dinner, declined a second glass of wine, and opted for the vegetable plate instead of the steak.

My eyes are riveted to the screen. A well-oiled man donning a construction hat massages another man's back. Both are impossibly fit and have absolutely no body hair.

"Why can't straight men look like that?" I ask.

"I've never seen a straight man who looks half as good," Cindy says.

"Hoss looks that good," Lizzy says.

"Is he gay?" Cindy asks.

"No," Lizzy says.

"Does he wax?" Cindy asks.

"No," Lizzy says.

"Then, he can't look that good. Men with pubic hair are gross."

"Do your men wax?" Natalie asks.

"Damn right. If I have to, then so do they," Cindy says.

"But how?" Natalie murmurs incredulous.

"If they want me to go down on them, they have to wax it," Cindy says. "Darling, they smell otherwise."

"I'm starting to feel guilty," Tommy Sue says as she looks back and forth between what she's eating and the men's toned bodies.

"Don't even think about barfing it up in my bathroom. I just cleaned it," Aimee says.

Tommy Sue puts down her food and squeezes her stomach.

"Oh, get off it. You're the size of a toothpick," Aimee says.

"I think I could lose a couple more pounds," Tommy Sue says, evaluating her body.

"Jesus, women like you really piss me off," Aimee screeches. "I exercise. I diet. I look pretty good. And then a waif like you says she's fat. How do you think that makes me feel?"

The alcohol has unleashed Aimee's inner feminist. She's voiced a universal feeling. We all turn to Tommy Sue for a response. She looks down at the picnic blanket as if she'll find the answer among the greasy chicken bones.

"I never thought about it. I don't think any of y'all are fat. Y'all look great," she stammers, and glances up at each one of us. "It's me. I'm the problem."

"You need to get some appreciation of yourself," Cindy says. "It's pathetic."

"I just . . ." Tommy Sue says.

"Don't speak. Think about it," Cindy says.

It's three a.m. We've alternated between *You've Got Mail* and *You Got Nailed*. We're all gloriously, deliciously overserved. Tommy Sue's mouth has gaped open and faint snores gurgle out. Natalie is in my bedroom checking Bradford's e-mail, voice mail, and credit card account. No rest for the wickedly paranoid. Aimee is making brownies. She bakes whenever she's stressed or drunk.

"That guy in the last video. I think he's what Baylor looks like naked," I say.

"What are you talking about?" Aimee yells, charging from the kitchen into the living room with a spoonful of batter in her hand. "Baylor isn't a target. He's not available."

"He's not dating anyone," Lizzy says.

"He doesn't have any of his own money," Aimee says.

"What are you talking about? He has a huge trust fund. I don't think he'll ever get married," Cindy says. "He's one of the toxic bachelors."

Toxic bachelors are the men who date women for two, three, five years. They wring their peak years of looks and reproduction out of them and then dump them when they're done. They simply move on to the next attractive woman while the dumped woman has to scramble to find an alternative plan of action.

"You know I love Baylor, but he's not part of the playing field. He's not your type. He's very finicky," Aimee says.

"What do you mean he's finicky?" Cindy asks, and then stops to consider what Aimee's said. "Yeah, I guess he is, in a way, but I don't see why that should matter."

"It should matter to Jenny and to all of us," Aimee says, like she's trying to cue Cindy into something.

"Finicky how?" I ask.

"He's off-limits," Aimee repeats and whips back into the kitchen. I detect traces of that same harsh tone in her voice.

Note to self: Don't mention Monday night date with Baylor to Aimee.

"Do you think Hoss will be happy?" Lizzy asks suddenly.

"Will *you* be happy? That's the most important thing. Darling, you're the one with the money. You have all the power," Cindy says.

But that's not what's important to Lizzy. Lizzy doesn't get a rush by just having the knowledge that she could walk into Hermès and buy anything she wants and pay it off the same day. She wears her Guccis until they fall apart. She used to think nothing of devouring half a pizza while watching a stack of DVDs with me. Lizzy doesn't want power. She wants what the consensus this evening says doesn't last and may not even really exist.

"I think he really loves you," I say.

"And, if nothing else, your checkbook will make him happy," Cindy says.

"Was marrying for money ever really worth it for you?" Lizzy asks her.

"Hell, yeah," Cindy says, examining the flawless diamond rings that populate her fingers.

"Then, why did you get divorced?" Lizzy asks.

"Because it wasn't so worth it to them apparently," she says.

Another awkward moment and we realize that, yes, Cindy Trammel does have a heart. Et tu, Tin Man? "I thought you always left them," I say gracefully, neglecting to mention the discovery of her first betrothed and the maid of honor making the beast with two backs in the bathroom.

"Well, I got a lot out of the deals—I mean, marriages," Cindy says.

The cold hard truth. Women leave men a lot less than they leave us, even if we do have cellulite-free legs. What did Robert Earl say? *Leavin's always easier, than bein' left behind.*

"Who would you marry now?" Lizzy asks.

"I don't know. I guess the only thing I need from a guy now is kids," Cindy says.

"You, a mother? Yeah right, how would you deal with the weight gain?" Aimee laughs.

"That's a problem, isn't it? Oh, what the hell, I'd do it. I mean, it's supposed to be the most special relationship in your life, or something like that, right? Or, maybe I'll change my mind and go back to being a class A sexual predator for as long as I can get away with it," she slurs.

Just then Natalie comes storming out of my bedroom with a piece of paper in her fist.

"Can you believe this? I can't fucking believe this," Natalie rants as she paces frantically. "I mean, we have sex almost every night. I'm not fat. I lift weights. I jog. I've had every plastic surgery I can think of. I'm smart. I can suck a golf ball through a garden hose and jump-start a Harley. Why would he do this?"

I pry the piece of paper from her fingers. It's a copy of an e-mail to Bradford from some nasty woman.

From: jlilly@capitol.com
To: bgoodnight@heliooil.com
Subject: Bump rising

Babycakes,
I ate two hot fudge sundaes today! My belly aches for you. When are
you going to come rub it? You make my skin feel the bestest.
xxoo, Sweetie

"Bestest? Who uses 'bestest' besides trailer trash?" Natalie yells.

"Do you know who this is?" I ask.

"Not a fucking idea," she growls. "She could be any number of
sluts in that bouncing bundle file. I think she's local, though. She
sounds like she is. Oh, what am I going to do?"

Natalie sits down on the floor, grabs her knees, and rocks. The
poor girl has invested years in Bradford. It looks as though that
time could be lost and she has nothing to show for it. If men aren't
interested in a commitment, there should be a law that requires
them to disclose that fact within six months of the relationship.
Otherwise it's false advertising. If Natalie had any clue what a
fetish Bradford had, she would have broken off the relationship
within the first year. Early on, some reports had come back to her
about his liberal attitude toward monogamy. But none of the stories on their own sounded too horrible, so she stuck with it. Now,
after three years of accumulated tales, she has become a paranoid
detective of adultery. She can't give up on him because of the investment and her reputation. She'd rather get her first marriage
out of the way and after a couple of years move on. Why? Because
a marriage, even a less than ideal one, establishes that there's nothing wrong with you. You can close a deal.

"Should I forget about it?" Natalie asks.

"Hell, no," Cindy says. "Honey, you figure out the next time
he's supposed to meet with one of these freaks and intercede. Keep
doing that 'til you get knocked up. Then say you have half a mind
to go over to his parents' house and show them the grandchild in
your belly. The only way you'll get him to the altar is if you make
the alternative seem much worse."

Natalie nods her head in silent agreement. She reaches for her makeup bag and applies her face. Makeup is to Natalie what baking is to Aimee.

"You're tough," I say to Cindy.

"You learn what men respond to and fear is one of their greatest motivators," she says.

"You should be a divorce lawyer."

"Don't you think Natalie can do better?" Lizzy says.

"She will in her next marriage," Cindy says.

"For damn sure I will." Natalie sniffles as she dusts her face with bronzer.

All the emotion has Lizzy looking frightened. I wonder if she's flashing back to her childhood, which consisted of knock-down, drag-out fights between her parents and then watching them pretend to make up. No wonder she's a little worried about lifelong commitment. She's told me some stories and gossipy women have filled in the rest of the details. Lizzy's dad's favorite pastime was chasing women of all sorts, including the maid, a vice president at his oil company, his sister-in-law, short women, fat women, women with teeth missing. You name it.

Lizzy's mother, who can be as sweet as Lizzy but also has a will of steel, wouldn't forgive these dalliances. She would get into fine fighting form with a couple of cocktails, then she'd explode at the dinner table, detailing exactly what her husband's life would be like without her—jobless, living in a condo with wall-to-wall shag carpeting and green wallpaper. Her dad would cower and become loving and apologetic for a few weeks, but only until he needed another taste.

You see, both of Lizzy's parents had money when they married, but the mother was the one with the business sense. She grew their fortunes to three times their original worth within ten years. Her father would have blown through his share of it in a couple of years if he were on his own. All he knows how to do is spend it. He's been allowed to represent the company because Texas businessmen still prefer to deal with other white businessmen rather than a woman or man of any other color. But her dad is really a figurehead, nothing more.

"Don't worry, you and Hoss will be fine," I say.

She nods. Tommy Sue wakes up, smelling the fresh baked brownies that Aimee is taking out of the oven.

"I found Chase with a hooker. That's why we broke up," Tommy Sue mumbles as she hoists herself upright. Chase is her second failed attempt at a fiancé. The first was the one who caught her going through his wallet.

"A couple of my friends dragged me to Secrets for fun and I'm there for a few minutes before I think I see Chase in the back room. You know, the one with the gauzy curtains. I walk over and there he is, having sex with a woman with a Smurf tattoo on her butt."

This is another Texas oddity. Keeping in mind that this is the Bible Belt, there are more strip clubs in Dallas than New York and L.A. put together, and there's no shame in going to them. Businessmen often have professional lunches there. One co-worker of mine invited me to what I thought was a bar but turned out to be a full-nude club. It was hard to tell if he thought this was seductive or normal. Many young Texas women think it's sort of avant-garde or dangerous to visit them, which is what had motivated Tommy Sue to walk on the wild side that night. But she hadn't counted on the long-shot consequences.

"I wonder if I should hire a private eye to follow him. Then I could figure out what the normal setup is with these women," Natalie muses.

"Absolutely, I have the perfect man for you. Caught my first husband with a seventeen-year-old. That was a good settlement," Cindy says as she reaches for her purse and pulls out her phone and a notebook. She writes down his number and hands it to Natalie. Natalie carefully folds the paper and puts it in her purse.

From there things get hazy, and my memory of the evening is scattered at best. I remember Cindy patting Natalie on the back and congratulating her for stepping up to the plate with her husband-hunting commitment. "We're gonna get that son of a bitch," she said. I recall Aimee telling Tommy Sue she loved her just the way she was and trying to get her to eat more brownies. I saw Lizzy eating a mountain of brownies with a look of ecstasy on her face. At some point I decided it was a good idea to lie down on the rug with a pillow and an edge of the down comforter.

At ten a.m. on Sunday morning, I wake up with a dry mouth, throbbing head, and the desire to go back to sleep until the pain goes away. I crawl to the bathroom, grab the large bottle of Excedrin, and carry it back to the living room. I hand out pills to all assembled and receive groans of thanks. We sleep for another three hours.

The end of a sleepover, like the end of a good movie, is always a letdown. You've had all this bonding excitement for hours and then you're left alone again. It's just you and the problems you had blissfully drowned out for a while. Problems like finding a husband. I have to get on that.

Chapter Five

Women Arrive Early and Dressed to Kill

It is eight a.m. My Gucci stilettos click-clack on the concrete floor of Whole Foods. I'm in prime husband-hunting territory. Rich men shop organic in the morning.

"What about that guy?" I whisper to Aimee and nudge her line of sight toward the olive bar. A man in a ratty old T-shirt with impressive pecs and buttery blond hair scoops up kalamata olives.

"Not a chance," Aimee sniffs and steers our cart away.

"Why? He's really cute," I practically whine.

"Yes, he's cute. Does he have money? No. Honey, you have to realize rich men aren't gonna be the most attractive," she says as she smiles at a troll of a man in a beautiful suit.

"So he's more my speed?" I ask about the man with only a few strands of hair left around his ears. I'm still learning.

"He's in the ballpark. Don't worry, honey, there are tons of options here," Aimee says as she propels the cart forward.

As I'm discovering, rich men like to purchase for themselves because it exudes power: *I am so wealthy that I can shop leisurely at eight a.m.* But they are hard to distinguish from the loser, *I lost my job and live off my mother but I am still interested in designer food.* At least for me, they are. I have to learn the subtle distinctions between the two. For instance, Aimee pointed out to me that rich men walk the aisles with confidence, their shoulders back and down, almost arrogant. The unemployed slouch.

As I scan the shelf for noncarbohydrate spelt flour, I can see who's checking me and Aimee out from the corner of my eye. So far I have been visually probed by a paunchy short-sleeved type (are they allowed in here?), a logo T-shirt bicycle shorts fellow, and one Brioni suit. The Brioni isn't bad. Nice thighs, no wedding ring, and a full head of hair. I eye-signal to Aimee, "What about him?" She waves me off with a quick nod of her head and an under-the-breath "psycho ex-wife."

I put the flour in the cart and head toward the cleaning supplies without even stopping to question how Aimee can tell that about him. She's the professional, after all. I am about to put dishwasher soap in the basket when I feel an icy cold death grip on my wrist.

"Put it back," Aimee sweetly commands. Her voice doesn't show her annoyance; it's all in her wrist. I drop the bottle like it's on fire. Aimee releases her grip.

"What?"

"You don't want these men to think of you cleaning," she says.

"It's dishwasher soap. It's hardly a Brillo pad and rubber gloves," I say.

"Cleaning isn't sexy. It says you're the help," she says as she moves us away from any type of cleaning product.

There are specific rules to shopping for men.

- You must be careful what food you put in your basket; it basically telegraphs who you are. In other words, you're getting tea not only because you like it, but because it says you're health-conscious and hip, implying subliminally that you know tea is now considered the new coffee.

- Always pay with a credit card. Cash is tacky.

- You must be done up. Something about the incongruence of wearing heels in a grocery store makes men remember you.

- Arrive early. The competition arrives at eight a.m. in the frozen food section dressed to kill or, at least, catch and release.

I am wearing a pencil skirt that gives a nice lift to my ass and a sheer silk Prada shell that is feminine and sexy. Aimee wears a Dolce & Gabbana dress that skims every curve. Both outfits are guaranteed to make men linger on your body and wonder what you'd be like in bed. The longer a man thinks about you sexually, the better he thinks your personality is. This translates to elevating your desirability. Shallow? Yes. But we're on a mission here and I'm an achiever. Though to be honest, I broke every grocery shopping rule the other day and landed a date with Baylor.

In New York, my friends didn't even start to think about marriage until they were thirty-six. And even then it was only because they were beginning to recycle old boyfriends. Here, if you're single at thirty-six, you're considered old, rich, or gay. It's the same thing with pastels. In New York, I only wore black, but bit by bit pink has begun to look like a nice color for a dress to me. Pathetic, I know. At least, I'm not wearing capris.

We walk over to the organic, free-range, cruelty-free fruit section and spot the same woman who took the underwear out of my hands outside my apartment. She's dressed in the standard high heels and body-hugging outfit of a husband-hunter—caramel pony hair shoes, drain pipe jeans, and a casual but expensive honey-colored silk blouse that highlights the golden glow of her skin. I notice as she handles the bok choy that she has a sizable ring on her wedding finger.

"That's the woman that Rafe got fancy with," I whisper to Aimee as I slow down our cart. "Who is she?"

Aimee looks over fresh strawberries while she surveys.

"That can't be. Are you sure?" Aimee says.

"We could drop something and watch her bend over. I guarantee that she'll have on C. Gilson underwear," I say. I resist my urge
to throw produce on the ground near her feet.

"That's Meg Koch. She married very well. No offense, but I
can't see a reason why she'd be remotely interested in a guy like
Rafe. I mean if you're gonna cheat, cheat with someone who has a
nice body or sex appeal," she says.

True, Rafe does have a chicken chest.

"I swear to God that's her," I whisper.

Meg looks in our direction. She must have attention radar. She
spots Aimee and waves. Aimee pushes our cart in her direction. I
follow.

"Hey, girl," Meg calls to Aimee. "I haven't seen you in a blue
moon. I've been too damn busy to keep up with you. Love the
stilettos. Gucci? Thought so. We have to sit down and talk some
talk."

I know this much, when women like Meg say "talk some talk,"
they don't mean they want to have a conversation. They want to
machine-gun questions and talk over your responses. She's the
type of woman who talks a blue streak to stay afloat, as though
stopping would give her pause to reflect on her circumstances. I
think she must breathe through her ears.

She hugs Aimee to the point of making her almost pass out as
she checks me out.

"And who's your friend?" she asks Aimee while eyeing me.

"I'm Jenny," I say and extend my hand.

"This is one of my closest friends and roommate," Aimee says.

"I'm Meg. You must've just moved in, huh?" Meg says as she
shakes my hand with all the warmth of a cobra. I know this is the
woman whom I met outside my old apartment. If I could just get
her to bend over to prove it.

"Yep, just over a month ago," I say as I extract my hand from
her tanned hide.

"Bad breakup? That's always when women search out the comfort of their girlfriends," she says. "Well, we'll have to get together
for some drinks to drown your sorrows. Are you going to Lizzy's
lingerie shower?"

"Yes, yes we are. How are you doing? Did you survive the family reunion?" Aimee asks.

Apparently, Meg's husband is rich but his family is even richer and Meg has to deal with a cantankerous mother-in-law who hammers her with questions about the arrival of grandchildren. Family dinners turn into interrogations when the two of them are seated close.

"Fine, fine. I had her in the palm of my hand, so to speak. A well-trained sheep will do that, you know," she says with a laugh.

Sheep jokes in a grocery store. Texans do love talk of bestiality. It's sort of a new coda of the West. Sheep joke punch lines. It took me forever to understand half of them. The first one I heard when I came out here, and the one Meg's referring to, is about a farmer on trial for alleged unnatural relations with one of his sheep. The witness, between sobs of disgust, describes the act, and, with further revulsion, notes that the sheep, postcoital, licked the defendant's genitalia. One of the jurors nods and says, "A well-trained sheep will do that." The farmer is acquitted.

Translation: Tell the mother-in-law what she wants to hear and she'll get off your back.

Aimee and Meg arrange to meet at Lizzy's shower. Even as Aimee talks, I know it's a bad idea. Meg is one of those women with whom you have a very pleasant evening, then pay for it dearly when she spreads gossip about you like manure on a lawn. She's a woman-hater.

She believes that any heterosexual male with a pulse is her territory and anyone with a uterus and Gucci heels is a competitor. It would be too kind to call her a rattlesnake; she never rattles before she sinks her fangs into you.

Meg glides off to the meat section, and I point out to Aimee a view of Meg's backside. We can see slate blue silk with delicate embroidery poking out of her low-rise jeans.

"Do you believe me now?" I ask.

"I don't get that. Rafe's not her type. Baylor was her type, 'til he broke off their affair," Aimee says.

Is every man I'm interested in destined to sleep with Meg instead of me?

"What? Her and Baylor?" I ask incredulous. "She's a snake. She's not even fifty percent human. She's jacked up with too much silicone to feel empathy anymore."

"What'd I tell you about Baylor? He's more dangerous than he looks," Aimee says as she steps on my foot, signaling me to turn.

I turn, knock over a whole pile of pesticide-free papaya, and find an attractive athletic man who I vaguely recognize staring at us. He bends down and helps me pick up the fruit.

"Thank you," I say, crouching, which I can barely accomplish in the skirt.

"I'm Jackson Ray. We met at Aimee's pregame party a while back."

"I'll do another one when your team is doing better," Aimee says as she takes papaya from us and arranges it on the table.

Yeah, that's right, Jackson Ray, huge sports fan. It all comes back to me. The kind that gets offended when you don't do the good luck things like crossing your fingers and putting them behind your back or wearing a baseball cap inside out during a two-minute drill. I remember him as being good-natured, even when he was demanding that everyone do the good luck rituals with him. And his family is loaded. They own a school uniform company that supplies all of the religious schools in Texas with their outfits. There are a lot of religious schools in this state. The Ray family owns a ranch out by Waco, where Baylor University, the Texas Baptist hub, is located. Jerusalem on the Brazos, as the unwashed call it. They also have a flat in London and a lodge in Aspen. Jackson is a VP of sales for the Cowboys or the Stars, or some sports team. He got the job through family connections. Let's be honest here: The rich hire the rich. Even though Jackson (or "Red," as his friends call him for reasons I may not want to know) doesn't need the money, I bet he makes more than the regular Joe does in his position.

"My team? Who's your team, Aimee? The Yankees?" Jackson asks.

"That's my team. I'm from New York and they do hold a record number of championships," I say.

It should be noted that the grocery store pickup is best if you have already met the man once in some other context. Then it's not as if you're some creepy, desperate woman picking up a guy at the supermarket, even if you are. You know him and you're just saying hi.

"How do you feel about college football?" he asks.

"Hook 'em horns," I say as I flash the hand sign.

We chat as Aimee pretends to be engrossed with arranging the papaya. We make a date. Tonight, dinner at his house. He'll cook. I'm sure that means grill. Texas men know how to char meat but that's about it. It's as if the act of baking fish in the kitchen would be an assault to their manhood. Any slight to manliness is taken here like a dueling offense. Sort of like saying something about your mother in New York.

He walks off toward the meat department. Aimee smiles at me with so much pride that I feel like I just won the sixth-grade spelling bee.

"That was beautiful, darling. You were witty and charming but not pushy. You gave him room to maneuver and now you have your first live bait on the hook," she says as we walk toward the checkout. "We're gonna have to go into all-out glamour mode to get you ready for tonight. Not only is Red attractive, he has his own funds, huge funds."

"Yeah, I'm lucky to get attractive, huh," I say.

"You have no idea," Aimee replies.

"How come you don't go for him?" I ask.

"Because I'm going for the billionaire level," she says.

"Maybe I should, too," I ponder.

"You're not that shallow," she says as she puts our food on the conveyor belt.

The thing you realize when you start looking for a wealthy man is that you have to narrow down the wealth you're looking for. Avoid the club scene. Those rich playboys are after a quick lay and maybe an enabler for their cocaine/sex/alcohol addiction. Run screaming from the ones who've never worked. They have no concept of reality and probably don't control their money. Say no to the "superstar" rich, the ones who are on a first-name basis with the media and have handlers. Those guys are pure ego and egos need conquests.

Humble beginnings are good, if they're not angry about it. The humanitarian rich, meaning the ones who donate money to homeless shelters and pass as Democrats, are the ones you want. Men with face-lifts are okay. Even a bit of liposuction is acceptable. But when you start getting into hair plugs and chest implants, you'll find a man who'll judge you as harshly as he judges himself.

According to Aimee, you should look for a man between ten and twenty-five years older than you. There's a very good reason for this. Most of the upper-echelon trophy wives pride themselves on not looking too ridiculous with their husbands but looking more like an attractive couple. If they're too old, you're Anna Nicole Smith. If they're too close to your age, you're in serious danger of replacement.

We walk out of the store just as Red climbs into a Ford truck. He has a big yellow Lab in the passenger seat, who licks him all over his face. Gross. Does he know where that tongue has been? Will I get some of the residue tonight? Okay, at least I know his type. Dog and truck guy with a soft spot for organic veggies and a sports obsession. He works but he doesn't have to, which shows some spunk. I'm being charitable; it could be evidence of greed. You can tell he doesn't flaunt his wealth, because, honey, he could afford a lot more than a truck. And he's health-conscious. Probably plays work-league sports and has a history of high blood pressure in the family, so he's taking precautions now. I'm not a reporter for nothing.

"I need to wear something washable tonight or else I'll get schmutz all over my silk," I say to Aimee as I point to Red and the dog.

"Schmutz?"

"Yeah, you know, unidentifiable crap you find on your clothing," I say as Aimee ushers me into her car.

"Honey, promise me you'll never say words like *schmutz* again," she begs.

"Okay, any particular reason why?"

"Honey, I don't want to offend your sense of religious or ethnic pride, and I'm not like this, but lots of people here don't like Jews," Aimee says.

She gives me the lowdown. The men we're chasing are upper-class Dallas society, which overall means Christians. In Texas, Jews and Christians still don't mix much socially. For example, there are country clubs in Dallas that to this day don't accept Jewish members. The motto appears to be: It's best not to mix unless you're trying to convert a person to the Christian faith.

"It's not a problem as long as you don't mention your mother is Jewish. I mean your last name, Barton, doesn't sound ethnic," Aimee says.

"My dad's not Jewish."

"Oh, you're only half. That's a bonus."

"What if I get serious with a guy? He's gonna meet my mother," I say.

"It's probably okay to eventually tell a guy. Once he likes you it's not gonna matter. It's not like you plan on raising your kids Jewish."

I pause to think about that. Would I raise my kids Jewish? I don't know, but I'd like the option. It's not like I go to synagogue or observe any holidays. But it's a solid religion. It's been around for millennia. Plus, what would my mother say? She'd be hurt that I pretended not to be Jewish, was planning on settling in a Jewish-ambivalent part of the country, and had basically agreed as a condition of marriage to be Christian. Though the promise of grandchildren may counteract all the negatives for her.

"So you're telling me to lie about my background?" I ask Aimee to triple-clarify.

"Honey, don't lie. Just don't mention it," she says, and glides back to the subject of Jackson Ray. "His family is big Christian. I'm glad we had this talk before dinner tonight. It wouldn't have gone over well on the first date. I remember that mutt is a big licker. You're probably gonna be in for baseball in some form, too."

I nod my head. I'm still reeling from the whole hiding-my-heritage-to-land-a-husband thing. Perhaps I was naïve. I didn't even consider that would be a factor. People intermarry all the time without as much as a second thought nowadays. The biggest problem seems to be finding a minister and a rabbi to mutually perform the wedding ceremony. Is Texas that far behind the rest of the country?

I try to picture my wedding to a Texan and all I can see is a wedding cake with a large Jesus painted on it. I don't think I can do this. I can't give up part of my identity to land a husband. That's too shallow even for me.

"I can't lie about being Jewish," I say, "and what does it matter anyway? Are people still so prejudiced here?"

"It's not that they're prejudiced. They don't know many Jews. If they did, I think their views would be different. You've changed how I think," Aimee explains.

"So you used to think what? That we're cheapskates who will screw you over in business?"

"Exactly."

"You're serious," I say as I give her a long, appraising stare.

"I could act all nice and gloss this over but I'm telling you the truth. The truth of husband-hunting here is that you have an opportunity to expand a man's mind about his views on Jews but you have to get his heart first," Aimee says.

She looks at my pale, shock-stricken face and smiles sincerely at me as she pats my arm in a comforting way.

"Promise me you'll keep your date with Jackson tonight. Give him one chance," she says as she pulls into our driveway. I get out of her car and jump into my own so I can drive to work.

I start my junky Honda and head downtown. As soon as I'm out of Aimee's line of sight, I grab my cell phone and dial my mother. She immediately launches into the latest crisis with my sister. Clomid isn't working. The doctors are discussing doing a procedure that would essentially Roto-Rooter out her fallopian tubes, but they're not sure it would help. My mother is in tears. She wails that she'll never be a grandmother. I try to console her but everything I say seems to incite a higher level of crying. After twenty minutes of this, I pull out the only other thing I can think to say to her. "Remember I'll be married within the year."

There's a pause in the wailing. It's like when you give a hysterical baby a pacifier. There's blissful silence on the other end of the line. She blows her nose and sniffles.

"You mean it?" she asks.

"Yes," I say tentatively.

"You don't mean it," she says and begins to whimper again.

"I absolutely do," I say as I recommit myself to the husband-hunt.

After that, she is ecstatic. She babbles on about her neighbor, Mrs. Kirschenbaum, and her two little grandchildren. The children came to visit their grandmother for a whole week and my mother made them macaroons, which they loved. She tells me about her other neighbor, Mrs. Taylor, whose daughter is expecting any day now. They're going to name the little girl Prudence. My mother strongly disapproves. It's like she's playing grandmother by proxy with these children, like she's practicing for her big moment as an official grandmother.

As she talks I make a mental map of my husband-hunting strategy. Tonight, I have the date with Jackson Ray. I have something else going on tonight, too, I think. What is it? I run through a checklist of possibilities—I'm not traveling anywhere, I don't have to work late, and I don't have any girlfriend commitments. Baylor. I have a date with Baylor. Jesus (practicing my Christian), since Aimee knows about Red I guess I'm going to have to reschedule Baylor.

The question is: Are Baylor and Red friends? Will Baylor hear about my date with Red? Highly doubtful. Baylor seems more Scotch and Red seems more Lone Star beer. Plus, guys don't talk about who they're seeing unless it's serious and they're forced to explain where they're spending all their time.

I wonder if I can husband-hunt two guys at the same time. Is that kosher? I mean okay?

Too bad, I'd like to see Baylor. I keep thinking about the line of his shoulders in a suit jacket. They look clean and in control. Then I go to his smile. He has this mischievous, up-to-no-good grin that I love. Maybe he's free Tuesday night. No, Tuesday night is a shower for Lizzy. Maybe I could see him later tonight. I could spend a couple of hours with Red and hightail it off to Baylor's house. No, that's bad. I have to be committed to my goal. Plus, should Baylor be all that attractive to me now that I know about his and Meg's past? I don't need to get involved with another un-trustworthy schlub with an affection for anorexic vipers. I did that already and I didn't even get to keep the underwear.

I should concentrate on Jackson. Forget Baylor. Focus on the dollar signs. And, of course, his other attributes. I'm sure he's kind, funny, smart, loving, and all that. I have to remember to use anticellulite cream before I go over there tonight. Wear jeans and be casual. Otherwise, all the while I'll be thinking, *Hey, I'm re-laxed but I don't want your dog to slobber all over my silk Prada.*

Chapter Six

Lick the Log—Time to Put On Your Game Face

It's been a day from hell. Not only am I sitting behind a desk in stylish and impossibly uncomfortable clothing, but I'm working like a dog and it shows no sign of stopping. Why is it that after twenty minutes of sitting, skirts seem to magically ride up to your navel, revealing every spider vein your mother endowed you with? Goddamn, I much prefer a good pair of Chloé pants. They make your ass look great and everything else is covered.

My work usually involves writing little paragraphs about earnings reports and public offerings. It's the kind of work that keeps me employed and takes about three hours a day. The rest of the time I report on stories that I hope will make the front page of the paper. Stories that people will tear out and put on their refrigerators and e-mail to their friends. Stories that *People* magazine will rip off. The top editor of the paper reads the magazine religiously. When he sees a story they've swiped from the paper it's a gold star on the reporter's record and helps lead to a promotion. A promotion leads to writing fewer little paragraphs and focusing more on writing great pieces.

So I focus on the possibility of making a minute step up the corporate ladder and spend the rest of the day making phone calls to sources, staring at my computer screen, talking to my co-workers, and waiting for something brilliant to occur to me. Trust me, this is a big improvement on what I did at the paper when I started four years ago. Then I was only allowed to write little boxes.

Today is the monthly retail report. I only have to do this twice a year since I share the task with retail reporters in other bureaus. Which means I do it just enough times to vaguely remember how to do it, but that doesn't prevent me from screwing it up. I'm supposed to collect monthly sales data from twenty different store chains across the country, put it in a graph, and get quotes from stores and analysts about what it all means. It usually means nothing. I then have to write something that bears some faint resemblance to what everyone said. This month, I'm saying that rain dampened retail sales. It's the writing equivalent of a root canal.

I've been calling sources since I walked in this morning. I alternate calling a source with calling Baylor to try to rearrange our date. He calls me back when I'm in the middle of an interview on durable goods. He leaves a message. I call back and he's in some meeting about family matters. We repeat the cycle three times before I get through.

"Your family must have a lot of baggage," I say.

"True, but why do you say that?" Baylor asks.

"Because you said you were doing a 'little' bit of work for your family when you talked to me, but your assistant makes it sound like you're running a Fortune 500 company," I say.

"It's all relative to how much you can handle. So I was thinking of dinner around seven," he says, changing the subject.

"I was hoping we could do something closer to Wednesday night. I have this deadline tonight and an angry editor headed my way," I say, which is completely true. I can see Carol's head bob as she stomps toward my cubicle.

"Tuesday?" he asks.

"Tuesday I have this lingerie-sex-party thing. Wednesday?" I reply.

"Sure," he says, again thrown off by my odd extracurricular activities.

"Great. Gotta go," I say cutting him off in time to make myself look incredibly busy as Carol puts her hands on the top of my cubicle wall.

"Done?" Carol asks in a voice that sounds more like a command.

It's only four-twenty. I have at least another hour before I'm obligated to turn my story over and I intend to take full advantage of that time.

"Almost," I say as I smile sweetly back at her. I'm trying to incorporate Aimee's technique of insincere kindness into my management of people.

Carol grunts and walks away. Normally, she would do more to chastise me, something like a verbal assault. I guess my kindness strategy is working.

I celebrate my victories at work and in husband-hunting while I wait for Kohl's to call me back with figures on acrylic sweater sales. I text Cindy, "Checked out of W. Foods w/Red Ray dinner 2nite."

She texts back, "Watch out for bank walkers."

Translation: You know when country boys are skinny-dipping in the river because there's always one who is walking on the bank talking up his ability to swim, dive, or use the tire swing. In this case, I am the braggart walking on the riverbank. In other words, I'm showing off.

I text back, "Far, Wide, and Handsome."

Translation: Far, Wide, and Handsome means that you did something well. In husband-hunting terms, I did Jackson Ray far, wide, and handsome. This doesn't mean I had sex with him; it means I made a good impression, and now I can reel him in.

So I've rewritten the story a dozen times in the last half hour. I'm trying to create a shred of something original. The story is due at 5:30. At 5:25 I grimace, punch SEND, and my story is instantaneously in the hands of Carol, the troll editor under the bridge. She has to look at it and ship the story to New York. If writing the story was painful, what comes next is even worse.

Carol's chin is hanging over my cubicle in moments. I can see the sarcasm dripping off the Velcro siding between us. I guess the kindness technique only lasts for so long.

"Was today Short Attention Span Theater Day or Bring Your Retard to Work Day?" she says sneeringly. "Does Jennifer Barton still work here? Did you write this pabulum? Walk this way, please."

If I walked that way I'd be in a zoo with the pachyderms. She waddles. I slink into her corner office. I absolutely hate this. An eight on the fear and loathing scale. She tells me to pull up a chair next to hers as she edits my story, so that I can see the carnage first-hand. She's always chewing sugarless gum, chocolate, or some nicotine product. She smells like Juicy Fruit in an ashtray. Without fail, she wants changes in the story that there's no way I could accomplish without a couple of days' lead time. So we beat the dead horse, wave the bloody red shirt, and regroup.

I race back to my desk to retrieve a notebook. When I take my seat again, I see that she's already cut and pasted. The story looks like disconnected scraps of paragraphs. It's the journalist's equivalent of surgery without the benefit of anesthesia, and it's going to take forever, with or without the sarcasm.

I curse myself. Don't try so hard. Next time just write the story in standard form. She loves that.

I don't escape until seven. I race to Rafe's apartment because it's my turn to take the kitty. Never agree to joint custody of a pet with an ex.

When I finally called Rafe back on Sunday after the sleepover, he insisted that it's in the cat's best interest to have a home with us both; otherwise it would always miss one of us. I was about to say no to the whole idea when I heard the cat once again plaintively meow over the phone. My heart broke a little. I have a huge soft spot for animals. I can never go to the pound because I'd wind up adopting at least half the animals in there.

So I agreed. I'm supposed to take the cat, Mr. Tatters (I didn't name him), for two weeks of the month and Rafe has him the other two. I wonder how Meg gets along with Mr. Tatters. He's not the best with new people or people having sex. He used to attack Rafe and me because he thought a mouse or something was moving under the covers. Wouldn't that be appropriate? A cat with real claws attacking Meg.

I don't have high hopes for our joint custody. Cats don't like change. I predict the poor animal will spend the first day at my house under the bed, too terrified or angry to come out. By the end of week two, he'll actually jump on my lap and purr. But then he'll be back in the kitty cage and back with Rafe.

I run to the elevator and down the hall, knock wildly on Rafe's door, and hear him rattling around in his apartment. Typical slacker behavior. They have a challenged view of the time-space continuum. Finally, there's a slow door-opening, like Dracula lifting the cover of his tomb.

I push my way inside. "Hey, where's Mr. Tatters? Is he ready?" I say as I scan for the kitty cage and cat. Neither is apparent.

"Yeah, why don't you come in and I'll round him up. Have a seat." He gestures to a newspaper strewn couch. Cabbage head ambles toward the living room, stepping over detritus—magazines, underwear, T-shirts, Cheetos. How did I ever live like this?

"I don't have time. I'm late," I say as I spy the cat licking refried beans off the floor and chase after him.

"Late for what?" he asks.

"A date," I say, scooping up Mr. Tatters and zipping him in the carrier.

"Yeah, a date? Well, can you spare some time tomorrow, because I'd like to talk to you about the cat? I want to make sure you're feeding Mr. Tatters the right thing," he says, while I'm running out the door.

"Not tomorrow, later," I say.

"This is important," he says as he follows me out into the hallway.

"So is staying faithful," I say as I round the corner to the elevator.

I can hear him pad back to his apartment and sigh as I press the button to the elevator. I can tell by the body movement and sigh that I've made a direct emotional hit. I feel like a complete jerk. I always go for the painful wounds.

As I get into the elevator, I give myself a mental pep talk. Why should I feel guilty about this? It's *his* cat, even though I love the kitty. He found it hiding under a Dumpster at the loading dock at work. Why do I keep enabling his neurotic attempts to manipulate me into "you owe me 'cause you dumped me" shit? Doesn't he owe me because he cheated on me?

Note to self: need to shift psychological gears from passive-aggressive to neutral.

During our phone call, Rafe and I decided to do that oh-so-mature "let's be friends" thing, now that I've cooled down.

I think the friendship thing will work, but it is subject to proper breakup etiquette. I can date right now if I'm discreet, but Rafe is supposed to be in mourning for at least six months. Technically, he should've stopped having sex with Meg, but since she's married it can't really go anywhere and is okay, sort of. He absolutely can't get a girlfriend. If he does, he's no longer allowed to be my friend. Southern belles seem to disallow that. What is it? Insecurity? Territorial imperative? Double standard?

Many Southern women assume there is no such thing as having a friend of the opposite sex because they know the single-girl rule of the South. An old girlfriend assumes that she can recycle her castoffs at some point. The incumbent girlfriend, knowing the recycling rule, sees any "just friends" relationship as a virtual betrayal, or at least tempting the edge of the slippery slope. Southern weddings are full of folklore about revenge-fucking the old boyfriend you haven't seen in months. There isn't a chance in hell that such a thing would happen with me and Rafe. I am perfectly fine to never date him again, but I'm not prepared to cut the cord of friendship. Even so, tonight I would give our attempt at being friends an "F" on both motive and result.

When I get to Aimee's house, I let out Mr. Tatters whereupon he instantly swats at my ankles as I attempt to slip on my jeans. According to the clock, which I set by the random last-time-I-overheard-it-on-the-radio method, I might have exactly fifteen minutes to get ready and drive to Jackson's house, or maybe thirty, or maybe five. Can I do it? I do love this sort of challenge. It's like those submarine movies where the captain yells "DIVE, DIVE!" and the submarine screams "Aoogah, aoogah," and everyone jumps through portals and slides down poles in seconds, while bombs are exploding everywhere.

"I have ten minutes to look like Sarah Jessica Parker cloned to Heidi Klum!" I yell to Aimee, who is in mid-sit-up on the living room floor. She forces herself to exercise whenever she watches television. I race to the bathroom. She jumps up and chases after me, ready to assist in my transformation.

The first thing I do is touch-up work—deodorant, perfume, eyeliner. Aimee hands me vaginal cream, which I put on my face. Sounds gross, but trust me: It makes your skin look as if it's been lifted.

"Preparation H," I command, like a surgeon on daytime television. Aimee slaps the tube in my palm. Also disgusting, but great for tightening the skin around your eyes. "I'm going on another rendezvous with Rance tonight," Aimee says as she commences pull-ups on the bathroom door molding. "He's flying me to Houston to hear Lyle Lovett. Front-row seats and backstage passes."

I would run over small animals for a backstage pass to meet Lyle Lovett. Even a Yankee like me can appreciate style, talent, and ugly sexy.

"He could be the one," she purrs. "This is far, wide, and handsome to the extreme."

I've heard this before. She thought Joe Ed Campbell could be the one until his annual hundred-thousand-dollar bash, when he implored her to get naked on the pool table and allow people to use her unmentionable as an additional pocket. That's something you can't predict from breaking into a guy's house and feeling around his underwear drawer. He had the cash but was lacking in basic human decency. Aimee refused but Natalie accepted. In some circles, she will forever be known as Eight Ball and blackballed (pun intended) from certain society weddings. Now you see why she's so desperate to land Bradford, pregnancy fetish or not.

I run to the kitchen and put my head in the freezer for a few seconds. It plumps up my hair and sets my makeup. I've seen lots of Southern girls do the arctic plunge, with flattering results. I've learned to trust some of their idiosyncrasies. These women look great, dammit, once you get past the image of some sorority sister in her underwear on a kitchen stool turned sideways, craning her neck into the freezer. It's routine. Think casual cool. I race into my bedroom. I find clean and sexy matching underwear—a miracle. I try again to slip on my Paper Denim & Cloth jeans (this time the cat isn't in hunting mode) and a Dolce & Gabbana top. I undo the top, apply liquid rouge to my nipples, and dust fake tanner on my chest, just in case. Aimee follows me.

"So I might not be back tonight or for a couple of days," she says. "I've sent Lizzy a note since I'll miss her lingerie shower—along with a fabulous Chanel negligee."

"What do you mean? Lizzy needs you there. I need you there. These women don't like me. I need a buffer."

"I'm sorry, honey. I'd be there if I could but duty calls," she says.

"What duty?"

"If I want to get married, I have to take this seriously."

"What about me? What about taking me seriously?"

"You'll be great."

Q: What kind of employer allows his paralegal to jet off at a moment's notice?

A: An employer who does the same kind of jet-setting. Aimee's boss thinks this is how most people live. I've often wondered if I've made the right career choice.

"So you actually like him?" I ask as I stuff my keys, cell phone, and lipstick into an Alice-in-Wonderland-small Versace purse.

Note to self: Check Neiman's post-Christmas sale for larger version.

"Honey, there's more to farming than fucking and knocking over fences," she says.

More coda of the West: A tractor salesman is driving down a dirt road and he sees a farmer plowing a field with his bull attached to the plow. Needless to say, the plowing isn't going very well. The salesman thinks to himself, "Now if I can't sell a tractor to that guy." He stops his car and waves to the farmer. The farmer waves back and walks over.

"That's a hard way to plow. Is your tractor broke? Your mule lame?" the salesman says.

"My tractor's brand-new," the farmer says.

"Then, why are you plowing with a bull?" the salesman asks.

"Because I'm teaching him that there's more to farming than fucking and knocking over fences," the farmer says.

Translation: There's more to a relationship than material attraction.

"My advice for self-preservation—make sure you like him a little," I say.

"Well, I hear he's a quick draw," she says.

When it comes to sexual gossip, sound travels faster than light. And nothing travels faster in female circles than word that a man can't get it up or falls short, so to speak. For younger women, gold-digging with an older male is a calculated risk, made somewhat more reliable by pharmacological breakthroughs, but if you're not particularly attracted to the fella you're dating, his speediness may be an asset. Two minutes with someone you're not smitten with is a lot more bearable than twenty.

I'm not sure what Aimee's hoping for exactly. Behind that husband-hunting exterior, I sense that neither is she. For her, it's always love versus happiness, never the conjunctive.

"Good luck with it. I hope you make it back for Lizzy's shower. Try, for my sanity," I say as I walk out the door.

"Remember, no strange words," Aimee calls after me and waves.

I am a few miles away from my house when I realize I don't know exactly where I'm going and I don't want to ask for directions. It's a fallacy that only men hate asking for directions. Another old saw: Why does it take so many sperm to impregnate one egg? Even at that biological level they won't ask for directions.

I find Jackson's house a half hour after I'm supposed to be there. It could be worse.

His place is a two-story stone town house on Turtle Creek with turrets and leaded-glass windows. There's a winding slate path to his front door with overly planned plantings of Japanese maple, lantana, and Silver Moon roses. It almost looks like an English cottage. Having little architectural culture of their own, Texans love to rip off others. Drive through the nicest areas of Dallas or Houston, and you'll cross over several cultural epochs in a few blocks: French châteaus, Italian villas, and English manors, one right after another. It's like wearing Chanel, Versace, Missoni, and Cavalli all at once—a visual assault.

I knock. I can hear what I think is baseball through the thick wood door, and rapid barking from what must be his yellow Lab.

Jackson opens the door and immediately loses his grip on Fido. His dog is doing that wiggly, all-over wagging that signals excitement and lots of jumping. He dives straight for my crotch as Jackson gropes for his collar while trying to maintain eye contact with me. This makes me incredibly self-conscious. Does he nose-dive into every female who enters his turf? Is he trained to do this as an icebreaker?

"I'm so sorry. Emmit, cut that shit out." Jackson yanks him back like a circus act. "Glad to see you. I thought you might miss the whole first inning."

So it's baseball. The Rangers are playing some other team on TV. Honestly, I do know sports, but I hate most Texas team owners. The Cowboys' Jerry Jones's bad eye lift gives me the creeps. He looks like a refugee from *The Rocky Horror Picture Show.* Mark Cuban, owner of the Mavericks, is testosterone on steroids.

"Great. You work for the Cowboys, right?"

"No, I'm with the Stars. Jerry's a little intense," he says as he tosses a salad in the kitchen. "Now, I think most of the things you had in your cart today are in this except for the papaya. They looked a little bruised."

Okay, nice joke. Great-looking salad. There are at least three different kinds of lettuce in there along with finely diced vegetables and dried cranberries. The man appears to be pretty good with a chopping knife.

He goes over to the oven and takes out an aromatic Chilean sea bass. It smells like he used lime, fennel, and lots of other herbs. No grilling. He turns out to be a more nuanced cook than expected. But not aromatic enough to distract the dog, who aggressively noses my pants. I not-so-gently place my knee on his nose and yank the nearest ear, all the while soothingly telling Emmit what a cute dog he is.

Jackson's place is done in Contemporary Guy. Green leather sofa, chairs, and foot rest. Beige carpets and blinds. Framed prints of French Impressionists and Southwestern adobes. A bike hanging on the wall. And a pile of gear stuffed in the corner. It's combination dentist office and REI. The table is set with matching dishware and cloth napkins. The wide-screen TV with subwoofers is on. Jackson leads me to the table, pulls out my chair, and pushes it in as I sit down. My ribs press into the table. I can't take a deep breath. I discreetly push back the chair while he lights a heavy silver candelabra that looks as if it came right out of his grandmother's chintz-soaked dining room, the wrong side of tacky.

"Is that an heirloom?" I ask.

"My granny died last year. I used to play with it when I was a kid, melt wax, pretend I was a vampire, things like that."

"It's something," I say as I calculate where I would bury it if we got serious.

"Yeah, it's beautiful," he says as he spoons bass, mushroom risotto, and salad onto my plate.

He places the serving plates on the table, dishes up his food, and sits down.

I start to dig in and catch Jackson looking at me. When he makes eye contact with me I put my silverware down. He closes his eyes and places his hands on the table. I imitate his hand movement but keep my eyes open. I don't want to miss any of the social cues about what he's doing.

"Dear lord, we thank you for this food," he says.

He's praying. I knew his family owned a religious-uniform company but I didn't think that meant he was religious. I mean, why would Aimee pair me with a super-religious guy? She'd have to know that the truth about my heritage would come out eventually.

After he says amen, he opens his eyes, takes my hand, and asks with an earnestness that is truly troubling, "Can you believe the Rangers are doing so well? I'm so glad we can watch the game together."

I haven't gone to someone's house to watch television since college and that was only because I didn't have cable.

As the game starts again, Jackson's facial expression fades from sentient human being to vegetable. During an especially tense play his mouth gapes open, exposing partially chewed food. He doesn't talk. He's an aggressive deaf-mute. I try to jump-start a conversation. "Do you like working for the Stars?"

"Uh-huh," he grunts, his eyes riveted to the screen.

"Are you from Dallas?"

"No."

"Waco, that's right I remember now."

"Uh-huh."

"Did you go to college here?"

"Uh-uh."

I feel like I'm talking to a non–English speaker.

"Habla English?"

"Sí."

When a commercial appears, his vocabulary increases a hundred percent.

"I went to SMU, majored in business," Jackson says. "I'm thinking about going back in a couple of years and getting my MBA."

The seventh-inning stretch is a wonderland. We actually have more than five minutes to further our knowledge of each other.

"Do you ski?" he asks.

"Yes," I lie again.

"Great! Me, too! Do you Rollerblade?"

"Yes." My turn to wax monosyllabic.

"Hey, you like to run?"

"Yes."

"Snowboard?"

"Nope."

"Water-ski?"

"All the time."

"Rock climb?"

"Yes, and I also kayak, mountain bike, bungee jump, and sky-dive."

This causes him to look at me askance before he lets Emmit lick his plate. "What about touch football, tennis, racquetball?"

"Uh-huh." I nod. And hockey, rugby, and polo. Plus, I box! If I said this out loud, Jackson would probably start drooling. This is how we determine if we're compatible. He figures out how many sports I'll play with him and if I'll get fat in my old age. Jackson, I've realized too late, is the überjock bachelor with a religious twist. He's not into work-league sports. He's into extreme-sweat-all-waking-hours-of-the-weekend sports. No books are in his living room except *Into Thin Air,* which doesn't count for obvious reasons, and the Bible. I'm betting that the sea bass is the sole flourish of Jackson's cuisine. There's a crate of PowerBars in the corner of the kitchen, right next to a row of Gatorade empties. I glance at the CDs on the shelves above his stereo, which looks as if it cost more than my car. Sammy Hagar. Limp Bizkit. Queen. Jackson is the kind of man who chants "We Will Rock You" and thinks Freddie Mercury died of a heart attack. Then there are his DVDs: *The Rock. NFL's Greatest Hits.* And, of course, *Cool Hand Luke. Cool Hand Luke* is required viewing (and repeated viewing) for affluent Southern white men, a cinematic substitute for rebellion.

This is the kind of boy who can justify spending five thousand dollars on a kayak and only thirty dollars on his clothes for a year. He spends most weekends in some remote part of Texas or Colorado in a tent, sometimes with other male-bonding types and large-caliber weapons, with a guide, of course. He doesn't mind bathing in fifty-degree water. He is immune to mosquitoes. To him, an ideal day is waking up at six a.m., going full throttle on some gruesomely intense sport like all-terrain mountain biking until sundown, getting lots of war wounds in the process, making a tuna casserole dinner over a smoky fire, and going to bed on a flat, rocky piece of field.

Many of my Dallas friends have been there before.

One of Janine Horton's saline breast implants actually ruptured when she slammed into a limestone cliff while rappelling. When she called out in pain that she needed to go to a doctor immediately, her boyfriend said, "This isn't life-threatening, right? So why don't we go to the doctor when we finish?" That was the last time she ever dated a guy who chalked his hands.

Abby Nelson, another friend of mine, is in good shape. She's muscular and skinny but, like so many other women, she has cellulite. She used to be pretty comfortable with what she previously considered a minor blemish on an otherwise yoga-instructor-toned physique. She even wore shorts on a hike, though she knew that her hamstrings were dimpled. In the middle of the five-mile path, her jock boyfriend swatted her on the ass and said, "Why don't you do something about that? Work out more or something."

Every guy should know by now that cellulite isn't something you can work off. It's like hair loss—there's nothing you can do about it. When it comes it's there to stay. Abby broke up with Ass Swatter shortly after that. She told him that she couldn't deal with the hair on his back. He said she was shallow.

I have to persuade myself that fleece can be glamorous. I must will myself to believe that I actually enjoy camping. I have to give this thing with Jackson a chance. Who knows—maybe if he falls in love with me I can convince him to give up camping. Say we have kids right away—you can't take a two-month-old into the deep wilderness. There's diaper disposal alone to consider.

"You know, I was thinking of doing a weekend kayak trip somewhere," I say.

"You like camping?" His perfect, tan skin crinkles at the crow's-feet, as he smiles broadly. His perfectly even white teeth come into full view. He looks like he should be in a commercial for what dairy can do for you.

"Sure, I mean I'm not the best at it but I want to learn," I say, knowing it's important not to paint myself as an expert and wind up on an arctic expedition. Enthusiasm is enough of an aphrodisiac. Real physical pain because of pretend expertise is above and beyond the call of duty.

"Really, most girls I meet are afraid of getting their hands dirty," he says.

"I'm not most girls," I reply and smile. I'm diving right in. I'm going to have to buy a lot of fleece and Handi Wipes if this thing works out.

"I love the outdoors."

With that, a budding relationship is fertilized. Jackson's face relaxes. I am a surprise and a find. The rest of dinner is all sports talk and camping plans. If things work out the way Jackson, a.k.a. Red talks, we'll be camping every weekend for the next six months. Let's hope he can be distracted from roughing it. Let's hope he's worth sleeping on a cold rocky ground for. Also on the wish list: a loose interpretation of religion, a willingness to negotiate about the identity of Jesus, a mutual love of New York bagels, and room service at four-star hotels. I wonder when I'll have to meet his mother. I'm going to have to go through mother boot camp with Aimee before that happens.

Chapter Seven

*Party to the Level of
Grade B Movie Star*

Getting married in the South, especially in Texas, means raising yourself to the status of a grade B movie star (grade A is not actually desired; their breasts are too small). Engagement implies consent to smile and wave and attend, as Aimee would put it, a shitload of theme parties in your name and never leave early.

First, there are the friends and family parties. One for each group: friends, family and parents' business associates. These are cocktail parties with a dozen kinds of tequila, but only two types of red wine. Ditto vodka. Usually there's an assortment of plantation-named drinks: mint juleps, Scarlet Sidecars, and General Lee tea. Then there's the kitchen shower for the unwashed masses whom the bride is soon to abandon—her work friends and hangers-on from her previous life. The gifts of choice are upscale kitchen utensils from Crate & Barrel, Williams Sonoma, and a little French boutique. There's an unofficial Christmas tree ornament shower for private school chums, where guests bring, you guessed it, ornaments. There's also a lingerie party for sorority sisters, where there is usually an overdose of La Perla, but hopefully Sabbia Rosa will make a showing. These are followed by generic events for both sets of their parents' friends. The couple is usually registered at Neiman's, Saks, or Stanley Korshak (like Barneys with a special 50 percent markup), and a furniture store somewhere in Europe. Nevertheless, the rate of return on these gifts is about 50 percent, including the recycled-for-the-in-laws Christmas gifts. For this reason alone, it's critical to keep an accurate list of gift-givers. There's also a charity donation event for the parents' business associates, which is one of the most ingenious ways to get on the A-list for the charity balls that year. Attendees donate money to charities in the name of the happy couple.

The tone of these parties varies according to the attendees and their gifts. Obviously, the lingerie shower, with blow-job lessons and sex toys traded like Tupperware, is not as understated as the kitchen shower, where quiche recipes and maid recommendations are the highlights of the conversation—unless, of course, someone suggests some novel application for the attachments to the battery-powered mixer.

Regardless of venue, these aren't exactly potluck affairs in church basements. White-gloved caterers serve precious food on silver trays and use one of Mama's sets of party crystal. The whole location is swathed in the bride's wedding colors. Pink is out, unless it's hot pink. Lavender is hip. White and silver are glam.

And then there are all the parties leading up to the wedding, including one for the bridesmaids with themes like "Paris" or "Rome." The girls eat caviar, drink champagne, get Louis Vuitton bags, a day at a spa with a French name, *Le* whatever, and a fashion show of the most upscale designers. Strictly Italian or French. Escada-rama. Chanel-ville. Ralph is passé. Gone the way of Klein. By the third glass of bubbly everyone is slurring fake French and pointing fingers at the fashion alert walking down the runway, shouting, *"J' accuse."*

The bachelorette parties usually involve a trip to Cabo, a male stripper, lots of tequila, shopping for Viagra and Valium on the street, and a one-night stand cherry-picked from the doctors' meeting in the hotel. Some "wild" girls may opt instead for a particularly muscular Mexican gardener. For the ultra-old money crowd (which means wealth obtained before the 1990s), there's a bonus party—shopping with the prospective in-laws in Paris or New York. If the parents have split, there are usually double parties—one set of parents are invited to each. If the families are from different cities, say, Dallas and Atlanta, expect duplications as well.

During the engagement period, most women don't work. They hire a personal trainer, nutritionist, event planner, private chef, and personal stylist. They are in the full-time mode of looking good and planning to look even better. Lizzy is in the midst of this whirlwind. She's halfway through the wedding march. For the past three months, she's stretched, run, and lifted weights five days a week while a personal trainer yelps at her. Her biceps ripple when she picks up a salt shaker. Her veins stick out like yarn. The bottom half of her body hasn't responded so well. Her thighs look like waves of flesh crashing to shore when she walks. Even the smallest hand could find something to grab on her love handles. She's in a full panic. Her dress is a size 4. Her hips are stuck at size 10.

This week, she launched an exercise program, nicknamed bikini boot camp. Her trainer submits her to calisthenics eight hours a day every day. Even with all that sweat equity, there's no guarantee she'll be the stick she wants to be, unless she stops eating entirely.

Lizzy begged me to go to her lingerie party. By my body language, she sensed reluctance.

"Unfold your arms and look at me, darling. This ain't no rodeo. You'll like it. I promise."

I wasn't convinced. "Who'll be there?"

"Don't make a shit. Ain't but the two of us."

Translation: Old Texas joke. Big-time lawyer drops out of society, buys a ranch in far west Texas, and just sits on his porch. Sooner than expected, he gets stir-crazy from so much isolation. Cabin fever. After several months, he notices a dust plume on the horizon, cutting squares along the section lines toward him. To his relief, a pickup pulls straight up his road and a slightly more grizzled version of himself gets out.

"Howdy neighbor. Been meanin' to git over here. Had to get the summer wheat in first. Looks like you could use some company. Gonna have a party over at my spread next week. Gotta warn ya. Pretty wild. Hope ya like lotsa drugs and wild sex."

The lawyer can't believe what he's hearing. "Hell yeah! What should I wear?"

Without missing a beat, the host replies, "Don't make a shit. Ain't but the two of us."

So the "two of us" are about to test-drive yet another prospective rites-of-matrimonial passage.

That night, when I walk through the large double doors of Lizzy's parents' house to a foyer ornately carved out of marble and mahogany, Lizzy can barely keep her head up. She nose-dives onto her chin between conversations.

"Hey there, great to see you." She tries for a smile, but it doesn't hold. I hug her and feel her body quaking from hunger and exhaustion. There is no rest for the bride who works overtime to be glamorous.

"Great to see you," I say and mean it. "Unfortunately Aimee got pulled away at the last minute for work."

"For work? I didn't realize Aimee had to travel for her job."

"Yeah, you know how it goes when a woman wants to divorce her husband so she moves to New York and files there. Better laws."

"But this is a community-property state."

"You look great. You've lost at least five pounds since I last saw you," I say, trying to draw the conversation away from a losing topic.

"You think?" Lizzy asks earnestly.

"Definitely."

Lizzy smiles appreciatively. She looks over to the next guest who walks in. "Hello, darling," she says as she tries to keep her head level and body conscious.

I head over to the living room but not before I turn around and examine Lizzy one more time. She is funny, smart, and rich. She's not sexy, thin, beautiful, pretty, or even cute. Her personality makes her gorgeous. But in Dallas that doesn't go retail. It stays on the shelf and gets shipped to the outlet. She's always suffered the usual commentary: *Great personality. Lots of money. All the girls like her.*

Of course, there are options for women like her. Dallas surpassed Los Angeles and New York in the number of plastic surgery procedures performed in the early '90s. The most prominent plastic surgeon here has a pool in the shape of a breast. The nipple is a hot tub. As Dave Barry would say, I'm not making this up. But Lizzy isn't that shallow. She doesn't want to be more silicone than flesh. She's also a realist. She wanted an attractive husband with a brain and she got him—a six-foot-two-inch former college football player, Phi Beta Kappa, golden boy. He netted a marriage to a woman worth more than twenty million dollars, no prenup agreement, and a mansion in his name. The only thing he didn't get was power of attorney. What price love?

I walk into the living room, which is transformed into what appears to be the inside of a uterus. The couches, rugs, drapes, and walls are swathed in varying shades of pink. Reams of condoms serve as streamers. There are more than a dozen dildos, standing at erect attention on the coffee table. They look like microphones. Porno-type electronic music pumps out of hidden speakers. Waitstaff in white vinyl bondage gear with large gashlike zippers hold silver trays with oysters, caviar, crackers and crème fraîche, dark chocolate and truffles. It's a sexual-mythology-food smorgasbord.

"Yoyster," one of the waiters mumbles at me from behind a zippered mask. A woman with cleavage the size of the Himalayas whips the waiter with a riding crop.

"Silence. Hello, have you given a blow job before?" the woman asks me as she hands me a champagne glass filled to the top with pink bubbly.

"Umm, hasn't everyone?" I reply, inching away from the crop.

She turns her attention to the waiter again as she grabs an oyster shell and lets the slimy mollusk slide down her throat. He tries to walk away while she's doing this but she hits him again with her crop and grabs his tray. She proceeds to pick her way through the other shells.

I throw my present on the heart-shaped satin table. It's lingerie from Agent Provocateur, but judging from all the phallic symbols around the room and the bondage motif, it may be too tame for this crowd.

"Aren't you Aimee's little friend?" blinks Meg, who is in her usual mode of looking like Barbie and being patronizing. I feel the hair on the back of my neck go stiff.

"Yes, I'm Jenny Barton. I'm a virgin to sex-toy parties," I say and extend my hand. How can she pretend to vaguely know me? "You must be the veteran. Didn't you almost win the contest for most attended last year?"

She doesn't miss a beat. "Miscount, darling. I was robbed. Here's a heads-up—when they get to the blow-job session just remember: Go deep."

"I'm sorry and you are?" I ask. I've decided to play the conversation her way.

"I thought everyone knew me. I'm Meg, you know, Coke," she says, holding up her hand to once again reveal a diamond the size of a large marble.

Aimee gave me more of the lowdown on Meg after our grocery store run-in. She married into the Coke bottling fortune, and from what I hear, she prefers the family beverage in its powdered variety. The last name is actually spelled Koch but they do indeed bottle Coke. She has the look of an Ethiopian refugee dressed in Narciso Rodriguez, and I'm guessing that she could string pearls through the hole in her septum. Her alleged hobby has led to some legendary stories. There's Meg putting Jell-O and dish soap into the university's fountain, so if the water ran cold the Jell-O would set and if it ran hot, the soap would bubble. This was no college prank. She did it last year during the annual trustees' gala. Meg is in her thirties.

My elbow moves and my body with it. The dorsal fin drifts away. Cindy Trammel spies me from the dildo display and latches on to me with the hollow-eyed stare of the incarcerated.

"What are you doing with that trash? You know she grew up in a split-level and has done more kneeling than Mother Teresa," she hisses. Meow.

"I'd say let's blow this joint, but I don't want to leave myself open for a comeback," I say.

"Baby, there's nothing wrong with the act of blowing. But it should be an end in itself, not a means to an end. At least, not all the time," Cindy says as Natalie walks up. In the few short days since the sleepover she's managed to plump herself up at least five pounds.

"You look so pretty," I say to her, startled at how her face has filled out now that she is approaching a healthy weight.

"I'm a stuck pig. My clothes are starting to get tight. I'm gonna have to go up to a size four," Natalie moans and then dutifully bites into a chocolate éclair.

"How's my man working out for you?" Cindy asks.

Natalie nods heartily in appreciation. "He's great. He tracked down Bradford's main girl here and he pages me whenever it looks like Bradford is headed to her place. Then I call him with some made-up emergency," Natalie says.

"Like what?" I ask.

"Oh, one time I told him I had a rattlesnake in my yard and he came right over. I made sure I was looking maternal—pushed out my stomach and put cutlets in my bra. We had the best sex," she says and laughs. She and Cindy clink glasses.

"You have him on the hook," Cindy says, gleeful that she's been able to mentor another woman through the husband-hunting experience.

I'm not ready to confide fully to these women about Jackson or my fascination with Baylor, but I know the conversation is headed in that direction.

"How's Jackson?" Cindy asks before I can escape.

"It looks like I'll be doing a lot of camping in the next few months," I say.

"Yeah, that is the problem with him. He doesn't understand the beauty of room service," Cindy says.

"Or a simple game of pool," Natalie says. She was dating Jackson when the whole pool table incident occurred.

"I need more courage for this thing," I say as I hold up my empty champagne glass. I head for the kitchen because I can hear lots of tipsy girl laughter emanating from that direction.

The silly girls always know where the drinks are. Three women—all in their late twenties with Tic Tac–size engagement rings—stand in the middle of the room and talk about sex. I slip some bubbly into my glass, minimizing the foam while eavesdropping on them.

"I told Chase that as soon as I got that ring there'd be no more nooky 'til the wedding day," says a blonde with Marilyn Monroe curls and tits. I think it's Tommy Sue. Either she's wearing a push-up bra or she's had the quickest breast job in history. She looks about two cups bigger than she did at the sleepover. It also sounds like she's had the fastest reconciliation and engagement in history. Just a few days ago she was calling Chase a creep because she found him getting more than a lap dance in a strip club.

"At least, not with him," quips the brunette.

"He asked if the Clinton rule was still in effect. I just glared at him. But I didn't know what he meant. Do you?" Tommy Sue has the deer-in-the-headlights look that only the rich and pampered have evolved into portraiture.

Raucous giggles burst from the buffy triplets.

"Sweetheart, it depends on what is, is."

More doe-eyed blankness. I'm not sure Tommy Sue should be allowed to procreate. Or vote.

The brunette decides to stop hinting and puts her hands on Tommy Sue's shoulders. She speaks slowly, as if to a child. "Mo-ni-ca. Mo-ni-ca."

Tommy Sue looks like she's having a bad moment on *Who Wants to Be a Millionaire*. I feel sorry for her, so I do the lifeline thing.

"President Clinton said he didn't have sex with Monica Lewinsky because, according to the president, a blow job lacked penetration, and therefore did not meet the legal definition of sex," I say. Tommy Sue smiles at me like she knows she's met me but she's not sure where.

High fives all around me from my newly bonded buffy pals.

Tommy Sue has one of those slow awakenings, like a rheostat brightening a room after a PowerPoint lecture.

"A blow job isn't sex, right? Or is that not okay?" she asks.

Now the kitchen has become a lecture hall and the entire room has filled with diamond-studded bleached blondes. I'm surrounded. Flashback to *Sesame Street*'s "Who doesn't fit?" Pick the one without a trust fund in this picture.

"You have to save something for the honeymoon," explains a short woman with shoulder-length blond hair and quarter-inch-long dark roots framing her face. Her button nose screams plastic surgery and head cheerleader. "Though I tell you, I did not even let him touch me on our wedding night. I was so tired that I passed out in my panty hose."

"I'm having the best sex right now," says Darby, a tall woman who looks like the not-quite-beautiful offspring of a model and a businessman. Her cheekbones are nonexistent, her eyes small and deep set, but her lips rival a water flotation device. Apparently, Miss Thing just got engaged and what she's not sharing with her fiancé, she's sharing with his friends. She stands there with the confidence of a knockout. "I can fuck anyone now because I'm not thinking 'Okay, what do I want this relationship to be?' I feel so much more secure. I'm so glad I found someone before I turned twenty-seven."

For the serious husband-hunter, serial monogamy isn't bed-hopping every two weeks. It's timing. It's pacing. It's not letting go. It's demonstrating your morality by restraining from sex for a respectable period. It's about knowing your target. When you finally pull the trigger, anything more creative than missionary and you're a slut. You can get more inventive later, once the deal is sealed.

Husband-hunting is about a strategy that telegraphs, *I'm not one of THOSE girls.* The subliminal message practically shouts, *I'm the one you can trust to meet your mother.* Its sole purpose is the right marriage as quickly as possible. Get the commitment before the passion clock runs out and you're fresh out of mystery and allure.

Then there's the other timing complication. The biological clock. In Dallas, it's not so much reproductive biology as physics. Get married for good money before you sag. Tighter deadlines, to be sure. Law of gravity meets law of economics. Unfortunately for me, I've already missed the sag deadline. Now I'm just shooting to make the biological one.

A bell rings. We are summoned to the living room for the organized humiliation.

I grab Tommy Sue on the way out of the room and pull her aside.

"So what happened? I thought you were done with Chase," I say.

"Well, he gave me this," she says, and shows me her Chiclet-size diamond.

"What about the strip club?"

"All couples go through their rough patches," she says and shrugs.

A blond returns to the kitchen to fetch us. She waves us into the living room. The woman with the Himalayan breasts stands on the heart-shaped satin stool that matches the heart-shaped table. She tells us to grab a dildo, or "snapper," as these women call them. Cindy motions to a waiter to bring us more drinks. That's one good thing about Cindy. She knows which social occasions require heavy drinking. I'm glad I'm standing next to her. I'm late in the snapper grab bag and wind up with a veiny, foot-long, porn-king version. How could anyone deal with this in real life?

"I've seen worse," Meg says, snuggling up next to me.

"Really," I say as I hold the pythonlike thing in my hands.

"Baylor Jones," she says.

Why is she mentioning Baylor to me? Does she know about our date tomorrow? How could she? Maybe she's the wicked witch of Dallas.

"First, you take the penis in your hands," says Himalaya. "Both hands, yes, that's right. But don't grab too hard, like you're trying to strangle it."

Himalaya peels Meg's hands off her snapper and repositions them. "You don't want to kill the penis, because then there'll be no fun for you. You want to massage it."

"Like this is fun," Cindy says loudly and chugs her Cristal.

I try to act casual and draw Meg out on her past with Baylor. "So when did you date Baylor?"

"I wouldn't exactly call it dating," Meg says. "We were engaged. But then, well, he got weird. Didn't want to have sex, went to bed early. I think he's gay."

"Baylor Jones?" Natalie pipes up. "He goes through women like Sherman went through Georgia." She's drunk enough that her eyes are slightly unfocused. She is actually addressing the armoire, twenty degrees to our right.

"Meg, you know he got sick of your stupid little games," Cindy says as she studies my face. I think she just discovered my interest in Baylor.

I want to be objective about this, but Meg is spewing a load of venom. I definitely didn't feel a gay vibe from Baylor. I never thought: *Hey, this would be a great guy to go shopping with.* And when the hell were he and Meg engaged? Meg, as I have learned, is famous for deriving fulfillment from fraternity-type behavior, like flirting with other women's husbands and buying near-extinct animals for her exotic hunting ranch. She thinks charity is giving her stepdaughters jewelry that she doesn't like.

"When was this?" I ask.

"Oh, I suppose four years ago. He was real sweet at first, rented a whole restaurant for a night, and it was just the two of us eating sushi. Romantic," she says.

"Weren't you married then?"

"Yeah, but it was in the beginning, and I wasn't sure what was going to happen. Oh, I know it was bad but Baylor kept pursuing me. What can you do when a man shows such passion?"

Yes, I remind myself, Southern women multitask, often arranging their next engagement while still, for all intents and purposes, being happily married.

The Himalayan instructor is now showing off Tommy Sue's no-gag reflex technique, and a group of women are standing around her in awe. Meg and I join the group. It's like a cooking demonstration mixed with a drinking contest. Women, two deep, make a circle around Tommy Sue, carefully observing her every movement so they don't miss a step or an ingredient. Some of the younger ones chant, "Go, go, go." Himalaya stands above Tommy Sue helping to guide the phallus. She looks like a proud parent from most angles. From behind, it looks like she's getting a blow job. The women applaud as Tommy Sue pulls the plastic penis from her mouth. She daintily dabs the saliva off her face and blushes at all the attention.

"I'm bulimic," she says shyly.

Miss Himalaya pats Tommy Sue on the back and ushers her back into the crowd. The woman doesn't like to share center stage for long. She claps her hands together to get our attention and with a passion in her eyes most women usually reserve for shopping she says, "Going deep on a blow job is all well and good but the secret to giving the kind of oral sex that will make a man never leave you is the pressure. You have to be a good sucker."

Vinyl-covered waiters appear with trays of unwrapped Twinkies delicately placed on their own individual doilies. Their yellow-sponge-cake outsides are moist and shine under the lights while their brown bottoms are gorgeously tan. They are the best-looking Twinkies I've ever seen. I reach for one out of sugar instinct, as does everyone else. I hold mine lovingly in two hands, joyous at the prospect of eating this much refined sugar.

"Who can suck the filling out of a Twinkie the fastest?" Himalaya asks as she holds a Twinkie in her hands. "Just put it up to your mouth like this and suck."

Lizzy eyes the sugar-laden treats like a bear coming out of hibernation. She reaches for one but Natalie smacks her hand away.

"Size four, remember?" Natalie says, and lifts a Twinkie for herself.

I see Meg out of the corner of my eye. She has that ate-the-canary look and she's headed my way. I don't pick up another Twinkie.

Advice for self-preservation: Avoid the bored and unsatisfied trophy wife. She's the meanest person you will ever meet. She's angry that money hasn't bought all the happiness she thought it would. She's enraged that she services a man she finds repulsive. And she hates the many men who now dismiss her as the wife of so-and-so. She's like a car coming off the lot, 50 percent depreciation automatically. She is, to put it simply, "no longer fuckable" (at least not by anyone at her husband's level) because she comes with the baggage of being one of the rich guys' wives. Being fuckable is her sole source of self-esteem. So she takes her aggression out on women who she deems to be the up-and-coming competition. Hell hath no fury.

I decide to head Meg off.

"I'm sorry it didn't work out for you and Baylor. You and Rafe are pretty friendly, though," I say.

"Really? I didn't know the two of you shared anything intimate anymore," she says, gliding into the conversation with ease.

"Yeah, we're close. Though I don't think I'd ever have sex with him again. Too sloppy. Do you two still talk?" I ask, trying my best to infuse my voice with honey.

"Oh, we're very close, have been for months," she purrs. Or was that a hiss?

With forced dignity, I pick up my twelve-inch penis from the table and glide away from the dildo-laden group.

Cindy, who came in second in the Twinkie contest, follows me into the kitchen.

"I think she's due to shed her skin and crawl under a rock," she whispers behind me. "If it's any consolation, she's gotten to the point where her options are limited to the shallower end of the gene pool—good ol' boys who barely walk erect—if you know what I mean."

"Or my ex-boyfriend," I say and nod in acknowledgment. Cindy saunters over to the refrigerator. She opens it and inspects its contents lovingly. She doesn't touch any of the food.

I glance in the pantry next to the kitchen and see waiters in various states of undress. Some have their vinyl unzipped and folded all the way down to their ankles. Others have only taken off their masks. They are all perspiring profusely, dipping paper towels into ice water and dousing themselves. The hairy pale chests of the men aren't a pretty sight. Squeezing a woman, no matter how toned, into one of those sausage casings doesn't do wonders for the thighs, either.

I put my dildo onto the counter next to the blender, bend over, plant my hands on the cold tile, and breathe out deeply the way they teach you in yoga. I'd like to find some inner peace about now. Instead, I pull out my cell phone and call Rafe.

"Hey," I whisper.

"Where are you?"

"Nowhere you ever want to be," I say as I plant a finger full of whipped cream in my mouth. There are vats of it in the kitchen. I shudder at the thought of how this will be applied in tonight's tutorial. I hope sweaty vinyl-covered waiters aren't involved. "Okay, I'm at a sex-toy Tupperware party, I just had a foot-long and I don't mean a hot dog."

"Wow, are there strippers?"

"It's not that kind of party," I say. "Though, who knows, maybe that's coming. Where are you?"

"I'm in class," he says.

"What class? When did you go academic?"

"Yoga class. It was Meg's suggestion," he stammers.

"That's great. Good for you." What the hell? No matter how nicely I asked or what I promised in exchange, he'd never go to a yoga class with me. Why is it that after you break up, your ex attempts to rehabilitate himself? "Gotta go," Rafe says. "Everyone's unrolling their mats."

I hang up. "Rafe's doing yoga," I say to Cindy, who's dabbing a finger into the whipped cream as if she's testing its temperature.

She nods her head in understanding. "He's trying to get you back."

"What? He's doing it for Meg."

"No, that's what he wants you to think. It's classic. They become the people you want them to be when you break up. My ex-husband did it. Be careful—they can only keep it up for so long. When we 'reconciled' it took Tom a whole month to cheat again," she says as she finally gives in and balances a glob of whipped cream all the way to her mouth.

"I don't think going to yoga at Meg's suggestion is a good strategy to get me back," I say.

"Watch, in a week he'll be begging you," Cindy says. She looks around the kitchen. The waiters have all zipped back up and marched into the living room. No one else is here. She concentrates on the outside door. "Wanna get out of here?"

"Only if we can get a drink somewhere else," I say.

Might as well go out with her, I think. Maybe she'll give up some good gossip. Anyway, it's refreshing to dish with someone who doesn't qualify every hot item she has to say with, *I don't want to talk out of school, but . . .* or *I'm not saying this is true, but . . .* Cindy throws her information out on the table, unapologetically.

"You're easy," she says.

"I'm desperate," I say.

I may be both but it's not going to be easy to navigate our way out of the party. We have to go out the front door since our coats and keys are in the foyer. We walk back into the uterus, a.k.a. living room, as Lizzy opens a gift-wrapped vibrator that's shaped like a branding iron. The women ooh and aah as if this is a fireworks show. It would be a slap in Lizzy's face if we left now.

Cindy and I grudgingly slide into an oversize armchair together. She's not as bony or devoid of a soul as I thought she was. At the sleepover, she seemed all about mentoring the weak-willed into militant husband-hunting. She was more drill sergeant than confidante. Tonight she's picked up on every emotional cue I've flashed and shown genuine concern.

The admiration of the crowd grows louder. Lizzy holds a pale pink negligee that looks like it could float on air—it's that finely woven—in her hands. I know it's Aimee's gift. A rush of guilt goes through me for attempting to lie to Lizzy about Aimee's whereabouts. I'm an accessory and not in a good way.

Lizzy smiles at me and puts the lingerie down. She takes a bite of a carrot stick and unwraps another package covered in breast-patterned wrapping paper.

"Do you think we'll get home before sunup?" Cindy asks.

"Do you ever get home before sunup?"

"No, but I usually have more to show for it than this," Cindy says and waves an empty champagne flute, prompting a waiter to run over and refill it.

"We're supporting our friend. Remember the world isn't all about you."

"I do forget that," she says as Meg circles our chair. Cindy lets out an actual hiss, which sounds completely in context to me but puzzles several other women who hear it. They turn and look at

Cindy, waiting for some sort of explanation. Cindy acts oblivious to their stares. She's at the point of wealth and confidence where she doesn't have to care what people think. Meg moves on. I realize she's a bit scared of Cindy. Cindy could easily take her in a catfight. Meg may be mean but so far she's all talk.

"I can't believe you hissed. Mace is equally effective," I whisper.

"It wouldn't fit in my purse," Cindy retorts as the other women turn back to watch Lizzy open presents. There are still twenty wrapped boxes by her side.

My phone buzzes and I rush to shut it off. Cindy turns the screen to see who's contacting me. I let her. It's a text page from Jackson: "Found some good hiking boots for you."

"Honey, he loves you," she says.

"Until he finds out I hate camping, hiking, and any prolonged exposure to the outdoors."

"By then he'll be too far gone," she says as she takes my phone from me and texts back, "I'm a size six . . . can't wait to see them."

"How did you know that?" I ask.

"Please, I can tell who's gained more than two ounces, who lies about her height, and who ain't anywhere near a size two. I've been doing this for years."

"He's gonna buy them now. I shouldn't let him do that," I say and try to grab my phone back.

"He has millions of dollars. He can afford to buy you a pair of hiking boots. Besides, you want him to be in the habit of giving you gifts."

She's right. I stop trying to text. I've found another husband-hunting mentor and a pair of new boots.

"I hope they're not ugly," I say.

"They're hiking boots. Of course they're ugly," she says.

Lizzy has opened yet another bunch of presents with the requisite clucks of approval. The last one, a spiky cage that I'm told fits on the penis, registers a shriek from one girl. I don't know if it was from excitement or disapproval.

I'm getting tired. I snuggle into Cindy's shoulder, preparing to take a nap.

"I want presents," I whine like a petulant child.

"Get married."

"No one will marry me," I say.

"Plenty of people will. They're not the people you want yet. Jackson Ray probably will soon."

"You think?"

"Absolutely, if you're encouraging whenever you see him but you make it difficult to see you, you become like a drug. He can't get enough of you and he realizes the only way to nail it down is to marry you," Cindy says.

"What if he doesn't?"

"Then you go out with another man a couple of times in a very public place and *wham*," she says as she slaps my hand. A couple of women look back at us with contempt. We should be oohhing and aahhhing with the rest of them.

"We're in love," Cindy says and kisses me on the cheek. They shake their heads and turn back.

The audience around Lizzy becomes deathly silent. Cindy and I peer over the heads of stunned women to see what's going on. Lizzy holds up a dainty lace nightie—Southern women still wear nighties—that is minuscule compared to its intended wearer.

"It's a size two," I whisper.

Lizzy smiles wanly as she appraises the pretty thing that her body will never fit into.

"Thank you, Meg. It's lovely," Lizzy says and lightly puts the garment back into its box.

"Why would she do that? She knows Lizzy isn't a two," I whisper again to Cindy.

"Some women can't even pretend to play nice."

"Why'd Lizzy even invite her?"

"She's part of the social circle."

"They're not friends," I say.

"Does that matter?" Cindy asks me as she sends another withering glance at Meg.

After Meg's clothing bombshell, the party winds down quickly. The shower girls can't seem to recover their pep. They each hug Lizzy in turn and tell her she'll be a beautiful bride while they stroke her hair. The gestures are kind and warm. This is how women should be with one another. I love how generous all these women are toward Lizzy right now. Their hugs and words are genuine.

When it's my turn to say good-bye I also hug Lizzy and tell her she's wonderful, but my warmth isn't as unabashed as that of the women before me. I do the pat on the shoulder, which means I'm there for her, but I can't do the hair stroke.

I walk down the winding path in her front yard to my car. I can hear heels clicking behind me but don't think much of it until I hear the icy voice.

"Have a good time with Baylor," Meg says as she passes me.

I shudder. How does she know I'm going to see Baylor? Will she tell Aimee or, worse, Jackson?

The clicking of the heels against the pavement gets fainter and fainter but sounds more menacing with each step, like little stabs into my chest. What does this woman want from me?

Chapter Eight

Don't Wear All Your Animal Pelts
at the Same Time

At work the next morning Carol grunts at me. She motions for me to come into her office. I walk over to her cave and take a seat. She continues to type on her computer and chew her gum, snapping it every few seconds. She doesn't look at me. I shift in my chair. I look at the ceiling, the floor, my hands, and her. It seems like an hour has passed before she stops typing. I think she's going to talk to me but she doesn't. She examines the papers on her desk. I feel like coughing or something to make my presence known, but then I think that would be rude. She knows I'm here.

A few seconds or minutes or maybe even a half hour passes before she looks at me. She leans back in her chair and studies me. She puts her fingers in the shape of a church steeple, places them against her mouth, and squints her eyes at me. I feel like she's trying to decide what species I am.

"I read your story on how Santa saying 'Ho Ho Ho' at Christmas is becoming controversial because 'ho' now means prostitute," she says.

"Did you like it?" I ask, moving to the edge of my seat. It's always nerve-racking to have a story judged.

"I don't get it," she says.

"What don't you get?" I ask as I start tapping my foot. I'm not quite sure what to do. It's a simple concept. What's not to get?

"I mean okay, ho is a bad word and mothers are upset at its usage so some Santas are saying, 'Ha, Ha, Ha.' I don't know. It doesn't grab me," she says.

"Okay, well, what would make it better? What would grab you?" I ask. I'm almost breathless from the rejection I'm starting to feel.

She sits back in her chair again and does the church steeple thing with her hands.

"I think," she begins slowly, "that nothing will."

Now I am unable to breathe. I worked on that story for weeks. I networked with mothers at day care centers all over the city. I called the Salvation Army to talk to them about their Santa policies. I bribed a Neiman Marcus employee to give me the goods on their Santas. I can't believe all that work was for nothing. I scramble for another option.

"Can I show it to the editors in New York and have them decide?" I ask.

"No, that's not the way it's done," she replies with a tinge of contempt in her voice. "Jenny, you're a bright girl with lots of potential but I'm not sure you're cut out to work here. I don't know if you think like the *Wall Street Journal*. Maybe you should focus more on earnings reports."

"Sure, okay," I say.

"You've been here four years? Writing a feature should be a breeze for you by now," she says. "I don't know."

"Okay, I could come up with some more ideas and send them to you," I suggest.

"No, no, we don't want to go through this again. I'll come up with something for you and see how you do with it," she says in a tone that suggests I'm on reporter probation.

I stumble out of her office toward my desk. Carol has once again dashed my dreams of reporting and made my work life a living hell. I slump into my chair and stare at my computer screen. What am I going to do? Am I cut out for this? Every time I think I've taken steps toward becoming a senior reporter, Carol draws me back. It's like she's decided that one out of every five long stories I write will be utter crap and she'll have to reevaluate my abilities as a reporter as well as my basic intelligence level.

A colleague leans over my cubicle. Skip, an Ivy Leaguer who's biding his time in Dallas, examines my body language and facial expression. Both are screaming agony.

"She did it to you again," he states and shakes his head. Skip and I used to be caught in the same abusive cycle with Carol. We bonded over our misery, our status or lack of it as young reporters, and our collective longing for good Italian food, something you don't find in Texas. But in the last couple of months something has happened with Skip and Carol. She doesn't yell at him or cut his stories to shreds anymore. She almost treats him as a friend.

"Yep," I say.

"You have to get smarter about this," he says in a low voice.

"What? What does that mean? Tell me what to do and I'll do it," I say with a desperation that makes my voice carry farther than I want it to. A couple of other reporters turn to look at us. Skip walks around the partition and into my cubicle. He squats by my chair.

"When you read a really good story what's the first thing that goes through your head?"

"I can't believe he got all of this. You know: quotes, descriptions," I say.

"Right, so what I've learned recently is a lot of times you shouldn't believe the reporter got all those good quotes and descriptions. You should think of the reporter more as a creative interpreter," he says.

"You're saying make things up?"

"I'm saying when you see an opportunity to embellish that won't cause problems, do it; because when you do, Carol notices and loves it," he says.

Okay, so my closest friend in the bureau lies in his stories and is encouraging me to do the same. This isn't turning out to be the day I expected.

"I can't do that. I'll get caught," I say. "Plus, I would never be proud of that story because I would know it wasn't real."

"If you're careful you won't, and if you don't, I don't think you have much more time here," he says.

"Has Carol told you something about me?" I ask. I stare right into his eyes. My fear and embarrassment are at an all-time high.

"Not exactly, but I can tell by how she treats you," he says.

"What does she say?" I ask strongly enough to throw him off guard.

"She says you're a lightweight," he says and stands up. He stretches and smiles pityingly at me. He walks away.

Great. Now it appears the only way for me to keep my career is to fabricate and show absolutely no respect for industry standards. Sounds like a great way to live with myself. I look over to Carol's office and examine her through the glass wall. She's wearing a particularly hideous dusky-rose sack of a dress with suntan, reinforced-toe panty hose and white sandals. Despite having lived in Dallas all her adult life, the fashion fairy evidently never found or blessed her with insight. I've often thought about throwing a Neiman Marcus catalog on her chair (or given my feeling today, directly at her head.)

What makes her better than I am? What makes her opinion valued over mine? Before I can stoke myself into a worker rebellion, Jackson calls.

"Hello, I have a pair of snake-resistant hiking boots for you" he says by way of a greeting.

"How thoughtful. I haven't gotten you anything snake resistant," I say.

"That's okay. I have all the gear I need. Wanna go camping with me next weekend?"

"Why don't we start with a hike," I say, trying to muster up enthusiasm.

"I'll bring a real nice wine and chocolate," he says.

Well, that doesn't sound all that bad. He can tell that I'm reluctant and he's willing to bribe me with food. Can jewelry be far behind? We hang up. I pull up files on my computer as I prepare to put in a full day of work. I examine my story list: the trend of ordering fish cheeks in restaurants, recess in elementary schools is becoming less common, and the crisis of wild ostriches (from all those ostrich farms gone bust) in Oklahoma. I don't have the desire to work on any of these today. I sneak out of work at four p.m. by feigning a late-afternoon interview. Really I'd rather be anywhere than in Carol's sight line.

When I walk into the house I smell bread baking—something must be wrong with Aimee.

The kitchen has become a pastry shop run by an eight-year-old. Mounds of lemon cookies, espresso brownies, and shortbread are stacked haphazardly on the counters. Some are on plates. Cranberry muffins cohabitate with incompatible partners like pound cake and peanut butter cookies. Judging from the volume of baked goods, Aimee must be borderline suicidal.

"We have to donate this stuff to a shelter. I can't be tempted like this," I say.

"I'll take it all to work tomorrow," she says.

"What's wrong?" I ask.

She stops whisking egg whites, brushes her hair back, and straightens her apron. She turns and looks at me, then quickly looks down. She studies her baked goodies.

"Aimee, what is it?" I ask as I move toward her.

When I place my hand on her arm she crumbles. She tries to stifle her crying but it comes out in strangled gasps.

"I don't. I didn't think it could be that bad," she says as she pulls me to the couch.

The postcoital report comes in a condensed *Reader's Digest* format. She speaks rapidly and in short, sometimes unfinished, sentences. Lyle Lovett was tremendous. They drank during the concert and had a great time. They danced and laughed. They were at that point of drunk when you're giddy and feel like anything can happen.

"I even thought he was attractive, a little," she says.

They got back to their hotel room and decided to order room service. They were like kids with a charge account. They ordered French fries, chili, ice cream, pie, cookies and milk.

While they waited for room service they kissed and went into heavy making out. It was good, she said. He was a pretty competent kisser and he was so enthusiastic. When the food came they dived in and turned on an on-demand movie. It was a comedy. They pigged out and laughed. It was a beautiful night.

The problem came when Rance started laughing really hard. He had just eaten cookies and drank milk. He laughed so hard that the milk spewed—no gushed—out of his nose with little chunks of cookie visible. It would have been recoverable if this was like a ten-second event and then it was done. But he kept laughing and laughing for at least two minutes.

"I timed it. I needed somewhere to look besides him. I looked at the clock," Aimee said.

So for two minutes, milk mixed with cookie and snot ran down his face and onto his nonexistent chin. It looked like a gang of snails decided to use his face as a path and left behind a trail of slime.

"I couldn't. I just couldn't after that," Aimee says.

"But he wanted to?"

"Oh, yeah," she nods.

"What did you do?" I ask.

"I went to the bathroom for a long time and then when I came back I turned off every light and closed the curtains. I could only see half a foot ahead of me."

"That sounds like it should've worked," I say.

"Except I swear to God I could smell sour milk," she says.

"So what did you do?"

"Well, at this stage of the game he's so excited I just have to lie there and it doesn't last more than a minute so it worked out, but, Jenny, I can't get that image out of my head. I don't know what I'm gonna do later," she says. "Oh God, I almost blocked this from my memory, and I wish I had: He drooled on my face. Splat right onto my cheek."

Luckily he rolled off her and fell asleep seconds after that, so there wasn't a long cuddling session to endure.

"He's just bad enough that he's on the edge of good," Aimee says as she walks back into the kitchen and pulls a pecan pie out of the oven before throwing in a loaf of sourdough.

"I assume you're not referring to his baking skills," I say, and she groans.

Aimee's fully made-up with perfectly painted red lips and modeling her Jimmy Choo "baking shoes" in a Marni housedress. Texas women are trained from the time they can walk to always have their makeup in place, their accessories matching (including underwear), and their hair sprayed to perfection. The highest compliment a woman can bestow upon herself is that in twenty years of marriage, her husband has never seen her without her face on.

"I should've given him a breath mint," she says. "I hear peppermint is an aphrodisiac."

Aimee preps to make a blueberry cobbler. I know what she's thinking. She'll have to fake it for life or at least a few years. Her only hope is that his personality will grow on her and she'll develop some emotion for him. But it's a slender thread she's grasping at. What if it gets worse? How often will she be required to have sex with him?

"Once a week?" I propose.

"No, honey, I think he wants it every day. He's a nerd, he's catching up," she says. "Maybe I can train him, like you said. He certainly hasn't had much experience."

"You like him, don't you?"

"He's real sweet, but I don't know."

"It's time to decide what you want—love or money. Are you going out with him tonight?"

"Yeah. We're going to the zoo."

"The zoo? How exotic. Okay, we'll talk when you get back. I have to run."

"Hey, wait a minute. Where are you going now?"

"A work thing," I fib, and rush into my room.

It's Wednesday and Baylor is supposed to pick me up at the house for our rescheduled date. I thought Aimee wouldn't be here. If she finds out that I've gone off her dating plan, she'll flip. She might force-feed me all those baked goods. What do I do? Quick, think. Baylor hasn't seen my rusty Honda yet but he doesn't seem like the type to be too freaked out by it.

I call him on his cell. He says he's walking out the door to pick me up.

"Well, I'm in my car right now, driving to pick *you* up. Where do you live?"

He laughs.

"I'm not joking," I say.

"Seriously, you, a female, want to pick me up?" he asks with disbelief so enormous that it borders on shock. This is getting insulting.

"Yes, I, a woman, am driving as we speak and I might add that I'm not too stubborn to ask for directions."

He gives me directions, but I can tell he's still questioning the reality of the situation.

It'll take fifteen minutes to get there and an hour to properly primp. I'm not going to give him the satisfaction of having me show up an hour late looking great, proving his long-held assumptions about women. I decide to go for the slicked-back hair, minimal makeup thing. It takes five minutes to assemble. I take off all my underwear and slip into a tan Celine halter dress with a tortoiseshell clasp. Visible bra straps might be hip in New York, but here they're as offensive as going topless to a church service, and panty lines are worse than mismatched underwear. I slather sparkly Stila moisturizer on my legs and wedge my feet into gold lizard Manolo stiletto sandals. Another good thing about Texas: No one walks anywhere. I can wear impractical shoes, such as the ones I'm standing in, just about all the time because I will never walk more than twenty yards. There ain't no subways or cabs. It's a door-to-door existence.

I race through the living room and yell good-bye to the maniacal baker.

"Wait a minute," she screeches.

I back up.

"What's going on with Jackson?"

"I told you all that," I say. I did text her and we had a couple of brief cell phone conversations.

"It sounds promising but I don't have all the details. When are you going to see him again?"

"He wants to go camping next weekend. He bought me a pair of hiking boots," I say as I edge toward the door.

"Why not tonight?"

"I'm playing hard to get."

"That's fabulous. We'll have to strategize. You shouldn't have sex with him this weekend. Definitely need to pack only long pants. Shorts make you look a little stunted," she rambles.

"Thanks. We can talk more about my midget status later," I say as I grab the handle of the front door and turn it. "See you later."

I throw my car into gear and squeal to a stop outside Baylor's door in twenty minutes. He's pacing his front walkway. He looks at his watch, smiles, and shakes his head. Not bad for a woman. He strides toward me dressed in a seersucker suit. In New York, he'd look like the ice cream man. Here, he's the pinnacle of style. He opens my door.

"I thought I'd drive," he says as he takes my arm and leads me to his Mercedes. "I don't know if that thing is safe to drive."

"Hondas always top *Consumer Reports.*"

"I'm not talking about Hondas. I'm referring to this rust bucket."

"I've been thinking about upgrading," I say, which is true except I can't afford it.

"We're driving to Fort Worth. My car will be more comfortable," he says as he opens the door to his car.

"Why are we going to Fort Worth?" I ask. Besides a mechanical bull, there isn't a lot that inspires driving forty-five minutes to another town.

"We're going to the zoo for the fund-raiser."

As he says the words, my heart sinks. Aimee's going to be at the zoo. I'm going to see Aimee when I'm on a date with Baylor, the person she'd least like me to date. This is bad. I feel like I'm skipping school and my parents are about to find out. I tap my fingers on the stick shift. Baylor catches my hand and holds it still.

"You okay?"

"Yeah, do you think we could duck out of this fund-raiser early? I'm really hungry."

"Sure."

"Maybe we could go eat now?"

"I have to make an appearance at this thing," he says as he squeezes my hand.

I like the touch but it doesn't ease my sense of impending doom. I look out the window and calculate how long I have to live without major trauma. Thirty minutes and counting.

"You sure you're okay?"

"I think Aimee might be at this thing."

"Oh."

"Yeah, she's a little fussy about who I date."

"She likes Jackson for you," he states, clearly knowing how Aimee works. "Don't worry we'll be in and out before she even notices."

"I hope so," I say, wondering how he knows about Jackson and if I should explain. I don't know what I'd say, so maybe nothing is best.

"Worse comes to worst, I'll pretend I don't know you."

"That's probably a good idea."

"Same thing with Jackson," he says.

"And Meg," I counter. He studies me out of the corner of his eye. We arrive at the Fort Worth zoo just as a throng of women in snakeskin pants and halter tops, dyed hot pink and turquoise, step out of their limo, throw their empty bottles of champagne (one per person) in the trash, and make a beeline for the fund-raiser.

Theme dressing is very big here. Even if a costume requirement isn't indicated on the invitation, many women will dress as if it's Halloween and they're out to trick-or-treat something.

"Let's follow them," Baylor says as he grabs my arm.

I'm giddy with our impromptu anthropological study. But I'm brought back to reality by the thought of what I am going to do about Aimee.

Not to mention the sixty acres of trails that the Fort Worth zoo is famous for. I'm not supposed to be walking more than twenty yards in these shoes. At least we have a good pack of hounds leading the way. We could wander around 'til morning without bumping into another human, which might not be a bad thing under the circumstances. We pace ourselves behind the women.

The fund-raiser is for the wildlife commission, which in Texas isn't as conservationist as it sounds. Big-time businessmen vie for spots on the board because a perk of the job is getting to hunt game in preserves that most people never see. The security in some of those places rivals the gauntlet I run every time I go to the airport. Suddenly, the herd ahead of us stops and applauds.

"How clever," says the one with the blue eye shadow that matches her outfit.

"Explains our way of life," nods another feathered blond.

They are in awe over a banner, which says TEXAS WILD: WHAT'S GOOD FOR HUNTERS IS GOOD FOR THE ANIMALS. Texas Wild is a new exhibit glorifying the world of hunting, complete with interactive video games where children shoot deer to thin out the herd. There's an exhibit of alligator and lizard purses with a laminated sign that says: DUE TO THE DEMAND FOR SUCH LUXURY GOODS, THE SPECIES POPULATIONS ARE ON THE UPSWING BECAUSE FARMERS ARE IN- CREASING THEIR STOCK. I look down at my lizard shoes and feel very Texan. I also feel that my vegan friends in New York would hate my guts if they knew I was here. There's a petting zoo with cows, chickens, turkeys, and goats. On each stall, another lami- nated sign explains what we get from each animal. For example, COWS GIVE US MILK, STEAK, HAMBURGERS, AND SKINS.

There's even a history of animals in Texas and the events that celebrate them, such as an exhibit with photos and artifacts on rattlesnake roundups. That's when people pour gasoline into rattle- snake holes, gather up a bunch of the fleeing snakes, and shoot them with pistols. In a stab at humanity, the exhibit condemns the practice because gasoline kills the bunnies who also live in the holes. But this hasn't done anything to stop the roundups. In fact, Aimee has given me an invitation to one taking place at Rance's ranch in a couple of weeks.

A crowd of about a hundred people mingle in the zoo exhibits, which are lit with glowing white Chinese lanterns. It feels so indul- gent to walk around this public place with only a handful of well- dressed people at each exhibit. I have time to read the information on the signs without feeling pushed by a traffic jam of other zoo- goers to move on.

The cobblestone path of the exhibit makes a figure eight. A bar sits where the two circles of the eight connect. The sides of the bar are covered with tortoise shells. The top is draped in tiger skin. The bartender and waitresses wandering alongside the guests wear a form of loincloth and offer mongoose martinis and Duckhorn merlot.

Stuffed dead animals are displayed throughout the grassy court- yard in the middle of the exhibits. There's a grizzly bear, buffalo,

lion, cheetah, moose, and a few other large furry things I don't recognize. The way they're organized looks like a large game of taxi-
dermy chess. My buffalo takes your lion—that kind of thing.

People lean on the animals like they're mantels or banisters as
they sip their drinks. One lady in a skintight Versace leopard-print
dress spills her full glass of white wine completely on the buffalo.
She shrugs and moves on.

"Isn't this sick," I say, looking around at all the evidence of carnage.

"Yeah, but I do enjoy a good steak," Baylor says.

"Oh no, are you a hunter?"

"Darling, I have much better things to do with my time than sit
in a deer blind for hours with a bunch of overweight men."

"Good."

"White or red?"

"Red," I say and he makes his way to the bar. I do a 360-degree
scan, searching for Aimee's blond head in a sea of blond heads. I
think I see her and move behind the stuffed buffalo, which feels
sticky from the wine. False alarm. It would probably be easier to
look for Rance's slumpy profile. From behind the buffalo I spot
Natalie. She's talking on her cell phone to what sounds like her
private detective.

"He didn't stop by the house, right?" she queries. "Great."

She is wearing an empire-waist dress that emphasizes her ex-
panding cleavage and a slight mound of a belly. I wonder if she's
stuffing her underwear to get that belly. Bradford walks over to her
and hugs her tightly.

"Something about you looks . . . You look good," he says and
squeezes her again. He absolutely has a thing for women with
more padding. He won't let go of Natalie's filled-out backside. She
has what could be mistaken as a pregnancy glow but what is, in
husband-hunting terms, the glow of an almost sealed deal.

I spot Cindy and Tommy Sue a few feet away. They're having a
very intense conversation. I can hear Tommy Sue using phrases
like *ironclad* and *one million per child.* Cindy speaks to her in
soothing tones and appears to be writing down the name of a
lawyer. She really is the husband-hunting guru.

I scan the place for Aimee again. The exhibit is packed with women who look as if they're about to go clubbing and men who look like they just came out of court. I bet they'll raise a few million tonight. But I'm not exactly sure how the money will be spent. In vitro fertilization of exotic game? Scholarships for inner-city kids to go on canned hunts? Snake-shooting classes?

"Hey there, darling, you're moving up in the world," Meg says, slithering up to me. She's wearing more animals than I can identify. Her shoes are lizard. Her dress may be snake or alligator, and it clings to her body like a second skin. Her wrap is something white and furry. Her purse is white with longer fur.

"I see you support hunting, or at least its consequences," I say as I scan her body head to toe. "What happens if you start to molt?"

"I grow a tougher skin."

"More leathery. And where's Mr. Koch this evening?"

"He's somewhere," she says.

"What about Rafe?"

"He's somewhere else," she says as Baylor walks up and hands me a glass of wine. Meg eyes me suspiciously.

"Darling, I've missed you so much," she says to Baylor and body-hugs him. He doesn't pull away.

The two of them become engrossed in conversation. I try to position myself so that I'm part of the discussion but Meg keeps moving with the opposite intention, like an NBA forward. Baylor doesn't notice. He laughs at Meg's jokes and grabs her arm a couple of times for emphasis. I haven't spoken a word or had a question directed at me for at least fifteen, maybe twenty minutes.

"Excuse me. Do you know where all the money goes tonight?" I ask. Lame, I know, but I'm scrambling for an opening.

"Not a clue," Meg says, then turns back to Baylor and starts speaking Spanish. He responds in español. My Spanish language skills are limited to bar drinks and some scatological expressions. I'm in social exile and getting *muy caliente*.

I move again. Now I'm facing their profiles. I am about to say something, when Meg holds up a finger and says, "Just a moment."

Screw it, I slam back the rest of my wine and stalk to the bar to refuel. Hopefully, my tactical retreat will buy me enough time to concoct a brilliant yet subtle way to humiliate Meg, humble Baylor, justify my presence to Aimee, and elevate me to the level of social goddess.

"Do you have anything stronger than wine? Vodka tonic? Tequila?" I ask.

The bartender pours straight tequila into my semi-empty plastic wine cup, giving it a slightly pink tinge. The herd of girls we followed into the exhibit are grazing the hors d'oeuvres, occasionally glancing over at Baylor and Meg, who has now moved within two inches of his face.

"Are they at it again?" asks Blue Eye Shadow.

"That's what I heard," says Feathered Hair.

"I thought he was gay," says D cup.

"He squats when he pees," says Blue Eye Shadow.

Translation: He squats when he pees basically means he's effeminate. It's usually used as a way to differentiate between someone who's effeminate and someone who's gay, thus making the alleged squatter tolerable to some of the more sexually conservative Texas rich.

I'm about ready to order another drink to throw in Meg's face, when I spot Aimee circling the edges of the party. Rance, ever the earnest dork, is jumping from exhibit to exhibit reading every word. I calculate that my trauma-free life has been extended another thirty minutes or so—the amount of time it will take for them to finish reading.

But Aimee turns and looks at me. She squints and walks toward me.

"What are you doing here?" she asks as she hugs me.

"You know, I'm working."

"But you didn't say you'd be working here when I told you I was going to the zoo," Aimee states.

"I didn't realize you meant Fort Worth," I say. By the end of the night the list of lies I'm going to have to keep track of will be a foot long.

"Oh, I'm glad you came."

"How's it going?" I ask and motion a hello to Rance, who is still reading and trying to casually look over at Aimee.

"It's about the most informative party I've ever been to."

"He didn't become a millionaire because he's dumb."

"Yeah," she says and turns to the bartender. "Could you get me the strongest thing you have?"

"That's what I'm having," I say and lift my empty glass, signaling to the bartender that I'd like a refill.

The bartender pours our drinks. Aimee takes a moment and scans the party. When her eyes fall on Baylor and Meg they stop. She stares and takes a long swallow of her drink.

"I don't understand why some married women still have the need to prey on other men. At least have the decency to be discreet if you're going to flirt."

"You think Baylor's interested?" I ask, a little too invested in the answer.

"No, he's done with that trash," she says as she finishes her drink and has the bartender pour another.

"What did she do to him? Why did they break up?" I ask.

"They both did bad things to each other. I have to get back but you should come over and join us."

"I have to get going pretty soon," I say and wonder how much a taxi back to Dallas will cost.

"Us, too."

"Where?" I ask, hoping to avoid whatever restaurant they may be headed toward.

"Rance has a lot of years to catch up on."

"The sex novelty still hasn't worn off."

"Oh, no," Aimee says as she walks over to Rance. He watches her. She watches Baylor. Rance's already in love with her. He hugs her and kisses her with the intensity one usually reserves for re-unions after six-month absences. Rance and Aimee walk hand in hand as they continue to read every word of each exhibit. Aimee occasionally glances up at Baylor and Meg. A clearly visible scowl paints her face. I know she doesn't like it when married women play the field they should've abandoned to the less fortunate single women. But she seems more upset by the Baylor and Meg flirtation than is warranted by anyone except a scorned lover. I don't think Aimee and Baylor ever dated but I'm not completely sure.

I notice Baylor noticing Aimee and Rance as they progress around the party. Meg pets his neck for a few seconds. It's going to be hard to approach him or, for that matter, leave with him without Aimee catching every movement.

I curse myself for not learning sign language, when a man in a tan suit and manicured hands comes up to me.

"That's mild flirtation as far as my wife is concerned," he says, nodding in Meg's direction.

Meg's husband? How unexpected. I pictured a toothless, sunken-eyed man with a bib in a wheelchair, but he's remarkably attractive and polished. He can form sentences with multisyllabic words. He's devoid of body odor. In fact, he smells of something expensive and French. He's prime, triple-A material. Why is Meg screwing around with Baylor?

"Yeah, well I'd hate to see her get serious."

"Byron Koch."

"Jenny Barton."

"She's insecure. She's turning forty soon and that's a hard number for a woman to deal with."

My smile grows tight. Is he insane? I'd skin him alive and feed him to the nearest predator if he outed me at forty. I wonder how many other people know this. My mind races with the various means at my disposal to expose this delicious bit of intelligence. Meow.

"Wow, I had her pegged in the low thirties."

"And, you know, we're trying to have kids. She has an incompetent uterus."

I keep my smile in place and hold back an almost convulsive urge to burst out laughing. What the hell is an incompetent uterus? Are her ovaries underachievers, or is she just vaginally awkward? I can't resist just a little levity.

"Did her uterus flunk the final exam?"

Byron smiles and laughs. "I don't have a clue about the clinical aspects. All I know is that it makes things difficult."

I have a brief pang of guilt, which is undermined by Meg's continued malfeasant attempts to paw Baylor, which I can see in my peripheral vision. I'm surprised that she has mothering instincts.

"Let me rescue you," Byron says and grabs my arm. We walk over to Meg and Baylor. His presence is a godsend. Anyone staring at Baylor will clearly see that I am being escorted over to him. I have no choice.

This time Meg and Baylor include us in the conversation, which is converted to English. But all the while we're talking, Meg keeps wrapping her talons around Baylor's arm. I can't imagine how her husband puts up with her. We keep the conversation brief. Then Byron physically pulls Meg away.

Before he swings her around, she manages to whisper to me, "I wouldn't get too comfortable."

I keep my temper in check. I see Jackson at the other end of the party and am very tempted to walk toward him. Maybe he can give me a ride back to Dallas. If I evaluate Baylor and Jackson side by side, Baylor loses. Each time I have met Jackson he's been nothing but attentive. Sure he watched the game while we ate dinner, but he talked to me during the commercial breaks. That's a lot better than speaking Spanish in front of me to some other woman.

"Why don't you start walking and in five minutes I'll catch up with you," Baylor whispers as we dodge paintballs some patrons are lobbing at each other. I'm too angry at the situation to openly mock the game.

"Fine," I say with clenched teeth.

I start the long trek back to the parking lot. I'm within fifty feet of it before Baylor catches up to me. He places his hand on the small of my back as if he's gently guiding me. I'm silent. I try to emanate my hatred toward him psychically.

"I'm warning you right now, this isn't going to be a pretty ride," I snarl as soon as I get into the car and punch the seat-heater button. I'm always cold in Texas because they crank the air-conditioning so high.

"What?"

"You completely forgot about me. You flirted with Meg almost the whole time and when I tried to enter the conversation, you started speaking Spanish."

"I thought you spoke Spanish."

"*Besa me cula.*"

"See?"

"I don't speak fucking Spanish. I speak swear words in many languages." The heat rises to my cheeks. "Why on earth would you think I spoke Spanish?"

"A requirement if you work in Texas?"

"Think again. Last I checked, the *Journal* is for English-speaking people."

"I'm sorry you were uncomfortable. I didn't mean to ignore you. These things sometimes happen when you're doing business at events, and we did agree to try to look like we weren't together because of Aimee and Jackson."

"What business were you doing with Meg?"

"She's a client."

"A what?"

"A client. I can't talk about it. It's privileged."

"Let's say you tell me what that means?"

"Let's say I knew that I was the only competent lawyer who would help her. I assure you that I have no interest in her. She's a snake."

"You think she's a snake?"

"I dated her before. I think I know," he says.

"Yeah, about that—" I try to angle more information.

"I'm not going to go any further than that. There are some things that should be kept private. For instance, would you like me talking to Aimee and Jackson about you?"

"No, but that's different. And how do you know about Jackson?" I ask.

"You don't think men gossip?" he asks.

"No."

"You don't know a lot about men," he says.

"Did Jackson confide in you in the locker room while he was taking off his jock strap?" I ask.

"He told some other guys that he thought you were amazing. They told me. All men were fully clothed at the time."

I squirm in my seat. Jackson telling people I'm amazing doesn't make me look bad or like I'm playing the field. The question is: Did he say anything else?

"Do you mind that Jackson finds me amazing?" I ask.

"I don't mind if you date him. I don't even know you yet," he says.

Where can I go from there? He said all the right derogatory things about Meg and followed up by pointing out my own hypocrisy in a subtle yet menacing way. Maybe it's a client thing, after all. I watch the freeway rush past for a few minutes and look for a diplomatic reentry into civil conversation.

"Meg's husband seems very nice," I try.

"He seems that way. Sushi?"

"Yeah, I love it and I know you do, too. Meg told me. She told me you rented out a whole restaurant for her." Give me some points for effort, even though my execution sucks.

"Those were my young, insecure days," he says.

"What are these?" I ask.

"My older, wiser days, when I don't need to rent out restaurants to be impressive," he says as we arrive at Kinichi and wait in a five-car valet line. There is a throng of people snaking out the door and into the parking lot. I start to walk to the end of the line but Baylor grabs my arm and leads me inside. I can feel the stares on my back from all the people we're cutting ahead of. Baylor waves to a short man who ushers us in and immediately seats us.

"I did some legal work for him. Immigration stuff a few years ago," Baylor says.

"Who needs to rent out a restaurant when you have connections?" I say.

I can't seem to play nice with Baylor. I play sarcastic with him extraordinarily well and he volleys back with the same skill. I'm not sure if this is husband-hunting and manipulating in the traditional sense or simply a road to working up sexual tension.

"I've always had connections. I didn't used to have as much confidence," he says.

The restaurant is all dark wood, silk pillows, and mood lighting. We sit in a booth that secludes us from most of the other patrons. Baylor orders for both of us, including the jalapeño salmon roll with salsa on the side that is my favorite. I look at him as he washes his hands and face with the hot towel provided by the waiter. Washing the face with a hot washcloth isn't something I usually see a cultured person do. He takes a sip of his sake and sinks further into the booth.

Maybe he's just rebound material, I think. He drums his hand on the table and loosens his tie. He looks every bit the privileged Southern brat I imagine him to be. He's so not my type.

"So tell me about your privileged childhood," I say and lean playfully across the table. He takes up my challenge.

He tells me he's an Eagle Scout (apparently you never stop being one) and that his dad and he used to spend weekends clearing cedar from the fields of their ranch in Big Bend during most of his adolescence.

"It teaches you a lot when you've peeled the skin from your hands on the weekend and your friends spent it joyriding in their new Porsches," he says.

"Didn't you have a new Porsche?" I ask.

"I had a Maserati but I didn't joyride in it. It would've been taken away from me for good if I did that," he says.

"Was it taken away from you temporarily for something else?" I ask.

"Minor infraction. I drove past curfew and left McDonald's wrappers all over the floor."

"What was the curfew?"

"Eleven o'clock. I came in at midnight. They were more angry about the wrappers. What if someone saw that was how I kept my car?"

He tells me about how his parents instilled a sense of manners and decorum in him. The whole family ate together every night, and every dinner was an object lesson in how to treat people. His mother and father used a new example of interactions they had each night and talked about the other person's motivations. For example, Why did the Republican party leader want twenty thousand dollars from Baylor's dad right then, and what did it mean if his dad wrote the check?

"My parents are real interested in what makes people tick. They're both exceptional listeners."

"Was that good or bad?" I ask.

"Growing up it was bad because I didn't get away with any- thing and it was good because I didn't get away with anything. It's probably about the same now."

His family's money comes from real estate but they dabble in ranching and a little bit of oil.

"My family has lived in Texas for six generations. We're a part of everything," he says.

"You'd never want to leave here, would you?" I ask.

"I might want to, but I don't know if I ever could," he says. "Whenever I'm in a plane headed back to Texas and they say we've crossed the state border, I always breathe easier."

His mother makes pies from scratch even though she never had to learn to cook. She has been surrounded by kitchen help since she was a day old. She is a small thin woman who uses the words *baby doll* and *precious* without irony. She's always holding Bay- lor's hand when they talk.

"I had plenty of nannies growing up but my mother was there, too. She read me a bedtime story every night," he says, sounding somewhat defensive.

"Hey, I didn't say anything," I say.

"Everyone who grew up without a nanny thinks that those of us who had nannies had parents who didn't care about us," he says.

"You've had a lot of people give you a hard time about this?" I ask.

"No, but I knew you would," he says.

"How often do you see your family?" I ask, deciding not to go the sarcastic route for once.

He sees his family almost every day because he's working with them. Before he became a lawyer he was at his parents' house every Sunday night for dinner. Now he's a little looser about the Sunday dinners, though he still does attend two a month. His mother desperately wants him to get married and have children. She says he's so rootless he's liable to blow away. He came close to marriage once. He fell for a society woman (is this Meg?) but she was too much of a mess. She had a liver the size of Rhode Island.

"I'm glad I found out before I was legally obligated to make it my problem," he says.

"You wouldn't help out if your wife was a drunk?"

"Of course I would and it wouldn't stop me from loving a woman if she had a drinking problem. I'd make sure she got some help and I'd stand beside her. This woman, she had too many other problems," he says.

"Was it Meg?" I ask, overwhelmed by my curiosity.

"You'd have to know my family to understand," he says cryptically.

"Ah, family can be difficult with prospective spouses. They have high standards," I say.

"Mine do," he says. "I've worked long enough and I'm smart enough not to care what people think of me. I just have to be okay with myself."

That's just about the best thing I've heard Baylor say.

The rest of the evening is noncombative. I tell him about my childhood: the time I shaved my head with my dad's razor and about my stutter, which was so bad that I refused to read out loud in class. For most guys that would be enough. We'd switch back to talking about him now. But Baylor persists in asking questions about who I am.

"Do you have brothers?"

"No, I have one sister and two cousins. They're all older than I am and used to torment me," I say.

"Can you give me some torment stories that I could refer to in the future?"

"I don't think you're strong enough to hold me up to the ceiling, tickle me, and pass me around. And I hope you're not mean enough to put poison ivy in my bed."

"God, they were bad." He's loosened me up so I tell him more about myself than I told Rafe in the first six months of dating. I grew up on Long Island. My mother is . . . What can I say about my mother? Aimee's words reverberate in my head. Don't tell the men here she's Jewish. Instead I say she's the epitome of a New York mother and quickly move on to the other members of my family. My dad's a lawyer. My sister and I had dinner with him every Sunday at Chang's Chinese restaurant. During dinner, he'd review our homework and bark orders at us like a drill sergeant. He was very big on grades, academics for their own sake, and reading.

"When I was in elementary school he stocked my bedroom with *The Fountainhead* and *As I Lay Dying*," I say.

"What about your mother? You haven't said much about her. I think you can tell a lot about a woman from what her mother is like," he says.

Once again, what can I say about my mother? I tell him my mother desperately wants grandkids. She'd steal one for my sister or me if she thought we'd keep it. For years she's stockpiled baby clothes and toys, thinking that this will be the year that one of us will get pregnant. She loves the smell of babies better than anything, including freshly baked chocolate chip cookies.

"My sister's married so it's more appropriate for her than me. She's trying but she's having problems," I say.

"That happens when women get older," Baylor says.

"She's not that old. She's in her early thirties," I say. "Women have kids in their forties."

"Those women are genetic freaks," he says.

"That's exactly what my mother said."

"She's right."

I stop talking to catch my breath and go over in my head all the information I just provided. Anything incriminating? I'm really trying to follow Aimee's rules even if I'm not with the man she picked for me.

"Did you really stutter?" he asks.

"Yes," I say, a bit defensive.

He laughs and reaches for my hands.

"That's so awful. I used to make fun of kids like you. I was such a bully in elementary school."

"And look at how the nerds turned out. I'm not so bad."

He leans over the table and kisses me, a small kiss on the lips but it's really nice. It gives me a high the way I used to get from chugging a Coke with a mouthful of Pop Rocks in junior high. I look down at our table. It's wiped off. All the dishes have been removed. The check has been paid. I let him pay without the slightest struggle—a thing I'm only starting to get comfortable with.

It's become awfully quiet in the restaurant. We look around. All the other customers have cleared out. The waiters are putting up chairs.

"I have an early day in court tomorrow," he says as he gets up and pulls out my chair. Then he takes my arm and leads me outside. He opens and closes my door for me. He drives without a hint of hurry. We stop outside his house with a slow easing like a train coming into a station.

We're in his car, parked by his condo. We've been here for an hour or more—talking. One topic leads to another and another and back to something we said a few minutes ago. It's free-form verbal association. We could do this all night. I'm so awake that I don't think I'll ever have to sleep again.

At this moment, no one could be more fascinating. There's nothing Baylor could say that wouldn't interest me. If he told me that playing bridge was his passion, I'd buy every bridge book I could find and practice shuffling cards until I could do it blindfolded with one hand.

He has the best smile. It's a little bratty and infectious. He smells like fresh lavender.

"So, dinner again?"

"Yeah," I say.

"Great. It's one a.m. and I have to get up at five," he says and kisses me. It's a long kiss and just right, firm and slow.

The great first date crush: he's perfect, at least for now; you're perfect, at least for now. When he touches the back of my neck, the hairs stand up. It's a better drug than caffeine, alcohol, or anything illegal.

Chapter Nine

Never Say No to a Nice Psychotropic

Aimee and I sip our way through our first sidecar of the evening and attack a large dish of heavily salted fries at the Inwood Bar, a pub separated from the Inwood Movie Theater by a glass wall so that you can sit in a booth and still follow the action, even if you can't hear the dialogue. The loudest scenes cause the glass to pulsate, sort of an unintended special effect. When the film is subtitled, you really luck out—like tonight, *Belle de Jour* is on. I always love what Catherine Deneuve is wearing.

We're regrouping. After Aimee's baking extravaganza, it was painfully obvious that she needed to readjust her strategy with Rance. I mean it's not practical to bake enough to feed the state of Delaware every time you have sex with your boyfriend. She called me at work the day after the wildlife fund-raiser and begged for an intervention because she said the sour milk smell wouldn't leave her alone.

"I have to have a powwow tonight. Call in some experts," she said.

"How many people do you want to know about your problem?" I asked her from my cubicle. I was trying to sound like I was interviewing a source.

"You're right, maybe just one expert. Meet me at the Inwood after work," she said and hung up. It's not like her to be so covert or abrupt. Last night must have been the worst yet.

I study Catherine Deneuve and eat the bar party mix. "Are you going to tell me anything?" I ask. We've been in the booth for twenty minutes already. She shushes me.

"So, when are we getting married?"

I don't know where the voice is coming from until I see Aimee smile and stand up to kiss someone behind me. I turn around and come nose to belt buckle with Drew Dalhart, her semi-closeted friend and a former Dallas Cowboy linebacker.

"As soon as you straighten up and fly right," Aimee says and laughs.

Drew is built like a refrigerator, but moves like a dancer. It's difficult to figure out where his shoulders stop and his head starts. A couple of rolls of fat or muscle, depending on how charitable you are, lie between his collar and neatly trimmed hair. He can still play football, but a blown-out knee, several compressed vertebrae, and countless concussions have put him on the permanently disabled list. The man is impressive and not just for his athletic ability. He's well read, mainly military history, and has a sharp, sardonic sense of humor. He travels in all the best gay and straight circles (he's also a friend of Baylor's) and faithfully offers up delicious society tidbits.

With Drew, the conversation devolves into gossip as fast as credits roll on the screen. Soon, he's regaling us on the most recent gay dish. Yet another prominent sports figure was caught by police with his pants down and a man attached to him in a public restroom. For the sake of the play-offs, the police officers walked the other way. He tells us about a certain society woman who is in such denial about her weight gain that she split open her pair of Dolces when trying to hoist herself out of a booth at Salt, a new Hungarian/Asian fusion restaurant. Imagine sushi goulash. The name of the establishment comes from some special kind of salt imported from Hungary and supplied aplenty at every rustic wooden table.

"She should've avoided the restaurant just for the name. As if she needs water retention and bloating in addition to all the pounds she's packed on," Drew hisses.

"I can't tell she's gained weight," I say.

"Well, my dear, then you see through rose-colored glasses. Her husband called her a heifer at lunch the other day, said that he would take home his leftovers but it would only encourage her."

"Are men really that catty?"

"More than you know. Darling, you should've heard what the other men were saying about *their* wives."

"And?" Aimee asks, poking Drew in the ribs.

"Okay, okay."

Drew gave us the highlights of his weekly lunch at the Capital Grille with his buddies, including a former mayor, an appellate judge, a lobbyist for the hemophiliacs, and Baylor.

"The ones who are married complained about how they're not getting any. Then they all took a couple of digs at their wives, referring to whether she's a lifer or not," Drew says. "I guess before they dump her for a younger woman, they do grapple with their conscience slightly, and I do mean slightly."

"Damn, men really do gossip. Seriously, they dump their wives just because they're not getting any?" I say.

"Doll, it's not as if these relationships are based on a whole lot more than sex."

Most of the wives are in perfect shape and ten to twenty years the juniors of their husbands. They put up with their husbands' beer bellies, back hair, and gas, which is a function of their steak, potato, and wine diet, until their patience with repulsion diminishes. Often the men come home too drunk to do anything more than talk, so their sex lives have dwindled down to vacations, occasional Sundays, and special gift-giving events.

Drew says a friend of his who married such a man said to him, "How am I supposed to feel romantic about someone who keeps me up most of the night by farting, snoring, and sweating as though he's lying on a bed of coals?"

Indeed, how? But then again she brought her looks to the marriage and he brought everything else. So when she stops treating him like the second coming of a porn star, his commitment to the relationship wears thin.

"These little biddies knew what they were getting into when they walked down the aisle. It ain't no fairy tale. They married the beast, not the beauty," Drew says.

"So let me get this straight. They all sat there and talked about their wives like trading cards?" Aimee asks.

"Not all of them. The ones who married for money sublimate their desire by talking about other women," Drew says. "Case in point: Five years ago, Judge Marc Whitehurst married Patty Banning, heir to a cattle fortune. Unfortunately, Miss Patty looks as if she's been eating the profits—she weighs in at two hundred fifty. It's doubtful the two have been intimate since the honeymoon. The judge, being an elected official in Texas, is limited to self-abuse and vicarious lechery to relieve his libido. You should have heard him." Drew then proceeds to re-create part of the conversation for us.

" 'Didn't I see you at the zoo with Big Boobs Walking?' the judge joked with Baylor. 'Personally, I would've skipped the exhibits and gone straight to the backseat of the car.' "

He's referring to Meg and Baylor's very public flirtation at that wildlife fund-raiser.

" 'Is that as erotic as you get?' said the lobbyist for the hemophiliacs. 'I would've gone to a hotel, at least. Might have even stayed the whole night.'

" 'No-daddy-no,' chirped the judge, to general leering and even one high five from the mayor."

Translation: A no-daddy-no is a woman so desirable that a man would make hard-core love to her on the fifty-yard line at Super Bowl halftime while his children pounded him on the back, yelling, "No Daddy, no!"

"The judge continued to bust Baylor about Meg, the silicone princess, saying things like 'She's a flotation device with legs' and 'Is she hourly, weekly, or an open-lease arrangement?' Baylor protested that he was only doing his legal duty. The group erupted in laughter when they heard that Baylor is actually working with her.

" 'Does she give good dictation?' the judge asked. 'If so, I'll work with her when you're done. I mean, when she's ready for *new employment.*'

"That's basically what men talk about," Drew finishes story-telling with his usual flair.

"What do you say when they talk about women that way?" Aimee asks.

"I usually take that opportunity to order more wine."

Most of his friends suspect that Drew "plays for the other team," but no one would even hint at his preferences. Homosexu-ality in Dallas, even among the enlightened and educated, is still firmly in the closet. They're even squeamish about hugging one an-other. The ubiquitous backslapping represents the outer boundary of male bonding rituals. Fortunately, Drew's obvious manliness re-moves any outright ambiguity.

"So what did Baylor say to all the ribbing?" I ask, trying to seem nonchalant.

"He claims Meg needs his help. She's not getting any from her husband," he says.

"She's not getting any, huh," Aimee says with a wink.

"Huh, so maybe this legal thing is about her husband," I say.

"Darling, if it involves Baylor and Meg, he better hope her hus-band doesn't know," Drew says.

"They're not together," I say emphatically.

Drew and Aimee both stop the conversation and stare at me. I've been caught. My interest in Baylor mixed with what sounds like intimate details about him can only mean that I have a story to tell them.

"It's nothing," I say.

They keep staring at me with their mouths closed. My neck is heating up. I shift positions three times. It's a silent interrogation.

"I think he's cute," I confess. I say the words so fast that they tumble out with the same abandon as cereal from an upturned box. Telling half the truth is better than not telling any of it.

"What?" Aimee screeches.

"I can't help it," I mumble.

"You can't date Baylor," Aimee says.

Aimee looks over to Drew for support.

"You really can't," he says with more feeling than I'd expect.

I look from one to the other of them. They both have stern looks of disapproval on their faces.

"What? He can't be all that bad. You both are friends with him," I whine.

"I'm friends with him but I wouldn't date him," Drew says, shaking his head.

They both look down at their drinks. They're hiding something from me. What could be worse than the things they've told me tonight? I've already heard about closeted homosexuality, chauvinism, and cheating.

"What? What is it about him that's so bad?" I ask.

Aimee takes a deep breath. Drew speaks. "Honey, Aimee told me your secret and I'll keep it with me forever, won't tell a soul. The problem is other people won't be as forgiving and Baylor, well, he's one of those people."

"What secret?" I ask, confused about what skeleton I have lurking in my closet.

Drew leans closer to me and hisses, "You're Jewish."

"What's your point?" I hiss back.

Drew sits up in his booth, assuming a scholarly look.

"Darling, Texas is a bit different from other places. We don't warm to people who are different from us that quickly," he says.

"That, and the fact that some churches here have more members than the population of a small town and lots of people have Arab business partners who specifically forbid them from hiring Jews, and you can see why there might be some issues," Aimee says.

"So why does Baylor specifically have issues?" I ask as I examine their faces for traces of lies.

"Baylor's family has a long, long history in Texas," Drew says.

"And with Jews," Aimee adds.

"So they're real anti-Semitic," I finish their thought.

"They're more than that. Baylor's done more than that," Drew says.

On the other side of the glass, we see J.T., or Hoss, his more

commonly used nickname (Lizzy's fiancé), scurrying into the subtitled movie with a bag of popcorn, candy, and bottled water.

"Hoss looks guilty," Aimee says to Drew, her attention momen-
tarily diverted.

"That food wasn't for Lizzy," he says.

According to Drew, Hoss was acting funny during the usual
Sunday afternoon pickup basketball game. He kept asking strange
questions about sex like: "You think a guy is better at sex if he's
had it with lots of women?" He was asking earnestly. This type of
earnestness puts the other guys in the awkward position of either
having to answer him with some true emotional sentiment, which
is difficult for Southern men under the best of circumstances, or to
deflect the question and quasi humiliate Hoss in the process.

They chose the latter.

His friends had been holding back their laughter, but as soon as
he finished they burst into peals of it and became a virtual Greek
chorus of ridicule.

"I feel like I became a more tender lover after I went to that
hooker in Abilene."

"I know my wife has benefited from the blow jobs my secretary
gives me."

And that was just during the game. Drew sits back in the booth,
looks into the movie theater, and smiles. "Never try to be sensitive
with a pack of men," he says. "I mean the son of a bitch was trying to tell us he's cheating on Lizzy. We don't want to hear that
crap."

"But does that really matter to men? That another guy cheats?"
I ask Drew.

"Look at it this way. Men like Hoss make us all look bad because we pay for their sins and freakiness," he says. "When one
man treats you badly, the next man pays for it. After Hoss is finished with her, Lizzy will be practically undatable because of how
he has messed with her head. If you want to chase women, dump
the girlfriend first."

It's true that after years of dysfunctional dating, I don't trust
most men, and the ones I do trust are so boring or unmotivated
that I don't want to date them. Aimee is intensely interested in this

conversation, so much so that she's discreetly taken my notebook and pen out of my purse and placed them on the seat beside her. She's actually taking notes.

"So what do men look for exactly?" she says seriously.

"Well, it depends on the kind of men you're trying to find."

"Rich," she says, set in stone.

"I'd say that men fall into three categories," Drew says. "The Uptight, the Crusader, and the Romantic. The Uptight man has a good pedigree and is religious to varying degrees. He's looking for a woman with a similar pedigree or a healthy dose of WASPy attitude. She has to sport an athletic body that borders on anorexia. Subtle plastic surgery only, we're talking Botox, no implants. She should be able to handle herself in any situation, and by this I don't mean she's the life of the party. She should be socially gracious enough to avoid saying something at a party that is talked about the next day in less than flattering terms or any terms at all. She is the social equivalent of socks, a basic part of a wardrobe that no one should get too excited about. There must be no hint of scandal. In addition to all this, she must be highly educated but do nothing with her degrees. She should play tennis and golf and attend church regularly. This is what political strivers, closeted gays, and old-money men want.

"For the Crusader, it isn't about the spouse, it's about the symbol. He marries to prove a point. This is a man trapped in a socially ambivalent old-money family, who wants to rebel by marrying a woman who's chained herself to abortion clinics in protest if he's a conservative Republican, or if he's liberal-minded, he may marry the organizer of Head Start or the chief fund-raiser for the local public television station. If he's new money and angry about it, he may wed a dancer or a hooker or a woman who looks like the other two to convey that he doesn't care what anyone thinks. He'll marry whomever he pleases and he'll rub your nose in it. The important thing to remember about the Crusader is that he's the most volatile. He may go from crusade to crusade, which means you either go with him or face becoming obsolete. Or, he could purge all his anger and decide to settle down to his family ways, which means you're out. Try to picture a Head Start director feeling at home with people who whine about paying property taxes because, after all, their kids are in private schools and don't use those public institutions. Imagine her enthrallment when the conversation turns to how they hide their money in the Cayman Islands so their tax dollars aren't exported to some poor, inner-city school district.

"Then there's the Romantic. He's the hardest to get. He usually appears to be a confirmed bachelor. He's dated lots of women, some seriously, but he never settles down. Most think this is because he wants to play the field. This usually isn't true. He wants to find the one person who's absolutely right for him. Though he'd never say it, he's looking for a soul mate. He can't put into words exactly what he's searching for and he doesn't talk about any of this with his friends. He appears to be sort of a lone wolf kind of guy. But he's the one who's going to be the most loyal, if you can catch him. The trick is, you must be worthy, and there's little you can alter in your personality to achieve soul-mate status," Drew said, once again with remarkable elegance.

"Sounds like the Romantic is what you're looking for," I say to him.

"It's who I'm looking for and who I am but you know what they say, 'To gay men, *monogamy* is a word without meaning.' It's an oxymoron, like Cowboy football." He sighs and takes a large gulp of his vodka tonic.

"Moving on, Aimee, what about Rance?"

Aimee blushes and claps her hands like a little girl at a tea party. After her emergency phone calls this morning, Rance took her on a shopping trip—he didn't become a millionaire by being dumb. He sensed she wasn't thrilled with the night before. To say that the shopping expedition exceeded her expectations would be like expressing disappointment at winning the lottery.

"I got a Hermès purse. A Birkin," she says. "Honey, he knows how to treat a woman and he's richer than I thought. He's diversified."

Her list of goodies included: a Hermès watch, a Chanel black chiffon dress, a Chanel driving coat and matching pants, an Yves Saint Laurent bag with a horn handle, and a J. Mendel chubby, meaning a short chinchilla coat. All that and all Aimee had to do was put out, but that's the problem.

"What category does Rance fit into?" I ask.

Drew thinks for a moment and says, "Uptight or Crusader. Sorry, babe, he's no Romantic."

Aimee looks a little nervous. "Well, am I a rebel or a WASP?"

Aimee's definitely not a WASP, but Rance isn't old money so he might not know what a real WASP is and he may have mistaken Aimee for something she's not, exactly. Rance is like the computer nerd in high school who gets the social cues a couple of years too late and then manages to misinterpret them. He still wears skinny ties with Zegna suits, tortoiseshell glasses, and drinks Diet Coke, for God's sake.

"I'd say he's Uptight Nouveau Riche," Drew says.

Aimee lets out a deep breath. "That's good. I don't want to chain myself to any clinics."

Drew stares intently at her. "So is Rance the one?"

She squirms under the scrutiny. "Umm, yeah. Maybe. I mean, I checked out his assets. They're in great shape. He knows how to treat a woman. . . ."

"But you can't imagine sleeping with him again," Drew declares. She obviously told him a little about the situation and why she needs his advice.

Aimee's shoulders cave. "God, no. I thought last night would be better. I was feeling real good. Thanks to the tequila. We went back to his place and I suggested we go straight upstairs to avoid any milk incidents. So we get to his bedroom and things are going as well as can be expected. I can still smell milk but I put some Chanel on under my nose so that's masking a lot of the fumes. We're making out and he excuses himself to go to the bathroom. The bathroom is very close to the bedroom and it has a thin door. I can hear that something he ate didn't agree with him. I can hear everything. I turn on the stereo. He comes out and we start making love, except his intestines aren't done talking," she says.

"He farted while you were having sex?" I ask for clarification.

"A lot of loud wet farts. All I could smell was rotting meat and sour milk and then when he was done, he drooled on me again," she says quietly. It's almost as if she's ashamed of being associated with him.

"Got milk?" Drew says scornfully.

"It was like kissing Spam."

This is the dark side of husband-hunting that no one tells you about and it is beginning to hit home with me. Sure, if you're attractive and bright you will probably be able to find a rich husband. But what people don't say is that you probably won't be attracted to him. In fact, more often than not, you'll be repulsed. This is because the attractive ones are gay, or looking for their equal in wealth, or acting out with model after model.

"It helps if you drink a lot beforehand," Drew says. "Alcohol is the great equalizer of sexual encounters. Partial blindness facilitates risk-taking and anesthetizes bad judgment."

"I might need something stronger," Aimee says.

"Turn off the lights?"

"Yeah."

"Use visualization?"

"Yeah."

"You know what I used to do when I was obliged to have sex with women?"

"Fake orgasms," Aimee says.

"Very funny. When I was a Dallas Cowboy I had to play along with everyone else. Hookers, groupies—I participated in all of it. The NFL didn't have a don't-ask-don't-tell doctrine," Drew says. "It was more like show-and-tell-your-hetero-inclinations."

"Wow, so what did you do?" Aimee perks up. I guess she's thinking that if a gay man can have sex with a woman, maybe there's hope for Rance.

Drew explained that first he would sit the woman down on his bed, spray some Cartier on her so that she smelled manly, tell her he was going to the bathroom for a minute, take a shot of tequila, and meditate. He would clear his mind of all thoughts except the one that he wanted to maintain—Vince Vaughn naked. When he came out, he expected the lights to be off and for her to be quiet. Then he'd get into bed with his eyes closed, his senses dulled, and go at the situation with the same intensity that he had playing football.

"I needed the winning mind-set," Drew says.

"Is there a video I can rent or a book or even a pamphlet?" Aimee asks.

"You mean like *Ten Easy Steps to Great Fake Sex* or *Bedroom Tips for the Good, the Bad, and the Ugly?*" he says.

"You don't have to belittle my pathetic copulation needs," Aimee says, and laughs nervously.

"Look, doll, it sounds like with him, the more you consummate, the quicker you'll get engaged," Drew says. "Jesus, he's a dork. He'll be in your debt forever for having sex a lot. Sit back and enjoy the ride. It's the quid pro quo for a grand lifestyle upgrade."

Aimee's eyes harden with determination. "You're right. I'll do it again tomorrow. All I need is a schedule II narcotic, nothing innovative, just an off-the-shelf psychotropic that distorts reality. Maybe I can get him to change his diet, too." She takes a big gulp of her sidecar just as Hoss walks out of the movie alone, from what we can tell; though there are plenty of attractive women around him. One approaches him in the lobby. She clasps his arm and hugs him. The gesture seems friendly but not overly so.

"He may be a jerk but at least he's doable," Aimee says of Hoss.

"Remember your mother saying, *You can't get everything you want?*" I say. "*They're either rich or attractive. You can't have both and, honey, the looks fade.* That's the speech Evelyn gave you your whole life."

"You had to remind me," Aimee said drily. "Are you trying to make me feel worse?"

The one time I met Evelyn, she would bring an object lesson into every aspect of life. The UPS man delivered a package, and Evelyn commented on the man's natural attributes, then sighed and said, "I'd like to see him in ten years. He won't be so hot then."

Evelyn married what passes for wealth in Gruene, Texas. She snatched up the town's biggest lawyer. Big, of course, is relative in Gruene, but it meant that they owned their three-story farmhouse outright, Aimee got to go to summer camp, and Evelyn didn't have to wear synthetic blends all the time. She wants more for her daughter, that's pretty clear. She visited for a weekend and it seemed as though the sole purpose of the trip was to pound into Aimee that she shouldn't lower her monetary standards ever, just her visual ones. I thought Aimee was resigned to these facts until tonight. The reality is much scarier than the morality play, I guess. Maybe Southern women don't have everything worked out.

"You know," I say to Aimee, "a guy like Rance might be open to instruction. Get him to do to your body exactly what you want and you may start to think he's the most far, wide, and handsome man on earth."

"That's a thought. Try to turn him into a vegan, too," Drew says before turning the spotlight on me. "What about you and Jackson Ray? He's a much better match for you than Baylor."

"You can't date both of them. You'll wind up like Natalie," Aimee says.

"So what's going on with Jackson?" Drew asks again.

I blush a little.

"I talked to Jackson earlier at work and we agreed to go camping from Saturday to Sunday. Nothing heavy, though, like remote trails where we have to hang our food from trees to protect it, and us, from bears."

"Why not start Friday night?" Drew asks.

"I have to go to Oklahoma for work on Thursday and on Friday I'll get out late because of it," I say.

"Ohhh," both Drew and Aimee utter. They sound disgusted with the thought of Oklahoma. I know that neither one of them completely understands what it is I do so they are a bit mystified about why I would have to do it in Oklahoma.

"I have to visit a JCPenney distribution center," I say.

I receive blank stares. I think it's best not to go any further into this. I let them devolve back into gossip as I check my phone. No messages. Baylor hasn't tried to contact me at all today. He can't be as bad as they say. He's too cute for that. Though I do think I'll use my reporting skills to figure out what about Baylor is so horrible that even Drew would warn me away.

Chapter Ten

An Ex Is an Ex for a Reason— Don't Go Back for Second Helpings

ateline: Tulsa, Oklahoma. I feel like I'm walking inside a blow-dryer. It's ninety degrees with ninety-degree humidity, and a thirty-knot wind, which kicks up enough dust to cause a permanent haze across my contact lenses. I landed at the Tulsa International Airport at ten a.m. It should have taken me fifteen minutes to scoot over to JCPenney's new mammoth distribution center. But it didn't. I'm lost in a maze of dead-end streets with names like Yale and Harvard (they had some big dreams here). An hour later, I find the five-story aluminum-sided behemoth that shines so brightly in the sun that I can only think it will be responsible for dozens of car collisions and UFO sightings. I step out of my smoke-laced Geo rental (Tulsa is all-smoking, all the time), and a perky PR girl in head-to-toe pink Escada greets me. Her lips are shining as brightly as the building's aluminum siding.

"Well, you must be Jenny Barton," she chirps. "Don't worry about the tour. It went on without you. I'll be your personal guide." She grabs my elbow firmly and leads me through a glut of cheap plastic merchandise. "As you can see, we're going more up-scale in an effort to reposition our brand."

I'm confronted with a synthetic, double-knit collection. If this got any uglier, it would bark at the neighbors and pee on the rug.

The tour with her lasts horribly long.

"Here you go."

She deposits me with a group of reporters who look as if they're well overdue for double lattes or something stronger. Their eyes are glazed and heavy-lidded. A man who must be a refugee from Department Store Central Casting drones on about their inventory control's technological breakthroughs. He's in a short-sleeve button-down shirt with what I believe is a clip-on tie. My professional objectivity slips into an aggressive dislike of this story. Do I actually have to write about this dreck? Most definitely. My job is on the line and if this is what Carol deems important, I'll try to pay attention.

I get lost again and don't reach the airport until six p.m. My flight is canceled. There's smog in Dallas because the farmers in Mexico are burning their fields to fertilize the soil. I'm stuck for two hours or more.

I sit down in a blue plastic airport chair, which feels like it hasn't been cleaned since the 1970s, pull out my laptop, and begin writing the two paragraphs that will be the JCPenney story. Rafe slides in right next to me.

"Hi," he says.

"What are you doing here?"

"I'm filling in for extra cash."

"I didn't see you on the tour."

"One of the PR girls gave me a special private tour."

"You were late. Have you written anything?"

"No, like what would I write? The story is garbage."

"Exactly what I'm thinking," I say as I type something verbatim from Mr. Clip-on about inventory control.

"So how is yoga?" I ask.

"Good, and your date?"

"Good."

"Gonna see him again?"

"Sure."

He slumps in his chair and pulls out some dip (chewing tobacco). He places a discreet lump in between his bottom lip and gum and spits the liquid chew into a Coke can that he's pretending to drink from. Not very sexy but definitely a trait he picked up in Texas.

"How's Meg?"

"Good."

"Are the two of you an item?"

He blushes. Can you call yourself an item with a married woman?

"I've been meaning to talk to you about that and about the cat. Yeah, um, I'm going away for a couple of days when I'm supposed to have Mr. Tatters. Could you take him?"

"Going where?"

This is a clear infraction of breakup etiquette. I'm not supposed to delve into who he's having sex with or where. But this is a little too much.

"I'm going to a ranch," he stutters.

"Meg's ranch?"

"Yeah."

"What if I already have plans? And more important, where will her husband be?"

"Look, if this is too weird for you . . ." he trails off.

Damn, now I'm being the psycho ex-girlfriend.

"No, it's fine. This week?"

"You have Tatters this week. I mean in two weeks."

"Sure, as long as you're happy with what I'm feeding him," I say as I finish my two paragraphs and punch SEND. Hopefully, there will be no frantic editing calls. Who am I kidding? Better inoculate. I shoot off another e-mail that tells Carol I'm about to board.

"Would you like to get a drink?" I ask as I'm packing my laptop. But Rafe has already locked in on the airport bar as if he's a self-propelled homing guidance system. I walk behind him several paces. He orders us two Dos Equises with lime. Twenty-somethings in Texas think this is a very suave drink because it's an import (Mexican) beer with citrus stuffed in it. Maybe it's the vitamin C.

Rafe fumbles in his jacket pocket, extracts enough crumpled dollar bills to cover both beers, and I give the waiter a tip. I wonder why he's doing this extra gig. He never attempted financial bet-terment when he was with me. He used to cultivate that cute artist-who-doesn't-care-about-money thing—cute until he asked you to cover his share of the rent for the fifth month in a row. The beer sharpens my already intense female search-and-destroy radar.

"So what's going on with you and Meg?" I purr.

He doesn't hear me. He's still concentrating on his pockets. He pulls out a cell phone, worn wallet, more dollar bills, and scraps of paper. The scraps have jokes scrawled on them. Rafe wants to be a stand-up comic but he presently lacks the self-confidence or work ethic to make the attempt. My armchair diagnosis is that his overbearing mother poisoned that well with her inability to rise to Martha Stewart standards of housekeeping and her own sense of failure over her divorce (she's Catholic). She always exudes a sense of doom when anyone tells her about their dreams for the future.

"Oh, honey, are you really funny enough to do that? How will you live?" she'd say to Rafe whenever he raised the idea of doing stand-up.

So he writes down jokes in small, illegible print, accumulates wads of them in his pockets, and then throws all the paper in a fishbowl. The bowl is almost full. I wonder if he'll ever cull the good ones or ignite the whole thing like a funeral pyre.

He's vulnerable and he has no idea how to get what he wants in life, so he takes small bites at the edges of his ambition. It won't get him anywhere, of course. And yet, I assume Rafe has always been and always will be happier than I am because he never lets anyone penetrate too far below the surface. He has the emotional depth of a cocktail party. He's a chocolate bunny with a hollow center.

Rafe looks up. "What?"

"So what's going on with you and Meg?" I repeat.

"Why?"

"You're dating, aren't you?"

"I wouldn't call it dating."

"Do you stay overnight?"

"Yeah, when I can."

"And?" I chug my beer.

"And what? Really, Jenny, I'm not going there."

"It sounds as if you've already been."

"How catty are you going to get?"

"Fine, I'll stop. Tell me about something else," I say, and remind myself that it's not okay to show my psycho side to my ex-boyfriend whom I don't want to get back together with.

He talks and I appear to be listening, a ruse. I'm in fake-listening mode, an acquired skill that I have nearly mastered as a reporter who listens to sources ramble about themselves for hours on end in order to get a sentence-long quote. I smile, nod, and mimic his gestures while my mind races: What the hell is going on here? I don't want Rafe back. Why am I being so competitive? Because I want Baylor, I think. I need to get the goods on Meg. The reporter in me was on autopilot, already doing the work before the rest of me figured out my emotional part in all this.

The best way to get a source to talk is to get him drunk. If you have a history, talk about the good old times to lubricate the flow of positive feeling and verbal diarrhea. I delve into the heart of what would be the good old times according to Rafe: the spontaneous sex experiences in the public park, which to me were truly uncomfortable and not erotic—I'd come home with grass stains on my underwear—and the one time I handcuffed him.

We slam down four beers, talk sex, and miss the plane. It's harder to pull out information on Meg than I thought. Whenever I circle the subject of Meg, Rafe smiles and wags his finger at me. "Oh, no you don't. I can't talk about that," and then he goes back to reminiscing about sex.

"Why can't you talk about that?" I press.

"Because it would end it," he says, but doesn't elaborate.

After we miss the plane, I go up to the airline counter to rebook on the next flight. There isn't one. Tulsa closes down early. Last flight is at eight p.m. We're gonna have to stay over. Maybe I can use this to my advantage. If I have more time with Rafe and provide more booze, there's a greater likelihood he'll crack. I walk back to his slumping figure from the airline counter.

"We're gonna have to stay the night," I say as I hit the table lightly with my ticket.

"Really?"

"Yeah, last flight left. We might as well share a room since my editor isn't going to be happy about paying for this. Yours probably won't, either," I say.

"Shit, yeah. I hope I wasn't supposed to do anything tomorrow," he says as he slings his arm over my shoulder. I hoist him to standing. He pulls me close as we walk toward the lone cab at the Tulsa International Airport.

"You know, sometimes I miss you," he slurs as we near a taxi. It's a burgundy minivan that I imagine does double duty as a soccer practice ferry during the day. A spunky woman named Sue Tucker drives us to a Marriott. She announces in a voice several levels too loud for inside a car, "My name is Sue. How do you do?" She offers us wet naps and breath mints because beer can get so sticky and smelly. Then she wipes off Rafe's hands herself because he isn't quick enough and dabs some drooled tobacco off his jacket. I think he ended up swallowing the rest of his chew with the beers.

Poor guy never did have any tolerance. At least I'm a functioning drunk. I can keep up with the big boys and still operate heavy machinery. It may be at a blood alcohol level that's far from legal, but my psychomotor skills work fine. It's my morals that go out the window.

Sue is dressed in pink capri pants, a denim shirt with lace that spells Jesus, and white tennies. She offers us juice boxes that are kept cool in a Styrofoam container on the passenger's seat. "So how long have you kids been together?" she asks.

"Two years," I say, hoping Rafe doesn't notice that I'm speaking in the present tense. Something tells me Sue wouldn't approve of us sharing a hotel room if we weren't together.

"That's right, two years. She stole my pen," he says. He's more cognizant than I thought.

"I met my Bobby and three months later we were married. It'll be our twentieth anniversary this June. Of course, I forgave him for a lot of sins," she says.

"We've never been married. I'm too scared," Rafe says. Interesting admission but enough of our personal dirty laundry. I'd rather hear about hers. This is a very Texas/Southern thing. These people like to talk, and the fact that you don't know them is no impediment to them acting as if you are their best friend. But it's not insincere. I've talked to women in elevators about yeast infections and alcoholic husbands.

"What sins?" I ask.

"Well, he got addicted to crank and spent most of our retirement money."

That's right, Oklahoma is a hotbed for meth labs, also known as homemade speed. Labs, which are basically any room with a Bunsen burner, electricity, and running water, were blowing up all over the state because the chemicals can explode if you're not properly trained, and a high school dropout stirring chemicals doesn't usually have a lot of knowledge. If you drive down the highways with the windows open, you're hit with a mixture of sweetgrass, ammonia, smoke, and cow manure. Felony aromatherapy.

"He never had much to say, except when he was high. Talked as if his tongue were tied in the middle and flapping at both ends."

Translation: He talks a lot but doesn't really say anything true, coherent, or of value.

We pull into the Marriott parking lot. This whole ride was a mood killer. They don't need to preach abstinence here, just make kids drive around with Sue and a couple of juice boxes.

I pay the fare and nudge Rafe, who passed out halfway through the life story of our born-again, denim-wearing driver. He stumbles out of the minivan, half-conscious. While he gets his bearings, I locate the front desk and secure a room. I walk back to the parking lot and find him still trying to figure out where he might be—airport, Dallas.

"Room sixteen," I say.

The room, nothing more than a metal box, bears wallpaper with tiny hearts and daisies, the curtains are gingham, and a wooden cow hangs above the bed, complete with a brass bell that sounds when the bed rocks. Behind the blue gingham curtains is the closet. I spot a minibar, the only possible savior for the evening.

"Minibar."

Rafe's head stops listing to one side.

"Really."

I throw him an airplane-size bottle of Wild Turkey and turn on the television. I can and do get *Dukes of Hazzard* on demand. I've only seen Rafe more thrilled stealing gnomes from people's gardens. There's a whole collection of them in his closet. They look as if they're having a members-only party in there.

"Cool, this is so cool." He bounces on the bed. "You know, I never really thought our breakup was the end," he says.

"Why not?"

"Because I like you and you like me."

"That's not enough."

"Why? What more is there?"

"Trust, plus it would get crowded with you, me, and Meg."

"Meg's not permanent."

"Really? What is she?"

"I'm doing a very altruist thing," he says and moves closer to me.

"By sleeping with a married woman?"

He tries to kiss me. I slip away and reposition myself to better defend from further amorous assaults.

"What do you mean by altruistic?" I delve further, correcting his vocabulary along the way.

"She needs something that I can provide. I have a very high sperm count," he says.

"Yeah, so," I say. I don't know what that has to do with an affair at all.

"Meg's under a lot of pressure to have children," he says as he positions himself closer to my face.

"Yeah, with her husband. Anyway, she has an incompetent something or other so they're having problems," I say.

"She doesn't have problems. He does. Only he won't get tested for it. Who told you she has an incompetent whatever?" he asks as he tries to gently stroke my arm. He's actually pawing at me with the same grace as a clawless bear.

"Her husband," I say.

"See, he's promoting the propaganda," he says.

He explains to me, between shots, stolen glances at Daisy's dukes, and clumsy attempts at seduction, that Meg found him through a sperm bank. She bribed a secretary at the bank to tell her what local donors had the highest number and most motile sperm. She got their names and addresses as well as their vital statistics. She found the best physical match to her husband, which is Rafe, and propositioned him. She'd pay him a hefty fee—five thousand dollars an encounter—to have sex with her and keep his mouth shut.

"But why didn't she just buy sperm from the bank?" I ask, dumbfounded by her intricate plot.

"She can't risk someone leaking that and her husband finding out the kid isn't his," Rafe explains.

"But *you* know," I point out.

"Yeah, but I'm only one person and I'm not gonna tell," he says as he collapses onto the bed. He's close to comatose.

"You told me," I say.

"You're the exception. I like her," he says as he closes his eyes.

I doubt Meg would trust Rafe with that information. There must be something more to this. How would she make sure Rafe would keep quiet? Also, she's almost forty. I doubt all the fertility problems are on her husband's side.

I sit back on the bed and look around the room. We've cleaned out the minibar including the NECCO wafers, demanded everything possible on TV, and uncovered one of Meg's deepest secrets.

I slide over to the plywood desk against the wall and set up my laptop. Even though this is Oklahoma the hotel offers free wireless. I boot up and sign into my *Wall Street Journal* account. There I have access to a story library spanning two hundred years of newspaper articles from every publication you can imagine. I type in *Jones* and *Texas* and get about two million matches. Jones is a common name. I try *Jones, Texas,* and *anti-Semitism.* I get nothing. No direct hits. See? Aimee and Drew were all wrong. *Don't be so sure,* I think to myself. If the Joneses are a powerful Texas family and have been for generations, they most likely have enough influence to keep their name out of the paper in relation to bad publicity. Baylor mentioned a small town that his family practically owned and still has property in. It was something weird. Palestine, I think it was Palestine, Texas, which, of course, is pronounced completely differently than the Middle Eastern country. I type in *Palestine, Texas,* and *Jews.* I get forty matches ranging in dates from the early 1800s to the 1990s.

I click on a headline, "Local Student Arrested for Hazing." The article goes on to talk about how a local resident, a freshman at the University of Texas and a member of a fraternity, was arrested for branding—branding!—another student with an anti-Semitic slur, *Hebe.* The student was a minor, and his name was withheld.

I click on another article, "Country Club Upholds Tradition." This one talks about the country club's decision to uphold its rules and not allow any Jewish members or Jewish guests access to the facilities because "people want to feel comfortable, like they're with their own." It was written in 1991.

I sit back in my chair. So there's a lot of anti-Semitism in Baylor's hometown, or I guess it's his family's hometown. I'm about 99 percent sure Baylor grew up in Dallas and attended some private Christian school (that probably didn't allow Jews, either). The question is: How much did Baylor's family have to do with the anti-Semitic stuff in Palestine? And the student who branded the Jewish kid at UT? Could it have been Baylor?

Instinctively, I feel myself distancing from thoughts of dating Baylor. He already seems less desirable to me and some of his comments now seem suspect. What did he mean when he said his family was particularly hard to please when it came to women he was dating? And what did Drew mean when he said Baylor did things worse than his family?

I have to find out more before I make any kind of snap decisions. I should call some people in Palestine, maybe the local librarian, to get some more information. I'll pump Drew and Cindy for details, too. Drew knows more than he's telling me.

I walk over to the bed. Rafe is sound asleep on his back. His mouth is wide open. A labored back-of-the-throat sound vibrates his whole face. I shove my hand under his shoulder and turn him on his side like a pancake. He moves without waking, smacks his lips, and asks for some tobacco. I can already smell the alcohol sweating from his pores.

I fall asleep and wake up around four a.m. I kick off the covers. I'm hot and thirsty, the prelude to a hangover of epic proportions.

It takes a few seconds to realize where I am. I lie still, hoping that if I don't move, I won't have to talk to Rafe. What do I do? Punch him in the arm and say, *Let's get some breakfast*? Will he remember anything he told me about Meg? Or worse, will he think we slept together?

And where is Rafe, anyway? I tentatively look across the bed. It's empty. I look over the side and he's curled up with the comforter on the shag carpeting. His head is wedged between the bed and the nightstand. He's snoring loudly again. I have time to figure this out. Would showering be too disruptive? Probably not.

The hot water runs over my head. I close my eyes. I do my best thinking in the shower. I've often wished that I had a waterproof notebook and pen. Think now. What did last night mean? *I can't believe he said those things and I can't believe the articles I read about Baylor's hometown,* I think as I exfoliate with a prison-grade washcloth.

It's now six a.m. I've showered, used the blow-dryer, and left a message at work that I'll be a little late. I've even chugged glass after glass of rusty tap water and reorganized my day planner.

It's time to wake up Rafe. I poke him. He's dead to the world. He's always managed to sleep the sleep of a clear conscience or no conscience. He mutters, "Mr. Tatters" and drifts back to sleep. I shake his shoulder and say his name. He swats at my hand and yells, "Not now." He's a sleep arguer, always has been. One time when I tried to wake him up, he thought he was a helicopter pilot and refused to land because there wasn't enough space. Another time, he thought I was his mother leaving him in the car alone. He screamed at me, "Don't you understand? This car can melt me in seconds."

I jab him again and say, "Your landing is fine." He wakes up, shaking the sleep off his body like a dog.

"What happened? Where are we? Meg?"

"Tulsa. Jenny. Let's get some breakfast," I say and punch him in the arm.

I have my answer about his feelings. He's been screwing Meg for three months tops and already he calls out her name instinctively. Maybe I'll open my mailbox in three months and find an invitation to their wedding (assuming she gets divorced), though I probably won't be invited.

He looks at me, dressed and showered, and at himself partially naked on shag carpeting, holding a gingham comforter around himself.

"We should go," he says and gets up.

Nothing about the whole Meg thing comes up until we're eating bacon and eggs. He studies me for a while, then says, "Yeah, I hope you don't think this means that you should tell anyone."

Hello, I'm not the one who blabbed Meg's secret life in the first place.

"Just think of it as part of the road to friendship. Your secret is safe," I say. "Where's Mr. Tatters?"

"Meg's taking care of him."

"Is that subtracted from the fee she pays you?"

"Sweet," he says. "Maybe you could try a little more discretion."

"It's Tulsa. I think we're safe," I say.

"I'm serious. This is really important to me."

"Okay."

"I mean, I don't want to screw this up for her. She has a lot riding on it."

"What does that mean?" I ask. He waves off my question.

"What do you know about anti-Semitism in Texas?" I ask as I butter my toast.

"There was a lot of it. Most of the prominent families in Texas were behind it," he says. "Why?"

"Looking into a story," I say as I take a bite of the toasted white bread.

"You're a retail reporter," he says.

"Jews are big into retail."

"I thought they never paid it," he says, waiting for a better answer.

"I'll tell you when I've found out more," I say and smile, "Reporter confidentiality."

Chapter Eleven

Don't Judge a Surgeon by His Lobby

arrive back in Dallas at nine a.m. I'll be a little late to the office but not horribly so, considering I'm commuting from Oklahoma. As soon as I get off the plane I check my cell phone. I have nine missed calls and eleven text messages. Has Carol gone off the deep end? Whenever my boss can't get ahold of me right away, she has an annoying habit of calling my number obsessively every thirty seconds until I answer. She must be convinced that I can see her calling all those times but am choosing not to pick up. I check my voice mail. Every one of them is from Lizzy begging me to come over to her house as soon as possible. She's sobbing. The text messages are also all from her, imploring me to drive to her house. Maybe she found out about Hoss cheating on her.

In the past few months, I've gotten to know Lizzy pretty well. We talk on the phone or text each other every day and of course she's at all the functions Aimee and I attend. She gets my sarcasm and I get her understated commentary of people. We click. Still I'm surprised that she's calling me out of all the lifelong friends and sorority sisters she could be calling. Though she might have called them, too. I could be invited to a massive support-Lizzy party. When I drive my car out of airport parking I head over to her house, the opposite direction from work. I call Carol's phone and leave a message about an emergency. I say I'll be in a little later. After last night's missed plane and this morning's detour, I know I'm going to have to endure a lot of yelling and lecturing from my boss about how important the news is, meaning nothing in my meaningless little life can compare to getting an earnings report in on time or being in the office for a minimum of ten hours a day.

Don't get me wrong, work is important to me, very important to me. I've spent the last four years grinding away at climbing up the corporate ladder. Most Saturdays I'm at the office. Most Sundays, too. I usually don't leave during the week until seven. I've struggled to write long stories that the editors in New York will notice. Usually, I get about four through Carol a year. It's just lately with the criticism from Carol that I've gotten tired of all the effort. Along with giving up on Rafe, I think I might be giving up on my career, or at least putting it into neutral.

I pull my Honda around to the back of Lizzy's house, where the help park. I pull in between a Lexus and a shiny new Prius. The staff have nicer cars than I do. I walk to the kitchen door. Lizzy opens it for me. Her hair is scrapped into a ponytail. Her face is tear-stained and puffy. She paces the floor in her Juicy Couture sweat suit. I watch her, waiting for her to land. She doesn't. There doesn't seem to be anyone else here, either. The next time she passes me I put my hand on her shoulder to stop her.

"What's wrong?" I ask, certain that she's discovered Hoss in a compromising position.

"I can't do it anymore. I need to eat," she says and starts crying.

Lizzy has cracked under the pressure. Months of eating nothing but almonds, chicken breasts, and leafy vegetables was too much for her. Her thighs plateaued at size 10, and she still has a size 4 wedding dress to cram into in two and a half months. Yesterday, she weighed in at two pounds more than she did the week before and it wasn't because she gained muscle. The sleepover might've had something to do with it.

She couldn't wrap her mind around two weeks of twelve-hour-a-day workouts to come.

In a rare act of rebellion, Lizzy inhaled a glazed doughnut in front of her trainer and fired him when he tried to protest. She decided on liposuction and called her mother's plastic surgeon to arrange for a rush operation the next day. You can do that when your mother's a repeat customer and your family name is on a hospital wing. Then she dove into an eating bender: a whole twelve-cut pizza, pasta Alfredo, and coconut cream pie. She ate and ate until midnight—when the doctor's office insisted she fast since she was scheduled for surgery the next day.

"Will you take me?" she asks as she blots her eyes.

"Sure," I say.

"Now," she says.

"Oh, okay. So you were serious when you said this was happening today. Let's go," I say and head toward the back door and my Honda. She doesn't follow me.

"What's the matter?"

"I thought we'd take my car," Lizzy says.

"You don't like the Honda?" I ask innocently.

"I'm sure it's very dependable," she says diplomatically.

"Knock it off, Lizzy. I know you've never even opened a Honda door."

"That's not true," she says as we change directions and head toward her BMW 700 series in black with mahogany accents on the dashboard.

"Oh, the help drives Japanese?"

"Well, they do have Lexuses."

"I know I need to get a new car."

We walk out the front door and I look back.

"Isn't your mom coming?" I say.

"She can't come. Last-minute conference call," Lizzy says.

"Hello. That's what cell phones are for," I say.

"She said the doctor's office gets bad reception," Lizzy says.

Well, her mother would know—being a frequent flier and all.

"I can't believe she just didn't change the time of the call. She's the boss, isn't she?" I ask as I get into Lizzy's car.

"Enough, okay," Lizzy says. I've hit a nerve, so I back off. Poor little rich girl—I wonder how much time her mother scheduled in while Lizzy was growing up.

Lizzy's car drives like it's on well-oiled tracks. This is what it feels like to have a good suspension.

"So how's Jackson?" she asks.

"We're going camping this weekend, tomorrow actually," I say.

"That's good."

"Yeah."

"He's real nice. Very moral."

"Is that a nice way of saying he wouldn't put up with Natalie?" I ask. As I said before, he broke up with Natalie after the pool table incident.

"He was a little too moral with Natalie. He was mean with Natalie, humiliated her. Told a bunch of his friends about the whole pool thing. I mean, he won't cheat on you," she says.

"That's something."

"Believe me, most men don't hesitate," she says as she turns off the car.

Does she know about Hoss? I wonder how much his cheating has led her to the decision to have plastic surgery. I wonder if I should talk to her about it before she goes under the knife.

"Is everything all right with Hoss?" I ask in the parking lot.

"Yeah, he's the sweetest guy I've ever met. Do you know he went and saw *Belle de Jour* because he knows it's one of my favorite movies?"

"Really, that's nice," I say, swallowing whatever words I was going to say about Hoss. I'm confused. He told her about his rendezvous? Maybe he wasn't cheating on her.

We walk into the doctor's office. It's a facsimile of real life, an upscale boutique masquerading as a medical facility. Potted orchids frame the entrance. The door is dominated by a human-size stained-glass panel of cranes flying over a Chinese village. I believe the awning is made of raw silk. The waiting area is a private lounge with white leather Barcelona chairs, Eames couches, and sixties-inspired glass chandeliers.

"Are you sure you want to do this here?" I ask.

"He's the doctor everyone goes to."

"Yeah, but. . ."

"But what?"

"Do you think that serious medicine is practiced here?" I ask her, as two Brazilian women speaking Portuguese sit down opposite us. They have on so much foundation that I have no idea what their real skin looks like or, for that matter, what color it is. Their pink pearly lipstick matches their Chanel suits and shoes—very old upper-crust rich.

"See, if they have traveled hundreds of miles to see this guy, he must be good," Lizzy whispers in my ear. "Brazil is light-years ahead of us in plastic surgery."

True, in Brazil being beautiful is considered a right of democracy. Free operations, including breast implants and nose jobs, are offered at the county hospitals because it's believed that even poor people have a right to look good.

A nurse marches into the lobby and shoves Valium at Lizzy and one of the Brazilians.

A few minutes later a short man with bags under his eyes and stubby hands shuffles into the lobby, Dr. Oliver. Why is it that plastic surgeons never avail themselves of their work?

"My babies, how are you doing today?" he says as he walks over to Lizzy, pats her on the head, and gives her a once-over. "We'll take excellent care of you, don't worry. It'll feel just like a massage. Come, come."

I take her arm and we walk into an office that looks like a mod bordello with shag carpeting and a glass-and-metal examining table.

"Strip, strip. We have a schedule to keep," he says.

I help Lizzy peel off her clothes. Dr. Oliver draws on her with a green magic marker as if she's a human topographical map. There are ovals and arrows covering 50 percent of her skin.

"Okay, we have a lot of work to do," he says, and makes a clicking sound with his mouth as he shoots us with his finger-shaped gun and leaves the room.

A few minutes later a nurse struts in, takes Lizzy away, and that's it. I return to the lounge for sixty scheduled minutes and wait with one of the Brazilians. The other must have been taken inside as well.

"So what have you had done? Here," she says pointing to my recently erased crow's-feet.

"Yeah, how'd you know?"

"When you have work done, you become an expert yourself."

"Just the crow's-feet. What about you?"

"Lots of things. Where to begin?" She stands up and performs a show-and-tell, highlighting the part of her body she's talking about. "Here, my thighs, my butt, my stomach. Tits, of course. Neck and eyes, Botox. Lift around my face. And hands."

"What have you done to your hands?"

"You know, laser resurfacing, fat injections, a lift."

"Why?"

"Because they tell your age more than any other part of your body."

She holds up her hands for me to examine. They are beautiful. They're plump, not bony and veiny, no age spots or any discoloration. They look like a twelve-year-old's.

"Wow."

"Five thousand."

"Really?"

"For one hand," she says.

I had no idea. I wonder how undersalvaged I appear to her. I've recently had a manicure, pedicure, facial, and a haircut. I feel decently groomed.

"What else do you think I should do?" I ask. She is thoughtful. She motions for me to stand up and turn around slowly, which I do. She scans me critically.

"Maybe here," she says pointing to my nose, indicating that I should thin it out. "And here, you need better grooming on your eyebrows, also an exfoliator. Lipo on thighs. Botox on neck."

That's it? I can afford most of that and the rest I can put on a credit card. I can do this. I slide back into my chair and feel satisfied, as if I actually did something—got a raise, ran a 5 K, did a full split.

Then I realize what I just thought. My mother would have a fit if I told her I was getting my nose done. It would be one thing to get my eyebrows waxed and change my exfoliant and it would be nice to have thighs that are skinny enough to fit into any kind of pants I want, but I've always been a natural girl and even with my new Texas preening habits, plastic surgery seems a little too much.

"If you don't mind my asking, why did you come all the way from Brazil for this?"

"Dr. Oliver is an artist. In plastic surgery, you need a creative mind," she says and leans toward me. "You can tell a good surgeon by how he decorates his office. Nice decor, good doctor."

"Oh," I say, wondering if there's a plastic surgery guidebook with pictures of doctors' waiting rooms.

"Remember thighs," she says.

Just then a nurse wheels out Lizzy. It's only been an hour. She is barely conscious and dripping. A puddle of clear liquid forms underneath her and the back of her Juicy Couture sweat suit is soaked.

"She'll expel fluid for a few days," the nurse says as she hands me a bag of pills and a garbage bag. "Put this on your car seat."

I drag Lizzy out to the car. She moans in pain. This isn't like any massage I've ever seen. I'm amazed at the amount of pain she's in after only an hour. When I close the car door, she places her head on the window and slumps down.

"Are you okay?"

"Sure, just need to lie down."

I drive and she groans whenever I take a corner too fast or go over a bump.

I pull into the servants' entrance of her parents' house and as quickly as I put the car in park, a crew of people descends. The servants carry Lizzy inside. I notice a puddle of liquid mixed with blood on the garbage bag. Lizzy's mother struts out and observes the scene. I can tell she's calculating the best way to manage and motivate all of us.

"You come here," she beckons to me and marches back into the house.

I follow her rapidly swaying backside across the marble floors. She's a few steps behind two men (the cook and butler?) who carry

Lizzy's limp body toward a silk damask couch. Liquid drips onto the floor from Lizzy's back.

"Not on the damask. Stop," Lizzy's mother, Ally, orders. "In here."

Ally leads them into a study and directs them to a leather sofa, "Wait. Trisha, put the sheet down," she orders a maid who trotted behind us. "Now put Lizzy down," she says. "Call the doctor. Go."

All the servants leave. The three of us are left alone. Ally surveys the damage.

"Goddamn bastard. Totally incompetent," she says as she caresses Lizzy's forehead. "Don't worry, honey, we'll make it right."

I look at the sweat suit. It's soaked with blood. So is the girdle she is stuffed into and been told to wear for three to four weeks to reduce swelling and bruising.

"There's some blood here," I say, trying to sound calm.

Ally looks at where I'm pointing.

"Holy hotness. I'm calling 911," she says and storms over to the phone. "You do something," she says to me.

"Like what?" I ask.

"Massage her feet. Circulate her blood. That's very important right now," she says.

I'm sorry. In the last few minutes, did Ally earn a medical degree and I miss it? I do what I'm told because doing something is better than nothing.

Ally puts the 911 operator on hold to correct my massage technique.

"Circular motions are better," she says to me. She gets back on the line with the operator and it sounds more like she's making a hotel reservation than reporting an emergency. She requests a newer ambulance and a private luxury suite ready and waiting by the time we arrive at the hospital.

It's two p.m. when the ambulance screeches into the driveway. Lizzy's temperature has spiked. There's lots of blood dripping from her legs now, which look lumpy and deformed, like a parade float. If you touch her thighs, she yelps in pain. Dr. Oliver has some explaining to do.

I call my office. Before I can even get a word out, Carol screams about my general incompetence, lack of maturity, and absence of brain cells.

"Do you realize where you work?"

"Yes."

"And the responsibilities it involves?"

"Yes."

"You always have to be available."

"Did anything happen on my beat today?"

"No, but that's not the point."

"I have to take a friend of mine to the hospital. Consider it a sick day."

"You can't keep doing this."

I stop and hold my breath, then speak, "You're right. I can't keep taking my friends to get butchered by plastic surgeons," and hang up. I call Baylor on his cell phone. He's on his plane. I can barely hear him above the engines. He yells that he's off to Arkansas on a family errand. I hang up. I'm not sure why I called him right now. The thought of his voice seemed calming. Even when I could barely hear it above the engine, it was nice to hear.

At the hospital, Lizzy is in a private room that looks like a hotel suite, except for the rails on her bed, the IV hooked up to her arm, and her general bloated appearance.

Apparently Dr. Oliver was overzealous in his fat removal. He got too close to the skin and burned it from the inside. Lizzy's lost a lot of blood and is susceptible to infection. All she wants to know is will she look good for the wedding. That's a Texas girl for you, always thinking about appearances.

A swat team of plastic surgeons examines her. They study every inch of Lizzy for about an hour, zip her back into her girdle, then leave with Ally in tow.

"Where'd they go?" Lizzy asks, happier now that she has a painkiller being pumped directly into her veins.

"To put together a game plan for Project Lizzy. They think they can rebuild you."

"Will I be bionic?"

She hasn't lost her sense of humor, that's good. Her legs are sausages, they're so swollen, and she's already soaked through an inch-thick layer of mattress pads. Typically, I'm told, you leak after liposuction because the doctor injects a lot of fluid into you to break up the fat.

"How do I look?" she asks.

"Like a million bucks."

Lizzy's top half looks pretty normal.

"But I'm worth a lot more than that."

"Should I call Hoss or your dad?"

"Don't call Hoss. He doesn't know I'm doing this. He wouldn't approve."

I liked Hoss until the other night when Aimee and I saw him acting mysterious at the movie theater. The fact that he wouldn't approve of lipo reassures me again. Lizzy's explanation about the movie confused me. I'm still debating whether I should tell her what I saw. It's not like I saw him with another woman. I just got a feeling that something wasn't right. I know if I try to communicate that feeling to Lizzy it will come out sounding mean for no reason.

"How are you going to explain where you are for the next couple of weeks?"

"I'll tell him I'm in Paris, getting ready for the wedding."

"Won't he figure out that you're not overseas from the 214 area code when you call?"

"No, I'll use my European cell phone. Could you help me with a few things? Ask my assistant to bring my phone to me. Also my laptop, and make sure I have a secure high-speed Internet connection here; the prospectus for Lando, this company I'm thinking about buying, and my subscriptions for the *Wall Street Journal, Investor's Business Daily,* and the *Financial Times.*"

The last request is barked out like an order. She really does take after her mother.

The doctors and Ally pile back into the room, but this time Lizzy's in control. She listens to all their findings, makes her decisions, and dismisses them. They'll perform another liposuction in a few days to even out the lumps Dr. Oliver left. In the meantime, she'll remain in the hospital on a high dosage of intravenous anti-biotics. She'll also have a dermatologist consult daily on her skin's recovery. Right now, her thighs look very bruised but that's actu-ally internal burns. The good news is that everything should return to normal for her wedding. The bad news is that the next few days are going to be pretty painful.

Now I know I won't do liposuction.

"You heading out soon?" Lizzy asks, prompting me to stop staring at her thighs.

"Yeah, but I'll be back shortly," I say.

As I leave, Lizzy and her mother are conferring about their re-turn on investment if they buy Lando. Ally also reassures Lizzy that she'll be better than new by the time they get finished with her. The bright side: She did get all that nasty fat removed.

I run back to her parents' house, where Lizzy has a home office, to give the list of requested materials to her assistant, Sara. She col-lects reams of paper, a laptop, half a dozen newspapers, an address book as thick as the Bible, and a date book the size of the *Oxford English Dictionary*. There's so much stuff, she zips it all into a weekender Goyard roller bag. She offers to take it to the hospital, but I'm not used to handing things off to employees, so I decide to bring it to Lizzy myself.

"Tell her I'll reschedule her face-time appointments to confer-ence calls. I'll cancel her trip to New York and send Charlie in-stead. I'll also arrange for a fax machine and a Bloomberg terminal to be delivered to her room tomorrow," Sara calls after me.

I swear Lizzy requires more paraphernalia than a seven-month-old child. I haven't called any of our friends to tell them about Lizzy's condition because she never told them she was going under the knife. I have no problem protecting her secret. It's one more to add to the list of things I know but don't tell: Meg's real age, Rafe's sperm donor status, and my religious background. Call me a situ-ational moralist.

I quietly open the door to Lizzy's private hospital room, think-ing she'll be knocked out on painkillers. Think again. She's talking a mile a minute to some business associate, making notes, and watching CNN on mute. I've never seen her in full business mode before. She's more than a little intimidating. She waves me in and directs me to one of the plush Italian armchairs. Her mother sits in the other chair and talks on her cell phone. A woman sits at her feet and gives her a pedicure.

I sit and stare at the silent television while she holds forth. I have to do something. I unzip the bag and unpack. I put the papers on a pull-up desk and program the computer to sync with the high-speed Internet the hospital offers. In the background I can hear Lizzy.

"Don't be an idiot, Sam. We're not doing that deal. Call me back when you have something that would impress me, not your mother."

She forcefully presses the END button and speed-dials another underling.

"Kim, get on Sam's ass. He has no balls."

Four calls later, she has time to talk to me.

"Sorry, it's hectic today. I'm trying to acquire this company," she says and motions me over to her.

"Anything I can do to help?" I ask.

"If a frog had a back pocket."

Translation: If a frog had a back pocket, he'd carry a pistol and shoot snakes. This means she'd love it if I could help, that is, if I had any of the skills she needs, but of course I don't. I guess it's nicer than saying, "Nope, you're totally unqualified."

Just then Aimee and Natalie burst through the door clutching a big bouquet of roses, a heating pad, and a box of Popsicles.

I glance at Lizzy, who's reaching for the phone. She's probably calling security. I mouth, I-did-not-tell-them, and shake my head.

"I heard from Shayla," Aimee says. Both of us stare blankly back. "You know, the cosmetic surgery consultant." Still blank stares.

In the evolutionary chain of personal assistants, the cosmetic surgery consultant is a relatively new mutation. She's basically a gossip columnist for surgeons and a blunt great-aunt. You pay her four hundred dollars an hour and she gives you a tough-love appraisal of what you need done, sort of like what the Brazilian did for me. Then she tells you about the latest techniques, which surgeons are on their game, and which celebrities have been sculpted by which doctor.

"Do you use Shayla?" I ask.

"Well, yeah, but for free. She's a friend and I give her good dirt. Anyway, she called me an hour ago to let me know about Lizzy."

"And Aimee called me," Natalie says.

"How did she know?" Lizzy asks, horrified.

"She has people on the payroll everywhere. Either some nurse here or at Dr. Oliver's called it in. This doesn't look good for his rating."

"Or my thighs."

Aimee and Natalie rush over and examine Lizzy up and down the way the doctors did. Aimee gives Lizzy the heating pad for the soreness she'll feel and the Popsicles for hot flashes from fevers. In total, Aimee's had nineteen surgeries in two years. It's a wonder she hasn't implanted wings. Natalie has a similar plastic surgery résumé. I'm not as clear on what she's had done, in part because I always hear about it when I'm a little drunk and also because after a while I zone out. There're only so many procedures you can hear about before they all sound the same.

Neither one of them ever had a bad reaction—Aimee steered clear of Dr. Oliver. Natalie went to him for liposuction but came out unscathed. Both have sailed through every post-op with minimum swelling and hardly any bruising. And this is the killer: They don't look like Frankenstein freaks. Aimee looks as if she's having a really good hair day every day. Her impeccable grooming isn't obvious to the untrained eye. She's always dead-on but not overdressed. Natalie's work veers toward Dallas Cowboy cheerleader. Her breasts are D cup and her tan is very deep. But her pregnancy quest has softened the plastic Barbieness of her appearance. Her face has filled out to the point of almost pleasantness from stark skin and chin bones. "Honey, this is totally workable," Aimee says as she lightly touches Lizzy's thigh and watches some liquid dribble out. "You're not a 'When good plastic surgeons go bad' story."

"If anything, this is a blessing. You have practically no fat left," Natalie says.

"She's not permanently disfigured," Aimee says.

I guess she should consider herself lucky.

"Are you going to sue?"

"Already started on it," Lizzy's mother says from her position in the corner. She's been listening while placing consistent cell phone calls to a variety of minions.

"No, I could never do that. Then Hoss would find out," Lizzy counters.

"But who cares, honey?"

"I do," Lizzy says.

"I don't," her mother counters.

"This isn't your marriage."

Her mother silently agrees and gets back on the phone to rein in her legal pack of hounds. She steps into the hall.

"Well, he'll find out anyway when he sees the scars," Aimee says.

"No, I'll just tell him they're childhood war wounds."

Meaning, they've never had sex and he's probably never even gone to second base with Lizzy.

"Honey, are you a virgin or just new to Hoss?" Aimee asks.

Lizzy blushes. This girl is a twenty-eight-year-old endangered species.

"Come on, you know how guys think of me—always the friend, never the girlfriend," Lizzy says.

"But still, you've had opportunities?" I ask.

"No, not really."

"Come on, even my hairy-chinned cousin Dora got action before she graduated from high school," Aimee says.

"Any girl who passes out at a frat party is basically fair game," Natalie says.

"Hoss is the first guy who's even asked me on a date."

"Baby, that's because you intimidate them," Aimee offers.

Lizzy shakes her head no. "Come on, I'm worth millions. That alone gets people over their fear pretty quick. Let's be honest, I'm one of those fat girls who won't be beautiful when I lose the weight."

Lizzy looks down at her deformed and bloated legs. I bet she's wondering why she even put herself through all the torture of plastic surgery to try to be something she'd never want to be.

"Don't be so hard on yourself," I say.

"Look, I know Hoss is interested in my money. That's obvious, but he's more decent than the other guys. He acts like he's actually glad to be with me."

"Then, why haven't you had sex?" Aimee asks.

"Because I want to wait and he does, too. Neither one of us has ever done it," Lizzy says.

We all gasp reflexively. A male twenty-something virgin is rarer than a legitimate e-mail solicitation offering to improve your love life.

"Why?" Natalie stutters, unable to comprehend.

"Yeah, why?" I second.

"He believes a man should only know his wife," Lizzy says.

"Oh, he's religious. That's real good, honey. Means he'll never stray," Aimee says and pats Lizzy's leg lightly. Lizzy cries out, "Stop!" Aimee automatically backs away a couple of feet.

"How come we never knew that about him?" Natalie asks.

"Because he doesn't want people to think he's a zealot. Thinks it will hurt him in business," Lizzy says.

This explains everything. When Hoss tried to broach the subject of sex with Drew and his other friends, he wasn't being a pervert. He was trying to get advice for the big wedding night. When he stumbled so awkwardly from *Belle de Jour* it was probably because the movie is more sexually risqué than anything he's experienced. He was embarrassed.

"I think that's real cute. The two of you are both brand-new," Natalie says.

"And to think what Tommy Sue is doing just to be the way you are naturally," Aimee says.

I'm completely clueless. "What are you talking about? What is Tommy Sue going to do?"

"You won't believe it," Aimee says. "As an extra treat for Chase, her dog of a fiancé, she is going under the knife to get her vagina tightened and her hymen repaired, so that on her wedding night it will feel like the very first time."

Lizzy gasps.

"I wonder if I should do that. Do you think Bradford would like a virginal pregnant woman?" Natalie asks.

"Jesus, what does that involve?" I ask, dumbfounded.

"The doctor lasers the vaginal channel, which tightens it, and either inserts sheep gut or delicately stitches together the existing hymen to create the virginal sensation. She won't be able to have sex for a couple of weeks after the procedures," Aimee says. I think she missed her calling. She'd make an excellent surgeon.

"Oh my God. That sounds so barbaric," Lizzy says.

"The hymen thing is weird, but I would do the tightening thing, right after I had kids. You'd feel like a twenty-year-old virgin. I heard men are supposed to love it," Aimee says.

"Me, too," Natalie says.

"Yeah, but what about you? Are *you* supposed to love it?" I say.

"Oh yeah, the sensations are intense. I swear to God, good vaginal muscles are wasted on the young," Aimee says and then proceeds to give Lizzy a tutorial on the use of rhythmic contractions during sex.

My phone rings and I walk to the other end of the room to answer it. It's Baylor.

"We landed and I thought I'd call you back when I could actually hear you," he says.

"So you're in Arkansas?"

"We have some property we're considering developing," he says. I can hear female voices in the background and high-pitched peels of laughter.

"Who's with you?" I ask, not liking how suspicious I sound.

"Family, some staff," he says.

I can hear a familiar hiss saying something with the word *darling* in it.

"Is Meg with you?" I ask.

"Not *with* me," he says. He's obviously cupping the phone, trying not to be overheard.

I don't know what to do. My chest tightens. I feel like it's become ten times harder to breathe in the last couple of seconds. Why am I so crazy about this? Baylor and I have had only one date. But I can't help myself.

"But she's there. Meg is with you on some sort of trip?" I ask.

"There were some things we had to sort out quickly and this was the only way I could do it," he says.

"Okay, y'all have fun," I say in a forced Southern nice voice.

"Stop it. It's not what you think," he says in the chiding voice of a teacher.

"Is this about Rafe?" I ask.

"Rafe? Do you know Rafe?" he counters.

"I know a lot of things."

"I get back tomorrow night. Would you like to get together?" he asks.

"No, I can't. I already have plans. I'll call you," I say and hang up. I can hear Baylor spurt from frustration before I press the END button. For the first time, I feel in control of what happens between us. I'm going to put Baylor on hold and move on. I have Jackson to focus on and my mother's eternal passive-aggressive guilt to worry about. I don't need another unfaithful Peter Pan.

"Baylor and Meg just landed somewhere in Arkansas together," I say to the room.

"Well, you can stick a fork in him, he's done," Lizzy says.

Translation: This probably means what you think it does, but to be sure, I'll define it. When baking a cake, one sticks a fork in it and if the fork stands up that means the cake is done. In Texas talk, when the phrase is applied to men, it means they are no longer viable.

"Do you think they're sleeping together?" I ask.

Natalie coughs and laughs at the same time.

"I don't know another reason a man would put up with Meg. But why do you care? He's not for you," Aimee says.

"Yeah, well, we all do things we shouldn't. He says he's representing her. He wanted to go out with me when they get back," I confess.

"Wow, Baylor is sleazy. I'm surprised," Lizzy utters from her bed.

Natalie, finally recovered from her cough and laughter fit, says, "Every man is sleazy. Some hide it better than others."

I slump my shoulders and sink into the armchair by Lizzy's bed. How can I be so wrong about men? I liked Rafe and thought he could be the one, and we know how that turned out. The first time I met Baylor I had this physical longing for him. I knew I liked him right away and once again I'm confronted with a lying jerk. I shouldn't listen to myself.

"You think Jackson is a keeper?" I ask the room at large. I think I might have better luck with men if I go by group consensus rather than my intuition.

"Absolutely. He's cute and rich," Aimee says.

"For the right kind of woman," Natalie says diplomatically. "He's very conservative. If you can live up to his standards you're golden."

"He's nice, but I think you can do better," Lizzy says as she hits the clicker on her morphine again.

Natalie pats her belly and changes the subject. "I think all those years of bulimia have screwed up my reproductive system. I haven't been on any kind of birth control for the past couple of weeks and haven't gotten pregnant."

"You're in your early thirties. It's gonna take more than a couple of weeks," I say, spouting the medical knowledge I've absorbed from my mother. "It might take more than a year to get pregnant."

"She doesn't have a year," Aimee says.

"I don't have a year. I have a few weeks to complete this," Natalie says as she starts to pace.

"Why a few weeks?" Lizzy asks. She's as clueless as I am about some of this husband-hunting gamesmanship.

Natalie speaks in a measured, teaching voice, which I think she picked up from Cindy and the number of times she has lectured Natalie on the very same subject. Natalie tells us that a man with a fetish like Bradford is more volatile than the regular rich guy. She needs to seal the deal while his fetish feelings for her are hot.

"Once he's in a committed relationship he can feel free to let his fetish out and be vulnerable. Before that he's always unsure of who to trust. He hops from woman to woman, afraid to fully give himself over to the relationship because he doesn't want to be judged," Natalie explains.

"You need a new plan," Aimee says, "something that forces the situation."

"I could bring a pregnant woman to the rattlesnake roundup and set up a sting," Natalie muses.

"Brilliant. If you can catch him in the act he'll feel like you have something on him and he'll have to marry you," Aimee concludes.

Lizzy's eyes have gone from Natalie to Aimee during the conversation. It's like she's watching verbal Ping-Pong. She's entranced.

"You girls are geniuses. I'd hate to go against you in business." Natalie smiles. So does Aimee.

"When's the rattlesnake roundup? And why?" Lizzy's mother asks.

Aimee explains that Rance is starting an annual roundup at his ranch in Big Bend for all the big business people. It's in a couple of weeks.

"You're invited. Everyone in Dallas is," Aimee says, looking around the room.

Lizzy examines her thighs. "I think I'll still be in rehab but Hoss will love it."

"That's sweet of you to think of him. I'm sure he'll enjoy the hunting with Rance and Jackson," Aimee says, firmly establishing that Hoss will have company just in case he wavers in his religious conviction.

Chapter Twelve

When in Doubt, Pretend You're Praying

Saturday morning came with Jackson knocking on my front door at six a.m. I opened it in my pajamas. He was fully clothed and showered with two lattes in his hands and a pair of snake-resistant hiking boots.

"Drink this. You'll feel better," he says as he walks into the living room and hands me one of the drinks along with the boots. He's clearly prepared for female resistance in the morning.

Sleep, a few more hours of it, would make me feel better. I check myself from whining. I have to play this right, which means perky exuberance. He may not be my first pick for marriage material, but he's a lot better than the bald rich guy Aimee pointed out in Whole Foods. I'm not going to blow this. Jackson has a full head of hair, nice body, and passable conversation skills. Sure, the merits of arctic versus mountain-weight fleece don't stoke my mental fire but I believe in the power of redirection in a relationship. I've seen women change men almost completely once they get to a certain level of influence in the relationship.

Jackson sits on the couch and unfolds a map on the coffee table. He traces a route with his finger.

"Come here. I want to show you something," he says. I move to sit by him on the couch.

"I thought we'd try to do this trail. It isn't that steep but it's a nice six-mile hike," he says, tracing his finger up the largest-looking bump on the map.

I can already feel my thighs scream with pain. How long does a six-mile hike take?

"Sounds great. I'll grab a quick shower and be ready before you know it. Want anything to eat? There's homemade banana bread on the counter," I say as I go off to the bathroom. Thank God for Aimee's baking binges. I look like I can cook, too.

We take his truck over to the path. It's only an hour or so away from Dallas. We are well into the hike before ten a.m. Jackson keeps up a steady banter as we walk. I do my best to seem like I hike all the time. I try to downgrade my breathing from heavy to casual. I look down at my feet, which are in an upgraded form of moon boot. The soles are so thick and stiff, I feel like I'm walking on a pair of logs tied to my feet. I stop myself from falling a couple of times by grabbing on to Jackson's arm. He doesn't seem to mind or think my lack of balance equals a lack of outdoor experience.

He tells me about the vegetation and the history of Native Americans in this part of Texas. He sounds more intelligent now than when he was spewing sports statistics at me. I do my best to sound interested, if not absolutely fascinated. It seems to be working. He talks and talks. I coo appropriately. I'm finding that being a husband-hunter involves a lot of cheerleading, sort of like active parenting.

"Cedar isn't indigenous to this area. It came from Mexican cattle. They'd eat the seeds in Mexico and shit them out here," he says.

"Wow, you know a lot of history," I say. He smiles shyly, a little embarrassed and pleased. I guess this isn't much different from what you do when you're dating anyone in the beginning. You flatter and please, except that when you're doing it with a financial goal in mind you're much more conscious of the mechanics of it. I'm breaking it down analytically almost like a math problem. Okay, after thirty seconds say something flattering. After five minutes ask a question. Look at him adoringly periodically, in two- to ten-minute increments.

Truthfully, I don't know why this is all mechanical. Jackson is attractive and sweet. He's attentive. I don't know why I'm not genuinely attracted to him. Maybe I have to try a little harder.

When we finally reach the top after two hours of upward movement, the view is beautiful. A green basin stretches out below us and clouds seem within our reach. We sit down. Jackson pulls food out of his backpack. He hands me a beef brisket sandwich with barbecue sauce. I wolf it down.

"You're not afraid of eating," he observes.

"I think I burned more calories than there were in that sandwich today," I say.

He reaches into his bag again and pulls out a ziplock bag of chocolate chip cookies.

"For you," he says.

"All of them?" I ask, eyeing the three cookies within the plastic.

"You look like you need them. Besides, I have another bag," he says, and pulls out more cookies. That's what I like in a man, a guy who understands that I don't like to share my dessert.

I lean back on a large rock and soak in the sun. Hiking isn't so bad, especially when you take a break.

"Can I ask you a question?" Jackson starts.

"Sure," I say, unsure of what's coming next.

"How's Natalie doing?" he asks.

"Well," I say, stalling for time. "She's doing pretty well."

"I know what Bradford's like and I know that she doesn't have a lot of options. I hope she's doing okay."

What does he know about Bradford? He can't know about the pregnancy fetish. I don't think he'd be friends with Bradford with that knowledge.

"What do you know?" I ask.

"I know that Natalie's rode hard and put away wet," he says.

Translation: Rode hard and put away wet is cowboy malpractice of a horse. The horse is worked into a sweat, then stabled without being wiped down, which has a tendency to make the horse ill, if not kill him. Nowadays, it refers to women and men who have not taken care of themselves, and look aged and worn out before their time as a result of serious partying.

I can only assume he's noticed Natalie's weight gain and chalked it up to her giving up.

"She's doing fine. In fact, I think she and Bradford are close to engaged," I say, slightly exaggerating Natalie's progress.

He lies back on the rock next to me and sighs. "That's good for her."

"Why'd the two of you break up?" I ask, deciding to play it dumb to hear his side of the story.

"She wasn't in line with me religiously," he says. "My momma wouldn't approve."

"What does that mean?" I press.

He takes me gently by the shoulder and says to me in a tender voice, "I believe in Jesus and I put myself in his hands. I can only hope my children get the same sort of spiritual fulfillment that I do from the Lord."

What do you think about Yahweh? I want to ask him. This whole half-Jewish thing is going to be a difficult sell. Instead, I take another bite of my cookie. I chew slowly.

Jackson gets up, walks a couple of feet away, and kneels. He's praying. I can hear some of the words: *forgiveness, wisdom,* and *Lord.* I'm a little uncomfortable. I feel like I walked in on a private moment. I think I should move farther down the mountain to give him some privacy but he knows I'm here. Maybe I should go and pray with him. I remember a time when I went to eat dinner at a friend's house during high school. Dinner was about to start and I was pouring my Sprite into a glass. It became very quiet in the room. All I could hear were the bubbles cascading from the can. I looked up and saw the whole family with their hands in prayer pose waiting for me so they could say grace. I feel the same level of embarrassment now. I opt to bow my head in silent reflection.

When I open my eyes I see Jackson staring at me. He's smiling. I guess he thinks I have a personal relationship with Jesus, too.

"You ever think about having kids?" he asks me as he helps me up and we commence our hike. Is he kidding? My mother has been mentioning me having kids since I turned twenty-one.

"Yeah, do you?"

"All the time," he says. "I feel like I need to get on it. I don't want to be an old dad."

"How many do you want?" I ask, shocked by his enthusiasm.

"Three, maybe two, but I think three would be better, don't you? More like a gang."

I walk slightly behind him. I don't answer right away because I'm comparing Rafe's attitude toward children with Jackson's. When Rafe thought of children he thought of accident—again part of the unwelcome but inevitable march toward middle age.

"What do you think?" he asks again.

"Three is nice but I guess you have to see how two goes first," I say.

"Can you imagine having a little baby right now? It would be so great," he says and practically skips for a few steps.

I've heard of this phenomenon but never experienced it first-hand. This is the traditional Southern man who wants to get married early and knock out a couple of kids. This is the kind of guy who thinks it's a treat to coach his son's football team and be scout-master. This is the kind of guy my mother would love, except for his most probable hatred of Jews. Maybe I can work on that. I think I heard Christians are supposed to like the fact that Israel exists, something about it being a sign of the impending rapture. Maybe I can spin that.

"Would you send your kids to a religious school?" I ask.

"I don't think so. Shocked? I think public education is a wonderful thing. It allows kids to be exposed to people they'd never know otherwise. I think Jesus wants us to meet and befriend our neighbors," he says.

"So you like meeting Muslims and Jews and all sorts of people. . . ." I trail off.

"You have to have a big heart to accept the Lord and all the children of the earth," he says and grabs my hand in a brotherly love kind of way. "I like the name August for a boy, or maybe Walter. What do you think?"

After a couple more hours of discussion about children, names, and views on parenting, we arrive at the truck. I expect us to pull out a tent and find a place to pitch it. Instead Jackson opens my car door. I walk over to it with a confused look on my face.

"I didn't think it was appropriate for me to ask you to stay with me on the second date, not that I thought anything would happen. I didn't think it was respectful," he says.

In addition to the kids bombshell, I don't have to sleep on the cold rocky ground. I could kiss him, and when he gets in the car I do. I lean over and give him a peck on the lips that evolves into a long, slow kiss. He's a good kisser. He rubs the palm of his hand along my arm. It's sexy and real confusing. I didn't think I liked Jackson that way.

I push myself back. Jackson doesn't persist. He's waiting to see what I want.

"I need to take it slow," I say, acting like the shy, retiring kind of girl.

"I understand," he says, and starts the truck. He takes my hand as he drives. I can tell I've scored well today. Aimee will be proud.

As he drives, he tells me about his desires—to be near his family, take over his father's business and expand it.

"I want to leave a legacy for my children that's more than what was left to me. Isn't that the only thing you can do to achieve some kind of immortality?"

"Yeah," I say, though I've never really thought of what legacy I wanted to leave when I die.

"And I think I'd like to raise them in a small town, maybe somewhere near Waco. There's nothing like the feeling of growing up in a small town, where everyone knows you," he says.

So part of the marriage deal with Jackson is moving to Waco? Maybe I can recalibrate that part of his personality, too. Believe it or not, Dallas has some of the best schools in the state. I'll have to start compiling data.

"How are Aimee and Rance doing?" he asks out of the blue.

"Good, great. I think he loves her," I say. "Why didn't the two of you ever get together?"

"I have to confess I've always had a crush on her but she never seemed interested," he says.

"She's a tough girl to figure out," I say diplomatically.

"I don't think I had the right assets for her," Jackson says, a little too aware of what Aimee is about.

"She's into the whole intellectual nerdy thing," I parry back.

Jackson smiles. He gets that I don't want to go there and respectfully backs away. That's another nice thing about Southern men. They don't directly confront. They smile and let arguments fade into the background of the conversation. I'd have to push very hard if I wanted to have an actual fight or disagreement.

Jackson pulls into my driveway. The lights are all out. I don't even know if Aimee's here. She's been spending nights at Rance's.

"So," I say as I gather my things together.

Jackson puts his arm on the seat behind me and watches me. It's making me self-conscious.

"What?" I ask.

"I think you're perfect," he says and leans over to kiss me again.

I walk out of the truck and to my front door. I turn around and notice that Jackson is still watching me. I blush and wave to him. He waves back. He waits until I open the front door before he turns on the truck again and pulls out of the driveway. Ever the gentleman, he waves again as he drives down the street.

I walk into the living room and don't see any signs of life. I look in the kitchen sink. There's a wineglass. Aimee might be here after all. I slink over to her bedroom and peer in. She's passed out on her bed. Her limbs stretch to all corners of it as if to say, "Thank God I get to sleep alone."

Chapter Thirteen

Brunch Isn't Just a Meal in Dallas

Brunch is huge in Dallas. It's a tradition right up there with barbecue. It's harder to get reservations at Breadwinner's on a Saturday or Sunday morning than the trendiest new concept restaurant on a Friday night.

Breadwinner's is a bakery/restaurant that operates out of an Arts and Crafts–era house. The oak floors are burnished a golden brown. The stained-glass light fixtures glow red. The rose garden is tended chaos. Dozens of blooming flowers bend the stalks almost to the ground. The food is soaked in butter and tastes fabulous, especially the jalapeño corn bread. But those aren't the reasons people come. It's all about female cruising, and I don't mean cruising in a sexual manner.

Women who normally have a hard time dragging themselves out of bed at eight a.m. for work bound into the shower in the wee dawn hours on Saturday and Sunday mornings. They pluck and primp and unwrap outfits they've waited all week to wear. They spend close to an hour in front of the mirror debating accessories. All to parade themselves in front of other women, who in turn nod appreciatively at a fabulously tailored dress, an adept mixing of stripes and florals, or the flaunting of an impossible-to-get purse. How do I know? Because I do it. It's like prom—all the giddiness of getting ready without the nausea from mixing rum with vodka. Let's admit something here—women dress for other women. Men don't notice anything other than skintight or cleavage. It's the other women who recognize the beautiful construction of a silk and cotton Yves Saint Laurent tuxedo shirt with defiant raw hems. It's the gentler sex that ogles a delicate gray satin Ungaro sandal with beaded iridescent butterflies sewn on the straps. It's females who bite their lips in envy at a retro-inspired rhinestone daisy brooch wittily placed on a belt.

I shower, straighten my hair, and fully dust myself with lilac body powder before I slip into the first pink dress I've ever owned. It's two shades lighter than bubble gum in a woven cotton that feels like silk with a tiny belt that cinches the waist. It is molded, constructed for the body, not sewn. I feel elegant and girly. The dress has been in my closet for weeks because I felt that donning pink is a betrayal of my New York roots. Every few nights I tried on the dress, danced around my room, and put it back on the hanger, realizing that I'm not quite able to do it yet. Now that I've turned a corner with husband-hunting and am really giving it a go with Jackson, I think I'm ready.

Aimee and I walk into Breadwinner's foyer. A full-size gilt-framed mirror is placed strategically opposite the door so we can watch ourselves enter the restaurant. We look film-perfect along with the dozens of other beautifully turned-out women who are crowding the foyer waiting to be seated. It's gonna be a long wait. Aimee whispers the open-sesame magic words to the hostess, *Rance Cox,* and the Red Sea parts. We sail through the throng of women who follow our progress with hungry eyes.

The hostess is decked out more expensively than some patrons in a chinchilla-cuffed blouse. She leads us to a table heavy with tea roses and nestled in the bay window nook. We sit in chocolate-painted wicker armchairs with yellow gingham cushions. Sun filters through the oak tree leaves outside and onto the table. The place smells like fresh baked bread and a good nap. A waiter brings us a double-decker sterling silver tray of pastries, a pot of tea with a lilies of the valley printed tea cozy, and delicate bone white china cups and saucers. I grab a couple of golf ball–size scones and three credit card–size pieces of corn bread. I ladle raspberry butter onto my plate and wolf it all down. It's my designated pig-out day.

Aimee has no interest in food. She stares at it like it's a television—entertaining and not edible. She has the vacant look of those who are lobotomized, sleep deprived, or heavily drugged. Her gaze matches about 10 percent of the women in the room.

She's perfectly made up. Her hair is loosely curled and casually put in a chignon. She wears a halter-neck dress in orange that shows off her tan. Her bag is white and constructed to look like it stepped out of the fifties. She doesn't look human. I don't think she sweats.

"Aimee, aren't you hungry?"

She jerks her head up.

"What?"

"Aren't you going to eat?"

"Yeah," she says as she picks at a scone.

"What's up?"

"My stomach's a little iffy," she says as she beckons the waiter and orders a Coke.

"Are you hungover?"

"No, I didn't really drink last night," she says as if she's not quite sure of what happened a few hours ago. "I tried other mind-altering substances."

"Not getting any easier?"

"Believe me, honey, I'm trying everything I can think of. Unfortunately, I'm running out of ideas. But it's getting a little better."

I'm about to suggest dumping Rance and looking at other well-invested pastures but I stop myself. In the past few weeks I've discovered just how hard it is to find a rich husband. I can't tell Aimee to forget all the hard work she's done and start over.

"It's okay. I'm positive it'll get better," I say as the waiter places lobster frittatas with rosemary home fries on our table.

Aimee smiles at the food, rummages through her purse, and pulls out a bottle of pills.

"It's going great. I mean everything else is going great. He's smitten," she says. "He had the best time re-creating a high school fantasy. We hung out in the hot tub last night."

"And?" I ask.

"That's it. He never got to hang out with a pretty girl in the hot tub. I mean we had sex in it, too, of course."

"He was more than smitten at the zoo thing. I could tell he was totally in love with you," I say.

She smiles and nods.

This is the first time I've had a chance to talk to her longer than five minutes without Rance in a couple of days.

"I don't always close my eyes during sex anymore," she says, as if it's a miracle in league with learning to walk again. "I really think he could be the one. Why don't we double-date?"

I decide to go with my earlier feeling and take a chance.

"Do you ever think about dating someone else?"

"You?"

"No, not me. You. Why don't you date someone you're more attracted to?"

"Maybe my third marriage, but I'm too close now," she says. For God's sake, she seems to be saying to me that marriage couldn't be much worse than sex in a hot tub.

Aimee asks me about Jackson. "What about you? How was the hike with Jackson?"

"It was good. Better than I thought, actually. Do you know he wants kids? And he didn't make me camp out. He even brought me homemade chocolate chip cookies."

"Really? I didn't know he was so sensitive," she says.

She decides we should all cement our couple compatibility at the rattlesnake roundup, which, as I discovered in Lizzy's hospital room and at that fund-raiser, is an event that celebrates rattlesnakes by scaring them from their holes, playing games with them, and shooting them to death. Who says Texans don't love wildlife?

"I don't have to shoot anything, do I?"

"No, but I think you'll want to. It's fun, like a video game," Aimee says as she pours her bottle of pills onto the table, arranging them into a heart.

"Are these a new kind of vitamin?" I ask.

"They help me remain healthy."

"How many of those can you take a day?"

"The doctor said that I can take as many as I can stomach. He said it's not like I can OD on them."

"Refreshing. An all-you-can-swallow program."

"They're harmless, nonaddictive," she says as she swallows a couple with her Coke.

She looks at me staring at her. "They take the edge off."

"What did the doctor say he was prescribing these for?" I ask as I try to grab the pill bottle. Aimee pushes my hand away.

"For nerves."

"For nerves. That's like getting a prescription for spells."

"Spells?"

"You know, old women who were on the painkillers because of their spells."

"I'm not like that."

"You're getting close."

"Will you look at that," Aimee says, diverting my attention. My eyes follow hers. A woman who looks like she greased herself up to squeeze into her Narciso Rodriguez dress slinks by. Poor girl, she doesn't know the Rodriguez secret. He downsizes, a size 6 in one of his dresses is really a size 2. But get a girl who is horrified at the thought of being anything more than a size 2 and you'll find a clothing disaster waiting to happen. She's not remotely fat, but the dress makes her look like a sausage in a wet suit.

Sure, it's an interesting view, especially her backside. The strain on the zipper is so intense, it looks like it could pop at any second. But Aimee's intention wasn't to point out the view, it was to change the subject.

"You wanna talk about this?" I ask, forcing her attention back to the pills.

"I wanna drink my Coke and check out the scene. Look, look at her. She has one of those new Vuitton bags with all the lizard. Where'd she get that? I've been on the wait list forever."

True, this woman has a killer bag, dress, and shoes. Her dress is a buttery chiffon cut on the bias. Her shoes harken back to the forties' dramatic wedge sandals. Looking at her immediately makes me wish I could go home and change. I need a wardrobe do-over.

See, this is what we're supposed to do at brunch. We ogle other women and feel alternately superior and inferior.

"Check her out. Can you tell from her nose what doctor she went to?" I ask.

Aimee turns, squints her eyes, and turns back in a matter of seconds.

"Dr. Blumenthal. He tries to do the cheerleader pug nose but never gets the profile right. She looks like she hit a window at sixty miles."

"Do you think any of her friends told her?"

"Oh, no."

"No?"

"These are all single women and even though they're all friends, pug nose is competition."

"That's so cold."

"We're not playing at going steady."

"Not to sound Pollyannaish, but shouldn't friends come first?"

"Okay, I would never do anything over a man to harm our friendship. But I'm different. These women have friendships that are about as deep as a puddle in July."

These women? Aren't we these women? I look around trying to distinguish the difference between us and them. We're all impeccably turned out. They seem like people I'd be friends with as they laugh and joke at their tables.

Aimee takes a bite of her frittata and then absentmindedly pops another pill and gulps her Coke.

"You just took another pill."

"Did I?"

"Did you mean to?"

"No, I wasn't thinking about it," she says as she scrapes her broken heart pill design back into the bottle.

She's flustered. I think she's embarrassed.

"You must've still been focused on the purse," I say.

"You know, I think I was. You know how I am about accessories."

"So where are you staying tonight?"

"Rance wants me to stay at his house. He says that you got me for all the morning so he should get me for the night."

"You can call in sick," I say.

"You think?"

"Yeah, I'll call him for you. I'll tell him you got food poisoning or something."

"But he might come over."

"I'll tell him you got something contagious. Flu?"

"God, that would be great."

"Come on, we'll slumber party, just the two of us."

"I swear to God sometimes I think men are more trouble than they're worth. They're so clingy."

"Let's do it."

"I can't. I have to go. I slept at home last night. I promised him," Aimee says after thinking for a moment.

The waiter places the bill on our table, which makes Aimee deflate. She grabs the bill and stares off into the restaurant.

"I'll split it with you," I say.

She waves away my money.

"Courtesy of Rance Cox. Wanna go shopping?"

"Sure, courtesy of Rance Cox?"

"Do you even have to ask?" she says as she signs the credit card receipt and stands up.

Aimee totters a little and grabs the table for support.

"Head rush?" I ask.

"Yeah," she says, regains her composure, and walks in the opposite direction of the exit. I wait for her to circle back to the foyer.

"Doing the scenic route?"

"Yeah," she says, laughing.

How confusing can a small restaurant be? To the pharmacologically impaired, it must be a wilderness of mirrors and blind spots.

We walk out to Aimee's Lexus. She's about to scooch into the driver's seat when I intercept.

"I think you should let me drive. You know I have car envy."

She grins like I've just solved nuclear fusion, hands me the keys, and follows the car's contours with both hands over to the passenger side. If she's this high when she's with Rance, I can understand why he's easier to stomach.

I straighten my dress, sit down in the driver's seat, and take off my shoes. My shoe repairman, who used to repair Sophia Loren's shoes in Italy, tells me she would never drive in good shoes because of the possible damage to the back of the heels. I can't figure out if he's telling the truth or is on the verge of insanity. But whenever I remember, I try to take mine off.

By the time I situate myself to actually drive, Aimee is wide-mouth snoring. I find a couple of tissues in my purse and place them like a bib on her dress. She doesn't need drool stains in addition to all the other stuff.

I pull out of the parking lot. Where am I driving? I want to take her home, but is our house still her home? I almost feel guilty for not wanting to drive her to Rance's estate. But I don't. The whole thing is creepy. I think she needs time to detox.

I pull into our driveway and lightly tap her. Nothing. She doesn't even move. I shake her a little. She's still dead to the world. I take both her shoulders and loudly call, "Aimee, Aimee." She half opens her eyes.

"Come on, honey, we're going to take a nap," I say as I walk around the car and open her door.

"I already am," she mumbles and tries to turn away from me.

"Your neck will thank me later," I say as I bend down, move her feet onto the driveway, and put her arm over my shoulder.

"Not now," she says.

"In just a little bit you'll be in bed."

She slouches toward the house, putting more weight on me than I knew she had in her body. I get her into the house and drag her to bed. There's no way I can change her—she's deadweight, plus she keeps slapping my hands away. I wonder if she thinks I'm Rance trying to score. I put a blanket over her, turn the phone on silent, and close the door.

She's a good five hours of sleep away from coherence, I think as I slip into my man pajamas, make some tea, and get out the paper. I think it's best if I wait for her to wake up before I leave the house.

I must've fallen asleep because after reading about Muslim strife the next thing I remember is knocking at the door. I stumble to the door and barely twist the knob to open it before Rance comes bursting in. He's sweaty and nervous. He keeps running his hands through what little hair he has left. His chin wattle swings back and forth quickly.

"Hi, how are you?" I ask.

"Fine, fine. I've called Aimee at least a dozen times and haven't gotten an answer. Do you know where she is?"

"She's asleep," I say and grab his arm before he charges into Aimee's room. "She's sick."

"Why didn't you tell me? Maybe I can help," he says, trying to break free of my grip.

"No, what I think she needs is sleep. I turned her phone on silent so she wouldn't be disturbed," I say as I grip his arm firmer and guide him back toward the front door. "I'm sure you understand. I'll have her call you when she wakes up."

"But she was supposed to spend the night at my house," he whines, and tries to free himself again.

"Another time," I say and push him out. " 'Bye."

Talk about pushy. I open Aimee's door quietly. She's still sound asleep/passed out. I pick her cell phone up from the dresser. Fifty-six missed calls, all from the same number. Rance called her that many times? Is this what one calls a healthy relationship?

I don't think I could deal with all that intensity directed toward me. Imagine the pressure of your boyfriend staring at you every second he's with you. You couldn't pick your teeth without him noticing. It'd be like prison surveillance. No wonder the girl is one pill away from comatose.

What's she going to be like at the rattlesnake roundup? That's four days of all Rance all the time. There must be something I can do.

I walk back into the living room and call Cindy, the husband-hunting mentor. I explain the situation. She laughs.

"Oh, honey. She's in tall cotton," she says.

Translation: He's really into her. The phrase comes from the farm, of course. When a field had tall cotton, workers were excited because they didn't have to bend down as far to pick it. Cotton-picking is backbreaking work because you're always bending over. It's worse when the plants are low. So when you're in tall cotton, you have things real good.

"She's taking drugs to stay that way. I mean, she's drugged to the point of incoherence," I say.

"Sounds like me during most of my first marriage," Cindy says. "I'll check on her dosage next time I see her. Honey, this is nothing to worry about. It's something a lot of women have to do."

"How do they work or drive if they're on so many drugs?" I ask as I try to imagine how I'd incorporate this husband-hunting custom into my life. Picture trying to write an earnings report when numbers look like pretty shapes to you.

Cindy laughs. "They don't. They don't need to. Besides, it's only for a couple of years usually."

We hang up and I get ready to go to bed, despite other husband-hunters' ability to not work or drive, I'm old-fashioned, I guess. I have to wake up for work tomorrow.

Chapter Fourteen

Reasons Why Trophy Wives Don't Work

There are an increasing number of moments in my job when I
think, "What the hell am I doing?"

I came into work this morning with the full intention to do my
best, work my hardest. I thought as I drove into work, *I will do
something meaningful* and *I'm going to write something I'm
proud of today.* Instead, as soon as I walked into the office, Carol
sent me out to a small town that I'd never heard of before today.

As the heels of my Manolos sink in mud and excrement, I bend
down to have a better look at the twisty cats. They are mutant fe-
lines with front legs that are two inches long while their back legs
are normal size. When they walk their bodies twist, hence the
name.

I observe them because I'm going to write about them. Not my
idea. In fact, it's not even my editor's idea, even though she kissed
up to her superiors and said it was a groundbreaking and revolu-
tionary story. It's the top editor of the paper's idea because his
twenty-something girlfriend read something about them in *Cat
Fancy.* He's at that stage, much like Rance, where he's so grateful

to be having sex with the same kind of women he lusted after in high school that he'll do anything to please her.

So, here I am writing a "groundbreaking" story on the twisty cats. The only controversy I can find is that one woman on a Siamese Lover's Web site said that breeding the twisty cats is sick and should stop. One woman will be the cornerstone of my story. I'm going to have to stretch this out a lot with descriptive scenes. Maybe I can get them to do a line drawing of a twisty cat.

I am in Prague, Texas (pronounced Praig), which is two hours from Dallas. It's a Czech settlement that displays its Bavarian heritage proudly with kolache festivals and parades featuring lots of peasant dresses and men in hats with feathers. And beer, gallons and gallons of beer. They even have a local brewery that has considerable mystique and a decent college following. I can't leave until I write the story.

I know I wanted to get away from retail reporting, but this isn't what I had in mind. Is this what journalism is really about?

I've pondered this last question so much lately that it scares me because the question that follows is "If this is journalism, what would I rather do?" Other than spend a week watching bad daytime television, I have no idea. I don't want a real job. Journalism has never felt like a real job. It's an extension of college. I hang out with my colleagues, drink late at night, and write the equivalent of term papers every so often. I'm not selling anything or networking or answering phones for someone. Maybe I'm more like the husband-hunters that Cindy talked about last night than I realize. Maybe I'd be happy staying home, shopping, and going to lunch with my friends.

I walk back to my hotel, another Motel 6, and prepare to write. I shower, deep-condition, and blow-dry my hair.

I eat. I try Aimee on the phone but get her voice mail. I've tried to call her several times but she never answers. I can say without a doubt she's heavily drugged and with Rance acting out another high school fantasy of his, I'm sure. I hope she doesn't have to dress up like a cheerleader or Little Bo Peep.

I watch television. I look at the clock and know I have to write.

Finally, I sit on my bed with the computer on my lap and type an article about a mutant breed of cats that some call Munchkins. I highlight the historic importance of cats in ancient Egypt. I squeeze in as many angry quotes as I can about how breeding the twisty cat is an offense to God. I make it sound like a battle of epic PETA proportions is bubbling in little Prague, Texas.

The poor owners of the twisties: The day this story is printed a battle will erupt. They'll have news stations and reporters swarming them. They'll wonder whatever did they tell me to give the impressions I printed in the paper, which aren't wrong but aren't right, either.

I call Carol. "I can't do this story. It's a nonstory. No one cares about the cats."

"Your boss does."

"What do you want me to write about? There's nothing here."

"Figure it out," she sighs and hangs up the phone.

I thought Carol was dipped in journalistic integrity but she's eaten up with ambition. No matter how mean she was to me or how demanding, I took it because I thought she believed in journalism and I needed to figure out how to believe in something. But I know "figure it out" means "make it up" to make sure this story comes in. Skip was right.

I call her back.

"Don't say another word about not being able to do this story. You will write it," Carol says.

"I wanted to know if you want pictures of the cats for a line drawing."

"Are you kidding me?"

"I think a certain girlfriend would think that'd be really cute."

"Fine, send them to me pronto," Carol says. "How close are you to finishing the story?"

"Why? You're not going to read it until tomorrow."

"I'm waiting here tonight until you send it."

This is insane. She didn't have this much interest in my front-page stories.

I punch SEND. I'm done with it.

I have to find a FedEx for my photos in a town that just stopped teaching high school typing courses in favor of computers. They're using Commodore 64s.

Prague is a two-stoplight town with a functioning main street shopping area, a rare sight in rural Texas. Most people shop at Wal-Mart.

I walk over to the drugstore to drop off my twisty cat film. They're the only ones in town who might have a FedEx link. I notice a procession of television vans parked outside the twisty cat house. Megawatt lights are trained on the front door of the sky-blue-and-green gingerbread porch.

Damn, someone else discovered the cats. I had better hurry up. I run into the drugstore, give them double the price of shipping the FedEx to make sure it gets there today, and fax a developed picture of the cats to my editor. First thing I learned as a reporter is to cover all my bases so I'm yelled at less.

I race over to the twisty house. A mob of reporters surrounds the couple and yells questions. They answer tentatively like they're speaking to a school principal.

I make my way through the crowd. I elbow Rafe in my effort to reach the front of the mob and cut off access to my sources.

"Slow news day?" I ask.

"The Christian Right issued a statement about how this is one step below the genetic experiments Nazis performed," he says.

"What are you doing here?"

"I volunteered."

Of course he did. He's obsessed with cats. Look at how he acts toward Mr. Tatters. Know how the cat got his name? Rafe added the Mr. to Tatters because he thought it was degrading for animals to have only one name and to never be addressed formally. The Tatters part of the name came from the loading-dock workers, who nicknamed the cat as they watched Rafe saving it from a certain death by crushing if it remained at the dock. Rafe thought it was presumptuous of us to change the cat's name. I think it's painfully apparent why I questioned Rafe's sexuality and sanity at one point.

"What are you going to write about this?" I hiss at him.

"The whole genetics debate thing. Pretty interesting huh?"

Just as I realize I have to sprint back to my motel room and rewrite my whole story because the Christian Right stuck their nose in this, the couple brings the twisty cats to the porch. The pack rushes the house like fans at a Metallica concert.

I elbow my way out. I open the door to my motel room as my cell phone rings. I know it's Carol.

"Did you tell everyone you know about this?"

"No," I answer.

"I'm watching CNN right now. Twisty cats are everywhere. You're in big trouble."

I think back quickly. Did I tell anyone I was coming down here? No. How can Carol think I have the power to gather dozens of news organizations to cover a nonstory anyway?

"I have to rewrite the story to take into account the whole religious element," I say.

"That's for damn sure," she says and hangs up on me.

Baylor calls my cell phone as I recraft my exposé on mutant cats. I don't pick up—too many mutants to handle in one day.

Carol and I volley on the story until nine p.m. It's done. It's going front page with a line drawing of the twisty cats. Carol calls me one last time to order me to write a memo on how I let the twisty cat story become a media circus. She reminds me about the story she made her name with as a reporter—the invention of skinless chicken breasts—and how she kept the story under wraps by wearing different disguises when she staked out the chicken counter of grocery stores to talk to customers. "No one knew there was a *Wall Street Journal* reporter hanging out in the poultry section because I didn't let them know."

Great, thanks for that life lesson, I think.

"I'm sending Skip in tomorrow morning. He'll handle the next twisty cat story. He's better at finding a unique angle," she says. More like a make-believe angle.

I take a walk to get rid of my homicidal urges. I stroll by the pub, where all the other reporters have been drinking it up for hours because they work for sane people.

Rafe spots me, gallops out of the bar, and matches his step to mine.

"Where's Mr. Tatters?" I ask.

"At the apartment. Meg's looking after him. I don't think she likes him very much, though."

"Why not?"

"He clawed one of her shoes, then took a dump in it, which she didn't notice until she stepped in it. He attacks her legs whenever he can. It's like he thinks she's wild game."

I love that cat. He's unleashed his fury on her tenfold. I've only experienced minor cuts and one ruined dress. She probably is considering keeping her clothes under lock and key whenever she visits. The one thing he can spot in people is insincerity.

"Getting pretty serious between you two?"

"I think we're getting close to a resolution."

Translation: Meg might be pregnant.

"What does that mean for you?"

"We're negotiating that," he says with his head down. "She doesn't understand that I've become invested."

"How invested? Do you love her or do you want compensation for your efforts?"

"Don't be catty."

"What's catty about asking you if you're being paid to stud? I mean, come on. You can't possibly think this is going to go anywhere. She's married and trying to pass the child you make off as her husband's offspring," I say.

"It's complicated," he says.

"What's complicated about her using your services?"

"I'm more than a sperm donor," he says as his voice cracks.

I doubt that's what Meg thinks. But I get it now. Rafe buys into this hyperinsecure female-hating hussy's vibe. He's in love. Probably for the first time in his life, he's seriously contemplating a long-term commitment that's legally binding. Only she's already married and I doubt she has any plans on changing that part of her life. I bet she reminds him of his mother.

"So you think the two of you might be able to work it out?" I ask, trying a different tactic.

"I hope so," he says quietly.

"You should keep Mr. Tatters," I say, knowing this small gesture will make Rafe think that I have some modicum of belief that his relationship with Meg could be a reality.

"Really? That's great."

"Yeah, it's getting too confusing and Meg doesn't like me," I say.

"This will really let him get to know Meg. Maybe she'll like him better," he says as we turn to walk back to the motel. It's the most awkward walk of my life. I'm next to a guy I dated for years who never wanted to marry me and now wants to marry a woman who isn't nice to small animals, is already married, and has used him for his high sperm count. I don't get men.

Things to understand before I marry: why men can't figure out which women are snakes, how to detect a cheater, why men can't remember—word for word—a conversation we had an hour ago, and why men can't bring themselves to say those three crucial words: "I don't know." Do they get it from their fathers? When they clearly don't know they will usually give an answer carefully couched and perfectly wrong. Then when the right answer is revealed they say, "That's what I thought."

I grab Rafe's arm, forcing him to turn toward me.

"What is it about her? Give me that. What does she have?"

Rafe sighs and looks like he's about to give me the "It wasn't you, it was me" speech. But he doesn't.

"I don't know. Sometimes I hate her. She doesn't ever tell me how she feels about me and she's always saying that as soon as she gets pregnant it's over. Who does that? She's shallow, conservative. But something about her makes me want to throw her down and . . . you know."

"So this is a carnal thing?"

"It's an I-can't-keep-my-hands-off-her thing."

Enough. Rafe and Meg have passion, something I've only been able to sustain with a man for two weeks, a month tops. I think I lusted over Rafe for ten days and after that it was a quick decline into married-couple sex: the five-minute, no-foreplay-necessary sex that feels more like a commercial break than an intimate act. Maybe it's me.

We hug.

"I'm saving up to buy her a ring," he whispers.

"You should have earned tons of money from her by now," I say back without thinking about his feelings. But come on, she is paying him five thousand dollars for every sexual encounter.

"No, I mean with money I earn working, reporting," he stammers, and breaks our embrace.

I smile at him and wave good-bye as I walk back to my hotel room. He goes back to the bar.

I keep smiling and saying to myself over and over again, "Breathe," as I walk. I can only manage a slow and steady gait. Getting my key into the door and unlocking it is near impossible. As soon as I open the door I start crying, the ugly cry—the one that mixes face-wrinkling squinting, a flood of tears and mucus, with occasional high-pitched shrieks. I fall on my bed and let myself wallow.

It was years of my life. That's a long time and here's the kicker: It meant nothing. Rafe spent five minutes telling me he's finally found the love of his life or at least the lust of it. I didn't measure up.

He didn't measure up for me, either, I think, as I head to the bathroom to retrieve a box of tissues and aspirin. This is so messed up. I'm crying over a man I wouldn't let carry my purse. I lust after a man whose family—and maybe he especially—hates people because they're Jewish. I have mixed feelings for a man whose personal relationship with Jesus is closer than mine is with my mother. My life is in relationship shambles.

I'm not going to let this happen again. I'm not going to let myself spend another two years wandering through a relationship that has no chance of becoming something permanent. Tomorrow, I'm driving to Baylor's hometown to do a little reconnaissance. I can't get him out of my mind. I have to do something to settle myself. I need to find out if he's a complete creep or something more human. I saw a sign for Palestine when I drove out here this morning. I'm going to make sure I know what he is, then I'll figure out which man is for me. Frankly, I don't have the time to waste and Jackson seems ready and willing, if I am.

Chapter Fifteen

Don't Talk Religion—
Everyone Assumes You're a Baptist

Whenever I think something will be easy, it's harder than I ever imagined. I woke up early. I checked out of my room by seven a.m. I purchased tea and strudel and procured directions by seven-thirty a.m.

It's nine-thirty a.m. and I'm lost on hard-packed dirt that I hope is a road. I don't know what happened. I took a right by the old red barn. I was supposed to follow the road for about two miles and turn right at the old dairy farm. But there's not a dairy farm in sight. All I see is waist-high grass and mesquite trees. It smells like baked clay.

I turn around. If I can't find Palestine soon, I'm going to have to go back to Dallas. I have to show up at work at some point.

I find another red barn and try the road by it. In a couple of miles, I see a dairy farm. I must be on the right track. I don't understand why rural Texas doesn't believe in street signs. I mean, "Turn at the red barn" isn't really a reliable directional tool since there are like five thousand red barns around here.

Awww, I see the WELCOME TO PALESTINE sign with a little cow on it. Cute. I drive down what looks like Main Street, which is a small two-lane road with faded-to-gray blacktop. The buildings look like a movie version of a Western town. Two-story clapboard houses share exterior walls. They look like they're smooshed together. There are about seven or eight buildings on each side of the street. There's a post office, diner, supermarket, newspaper office, police station, bakery, manicurist salon, doctor's office, and one of those knickknack stores. I have no idea how they survive. Who shops there?

I park by the diner though I could park anywhere. I've seen a handful of trucks parked and moving since I drove into town. I get out of my car and walk into the diner. It hasn't been altered since the fifties. Formica countertops and lots of chrome. I sit down at the counter next to a couple of locals and order some grits with cheese.

"Gonna be a nice one," an older man at the counter says to no one in particular.

He's in stiff dark Wranglers, a plaid shirt with mother-of-pearl buttons, a belt buckle the size of a saucer, and worn-down boots. His legs are as small as baseball bats but his stomach is the size of a six-month pregnant woman's belly.

"Sure is," I say back.

"Seventy degrees without a drop of humidity," he says.

"You live here all your life?" I ask.

"Yep."

"Do you know my friend Baylor Jones?"

"Everyone knows the Joneses," he says.

"They own the big house on the top of the hill. We call it the white house because a Jones is always ruling this town," the waitress behind the counter cracks.

"Hush now," the old man says.

"What do you mean?" I ask.

"The Joneses own most of the people in this town," she says.

"How?"

"Lots of people work at their ranch. Let's leave it at that," the old man says sternly.

With that the conversation is dropped. What did they mean? My reporter antenna goes off. I need to check the newspaper archives or the library.

I finish my grits, put my money down on the counter, and race out the door.

After a five-minute conversation about the importance of the local paper and how it's the first thing I read when I get up in the morning, the newspaperman lets me sit in the back of the office and go through the bound archives. This is a real old-fashioned paper. There's one owner, editor, and writer, and it's all the same person. He still types his stories on a typewriter and takes his own pictures.

I flip through the archives in the back of the room while he writes a story.

I read yellowed stories about Baylor's performance on the football field, his volunteer service in a food drive, and his academic success on the honor roll. There are several pictures of him. He's young and skinny with big ears and short hair. According to these articles, Baylor was the perfect child, a golden boy. In one picture he's standing next to an older child, who looks like him, but with darker hair and more guarded eyes. The photos identify him as Baylor's older brother, Clayton. Baylor has a brother? How has this never come up?

I keep flipping and find an announcement of Baylor's high school graduation. Crap, he graduated just at the time I'd feared—just the right age to start his freshman year during the branding incident. A few pages later I find something I really didn't expect—an obituary for Clayton. He died nearly ten years ago, in a car accident. Left a wife but no kids. I can't believe this is something I never knew about Baylor. Why doesn't anyone ever talk about his brother? Is it possible they don't know?

I need to find out more.

"Hi, thanks for letting me look at the archives. Where's the library?" I ask the newspaperman.

He gives me directions involving a red barn. I walk the half mile to the library. It is a beautiful day. Early spring is just about perfect in Texas. The sun is bright and a cool breeze brings the smell of hay to you. It feels clean.

I walk into the library. I explain that I'm putting together a little scrapbook for my boyfriend, Baylor, and I want to get some of his family history. The woman behind the counter jiggles with excitement.

"Little Baylor has a girlfriend. We've never seen him bring a girl around here," she says as she leads me into a dusty windowless room with old books. "I'll get a librarian to help you."

"Thanks," I say.

A creaky old man shuffles into the room. He smiles at me behind thick glasses and yellowed dentures. He sits down in one of the old mahogany chairs, settling in for a long-winded diatribe on the lustrous history of the town. He talks for two hours without stopping. I didn't know there was enough air in those old lungs to sustain such an effort. I smile and act fascinated, waiting for my chance to ask uncomfortable questions about the town's most powerful citizens. I manage to discreetly check the time. I'm not going to make it in to work today. I should formulate a good reason why not while I do the polite listening.

I sense a conversation lull at the point when the town recovered from the drought of 1906. I plunge in.

"I'm interested in the Jones family history."

"Uh-huh," he says.

"I'm going to be straight with you. I'm part Jewish and I like Baylor but I can't be with a man whose family hates half of who I am. How anti-Semitic are they?"

"You have to understand the social climate in Texas at the time," he says.

"In 1991, when the town voted not to allow Jewish people into the country club?"

"Honey, let me be straight with you. The Joneses are a good Christian family. I don't think they'd ever let their son bring you home for Christmas dinner, never mind marry you. I'd cut my losses if I was you," he says with a smile and pats my hand. That's the most direct a Southern man has ever been with me and I don't feel like he was doing it for my benefit. It felt like the New York equivalent of "Screw you."

"You know, a lot of Christians like Jews now. . . . Israel and all," I sputter.

He smiles at me again with a cruel glint in his opaque eyes. "We're different people, that's all."

"Tell me this, is Baylor anti-Semitic?" I ask.

"He's never gone against his family," the man says, and taps the table with his fingers for emphasis.

I think a quick exit would be best. I don't want to make more of an impression on him, and therefore make me worthy of gossip, than I already have. I wave to him and depart.

I decide to swing by the diner one more time. The old cranky guy has left. The waitress is alone at the counter, filling saltshakers. I sit down next to her.

"Back for more food? You must have the metabolism of a hummingbird," she says.

"I want to know more about Baylor Jones," I say as I smile and stare at her. I find that when I'm quiet, the people I'm with will rush to fill the silence—old reporter trick.

"What? Who are you?" she asks, pulling back to better inspect me.

"I went on a couple of dates with him. I'll level with you. I really like him. I need to know if I'm making a mistake," I say.

"If I start talking to you—" she begins.

"I'm not from here. I'm not even from this state. I won't tell anyone. I need to know for me," I say.

"Don't get involved with him," she says.

"Because?"

"He'll leave you without taking a glance back," she says.

"Did you date him?" I ask.

"No, I slept with him in high school but we never really dated. That wouldn't have been okay with his family. I've watched him over the years. He only brought one girlfriend here and the way he treated her, well . . . you're better off alone," she says.

"I thought he never brought girls here," I say.

"Not never, just rarely," she corrects. "It's a shame what he did to that Koch woman."

"What'd he do?" I ask as the cranky man walks back into the diner and sits at the counter near us.

The waitress gets up and walks into the kitchen.

I walk back to my car and drive off. The miles tick off as the same thoughts circle my brain—Baylor branding a Jewish student. Could he have actually burned another human being's flesh? The old man looking at me like I'm some lesser life-form because I'm not Christian. I'm creeped out that I even walked into that town. I ate in that town. And it's named Palestine—a completely appropriate moniker.

How do I deal with this? What did he do to Meg? I worry as I nearly swerve into a tractor trailer climbing up the Interstate entrance ramp. I'm about two hours from Dallas. I should be able to sort through this before I hit home. Sure I can solve religious prejudice in two hours.

God, it's two p.m. I have to call Carol.

"Carol, there was an accident on the highway. It's taking forever to get back. I think I'll just go home," I lie.

"Fine."

"Any word about the story?"

"Uh-huh."

"What'd they say?"

"You're not being fired," she says and hangs up.

Well, that's one good thing. I call Baylor.

"How are you? Are you still in the state or have you moved back to New York?" he asks as soon as he picks up.

"I'm in Palestine," I say.

"I haven't been there in months. Dinner?" he says.

"Can't. Have to work late," I say. I don't know what I wanted when I called him and mentioned Palestine. Part of me was expecting him to confess his family's history, and his own, as soon as I mentioned the town, but why would he? He doesn't even know about my heritage. I do know dinner didn't figure into what I wanted.

"Another time?"

"Yeah, I'll call you. I have a hectic week," I say, hedging. I'm still attracted to him but I have no idea what to do with it.

"I'll see you at the rattlesnake roundup," he says.

"Really, you're going to be there?" I perk up instinctively. I do want to see him.

"Absolutely," he says. "Are you okay? You sound distracted."

"Lots of deadlines," I say. "Lots to do before the weekend."

Chapter Sixteen

What Your Mother Doesn't Guilt You Into Makes You Stronger

I avoid all contact with men for the rest of the week. I need to work hard and get distance from all the guys. Jackson and Baylor are too confusing to me—it's like both of them almost fit, but not quite.

My mother calls me for our weekly powwow. She makes sure she doesn't go more than seven days without talking to me. It's like she thinks that I can't go horribly off course in six days but in eight I could become a cocaine addict married to an abusive unemployed high school dropout.

The first thing she does is ask for a progress report on my marriage status with the seemingly innocuous phrase, "So how's it going?"

"Good," I say.

"How's Jackson? How's Baylor? How's Rafe?" She demands an accounting of all the men in my life.

I tell her Jackson wants kids, at least three. She lets out a squeal of glee.

"He sounds like such a nice boy," she says.

I tell her Baylor's parents were very strict, but that I haven't seen him much because he's been doing lots of family business.

"He's close to his parents, that's good," she says.

Jackson and Baylor sound good when I don't include all the details. I tell her about Rafe and Meg in all its specific, gruesome, detailed glory.

"That's gross. I'm so glad you're not dating him anymore," my mother says, completely changing her tune. I can cross one man off the update-my-mother list.

I ask her how my sister is coming with all the fertility stuff.

"Well, Clomid still isn't working. They're going to try the whole in vitro thing."

"That's horrible. I know she's gonna hate that."

"You should call her," my mother chastises.

I probably should but I hate those calls when you ask the person if there's anything you can do, she says no, and then you try to make awkward small talk. Usually something you say unwittingly sets off a bad memory and the person starts crying. I don't know if everyone is like this in a crisis, but my sister sure is.

My mother tears up. I can feel her grandmother desperation over the phone.

"Within the year, within the year," I repeat. "Have you found a dress?"

"I have a couple of options," my mother whimpers.

"Well, keep looking," I say and tell her good-bye.

The level of passive-aggressive unhappiness in my mother is only equal to the amount of guilt she can administer. Don't get me wrong—I love my mother. It's great that she's so invested in her family. It also sucks because you feel like she's always trying to live your life for you and when you tell her in nice and not so nice ways to back off, she acts like you're an ungrateful, horrible child. I hope I will never be so involved in my child's life that I'm happier than she is when she gets married or pregnant.

I wish I could talk to Aimee about all this. But she wasn't around this week. I think she's moved into Rance's house but hasn't broken the news to me yet. Do I get to keep her house if she moves out? A consolation prize or a really good bridesmaid gift?

I know she has to stop by the house before the roundup this weekend, so I can catch up with her then. I took Friday and next Monday off so I can fully experience the rattlesnake roundup.

Rance agreed to let me catch a ride with them on his private jet. I have to be showered and packed by noon, when his driver picks me up. I didn't expect Aimee to show up at eight that morning and crawl into my bed.

"What are you doing?" I ask as I roll over and cover my head with a pillow.

"I had some free time."

"Go be free with it, then."

"Aw, is little Jenny tired?"

"I'm not getting up until ten."

"Good, I'd like to take a nap," she says and falls asleep or passes out—you never can tell—next to me.

At ten a.m. my alarm clock chimes. I reach over Aimee to turn it off. She doesn't stir. I climb over her to get to the bathroom. She's wide-mouth snoring again.

I shower and primp. Now comes the difficult part: packing. What does one wear to a rattlesnake roundup? All the snakeskin one owns? Or is that considered too obvious?

I throw a pair of Blue Cult jeans and Vega jeans, a funky Catherine Malandrino Western shirt, a lacy camisole, C&C T-shirts, a belt with a large mother-of-pearl buckle, a couple of summer dresses (i.e., dresses costing less than one thousand dollars), a pair of Jimmy Choo slides, Prada sneakers, Gucci boots, and workout gear into my suitcase. I will never, with God as my witness, wear cowboy boots, a prairie skirt, or a cowboy hat.

Urban Texans love their hats, but only for parties and ceremonies. At President Bush's inaugural, the hottest ticket was the "black tie and boots" party, where Texas's elite sported cowboy hats, boots, jeans, and tuxedo jackets. Stetsons and Resistols of various shapes and colors flooded the ballroom. But at most special occasions you don't see cowboy hats. Real working cowboys prefer the "gimme cap" with a long visor from a feed store.

Aimee stirs as I finish packing.

"And she wakes up when the work is done," I say as I zip up my bag.

"Is there any other way?" she asks as she slithers off the bed and heads for the mirror.

"Can you tell me if I'm bringing the right stuff?"

"As long as you look good, you're in the right stuff," she says as she finishes her face. "You ready?"

"As much as I ever will be."

Aimee skips to the front door. The limo is waiting in the driveway and the driver stuffs her many bags into the back. She doesn't seem as drugged-out as the last time I saw her. But she did take a three-hour nap, so the drugs could have worked through her system. Even so, she puts her head on my shoulder and dozes while we're driving to the airport.

We pull up to the plane. That's right. We pull right up to the plane. There's no security or airport waiting area you have to walk through if you're privy to a private plane. It's door-to-door service—so much more convenient for the woman permanently planted in stilettos. The whole look of a private airport puts the glamour back into travel. The tarmac is pristine, and the blacktop is a dark black with bright yellow lines, resembling abstract art more than meaningful airplane directives.

When we come to a stop, I push Aimee into an upright position, get out of the limo, and feel the sun, which is low but hot. The moisture has already baked out of the blacktop and in an hour it will be hot enough to cook on.

The airport terminal itself is a shiny low-slung metal-and-glass box framed by potted palms. White-gloved men run out of it, haul our luggage from the trunk, and race to the plane. A revived Aimee jumps out of the car, just as Drew and Cindy come whirling around the corner.

"I didn't know Drew and Cindy were coming!" I say. "Why didn't you tell me?"

"I wanted to surprise you," she says and smiles gaily. "I know you've been reluctant about the whole rattlesnake thing. So I thought you should have some reliable companionship on the plane."

I must admit I feel relief at the sight of them.

Drew is casual in jeans and a button-down baby pink shirt and linen jacket. He heads toward me with wide-open arms and I'm engulfed in steamy pro-football flesh.

"It's good to know that we do have the deeper end of the gene pool represented here," he says.

Cindy's in a pencil skirt that makes her hip bones look like two halves of a tennis ball. She gives me a real hug, too—not the lady-pretend kind that feels like skeletons rattling.

"I was afraid you'd back out at the last minute," she says without a trace of false nice.

"What—and miss all the snake pits?" I ask.

Drew smiles playfully. "You know, I'm not one to pass up a free ride."

"It's almost like car pooling," Cindy says. "But we don't have to drive and we can drink."

Just then we hear some kind of slapping or thumping and turn to see a blond woman inspecting the body of the plane. Tommy Sue is knocking on it with her knuckles as if she's checking to see if it's hollow.

"She must think she's on a used-plane lot," Drew says. "I expect her to kick the tires any minute now." And right on cue, she kicks a tire with short, efficient taps as if she's testing its reflexes. Tommy Sue turns and points in the direction of the Dumpsters. A homeless man, dark-skinned from living outdoors in the Texas sun, has caught her attention, perhaps because he's moving so rapidly. He glances around, stares at Tommy Sue for a moment, then adeptly vaults into the Dumpster and proceeds to sort through the detritus. He picks up promising paper bags, smells them, opens them up to examine their contents, and throws them into one of two piles. I'm guessing food groups?

"Homeless people have the best tans," Tommy Sue sighs, examining her own skin tone.

"Maybe if you start Dumpster-diving, you'll be real tan for your wedding," Cindy says.

Tommy Sue seems to seriously consider this possibility.

"Maybe. Thanks for the attorney referral. He's getting everything straightened out with Chase's parents," she says.

"What's he using as leverage?" Cindy asks.

"Pictures of Chase having sex with a hooker," Tommy Sue says.

Tommy Sue's lawyer is threatening to take compromising pictures of her fiancé to the press if his parents don't agree to her prenup terms. The parents have always dreamed of him having a political career so they're doing everything they can to make the pictures "go away," including giving Tommy Sue a nice financial settlement from the family if she ever divorces him. Holidays may be a little strained for a few years after these negotiations but at least Tommy Sue knows she'll be in the family for a while because it would be a financially painful divorce for them.

A stewardess in a wrap dress and mules has stepped down from the plane's open gateway to serve us ice-cold mimosas on a silver tray. The drinks are equal to an ice cube in hell, a little bit of coolness that will soon be overpowered by the oppressive temperature. I can feel the waves of hot air rising up from the pavement, tiny pinpricks of heat assaulting my skin. It's the kind of weather that makes breathing difficult, as if you could scorch your lungs by inhaling. Drew hands me a glass.

Aimee lays her hand on Drew's arm and leans into him. "How about two kids and a ranch house in Plano?"

"Sure, you'll love the synthetic," Drew says.

Aimee shudders at the thought and waves to the stewardess with two bent "come here" fingers. She grabs a mimosa, pops a couple of pills, and chases them down with her drink. She's back on the barbiturate train.

"Aimee?" I say, watching her take the pills.

"You know I'm not good on airplanes," she says. "Come on, everyone, let's go." Aimee heads up the stairway and Tommy Sue follows like a baby duck.

"Aren't we waiting for the owner?" Cindy asks as she rolls an unlit cigarette between her fingers. She's trying to quit but finds that fondling cigarettes calms her nerves.

"I'm owner by proxy," Aimee says.

Cindy doesn't buy it. She's planted on the tarmac. Drew and I follow her lead and stay put.

"He's late," I say.

"That boy is always late. Frankly, I think it's bad manners," Cindy responds.

"I knew him when he made his first million. He's just as awkward now as he was then," Drew says as Rance's limousine pulls up to the plane.

Rance barks into the phone as he jumps out of the car, jacks up his pants, and spits on the ground. Some of it lands on his shirt. Natalie gets out of the car behind him. He shakes all our hands while mouthing *hello,* then struts toward the plane and beckons us to follow with a hurry-up hand gesture.

"He needs a good tailor," Drew says.

I see what he's talking about. Rance has on what looks like a wet diaper in the butt of his pants. He is short-waisted and must buy off the rack.

"That's not all he needs," Natalie says. She seems shaken up by the car ride with him.

"What's wrong, honey?" Cindy asks.

"Nothing good earplugs won't solve," Natalie says.

"Where's your pregnant woman?" Cindy asks.

"She's meeting us there. I thought it'd be too obvious if she rode on the plane with me. I want Bradford to think I don't know her. Might make her more appealing. Then I can reel him in."

We walk up the steps behind Rance.

The plane's interior is completely white—white leather seats and paneled walls, a plush white carpet, white cashmere throws. The metal accents are silver. It feels like a deluxe refrigerator.

Drew breathes in the air-conditioning. "I don't know what people did before compressed air," he says.

Aimee is sacked out in the front seat, which is more like a couch than the slightly padded cousin of a folding chair that one usually finds on most airplanes. Rance flops down beside her and goes in for a few unsanctioned gropes while talking on his cell phone about market share. He's in the middle of a deal, shotgunning orders at two decibels louder than required. I feel like a captive on a conference call.

"No, I said I wanted the poison-pill provision. Also, the stock-to-stock ratio isn't right. You need to revise that so it's a 3.5 to one distribution," he yells just as we're taking off. He must have one of those global-positioning cell phones because he doesn't lose his signal as the plane climbs.

"What is it that I always say? That's right, if you give a man a fish, you widen your customer base. If you teach him to fish, you screw your market share," Rance says and laughs at his own joke.

I didn't realize that he's a cutthroat businessman. I had this image of him as a dork who got really lucky with money and had an *aw shucks* idea about financial power. Boy, was I wrong.

"If he comes back with a counteroffer, walk away. Yeah, he'll come crawling back in a couple months, and then we'll cut our offer in half. He doesn't have enough liquid to last any longer," Rance advises as he ignores the FASTEN SEAT BELT light and paces down the aisle.

Drew cracks his neck by twisting his head from side to side with both hands.

Cindy looks over at Drew, who is sitting opposite us. "Is that really necessary?"

"It's a football thing," Drew says drily.

I can't take my eyes off Aimee. "I think she's going for co-matose. What do you think?" I say quietly to Cindy and Drew.

"More like maxed-out," Drew whispers. "Rance, on the other hand, appears to be going all the way."

I peek over at Rance who has sat down beside her and seems to have one hand under her butt.

Cindy snorts. "From what I've heard, this is the warmest response he's ever gotten," she shoots.

"I can't tell you the number of times I've wished for an unconscious hottie to toy with during a conference call," Drew whispers.

"I'd take Rance's fetish over Bradford's any day," Natalie says, "though Bradford's family has better social credentials."

It's at moments like these when I realize that the rich aren't like the rest of us. For instance, it would appear to the casual observer that everyone on this plane is friendly and having a good time. But look closer. Rance is a social Bambi. He struts around on his cell phone so we all know how important he is. He also doesn't realize that being accommodating is a sign of weakness in this social set—

that's what you have help for. In the last hour, he's approached me twice to ask if I have everything I need. He put his hand over the mouthpiece of his phone and offered me a blanket and a martini. The second time, I pretended to be asleep. Drew, Natalie, and Cindy did the same. Tommy Sue took the opposite tack and asked him for more elaborate things with each approach. Her last request was for dark chocolate–covered smoked almonds from Peru. He went back to the plane's kitchen and didn't return before landing. Out of one half-open eye I could see the pained expression that spread across his face over the possibility of not being able to fulfill her request. I can't imagine that his adversaries have seen this side of him. If they did, they'd know he's a pushover.

The plane starts to descend after two and a half hours of flying time (and that's all inside Texas—see, this is what Aimee was talking about—why Texans need planes). I can see stubbly patches of green cacti dramatically eclipsed by stark cliffs jutting up from wide river waters. Then suddenly we're on the ground surrounded by long, yellow grasses and craggy cedars.

"We're here, I guess," I say, unsure if this is something I'm happy about.

"No doubt about it, this is West Texas," Drew says. "I can tell because the cacti outnumber the people ten to one."

Rance pulls Aimee up, takes her by the hand, and leads her outside while still talking on the phone. Drew and I stumble off the plane into sunlight so bright that it's painful.

The sky is dark blue and limitless over bare mountains. It smells dry, like pine. Sagebrush sprouts next to prickly pear cactus whose oval, meaty branches are long and rambling like the tusks of elephants. They're the only plants out here that look like they hold water. Their waxy yellow flowers stand alongside plants with burnt skeletons. This place is more remote than I've ever been.

The heat reflects off the asphalt right into my eyes. My lightly tinted glasses don't help at all. Cindy came prepared. She's wearing dark glasses and a sun hat. She pulls out a small, black cotton Ralph Lauren umbrella—a gift from a friend living in Tokyo—not for rain, but especially made to block out the sun's ultraviolet rays.

"They're all the rage there," she says, flipping it open. "They're not even sold in this country."

It's a bit eccentric, even for Texas, but I must admit, it's adorable. She looks like a Japanese doll underneath it. Natalie scoots over and huddles underneath the umbrella with Cindy.

Because of the sun we race to the limo fifty yards away as a van is being filled with our luggage. Rance and Aimee stand by the car while he untangles her from his headset. Cindy struts into the car. Rance and Aimee get in next, slumping into the backseat. The rest of us pile in after them.

Rance forms a human C around Aimee. Her eyes are slits. I don't think she's capable of seeing more than a few inches in front of her. This pairing would never occur in nature, if for no other reason than most animals don't have regular access to psychotropics.

For the short time we've been driving, the landscape has changed to irrigated pastures among fields of wildflowers and sweetgrass, which seem to be pulsing. Butterflies are fluttering their wings on each flower—bright oranges, yellows, and reds blink at us for acres. I remember that someone told me that this is a refuge for butterflies as they migrate to Mexico.

"Incredible," I say.

"They're glorified moths," Tommy Sue says.

Aimee coughs and gurgles and doubles over. Rance rubs her back. Did she choke on his tongue? Her hands cover her mouth and, as she lifts her head, I can see a little white pill in her palm. I watch as she stuffs it into a crease in the upholstery. I guess she's had enough.

Rance gently kisses her cheek as she collapses back into the seat. Her face is pale and sweaty.

"Are you okay?" I ask her.

She closes her eyes, waves at me, and says, "I'm fine."

I exchange glances with Cindy and Drew.

Aimee says in a voice as flat as Kansas, "Tell Jenny about what Jackson said to you, Rance."

"Jackson has it bad. He says you have childbearing hips."

"I don't think I want to be known for wide hips," I say.

"Really, Rance, women don't like to hear that. Tell her something else," Aimee scolds.

"He said he loved your ideas on child-raising and that he thinks you'll be a good mother."

"Why?"

"Why?" Rance asks back uncertainly. His hand is wound so thoroughly in Aimee's hair that I don't know if he can get it out.

"Why does he think I'll be a really good mother?"

"I don't know. Guys don't talk about that. I think he's impressed with your intelligence and humor."

"Yeah?"

"I've never heard Jackson so excited about a woman. Not since Natalie," Rance says.

Natalie cringes a little and looks out the window harder than she did before.

"That's saying something. He loved Natalie," Drew says as he pats Natalie reassuringly on the knee.

"He's a good catch," Cindy echoes. I can hear traces of my mother in her sentiment.

We pull off the blacktop onto a dirt road. The rocks sound like hail against the limo until we come to the limestone driveway.

"I'd trade Chase for him," Tommy Sue says.

A heavy wrought-iron gate opens as we approach. Tommy Sue makes pigeon-cooing sounds. Drew lets out a low whistle. Cindy nods appreciatively. A sly smile crosses Rance's face. Aimee looks starstruck. I've forgotten that she's seeing this place for the first time. I'm sure she's recalculating Rance's net worth even now. She squeezes his arm, and he beams.

"It's real pretty, honey," she says.

"I feel like I'm in another country, United Kingdom of Rance," I say.

"This is one of the biggest ranches in Texas," Rance says.

"Just one of the biggest?"

"The first is bigger than Rhode Island."

That's right, brag away, Rance.

Rance's ranch is ten thousand acres of scrub brush and limestone. A tributary that feeds into the Rio Grande runs through his property. There are several ponds stocked with bass, catfish, and perch for fishermen. The electric fences are twelve feet high and heavily fortified because it's loaded with deer, antelope, quail, and exotic game not usually seen outside of Africa, so most of the year Rance entertains hunters as well.

There are a few hundred head of cattle roaming around, a dozen horses in the stables, and some chickens. Except for the horses, all animals will eventually make it to the dinner table.

"We're pulling up to the house," Rance says and presses his face to the glass.

I can finally make out buildings. I can't believe I'm looking at Rance's house. It's the size of a motel. It's at least four stories of yellowish stone combined with weathered wood and stucco. The aluminum roof, wide windows and doorways, and lots of large, expansive porches are pure Texas. Nouveau house designs in Texas, which I love, are all straight ninety-degree angles. Comfortable and unassuming, they're made of a hodgepodge of materials that give homes a patchwork quilt effect. But I've never seen a house this big before. I'm impressed with Rance's style—a hybrid of old barn, ranch, and sod. True, the house is huge, but it's also homey in a weird sort of way.

"This is beautiful," I say. "It looks like a contemporary castle."

"I used stones from the ranch and pines from the land," he says. "A new era needs a new kind of grandeur. I didn't want to build another Victorian replica or English Tudor."

He opens his door and jumps out. He pats himself down to make sure he's wearing all of his electronic devices. BlackBerry, *check*. iPod, *check*.

"Here, I'll give you a tour," he says and offers his hand first to Aimee, who is woefully wobbly, then to me and Cindy and Tommy Sue. Drew would've taken his hand but Rance doesn't offer it.

The "house" is eleven thousand square feet of stone walls and terrazzo tile floors. It has an interior courtyard with wisteria and trumpet flowers climbing an arbor. Mimosa and laurel trees provide shade as well as fragrance. A swimming pool that has tiles the same color as the courtyard is a seamless accessory. A twelve-foot-high statue of a missionary holding a sword above his head stands in the middle of the courtyard. He looks angry and menacing. It seems like the sculptor caught him just before he swung the sword down to injure one of the several cowering Native Americans at his feet. I hate it.

"This is my favorite piece," Rance says as he circles the angry statue. "Gives you the shivers, doesn't it?"

Oh, yeah, shivers of disgust.

He leads us through the kitchen, which looks like a behind-the-scenes view of a four-star restaurant on a slow day.

"There's a full-time staff for every aspect of the estate—livestock, grounds, cleaning, kitchen. You can order room service at any hour," he says.

"Really? Can I order lobster thermidor or baked Alaska?" Natalie asks. She's still packing on the pounds.

"You can request anything from a Bob Armstrong to a Brown Derby with legs and loafers," he says proudly.

Translation: A Bob Armstrong is a melted cheese dip with guacamole, ground beef, and salsa mixed in. It is deadly good. It was created by then Texas land commissioner Bob Armstrong who requested it whenever he dined at a Mexican restaurant in Austin.

A Brown Derby with legs and loafers is a dipped ice cream cone with a dollop of melted chocolate squirted into the bottom of the cone—that's the loafers. The legs mean you want it portable. The term was coined at Dairy Queen but is used everywhere dipped cones are made. People do love their Dairy Queens here. Most small-town Dairy Queens still have morning whittle clubs, which are a group of people who sip coffee and whittle things at the restaurant. I should note that the only thing Dairy Queens serve in the morning is coffee.

We walk through hallways that are bigger than most people's bedrooms. I'm not sure if that's good or bad for sneaking around.

Rance's house is more of a resort than a home and can easily handle the thirty-odd prospective snake killers that will assemble here.

"So are we killing snakes tonight?" I ask.

"No, we don't have them all yet. We're doing a reception tonight," Rance replies.

"When do you get the rest of them?" I ask.

"We get the rest of them tomorrow," Drew says, and puts his arm around me.

"I don't think I have the right clothes."

"We'll find something for you," Cindy says.

"I have extra gear. I'm always prepared," Natalie says. I heard she's a big hunting advocate, which is probably why Jackson loved her so much.

"Aimee, are you going?" I ask.

"It's just like a video game," she mumbles and sits down in the middle of the hallway like a three-year-old would do.

Time for a nap?

"Honey, you need to get up," Cindy says as she tries to pull Aimee up. I take Aimee's other side as I notice other guests entering the house at the other end of the living room. This isn't the greatest welcoming picture.

Aimee stumbles to vertical.

"I want to go to the spa," she whines.

"We will when we get home," I promise her like you would bribe a child.

"There's one in the basement," Rance offers helpfully.

"We should go," Tommy Sue claps her hands with excitement.

"We should go now," Natalie says, urging us to move.

Cindy and I propel Aimee in the direction of the stairs as Meg comes into full view. Why did they invite her?

"Ladies, where are we all off to?" she asks with a horrible look of satisfaction as she notices Aimee's state.

"Spa," Tommy Sue says, a little too forthcoming.

"Good, I'll join you," she says as she matches her steps with ours.

Once we start navigating Aimee down the stairs, she shouts, "Delta, Delta, Delta." Then she tries to take off her shirt. I pull it down.

"It's so fucking hot in Texas," she says.

"I see someone has overindulged," Meg says.

"Come on, darlin', let's get us a little treatment," Cindy says as she pulls on the other side of Aimee's blouse. Tommy Sue and Meg follow a couple of paces behind, serving, I think, as a safety net. Natalie trails behind them.

It's odd how Aimee can adjust her behavior, going from completely coherent to a lump of flesh to a frenzied cheerleader in a matter of minutes. I'm not sure what's in the drugs, but I hope they're prescribed for bipolar disorder.

The spa is wall-to-wall beige marble, with treatment room after treatment room lining the corridors. A man in white jeans and a white T-shirt greets us.

"Hello, ladies," he says in a hushed voice, with his hands behind his back. "What can I do for you today?"

We stop to look at the menu of treatments.

"We're going to the sauna," Cindy says, taking Aimee by the hand and walking past the desk.

The spa attendant rushes ahead of Cindy. "The changing rooms are to the left. You'll find plenty of robes and towels in there. The sauna is straight ahead," he says, then turns back to assist Tommy Sue and Meg.

Cindy and I push Aimee into one of the changing rooms, then pile in behind her and close the door.

"Time to kill a snake," Cindy says.

"Which one of you is going to take on Meg?" Aimee huffs, then takes off her clothes in a lethargic striptease.

"Good question," I say and open a closet filled with white terry-cloth robes. There must be twenty of them in here, all monogrammed with "RC." I hand one each to Aimee and Cindy, then fold our clothes as we undress and place them in the designated wicker baskets.

In the sauna, Aimee drops her robe and prances around the large, cedar-lined room unapologetically naked, as if she's waiting for applause. Modesty is one of her long-forgotten virtues. Then she grabs a towel, wraps it around her body, and sits, almost in the shape of a bow, on the cedar bench.

Cindy and I collapse on the wooden benches. Soon Meg and Tommy Sue file in, hang up their terry-cloth robes on the wooden hooks dotting the walls, and stretch out on the decks above us— right where the heat rises. I can't help but look at their naked bodies. Tommy Sue's ribs are so visible, they look like they've been enhanced with blush to make them more obvious. Meg has some of the roundest, highest, most unnatural breasts I've ever seen. Cindy's look is modest by comparison. Meg's must be an E cup. I can see veins popping out of Meg's calves even when she's resting.

"This is exactly what I need," Meg says.

"Yeah, lots of hot air," Cindy says and throws water on the black lava rocks, sending the temperature up ten degrees. I'm guessing she's trying to steam Meg out, but Meg's a Texas girl—she's heat-tolerant.

Meg is scowling, but I think she's decided to give Cindy a wide berth. I'm surprised she's even come in here; clearly Meg wants Cindy to think she's not completely intimidated.

"Jesus," Tommy Sue says. "There's enough steam in here to roast a pig." She moves down to the lower benches.

"It's good for the pores," Cindy says.

This is where the New Yorker in me comes out—I hate the heat. I rub ice on my neck and other pulse points. Natalie walks in. She hangs up her terry-cloth robe and takes a position on a bench.

"Feels like Texas," Natalie says.

"Am I sweating?" Aimee asks. "I feel like a cold fish."

"Only where Rance is concerned," Cindy says.

"Sometimes I feel like I'm losing my mind," Aimee admits in a rare moment of clarity.

"You need to sweat a lot more to get some sanity going," Cindy says and pours some more water on the coals.

"I think he's sweet," Tommy Sue says.

"Yes, he is," Aimee says and closes her eyes. I see her shoulders relax for the first time since we got here.

"He's a great catch," Natalie agrees.

"I think my flesh is melting. Can I lose fat through my pores?" Tommy Sue asks.

"Baby, you look great," Cindy says.

"I'm already two hundred calories over where I should be today," Tommy Sue whines. "If I can't lose weight in a sauna, then what's the point of having one?"

"I can see you're getting skinnier," Aimee says with closed eyes.

A smile bubbles up on Tommy Sue's lips.

"Won't improve your intelligence, though," Meg mumbles.

My skin feels tight and hot. I can't tell what's sweat and what's steam anymore. I am drenched in water. Sweat is flowing over my eyebrows and streaming into my eyes. Cindy and Meg are in their glory. Neither will be steamed out. Everyone is basking in the unbearable vapor, even Tommy Sue, now that she believes she's losing weight. Aimee is glistening. Water droplets are collecting in her hair and reflecting the light. She sits up on her own and opens her eyes, examining her surroundings like an old woman in the first stages of dementia.

"Aimee," I say and study her face for a hint of how she's really feeling.

"Yeah." She smiles a little and pats my face.

"You all right?"

"Of course, honey," she says, then looks under her towel as if to see what she's wearing.

Meg starts doing yoga stretches using the bench as a piece of equipment.

"Baylor is coming in early tomorrow morning. Seems he has a date in Dallas tonight. Did you know about that, Jenny?" Meg says to me.

I shift my towel to cover more of my breasts and try to ignore her. Does she have to let everyone know I'm interested in Baylor? Yes she does, because she wants to inflict the most damage she can. She's a truly vengeful person.

"'Course, I hear you're dating Jackson so I guess it doesn't matter what Baylor does," Meg says and goes in for the kill. "Natalie, honey, you sure are a true friend if you don't mind Jenny here dating the man who humiliated you a couple of years ago."

"At least I only have one man who humiliated me," Natalie says.

Meg's head whips around. She stares at Natalie but doesn't say anything further. Natalie smiles sweetly at Meg. Aimee's eyes have snapped open. Her eyes swivel back and forth between Natalie and Meg and me. Tommy Sue intently examines her thighs. Cindy watches Meg as she pats her pulse points with ice.

"So what's wrong with Byron Koch?" Cindy says to Meg. "He's rich as Croesus and funny as hell."

"Rich as creases?" Tommy Sue asks.

"Unimaginable wealth," Aimee elaborates. "Croesus is the name of an ancient Lydian king."

Told you she was smart.

"Wow. Imagine meeting a king," Tommy Sue says while twisting her thighs to get a better look at the backs.

"We're perfect together. I don't know what you're talking about," Meg says as she douses her head with cold water.

"I heard he hired a certain lawyer and that you also have representation—different representation," Cindy says, obviously undeterred.

"We have different lawyers because we have different investments," Meg says lightly.

"I didn't realize you had any money without him," Cindy says.

"I'll take him if you don't want him," Tommy Sue says. Meg glances at her with nasty eyes. Meg goes into a full split on the cedar floor.

God, that must chafe—at least I hope so.

"So when's your wedding, Aimee?" Meg asks.

"There has to be an engagement first," Aimee says.

"Oh honey, he loves you. I'm sure it's there if you want it," Natalie says.

"Isn't that the sixty-four-thousand-dollar question?" Meg says. "Whether you want him?"

"Yeah," Aimee exhales. "I do."

I'm reluctant to talk about her less-than-perfect love of Rance, no matter how obvious it is to everyone present, because Aimee's friends are, after all, husband-hunters themselves. Who knows which one of them might use the information against her in some calculating way.

Note to self: Never underestimate the hunger of a woman who's on the prowl for a wealthy man.

Sounds paranoid until you hear Vida Franklin's story: Her husband, Bo, was itching for a divorce but wasn't so keen on losing half his wealth (no prenup, silly man). So he bribed all the major people in her life—hairstylist, colorist, dermatologist, facialist—to tape their conversations and to specifically see if they could get her to admit to infidelity. Boy, did she.

There was the time in New York when Bo was at a shareholder meeting and Vida slipped into New Jersey to meet the Texas lobbyist for hemophiliacs who just happened to be wasting time in Newark. Vida had the audacity to come back to New York after her afternoon delight and scold her husband for not paying enough attention to her, a textbook misdirect strategy. After that and a taped discussion involving several kinds of phallic fruit were sent to Vida's attorney, they settled for a small lump sum that amounted to the cost of Bo's Vail house. Now he's dating Vida's best friend.

Beware of the tenacity of a successful businessman who is threatened with the loss of face, not to mention money.

I feel like I could dissolve into the bench. "Listen, kids, I'm a New Yorker. I have to get out of here," I say and shuffle out of the sauna with the springiness of an eighty-year-old man.

I get back to the changing room and lie down on a bench, praying the room will stop spinning. This is what it feels like to have your skin dry-roasted. I turn on my side. Aimee's large lavender purse stares up at me with its huge silver buckles. I stare back at it for several minutes before a plot flits through my mind—how to make Aimee a more well-rounded person. I grab the purse strap and drag it toward me, then dive my hand into the bottom. I can feel her fabric makeup bag, her hard leather sunglasses case, a bottle of water, and, aha, a bottle of pills. I pull it out and read the label. Hydrocodone, which, if I'm not mistaken, is generic Vicodin. The doctor has prescribed it for back pain. It's over half empty with two refills left—they must be having a lot of sex. I tuck the bottle into my woven orange leather purse—a Bottega Veneta number that's slouchy without looking like a gym bag—and shove her purse underneath the bench. I take a deep breath. I'm not sure if this is the right thing to do, but if I don't do something about Aimee's addiction, she'll end up in a psycho ward.

I swing my legs off the bench and test my ability to stay upright. Not bad. The room sort of slants instead of spins. I inch toward the wicker basket, sort of half standing, half squatting, and pull out my things. I wrap a new robe around me and sling my purse over my shoulder, then make my way out of the changing room.

As I stand in the hallway, I watch two worlds collide—Meg and Tommy Sue come out of the sauna just as Drew is rushing out of one of the treatment rooms in a towel only. He sees them first and searches frantically for a place to hide. I watch his expression change from panic-stricken to manipulative in the span of seconds. Then he faces the situation head-on.

"Ladies, you look pink," he says, startling Meg.

"Drew, what in the world?" Meg says, examining him up and down. "You look pretty pink yourself. Judging from the traces of mask on your hairline, I'd say you've just had a facial."

"No, a massage. It must be some of the oil," Drew says, backing off.

"And look at those nails," says Meg. Drew's neatly trimmed nails have a splash of clear, shiny topcoat. "I'd love a manicure."

"Manicure?" Tommy Sue asks.

"You know, Southern men have always prided themselves on keeping neat appearances," he says. "I have to shower."

Meg watches him walk away. "He's playing for the other team."

"I thought he stopped playing football," Tommy Sue says.

I peer through the sauna's glass door. Cindy is lying on an upper bench. Aimee glistens on a lower bench. Natalie examines her stomach, where there's absolutely extra weight, which gives her a sexy look. There's not a lot of steam left in the room, so Cindy must have stopped her steam-out campaign.

I turn and run into the same man in white jeans, waiting to take me to my room.

"Let me show you where to go. It's easy to get lost in this place," he says as he takes my elbow and ushers me to the elevator. Even at the slightest movement, his arm muscle snaps to attention. He is toned to the point of cement. He holds open the elevator, allowing me to walk out first.

The first thing I notice when I enter the room is the fantastic view of rocky red cliffs. The windows are large and shaded. It'll be wonderful to sleep with the breeze skimming over me tonight.

"Thanks," I say, wondering if I should tip him. I never handle these situations appropriately. It's so awkward—if I tip him, I'm implying he's less than me. If I don't, it's like I'm saying he's not doing a good job. So I compensate by heavily tipping waitresses and cabdrivers, because those are the only tipping protocols I understand. I decide against it.

"I give excellent massages, too," he says, winking at me as he leaves.

I scan the room. There's a plush white fur rug in front of the fireplace. I'm not sure who or what was the previous owner of this enormous pelt but I don't feel any remorse for lying down on it. It feels soothing, like lying on a dog that doesn't stink. There's a beautiful toffee silk-covered love seat with wooden claw feet, a club chair, and antler-based coffee table surrounding the rug. The bed is a mahogany four-poster number with lots of carvings. It looks like it could have come out of the Old West. An old-fashioned canopy and the bedspread are covered with rose-patterned silk.

After unpacking and hanging out in my room for a couple of hours, I feel like I've stepped back in time. I decide to dress more modestly for the cocktail party than I normally would for an evening affair. I pull out my Blue Cult jeans and button up my Catherine Malandrino blouse, which is a mixture of cowgirl and Victorian. I lay them on the bed. I'm about to head for the shower when I hear a knock on my door. I open it and find a very awake and sober Aimee wrapped in a robe matching mine. She walks into my room and collapses on the sofa. Her face is still bright pink from the sauna heat. I sit next to her.

"Baylor is off-limits," she mumbles.

"I know. I'm here to spend time with Jackson," I say.

"Darling, you can't play two men," she says shaking her head. "You know what happens when you look like a player. Natalie's bloated stomach should put the fear of God in you."

"So what's the real story with Rance?" I ask, trying to get the spotlight off me.

"What, honey?" Aimee asks.

"Don't honey me. You have to be higher than a helium balloon to even let Rance touch you," I say. "And then, when he's out of sight, you become the model of health."

Aimee closes her eyes.

"Aimee?"

"This is too good a deal to pass up," she says. "I have to stop being a baby and suck it up." Her face is expressionless.

"Are you sure?" I say and wait for a change in her demeanor.

Then Aimee jumps off the sofa and twirls around the room. "Look at this; look at all I could own."

Someone who didn't know her any better might say she looks joyous. To me, it seems like a manic desire for possessions.

"But you'll never get to have enjoyable sex again."

"Marriage isn't a lasting institution, you know. This is just another phase of my life," she says.

"What about the pills?"

"You have to stop worrying about me," Aimee says, and I sense a new edge to her personality that I've never seen before. "I know what I'm doing." Then she gets up, gives me a kiss on the cheek, and says, "See you at dinner. Sorry about Meg."

After she leaves, I realize that I've made a decision that could end my friendship with her forever. I spill out my purse onto the bed. The pill bottle drops to the floor. I pick it up and open the bottle, heading for the bathroom. It feels like slow motion as the little white pills form an arc as they fall into the water. I flush the toilet. It's done.

Chapter Seventeen

The Time to Kill a Snake Is
When You Have the Hoe in Your Hands

By the time I walk out back where the evening's party is being held, there's already quite a crowd on the porch, which is the size of a football field, with enough teak seating that one could easily mistake it for a restaurant. Waiters, duded out with red bandanas and Stetsons, mill through the throng and offer rattlesnake martinis and the ever-present frozen margarita, nicknamed DQs after Dairy Queen's swirl slushie.

There's a barbecue pit off in the distance. I can see big plumes of smoke rising above the house. I hope there's a fire department on hand in case they need help putting it out later.

The help, a.k.a. cowhands, offer hunks of pig and brisket, white bread and pickles. I have no idea how to eat the combination.

"You look confused," Jackson says as he puts his hand gently on my shoulder. Speaking of shoulders, his are looking mighty good tonight. He's wearing a gray T-shirt, no logos, we're talking Egyptian cotton, and his muscles pull against the hem of the sleeves. He has on dark boot-cut jeans and flip-flops with plaid soles. The man has the instinct to defy Western dress code.

"I'm not sure how one eats that," I confess, and point to the white bread and barbecue. "Do you make a sandwich?"

He beckons the waiter over and picks up two paper baskets. He places one in my hands. He puts two pieces of white bread on the bottom of both of our baskets. Then he loads us both up with meat, extra sauce, and pickles on the side. He leads me over to the chairs.

"So do you fold the bread together?" I ask, still mystified.

"No, you eat the barbecue and save the bread for later. The bread sops up the grease. You eat it sort of like a dessert," he says as he digs in.

"I see you don't want to miss out on an ounce of grease if you don't have to."

"You understand."

"I do," I say, looking disgusted over the idea of eating grease-soaked bread.

"It's not like this is something we do every day. It's a greasy treat like fried dough."

"Mmm, fried dough. The only reason I go to fairs is to eat fried dough." I bite into my barbecue, half hoping it tastes like powdered sugar and peanut oil.

"See, you understand."

"There's one thing I don't get. Why all the different sauces?" I point to a bar in the corner that is stocked with nothing but different types of barbecue sauce. There are more than a dozen different bottles.

"The big differences between the schools are tomato content and heat," he says.

"Schools?" I laugh.

"There are barbecue adherents who refuse to stray from their beloved," he says. "I believe in the school of habanero. It can burn a hole through a penny but it's worth the pain."

"An acquired taste," I say.

Aimee plops down next to us with a margarita in hand. I didn't even see her coming. She doesn't have her usual veil of Southern charm intact. She looks annoyed.

"What's up?" I ask.

"Nothing, I lost something is all." She scans the scene and composes herself. "Oh, I'm so glad you two found each other. Jackson came up early to see you."

"I did," Jackson says and smiles.

"Isn't this great? Look at all the people," Aimee says and gulps her margarita like water. Her feet tap nervously. She runs her fingers through her hair over and over again.

"God, check out Meg. Do you know she came without her husband? What's Byron up to these days?" Aimee pointedly asks Jackson, making him very uncomfortable.

"I think Byron is on his hunting lease this weekend," he says as we all look over in Meg's direction. She's wearing what barely meets the requirements of a shirt. Pasties would be as covering.

"You sure you're okay?" I ask her and touch her shoulder. She feels clammy.

"I have to find something," she says absently and leaves.

"Maybe she's coming down with something," Jackson offers.

Painkiller withdrawal perhaps?

"I'm sure she'll be fine," I say as I watch a heavily pregnant woman glide by. Bradford follows her, entranced by her belly. He's asking her about what kind of cocoa butter she uses. Natalie trails behind a few paces. Jackson watches her.

"Natalie was hard to get over," I say.

"I told you. We were together two years. Everything was going great but I knew it was time to move on after I saw we had different values," he says.

"What about forgiveness?" I ask, getting a little hostile for her and myself. I'm scared of how he'll react when he finds out about my mother's heritage.

"Settle down. I didn't break up with you. I think there's something in you that tells you when you've met the person you're going to spend your life with. I didn't feel that for her. Under those circumstances, it was wrong to continue."

"That's understandable."

I mean it, too. I think there can be something special that you feel when you meet the one. Something clicks. I've never felt it but I could see it happening.

He says more good things about his philosophy on dating, religion, and sports. He's looking for love and marriage. I already
knew that but he reiterates it and expands on his feelings. He men-
tions Jesus a few more times than is comfortable. He grabs my
hand with sincerity and a fervor that says to me, "Let's go up to
your bedroom right now and procreate."

His desire is appealing. I could see following him up to the
room and into a life with three small children and a nice backyard.
I could see my mother being so happy that she allows me to slip
occasionally on the weekly required call.

"Do you hunt?" he asks.

"I've never tried."

"Let me teach you tomorrow. We'll go to the shooting range
and shoot skeet."

The thought of hitting an inanimate object rather than a live
blood-filled one is encouraging.

"Sounds good," I say as I watch Baylor in the distance. I didn't
realize he was already here. Guess Meg's information was bad.
Meg hovers not far from him.

"We'll have to do it early so we don't miss the snake hunt,"
Jackson says, trying to gain my attention again. "I'll pick you up
at your room around seven."

"Nine."

"Eight."

"Eight. You really like this early-morning thing. Don't expect
anything fancy. I'm not going to wash my hair."

"That's fair."

As we shake on it, Rance's disembodied voice comes over the
speakers. We instinctively stand up and look around for him. He's
on a platform. He holds Aimee's hand tightly. She rolls her eyes
and tries to free herself. Champagne is handed out to everyone. He
raises a glass to toast Aimee, while she yawns and gazes with intense hatred at the crowd. She must've drunk a pitcher of margar-
itas to compensate for her pill loss. Unfortunately, alcohol doesn't
hide her emotions as well as pharmaceuticals.

"I'd like to introduce y'all to Aimee. Aimee, I'd like to introduce you to the crowd as my fiancée if you agree," he says and gets
down on one knee.

The crowd claps and hoots. This is the first time any of them are associating Rance and Aimee with terms like *forever together* instead of *good enough for now*.

Aimee, glassy-eyed, stares at Rance for a beat. Her face is transformed into a look of forced exuberance. She smiles wide and chirps, "Oh, yes." She throws her arms around Rance, knocking him off balance. He tumbles onto the stage. He staggers up, wipes off his pants, and as an afterthought pulls Aimee up. Geek supersedes Southern manners in Rance's mind-set.

Fireworks flare into the sky in the shape of a yellow rose, while Rance calls Aimee his yellow rose. I know he means it but it comes off hokey to the point of cheesy. I'm remembering with some horror that the Yellow Rose was a San Antonio prostitute in the frontier days of South Texas. Poor Rance, I swear I can almost see milk coming through his nose.

Jackson hoots with the best of them. He's cute enough that I don't hold it against him.

"Did you know about this?" he asks.

"No, but I'm not completely surprised. They spend all of their time together."

"How long have they known each other?"

"Like a year," I stretch the truth.

"Must be true love," he says without a hint of irony.

"Absolutely, true love," Cindy says, walking up to us with Drew in tow.

"I love a good union," he says.

"You love access to a private plane," Cindy says.

Jackson looks at her, dismayed at her snarkiness. He does have a lot of the earnest in him. I think with enough time I could up his sarcasm factor.

I plead migraine. I've had enough excitement for one night and I want to look good tomorrow morning. I head inside.

Baylor meets me in the hallway.

"Hello," he says.

"I thought I recognized you. I wasn't sure because there was no skeletal blond attached to you," I say.

He walks down the hall with me.

"I'm glad to see you," he says.

He looks at me with a playful smile. I smile back. I'm resisting the temptation to invite him to my room. The bubbling-on-the-surface attraction I feel for Jackson is nothing compared to the deep-down-in-my-stomach pull I feel for Baylor. Why is that? Think about what he did, I tell myself.

"Have fun in Arkansas?" I ask.

"Fun isn't the word for it. Productive is," he says.

"What'd you do? I love details," I say.

"Attorney-client privilege," he says.

"I know some of this involves a naïve friend of mine who's about to get very hurt. Is there anything I can do to soften the blow?" I ask.

"Men go to places with a hard dick that they wouldn't dare with a loaded gun," Baylor says.

True, Rafe isn't the most emotionally evolved individual, but that doesn't mean he deserves to get screwed over by a woman who's lower down on the emotional evolutionary chain than he is.

"I can't believe you're helping her," I say.

"I'm trying to get a good outcome for everyone," he says.

"What does that mean?"

He stops me a few feet from my bedroom door. He tries to kiss me. I dodge him and march over to my door. He follows me to my room.

"I should go to bed," I say.

"Okay," he says, but doesn't move.

"I'm not going to invite you in. I'm not that kind of girl."

"I understand. You're a good Southern lady," he says, smiling but still not moving.

I open my door a crack and slide inside. I close the door.

"Good night," I call.

"Good night," he says back. It sounds like he's still in the same place he was a few seconds ago.

I get into my men's pajamas, open the windows to my room, and snuggle into bed. I can hear the party below. It's comforting to hear bursts of laughter and glasses clinking for toasts. Maybe I'm overreacting about the Rance and Aimee thing. Maybe they have a different brand of happiness than I do. I know plenty of people who have never been in love but are happy.

I hear a cough outside my door. Is Baylor still there? I get out of my bed and open the door. He's leaning against the wall with his hands in his pockets.

"What are you doing?" I ask.

"I wasn't ready to leave yet," he says.

"I'm not inviting you in," I say.

"Not tonight," he says and walks away.

Not ever, I promise myself.

I close the door and climb into bed again. I swear to keep an open mind about Jackson as I doze off.

I open the door at seven to a tray of pancakes and hot tea. How I love room service. The waitress?—I don't know if you have "waitresses" in private homes—the serving woman puts the tray down on my coffee table, sets up my tea service, and lays out a crisp copy of the *Dallas Morning News*. She leaves as quietly as she came in.

I sit back on the plush couch, daintily slice pancakes, sip tea, and read the paper. The birds chirp outside and in the distance I think I hear the hum of a lawn mower. This is pretty perfect.

I'm still in my pajamas when there's a knock on my door. I look at my cell phone clock. It's already eight. Damn, damn, damn.

"Coming!" I yell.

I grab a bra and T-shirt, slip on some jeans, brush my hair, and down some mouthwash.

"You're timely," I say as I open the door.

"You look great," Jackson says as he walks into my room. What? It must be the relaxing breakfast.

Jackson waits expectantly.

"I have to put on some shoes," I say as I sit down on the couch and put on my green Prada sneakers that I got on sale for nineteen dollars, marked down from three hundred. I love a bargain.

"I think we can get in a good hour at the range before the snake hunt," Jackson says. "I'm thinking I'll start you off with a .22, see how you do with that, and play around."

"How many guns do you have?"

"Six with me. I don't know how many I have altogether," he says as we walk out the door.

How many guns does one need? Are they like purses?

The range is about a half mile from the house. We walk the distance. It's a nice hike. The grass is still damp. The sun is bright and warm. The trees leaves are the neon green of spring growth. It smells like sweetgrass and wisteria. The hum of bees and dragonflies is low and constant.

Jackson picks up a stick and plants it in the ground periodically. With his hiking boots, jeans, and fitted T-shirt, he looks like a regular Greenpeace activist.

"Beautiful day," he says.

"Yeah, it is. It'd be sixty degrees in New York today," I say.

"Another reason to live in Texas."

We get to the range. A white canopy covers where we shoot from. Servants stand under the tent with mimosas in one hand and boxes of shells in the other. Hay bales create a wall between us and the range. Several feet away are targets shaped like deer. Jackson's six guns lay on felt on top of the bales. Their barrels shine like they've never been used.

Jackson practically skips toward them. He runs his fingers over each one, picks them up, and checks them out from every angle.

"They're so clean," I say.

"You have to take pride in your equipment."

"Okay, so what do we do with these bad boys?" I say as I pick up a gun and aim it at a target.

"Whoa, whoa," Jackson says as he gingerly takes the gun away from me. "Never point a gun—loaded or not—at anything but the ground until you're ready to shoot."

He turned so somber.

"Sorry," I say.

"Gun safety is the most important thing to learn before you go hunting. You don't want to make other people nervous," he says and proceeds to give me a forty-five-minute lecture on the finer points of firearms.

I pay attention and get the rules. This easily could've been a ten-minute lecture instead of the safety extravaganza it turned into.

"Are we ready to shoot?"

"Yeah," he says and hands me a shotgun and puts ear protectors on my head. I take the gun carefully as I try to simulate his instructions.

"Now, what you want to do is aim at that target, brace your shoulder, and shoot."

"What's the good place to aim at?"

"The heart."

I pull the trigger. It happens so fast. I hear an explosion and feel a force hit my shoulder, which throws me a couple of feet back.

"What the hell," I say.

Jackson studies the target.

"You got it through the heart."

"Really?"

"Yep, try it again."

I aim and shoot.

"Damn, you're a natural," he says and smiles.

I feel, I don't know, invigorated. It's like diving into a cold lake on a hot day. At first the shock is so great you're not sure what you think and then a few seconds later you feel good. Very good.

Shooting a target well feels like an accomplishment on par with finishing an article before it's due.

Jackson smiles at me. I think finding a woman who's a good shot is an aphrodisiac for him.

"Why don't you try this one?" he says slyly, and hands me a beretta.

"Don't mind if I do," I say and aim at the target, letting off several shots.

"Perfect," he says as he eyes my shot pattern. "Why don't we try skeet?"

"What is skeet, anyway?"

"Small clay disks that mimic birds in flight. There are three different machines that release randomly. Ready?"

"Sure," I say and notice he's picking up a gun as well.

"Thought I'd make it more interesting," he says.

The servant stands ready. Jackson gives him the word.

Objects fly randomly from all directions. Jackson shoots. Clay shards erupt. At first I don't quite comprehend what's going on or how to shoot. But when I let my instincts take over, that's when things click.

Jackson makes the signal to stop. We put down our guns and pick up mimosas.

"Aimee's right. It is just like a video game," I say.

"You are a natural. You've never shot before?"

"Never."

"You've found your calling," he says.

"What? Can I make money at this?"

"It's not about money. It's about finding a passion."

"I wouldn't call this a passion. It's just something I'm insanely good at," I say. He laughs.

"Would you like to team up with me on the hunt?"

"Tomorrow?"

"That's the one."

"I won't slow you down?"

"You? You're a better shot than most of the guys here. Though I wouldn't say that to their faces."

"Sure."

"Great, I'll get all the gear you need ready for tomorrow. Be ready and downstairs by six a.m."

"What is it with you and early mornings?" I ask.

"You get to accomplish something while the rest of the world is sleeping," he says.

I can feel the sun baking through my shirt. The grass steams with evaporating dew. It's going to reach eighty pretty soon.

"We should get going, huh," I say.

"Yeah."

We walk back to the house. Jackson takes my hand and stops me in the middle of a field that bursts with bluebonnets.

"Let's try something. Do you mind?" he says as he leans in and kisses me.

His lips lightly touch mine. Like I thought the first time he kissed me, he's good at this. Why am I thinking during a kiss?

"Nice," he says.

He keeps a hold of my hand as we walk the rest of the way back to the house.

When we get to the back porch Jackson gives me another light kiss on the lips and goes off to change for the snake hunt.

I am about to run upstairs for an outfit change, too, but I spot Aimee slumped down in a lounge chair. She looks half dead. Her skin is pale and sweaty.

I sit in the empty lounge chair next to her. On the other side, Natalie is sprawled out in a tank top that inches up past her pudgy stomach.

"Catching a tan?" I ask Aimee.

"What?" she croaks.

"Are you okay?"

"No, I think I'm dying," she says.

I pick up the glass of orange juice on the table and take a sip of it to confirm that it's at least two parts vodka.

"Is this helping?" I ask.

"You should've seen her before," Natalie says.

"A little," Aimee says and turns toward me. "I can't find my pills."

"So?"

"I need them."

"I thought you said they were nonaddictive."

"I'm not saying I'm addicted. I'm saying I need them mentally, not physically," she says as she vigorously scratches her arms.

"Don't worry. I'm sure they'll turn up," I say, which is a total lie since I'm the one who flushed them down the toilet. But I feel I have to give her some hope.

"Shouldn't we be getting ready for the snake hunt?" I ask.

"I'm not going anywhere. I feel like hell."

"Come on, I'll have the maid put together a couple of thermoses of mimosas."

"I'd suggest something stronger," Natalie interjects.

"I think I'll retch if I have to smile and laugh at all of Rance's god-awful jokes and his stupid Civil War reenactments," she says.

"Is that what you're doing as foreplay now?" Natalie asks.

"Yep," Aimee answers in a disgusted tone.

"I thought I heard references to charging the left flank when I walked by your room," Natalie says.

"I'll act as a buffer," I offer.

"No."

"How will it look if you don't go?"

"She's right. You'd be rude," Natalie echoes.

"Fine, but you better have more than a couple of thermoses of champagne," she says as she tries to get up. I grab her arm to steady her.

"Anything you say, princess," I say.

"I don't know what you're so happy about. You've never been to one of these things."

No, I haven't, and her comment doesn't do anything to calm my worries. Once we're out there, if I hate it I can't escape. I'm going in a bus with all the other guests and if I do despise it I can't show it because that would be rude. Rude is like the cardinal sin of Texandom. Take Aimee's example. The girl is in the depths of chemical withdrawal. I'm sure her idea of a perfect day would be a cool bed in a darkened room. But as soon as I mention to her that it wouldn't look good if she didn't attend the snake hunt, she rushes upstairs to change.

I follow her and I walk into my room. My shirt is off when I realize I have no idea what I'm doing. Why is everyone changing? I'm in jeans and sneakers. Isn't that good enough?

I put my shirt back on and walk downstairs, or start to. I see Meg in the hallway. I duck into an alcove. I can hear Meg talking on the phone as she paces.

"What do you want? I told you what the deal was," Meg hisses. "I can't believe this. No, no, don't you dare. Byron and I are going to stay married."

She's quiet for a few seconds. She listens to the person on the other end as she bangs her fist into the wall. She lets out a couple of bursts of air like a teakettle on full blow before she launches into a response.

"No, I'm not. Baylor isn't going to wind up with that stringy little bitch. Yeah, I know you used to date her. Didn't treat her very well then. I don't know why you're defending her," Meg says.

Silence again. Then Meg's tone changes completely. Her voice is as sweet as chocolate syrup.

"Honey, why don't we talk about this next week when I come over? I'll bring something real fun with me. I promise," she says.

She hangs up her phone, mutters "Asshole," and marches down the hallway, away from me. I guess Rafe isn't going quietly.

I skulk out from my alcove and head downstairs.

Chapter Eighteen

Never Take Your Eyes off the Rattle

I peer out back to see what everyone has on. They're in jeans like I am. Jackson looks the same. He waves. I walk toward him. He kisses me on the lips. Firm lips. Again, why am I thinking during a kiss?

"Did you change?" I ask.

"Yep."

"What did you change into?"

"I put on steel-toe boots that go up to my knees and canvas-treated pants."

"Why?"

"Some of those snakes are a little ornery."

"Huh."

"They bite."

"No one told me that."

"They're snakes. What did you expect them to do?"

"I don't know," I say defensively.

"It's okay. Here," he says and hands me a pair of boots. "Don't go on the front line and you'll be fine."

Front line. Now I'm scared.

"Oh, you got me more snake-resistant boots. That's sweet," I say, a little embarrassed. I turn to embark on a search for Aimee.

"Wait," Jackson says and hugs me.

"Am I doing well?" I ask Aimee as I walk toward her.

"Jackson's smitten," she says in between gulps of vodka tonic.

"Yeah, it's because he found out I'm an incredible marksman."

"Oh, that's the best aphrodisiac there is," Natalie says.

"That and a keen interest in camping," I say.

"You have to mirror his interests. It'll be like he's falling in love with himself," Natalie says with all the psychobabble knowledge daytime television has endowed her with.

"Once you're married you can reclaim your personality," Cindy says, walking up to us.

"What happened with Bradford last night?" I ask Natalie.

"Nothing. He sort of circled the pregnant woman. Never made a move. I think he'll go in for the kill tonight and I'll be there. I'll walk in and expose his fetish. He'll have no choice but to ask me to marry him," she says.

"Any luck with your pregnancy?" Cindy asks.

"Not yet, but I think I'm ovulating," Natalie says as she takes a gulp of her vodka tonic.

"Well, this could be a banner weekend for you," Cindy says as Tommy Sue walks up. I don't think I've seen her since yesterday afternoon.

"Where'd you go last night?" I ask her.

"Jogging," she says.

"For the whole night?" Cindy asks.

"For a few hours. I needed to burn a few calories," Tommy Sue says.

"Honey, you have to stop this all-out assault on your body. You're engaged. You don't have to kill yourself anymore. You can gain two to five pounds," Cindy counsels.

"Just don't go above six. I've gained ten and I'm a cow," Natalie says.

Tommy Sue looks Natalie up and down. Warning taken. I

wouldn't be surprised if Tommy Sue ducked out of the roundup to do some more jogging.

Meg slithers up to us. "Hello, ladies. Ready to catch some reptiles?"

"I am. I plan to catch a whole mess of them," Natalie says as she perks up.

"You can start with her," Cindy says in a sweet voice. Meg smiles hard.

"Still bitter from your last divorce," Meg says brightly.

"Not as bitter as you'll be when Byron divorces you. I've read your prenup. Maybe I'll hire you as a personal assistant. You'll need the work," Cindy says and hands Meg her empty champagne glass.

The last comment silenced us. Cindy has gone beyond the biting Southern repartee into plain mean. Meg takes the glass and heads toward the house. I've never seen her in full retreat.

"Was that true, what you said?" I ask.

"I don't bluff," Cindy says.

"That was mean, real mean," Natalie says.

"Sometimes you have to drive the knife in. She has to know who's the alpha," Cindy says as we watch the men parade around in leather chaps, thigh-high wading boots, and leather pants. They must be hot in the temperature sense. It's at least eighty degrees.

"Do you have any armor against the snakes?" I ask Aimee.

"No, we're not going to be on the front line."

"What does that mean? It's not like we're doing battle with them, are we?" I ask.

"It kind of is like that. You'll see," she says as she gets up and walks toward the bus.

"I'm going to be right out there," Natalie says. I see she's wearing steel-toe boots.

Dozens of people step onto a large silver bus that glistens in the sun. It's a tour bus for snake fighters. Aimee and I get to the back of the line. Natalie pushes her way up front with Bradford. Cindy walks with us and gets in line. Tommy Sue looks like she's going for a jog. Meg comes toward us, ready for a second round. She doesn't look like a big hunter.

"Beautiful day to rile up a few snakes," she says as she stands behind Cindy. She's acting like nothing ever happened.

"Have you hunted snakes before?" I ask Meg, feeling pity for her for the first time.

"Sure. Nothing wrong with a few less snakes in the world, right? Almost as bad as all those lawyers and Jews," she says, laughing.

"What about all those Muslims and Mexicans and let's not forget the blacks?" I shoot back sarcastically.

"The Muslims keep to themselves, thank God. The Mexicans, well they're the help. The blacks are less reliable help than the Mexicans. What I can't stand is when a minority doesn't know its place. Jews think they're just as good—no, better—than the rest of us," Meg says.

"And that's arrogant?" I ask, trying to get to the specifics of her prejudice.

"No, it's wrong. Jews are shorter than us, darker, and with bad noses. They might be good with money and they're funny, but they're not an attractive or pleasant people."

"You think Hitler was right?" I ask.

"Nooo, I'm not saying killing millions of people is right. But look at the history. How many countries have they been thrown out of? There's a reason for it," she says. "For God's sake, they couldn't even keep their own country. We had to go and get it back for them."

That's it. I can't take it anymore. I knew Meg was evil, but she's crossed a line. After her "there's a reason for it" line, I'm not worried about Jackson, or Baylor, or what anyone else might think. I need to take a stand.

"How should I thank your Aryan counterparts for all they've done for my people? Maybe a thank-you note or an unlimited supply of bacon and shellfish," I say and soak in the confused expression on Meg's face. "I'm half Jewish. I'm surprised you couldn't figure that out from my nose, shortness, and love of money."

Meg's eyes light up. She doesn't look upset that I'm confronting her. She seems happy—and that's got to be worse.

"The money-grubbing should've tipped me off," she says,

smirking. "Please excuse me. My powers of observation are off. It's a mistake I won't make again."

She tips her head and walks back into the house.

Cindy and Aimee exchange glances. "She's going to tell everyone she knows," Aimee states. "I'm not saying you shouldn't have spoken up, but be warned. She's going to turn it into a statewide incident."

"Can't do anything about it now. Look at his quick hands," Cindy says as she motions to Baylor, who is now standing just a few paces in front of us. "He's one of the best."

Baylor gets on the bus. He looks back at me and smiles. I look away.

"My best advice: Don't let Meg see you looking at Baylor," Cindy says as we climb on the bus.

The bus windows are tinted purple. Inside, the air-conditioning has dropped the temperature to see-your-breath level. The seats aren't the normal bus ones, either. They are easy chairs that twist completely around and recline. There's a bar in the back. The bus smells like oranges and gardenias, sweet and strong. Aimee, Cindy, and I take seats in the back.

Jackson waves from up front. I wave back and he sits down with a group of boys in the front of the bus. He must want to get all the good snakes.

"Where's Rance?" I ask. I haven't seen a chin waddle all morning. Strange since he's normally stuck like double-sided tape to Aimee.

"Oh, he has some business. He's been on the phone since six a.m."

"Is he going to miss the snake hunt?"

"No, he'll come in a separate car."

"It must be a pretty big deal to keep him on the phone so long."

"It's tedious."

"Come on, Aimee, not all business is tedious."

"It's about the pharmacy benefits, specifically copayment issues at a start-up data collection company that Rance bought for two and a half million dollars. It's hardly an exciting issue."

"I guess you would know. How do you know?"

"It's my business to be up-to-date in all of Rance's financial issues."

"Good girl," Cindy says and pats her on the arm.

"Where's Drew?" I ask.

"Up front. He's putting in his manly hours," Cindy says.

The bus drives down a dusty, cactus-filled part of Big Bend. It's bright, rocky, and yellow. The men rush out of the bus as soon as it stops. Some of them pull out jugs of gasoline. Others start to make a fire.

"Isn't that a dangerous combination?" I ask Aimee. We're still on the bus.

"Sure, but so is drinking and driving and everyone does that. Let's go," Aimee says, grabbing a thermos. "Don't worry, we'll watch from a distance," she says. "Even though they're confused from the gas fumes, they still bite."

"I'm gonna land me some snakes," Natalie says as she walks out with Bradford into the field. She would have been the perfect match for Jackson.

I look around for the pregnant woman. She's not here. I guess that's smart. Pregnancy and poisonous venom don't mix.

"I'm going to get me something to drink," Cindy says, making her way toward a cooler that was moved from the bar and placed at the front of the bus.

We walk out of the bus and into the blinding sunlight. What you can't hear from the bus is the men calling to one another as if they were in battle.

"Got a live one here."

"Bring the tongs. Good God, I need the tongs."

There are pairs of long silver tongs used to snare the snakes once they come out of their holes.

"He's on the move. Watch out. You have a hostile at two o'clock."

"Watch your right flank. Five o'clock. No, five o'clock, dipshit. Incoming."

"J.T., you can head him off at the pass. Go left and down."

"I'm hit. I'm hit."

"Man down. Man down."

A man with a fluorescent orange hunting vest trots into the battle and drags out a man who is swearing to God about the motherfucking pain. He's sweating so much it drips off his shirt and forms small streams on the ground. His eyes roll around. It's Drew.

Aimee and I watch the whole scene like it's some kind of interactive play. I don't move because I have no idea what's safe ground and what's the battleground.

"Don't worry. He'll be fine," Aimee says, gesturing to where Drew is now lying, out of the fray. I can't tell if she's reassuring me or herself. She gets up and walks over to Drew. Her quick pace makes me think she's more worried than she lets on.

"I thought the bites could be lethal," I say.

"They can be and they hurt like hell," the man wearing the fluorescent-orange vest says as he fumbles to open a firstaid kit. "The thing to do is not panic and run around screaming your head off because you'll accelerate the venom pumping through your system and you'll probably go into shock."

Drew clenches his fists and widens his eyes. He looks scared.

"Motherfucker," he screeches.

"Seriously, how many people die from the bites?" I ask Aimee as she grabs the first-aid kit out of the orange-vested man's hand and takes out a syringe. She plunges it into Drew's vein.

"It'll be okay, baby," she says as she pats his arm.

We all look on in shock.

"Antivenom," she says. She goes back to the first-aid kit and rummages around for a few seconds. She pulls out a pill bottle, opens it, and takes out a pill. She puts it in Drew's mouth and holds a bottle of water up to his face.

"There, there. You'll feel great in a few seconds," she says as she pats his throat to make sure he's swallowed it.

I hope she didn't pocket the rest of the bottle.

Drew looks happier and he's a lot quieter, but his calf is swelling to the size of a car tire. The orange-vest guy pulls Drew onto the bus with the help of three other guys.

"Will the swelling go down now that he has the antivenom?" I ask.

"Oh, no, he's gonna be swollen for a few days."

"Ouch."

"Yeah, it's not going to be pretty. Poor guy is going to be laid up for a while," Aimee says as she walks a little farther out into the battleground and surveys the scene. Her earlier urgency to help Drew has faded again to the detached Aimee of before. Men hoot and holler as the snakes slowly slither toward them.

Aimee walks past me, heading back toward the bus. "I'll go check on him—make sure Drew is comfy on the bus."

I hear Jackson's now-familiar hoot and I turn from Aimee's slightly unsteady progress to the bus. Jackson's about fifty feet away with three other guys. They shove snakes into gunny sacks with their bare hands. Way too much testosterone going on over there. Jackson looks up and waves at me. I point to the snake in his hand who looks like he's ready to strike. Jackson quickly drops the snake in the sack and waves again. I wave back. I feel like a mother at a school track meet. "Yep, I'm proud of you, son, and I signal that pride by this wavy motion with my hand." I'm glad he didn't ask me to join him in the field on this one. I couldn't feign enthusiasm or lack of fear. No man, no matter how rich, is worth risking life or disfigurement for. That's my viewpoint. I think Natalie, Aimee, and Cindy would disagree.

I walk over to Aimee's perch on the bus bumper and see men dancing barefoot among the rocks.

"What the hell are they doing?"

"It's a macho thing. Who can handle snakes bare-handed? Who can walk with snakes barefooted?"

"It's so stupid."

"You haven't seen the worst yet," Aimee says, and she points to a group of men, including Hoss, holding a snake wide-mouthed over a glass jar.

"That's venom, right?"

"Yep, they're milking the snake. We use the venom to make antivenom."

"Sort of like recycling."

"Sort of," Aimee says vacantly. She looks pale and clammy again.

"This is the first time I've seen Hoss here. Where's he been?" I ask. I am still on the fence about him even though Lizzy confessed to us that he's a virgin.

"Don't worry. I asked Rance to keep him busy. Rance has him doing all sorts of men-only activities," she says.

"Such as?" I ask.

"Like hunting and, I don't know, macho stuff," Aimee slurs and trails off. She looks ready to bob and weave and pass out cold.

"Why don't we go back on the bus?" I ask, and lead her up the steps into the air-conditioned monstrosity. We pass Drew, who is sprawled out across three seats. He babbles to himself incoherently about cattle prices. His calf, propped up in its own chair, is twice as big as last time I saw it. I take Aimee to our original seats and pour her some water.

"Drink," I say as I notice Baylor saving another man from getting bit by a snake. He quickly pulls the snake's head from the guy's wrist in one deft move.

"What is it?" she asks, pushing the water away before I even hand it to her.

"Vodka," I say and dangle it in front of her.

"Good," she says, lurching for it and chugging it. Her face twists up in disgust. "Liar."

"You do what you have to do," I say. "Rance is here."

Rance's Land Rover pulls up next to the bus. He reclines in the backseat and talks on the phone. Reclining does nothing for his weak chin. He appears to have three when he pulls his head back. Occasionally he fiddles with the folds of skin as he talks. I hope Aimee doesn't turn to look. Her repulsion would only grow.

"Don't worry. He's on the phone. You're safe," I say as I position myself between the window and her. I've already taken her drugs from her. I don't need to add to her pain.

"So tiresome," Aimee says and closes her eyes. A few seconds later she slumps onto the wall of the bus and a faint whistle of a snore comes from her. She sleeps until the hunt is over, everyone piles back on the bus, and we drive back to Rance's spread. I wake her by saying her name loudly. I don't want to touch her and get my hand swatted away because she thinks I'm Rance, like she did after brunch.

"Aimee, we're at the ranch," I say.

"Okay, let me know when it's time to get off the bus," she says and snuggles close to the wall.

"It's time," I say.

She opens her eyes and scans the interior. We're the only two people left.

"Where're Cindy and Natalie?" she asks.

"They rode up front with Drew," I say as I motion for her to get up.

She stands up awkwardly. She looks outside the window at the mass of people headed toward the house.

"Did anyone think it was weird that I was sort of passed out?" she asks.

"Drew distracted them with his moans," I say.

"Good," she says and follows me. I stop her.

"Rance is waiting out there for you. You sure this is what you want?" I ask.

"Yes, yes, yes. I admit it's not perfect, but he's a starter husband," she says.

"Do you like him even a little?" I ask.

Aimee looks outside at Rance, who is furiously BlackBerrying. His tongue touches his nose every now and then. Aimee smiles slightly.

"Yeah, I do. If he only could tone it down some and become a bit, I don't know, cooler, less needy," she says.

We walk off the bus. Rance immediately reattaches himself to Aimee. She goes with it but I can tell the onslaught of overpowering attention is a bit much. I want to tell him to chill out.

"I need to take a shower alone," she says quietly.

His face falls. The waddle slumps. He walks away from her into a group of hunters.

She goes inside. Her shoulders cave in a very non–Southern debutante way.

If I can keep Aimee off the drugs, I might be able to knock some sense into her. To make her examine whether giving away two years of your life to someone you can only tolerate as an acquaintance is worth it. I mean, to take drugs and trade her consciousness for a million-dollar marriage seems like a high price to pay.

We have a couple of hours of free time before the nighttime postroundup festivities begin. I shower and decide to dress up for the event so I won't be asked to handle any kind of reptile. I call Aimee and ask her to bring her dressy clothes over since I didn't bring any. Aimee jumps at the chance to leave her room. I can hear Rance in the background on the phone—it's obvious why she wants to flee. He's in complete business mode. He's practically yelling about a deal.

Aimee knocks on my door minutes after we hang up. She lays out a whole outfit on the bed in my room: a Versace dress that doesn't permit a bra and punishes any woman without sixteen-year-old tits; a thong with a rhinestone message on the back that spells, "U R Sweet"; and a pair of four-inch heels.

"You need a little lift," she says as she pulls out the duct tape, cuts off a piece, puts it on her pants, pulls it off, and then places it under my breasts. "It's less sticky this way and won't hurt as much when you rip it off."

"I went braless a couple of weeks ago and you didn't say anything about droopy breasts."

"You didn't ask me," she says.

She applies duct tape to my other breast.

Texans and duct tape. Even in the highest elevations of society, every debutante and maven uses duct tape, and probably keeps a roll in the pantry and a backup roll in the trunk of the Mercedes. There's a joke book that circulates in the newsroom every now and then called something like *How to Tell if You're Not a Texan*. It lists various phrases, which are dead giveaways, including, "You can't fix it with duct tape."

Aimee tells me to get into the thong and makes me twirl as she showers me with Coco perfume. No one has so thoroughly dressed me since I was two.

The dress hugs the right curves and skims over the rest. My breasts look perkier than I've seen them since prom night. The shoes make my calves look toned to the point of an Olympic athlete. I should get her to do this more often.

"Really nice," I say, appreciating her work.

"Years of practice," she says.

"What about you?" I ask.

"It'll only take a minute," she says and slips into a bias-cut Cavalli she brought with her. She doesn't do any of the prep for herself that she did for me.

"What about duct tape and all that?" I ask.

"I've done it all surgically. Really makes my routine a lot simpler," she says.

We walk downstairs to the party, which has started without us. Twenty or so people are two drinks into a good time. I see that other women thought the same thing I did. They are, for the most part, dressed to the nines. The men are a different story. They're in jeans, plaid shirts with the sleeves rolled up, and cowboy boots.

I see Jackson leaning against the deck railing. He holds court with a group of men, swapping war stories. He waves at us.

"You think he's cute?" I ask Aimee.

"Definitely."

"Even with all the cheesy machismo stuff and the waving."

"That does detract."

"I know. He's attractive, sensitive, smart, and dresses well, but I don't think I'm feeling it."

"You have to give it a chance."

"I have."

"For more than a day."

"He kissed me."

"And?"

"I keep rating his kisses while he's kissing me. That's not a good sign."

"How do you rate him?" Aimee asks.

"Good, firm. He's a sold kisser. Absolutely a B-plus. But it's not enough. It's like kissing a good friend."

"At least you didn't feel vomit in your throat."

"You're right," I say.

"You seem more chipper," I say.

She nods. I knew it. She swiped the pill bottle from the first-aid kit. I have to find it.

"You can't have it all in a relationship. I think you're real lucky," she says.

"What about when he finds out I'm Jewish?" I ask.

"I've been thinking about this and frankly I think it will work to your advantage as long as you're willing to convert to Christianity. If he can convert you, it'll be like an aphrodisiac."

I see Rance making a beeline for Aimee's ass. He reaches for her hips and doesn't let go.

"How are we all doing?" Rance asks and kisses Aimee's neck.

"Delightful," Aimee says as she maneuvers out of Rance's grasp, takes a step away, and grabs his hand with hers. She plunges her other hand into her purse.

"How was the call?" I ask Rance.

"We finally got it done," he says as he nuzzles Aimee again. She pops a couple of pills into her mouth.

"Do you have gum?" I ask her.

"Let's see," she says as she paws through her handbag. I take the bag to help her and palm the bottle. I think she needs just a little more time free of narcotics to contemplate a marriage to Rance.

"Never mind. I should eat something more substantial."

"Let's go see the gutting," Aimee says.

Not my idea of how to quench hunger.

A few feet away, hired men cut the now-dead snakes in two and scrap out gray guts. They tack the skins to long flat boards and salt them.

"Lovely," I say.

"It's really good to eat," Rance says as he queues up for a sample.

They actually grill the meat and eat it, usually with French fries and tarter sauce. As one might expect, there are annual rattlesnake cooking contests, with rattlesnake fritters, rattlesnake jam, rattlesnake chili, and other unsettling recipes.

Rance gets a snake kebab. I try a piece. It tastes like dry chicken. I bet it's low-fat. Still, I don't want more than a taste. I should have packed some protein bars or something to get me past this part of the ritual.

I see the pregnant woman and Bradford in line for kebabs. It looks like he's made some headway with her. He discreetly rubs her arm and she gives him an adoring smile. The sight of the two of them is almost enough to distract me from the women walking around in bikinis and high heels.

"What's going on?" I ask.

"Miss Snake Charmer," Rance answers.

During a roundup, a Miss Snake Charmer is named. Besides a bikini competition, the girls must show their prowess in handling the snakes. I wonder what kind of job application would include a place for this particular honor.

"Where'd you get these girls?" I ask as I watch women with fake 'n' bake tans and Vaseline-coated teeth strut around.

"Local high schools. They love to compete," he says as he eyes them with pride. Other men eye them with lust and bad intentions.

"What do they get if they win?"

"A ten-thousand-dollar scholarship."

"Not bad. Why didn't I do this in high school?" I ask and then the answer comes to me—I didn't live in Texas, the land of beauty contests.

I grab a margarita and head over to Natalie. She's staying on the outskirts of the party, tracking Bradford's movement.

"It looks like he's getting more comfortable with the pregnant girl," I say to her.

"Yeah, I think it's gonna happen tonight," Natalie says as she moves slightly to get a better viewing position of Bradford and the pregnant lady.

Meg walks up to us with Baylor and Jackson in tow. She has a smile on her face that spells trouble for me. I can feel it.

Jackson reaches me first. He grabs my hand.

"You look amazing," he says as he intently stares at me. Meg watches for a second, absorbing the scene.

"Honey, I was wondering if you could settle something for me. Are snakes kosher? I figured you'd know since you are of the Hebrew persuasion," Meg says.

"What?" Jackson says. The look of horror on his face says more than his question. As I suspected, Jewish women aren't high on his list of dating opportunities. He instinctively drops my hands and takes a step back. His eyes scan my whole body. It looks like he's trying to find proof of my heritage.

Baylor is quiet. His expression hasn't changed at all. His body language is the same as it was moments ago.

"My mother is Jewish," I explain, though I'm not sure why I need to.

"Doesn't that make you Jewish? I mean, they track it on the momma's side, don't they?" Meg asks.

"Yep, that's true," I say. "But I wasn't raised Jewish or with any religion, really."

"You never went to church?" Jackson asks, shocked.

"No, I didn't, except for funerals and weddings," I say.

"Wow," Jackson says as he starts walking in circles.

Meg's smile broadens. She's eating up Jackson's near hyperventilation. Baylor is silent, nonreactive. I can't tell what this means to him. Normally he's the one smoothing these situations over but now he's the passive one in the social crisis. I guess that tells me a lot.

"Come here," Jackson says and pulls me into the kitchen, which is the size of a gymnasium. We're talking four full ovens, an island with every cooking surface you can imagine, and two industrial dishwashers.

We dodge waitstaff and duck into the breakfast nook. Jackson tries to regain his composure. He nods to the staff as they walk by and waits for a calm moment. He takes a couple of passes at trying to talk and stops himself. He shakes his head and turns around twice.

"I want you to know that I'm not prejudiced," he starts off and points his finger at me. "Hell, Jesus was a Jew. You're the original tribes from which Christianity sprang. Meg caught me off guard."

"So what are you saying?" I ask, pointing my finger back at him.

"I want you to go hunting with me tomorrow," Jackson says.

"Why?"

"You're a natural and I think it would be good for us," Jackson says as he fiddles with some carrots on the counter. It looks like he's trying to build a carrot house. "We need to bond. We need some quiet time together."

"Okay, eight a.m.," I say.

"Six a.m. like we agreed to before, and that's late by hunting standards," he says.

"Fine," I say as he gives me a peck on the cheek and walks out of the kitchen. I rearrange the carrots on the counter. I'm not sure why I've just agreed to this date when I was pretty sure Jackson wasn't the one, but he's exhibited an open-mindedness that I didn't think he was capable of. Sure he freaked out like he found out I had AIDS when Meg said I was Jewish, but he recovered quickly. He's trying, which is more than I can say for Baylor. He didn't even talk to me.

Maybe this Jewish thing isn't such a big deal after all—for Jackson, that is. As long as I don't wear wigs during the day and a Star of David around my neck, it could be that Aimee was overreacting when she warned me not to talk about religion.

I walk out of the kitchen onto the deck. Meg is several feet away, being pinned down by Cindy. I can tell by the closed-lipped smile on Meg's face that Cindy is once again bringing up the subject of Byron. This is why I'd never want to get on Cindy's bad side. She's like a mole once she gets on a topic. She won't put it down until all her questions are answered. Right now, she's burrowing down into Meg's marriage and she's not going to let go of it until Meg cracks or leaves the premises. It's a nice reprieve to see Meg get screwed to the wall instead of her screwing someone else, namely me.

Aimee hangs on Rance. She looks content and drugged. She took enough of the pain pills before I swiped them from her purse to last her a few hours. I'd say she has until midnight before her serenity turns into disgust and panic.

Natalie is nowhere to be seen. Neither are Bradford or the pregnant woman. That's a good sign, I guess.

"Jewish, huh?" Baylor says.

"Yep, problem for you?" I ask. I can feel the cotton of his shirt brush up against my arm. I'm pissed off that he stood there and let Meg explode on me.

"No."

"That's a surprise to me, considering your college 'activities,' for lack of a better word."

Baylor looks shocked and hurt. "Why don't you let me explain somewhere more private? Let's go to your room," he says, gently pulling me back into the house.

"No, your room," I say, following him upstairs. I want to make some decisions here.

As we walk he tries to make conversation. I don't say anything. I want to make him feel what I did when Meg outed me. I never thought I would try to hide my heritage. The whole scene tonight made me feel dirty. Baylor's reaction topped off that feeling.

Baylor's room has a four-poster bed, an antelope head hanging above the mantel, a tortoiseshell lamp, a bear skin rug, and lots of plaid. I can feel the testosterone. I wonder if Rance asked the designer to make girl and boy rooms. The window of the room is open. It overlooks the party. We can hear the swing band from up here.

I plop down on the plaid couch. "So what do you have to say?"

"About my ancient college history? I know this won't be easy, but whatever you heard, I promise you it isn't true," Baylor says. He stands in front of the couch.

"So it wasn't you that was arrested for branding a Jewish student with a horrible insult? I believe it was 'Hebe.' I've read the articles, I've asked around—if it wasn't you, you'd better have a good story. Or are you just waiting to get me in a vulnerable position so you can give me a matching brand?"

Baylor seems even more miserable. But not like he's been caught. More like . . . he was remembering something that he never wanted to remember or talk about again.

"This was years ago. I was a freshman, and under eighteen. I'm not saying the branding didn't happen, that it wasn't my fraternity, and that I wasn't arrested. . . . but you have to believe, Jenny, it wasn't me."

"Who was it, then? Why the hell would you take the heat for something so heinous?"

Then it all made sense in an instant. His brother, Clayton. The obituary said he went to UT, too. He wasn't a minor and could have been arrested—and his name would have been revealed.

"I love my family. That's all I want to say. It's ancient history now, anyway."

"The year 1991 and banning Jews from the country club aren't so ancient," I say.

"My parents are wonderful people but they're members of some old-fashioned institutions. Just because they didn't speak up in public doesn't mean they agree with what happened," he explains.

"Would your parents welcome me to Christmas dinner?" I ask.

He thinks for a moment. "Of course they would. Do you even celebrate Christmas?"

I ignore his question.

"What about if we got married? What would they think of that?"

"It wouldn't matter," he says slowly.

"If I wanted to raise the kids Jewish?" I ask.

"We're getting ahead of ourselves, aren't we?" he says as he moves toward me.

"Why didn't you stand up for me?" I ask.

"What did you want me to do?" he asks.

"I wanted you to do what I've seen you do countless times. I wanted you to save the scene, swoop in and smooth everything over. Why did you leave me there?" I ask.

"I thought you could handle it yourself and I didn't know what Jackson knew," he says and plants a kiss on me. I don't have enough time to do anything but kiss back. My mind goes blank for a moment. I struggle not to lose myself in the kiss and push Baylor away.

There's a knock at the door. Meg says, "Baylor, Baylor."

We both freeze. She knocks again, tries the knob—which is locked, thank God—and hovers for a few seconds. She knocks again and says, "This is really important." She sounds drunk. She kicks the door lightly. We hear her stalk off.

"That's a little weird for the typical attorney-client relation-ship," I whisper.

"We'll deal with it later," Baylor says.

"But don't you think that was a little weird?"

"I swear to you I am only counseling Meg. That's why I didn't answer the door. But while we're on the subject, how do you know what you know about her predicament? You mentioned Rafe?"

"What does this have to do with Rafe?"

"I'm sure you can understand it's a delicate situation."

I'm giving him the coldest and meanest stare I can. I hope it works better this time than it did at the wildlife fund-raiser.

"I didn't know the whole story until I was deep into representing her. Now I have to finish it."

Okay, now we're getting somewhere.

"It's tricky."

"Are you going to tell me more than that?" I ask.

"Soon," he counters. He smiles and pats me on the arm.

"Now?" I ask.

"And ruin a pleasant evening?" he asks and walks toward the door.

"Wait. This is your room. Where are you going?" I say, and he pauses in the doorway.

"Do you want to leave, then?"

"No."

He starts to walk out again.

"I don't want you to leave, either."

Baylor stands there, drops his head, and measures each word as he says it, "Do you know what you want?"

The million-dollar question. I know Baylor is talking about more than which room I'm in. He's opened up a can of worms. We've been dancing around. What do we want from each other? From life? No, I never know what I want exactly and I sure don't know what I want from Baylor. I don't even know who Baylor is really.

"What do you want?" I ask him, instead of answering him.

He walks back into the room and shuts the door. He uses a voice that is earnest. I don't even find his lack of guile irritating.

"Relationships come down to those moments that are incredible," he says and paces. "The time you belly-laughed with her for a half an hour over nothing. The moment that you felt so incredibly passionate that you didn't care you were walking around the house naked."

Men have issues with their bodies, too? Or maybe he meant he didn't care if anyone else saw him walking around naked? This isn't the time to speculate. Focus. I study Baylor's face. He is con-centrating so much on what he's saying that I'm not sure he knows where I am in the room. He's trying to get this all just right. I can tell these aren't lines he's spoken before.

"The moment she was such a brat that you hiked her over your shoulder and swatted her bottom and she liked it," he says with a sideways grin. I can picture him giving that grin as a little boy be-fore he did something awful.

"They're the intangibles that make a relationship hold. Those moments sustain you during the mundane routine of life. You know, the times when you're washing dishes or changing a dirty diaper and you laugh because you think about the other times," he says and stops pacing for a moment to look at me.

"I think that a relationship works when you can find something to laugh about with your boyfriend while he's washing the dishes," I say without thinking.

"You're right. You should be able to find humor in every aspect of life"—he stops for a second to readjust his thoughts, then starts pacing again—"because those moments of humor reassure you that there will always be magic and the promise of spontaneity. It's part of what can only be explained as the underpinnings of trust, a belief that there will always be sparks."

"A belief you'll always be valued," I add.

"Exactly. I don't want to be a part of one of those couples that treat each other like good friends who have sex once a month," he says as he sits down on the bed next to me.

"This is about the sex. You want to make sure you have sex a few times a week," I say and move closer to him.

"It's not about the sex. . . . okay, it's about the sex and it's about the intimacy. I want to feel like the relationship I have with my wife is the only one like it in the world," he says and gets up. He starts to pace again.

"What's that mean?"

"It means I don't want to feel the same affection toward my wife as I do a golfing buddy. I want to feel more. I never want to be in a position where cheating is a more attractive option than coming home," he says.

"I'm with you there," I say.

"That's what I want," he says.

"So that's what you want? Not asking too much, huh?"

"I've learned from experience," he says, sitting down next to me again. He runs his hand along my arms, to my face, and back down my neck. He has the softest hands. His touch makes me lose my train of thought. I have to concentrate to formulate my response. I want to tell him the truth of what I need.

"I want someone I can feel good about being with. I want someone who's decent. Are you decent?" I ask and look him in the eyes.

"Yes," he says, looking right back without flinching.

"What did you do to Meg to end the relationship?"

"I told her she was trash and she'd never be anything different. I told her there was no way my family would ever accept her," he says, still looking me directly in the eyes.

"And?"

"And that meant I wouldn't accept her. I told her all of this Christmas day at a diner in Palestine in front of twenty or so people," he says.

"You gave a speech about Meg in front of these people?" I ask.

"I spoke very loudly at our booth," he says.

"You were a jerk."

"I was an absolute jerk. I'd never do that again," he says as he rubs his fingers up and down my arm.

"How does that fit into your definition of decent?" I ask, once again questioning if I should be alone with him, while getting distracted by his touch.

"It doesn't. I wasn't decent in that relationship. Neither was she. Meg brings out the worst in people. I was going crazy. I was in love with her, but she was married. She kept saying she was going to get a divorce but she didn't do anything. I kept trying to break up with her but then she'd do things like go home with me for the holidays," he says.

"How did she do that? Where'd Byron go?" I ask more out of amazement than actually searching for an answer.

"He was hunting with some buddies," Baylor says.

"Still, I can't believe you humiliated her like that," I say.

"I would never ever do anything like that again. That's part of the reason I'm helping Meg now," he says.

"Huh," I say. Not even in my circular logic does that make sense.

"I have to be decent," he says as he eases me down on the bed and starts to rub my shoulders and upper arms.

"We have to stop this. I'm not even sure I like you as a person," I say as I make a weak attempt to get up.

"I've made mistakes like everyone else in life," he says as he lifts my hair off my neck. The tips of his fingers brush my skin and send a crackle of electricity to my head. The small hairs on my skin stand up.

He rubs my shoulders. His hands are so big they make my bones feel as small as a chicken's, easily breakable and delicate. As his hands travel down my back, my head sinks to the pillow and I lay on my stomach. Both of his hands run slowly up and down my spine, kneading the muscles. It's a gentle rhythmic motion that I hope will never stop. The palms of his hands press into my skin as his fingers search for tension in my back. When they find a tight muscle his hands descend upon it and make it melt into something resembling gelatin. He mutters something to me in a soothing low voice about living on a farm. He talks about the morning routine of taking care of the animals and making a huge breakfast after.

"I thought you grew up in Dallas," I say.

"On the weekends I was always on the farm," he says, and then explains how you wipe down a horse after you take your morning ride, and that's all I remember. I must've fallen asleep.

I wake up early in the morning. I can see the light spilling through the window and smell lavender in the sheets. They must've ironed them with lavender water.

Baylor's still asleep on his side. His feet are touching me. I think we touched throughout the night, always seeking each other out. I know that as the sun was rising his hand was on my shoulder and I instinctively wrapped his arm around me.

His back looks delicious—browned and firm. The curve to his behind, the insistence of his shoulder blades poking out from the roundness: He is beautiful. The skin is unblemished. It holds the promise of something sweet and kind. I feel it in the back of my brain. Instinctively, I know he's a good guy. He has to be. No one that I want this much can be bad.

I peek at the rest of him. Judging by his chest hair, all dark brown, he doesn't dye the hair on his head. Good genes. His fingers are long and manicured. They seem like they could handle anything. His legs stretch on forever. He must be over six feet tall. His calf is probably the length of my whole leg and does a beautiful curve like a gentle S down to his ankle. I bet he looks good in shorts.

I must've studied him for several minutes. The sun is a couple of inches higher and is starting to spill onto the sheets. He moves his face away from the light. I slip out of bed, gather my shoes, and sneak out of the room. I'm sure the deer will still be around at noon. I'd love to walk back into Baylor's room and climb into bed. But I promised Jackson I'd meet him and I want to be a decent person, too.

Chapter Nineteen

Once You Have Them by the Balls,
Their Hearts and Minds Will Follow

—Originally Attributed to President Lyndon B. Johnson

drag myself to my room and get dressed. No time for a shower this morning, either.

I'm conflicted about this whole hunting enterprise. Shooting targets was fun, but I'm not sure about shooting a live animal. I'm also not real comfortable with spending time with Jackson on the pretense that we're building a relationship. It's becoming too difficult to juggle two men.

I throw on a pair of Maharishi cargo pants, my green Prada sneakers, a T-shirt, and a baseball cap. I toss sunscreen, breath mints, and a magazine into my pockets. *Who knows how long we'll have to wait for prey?*

I get to the deck. Dozens of people pack as much ammo as possible into their pockets. I didn't realize this was a group activity. I thought just Jackson and I were going.

I'm surprised to see Drew there, expertly chambering his large pistol, with another on his hip. His one calf is swollen so much that he has cut the leg of his pants up to his knee. He stands braced on his good leg.

"Hey, cowboy. Didn't know your feminine side allowed for massacring defenseless animals?"

"You will recall I am a professional athlete and hunting is a sport."

"What does one do with that many pistols?"

"Don't go phallic on me. Every red-blooded Texan likes a warm gun in his hand."

"You weren't even born in Texas."

"Honey, it's a state of mind."

"Seriously, it doesn't seem very safe to have all those guns. You could accidentally shoot yourself," I say.

"Yeah, but probably nothing vital. Maybe a foot. You notice how all the guns are pointing down."

"Speaking of your foot, how's the snakebite?" I ask.

He pulls his pant leg apart, revealing an angry, purple, swollen knot of flesh.

"Ouch, that's painful to look at," I say.

"If Aimee didn't act so quickly it would've been a lot worse," he says.

Jackson walks up to us, smiles broadly, and hands me what looks like a rifle, only larger.

"Hey, big fella. Gonna blindside some four-legged running backs this morning?" Jackson asks.

Without giving a reply to Jackson, Drew kisses me on the cheek and walks over to another group of burly men. He's used to weak football metaphors and no longer even tries to be polite when one is trotted out.

Jackson watches him go. I think he's a little upset that he didn't achieve maximum male bonding. He turns back to me with a brave face.

"This is your basic Winchester .270. Packs a wallop compared to what you used before. Don't rest it on your collarbone or the kick will snap the bone like a matchstick," he says.

"Can't I use what I had before?" I ask as I notice his left arm is bandaged and swollen. He must have come in second in the rattlesnake sack-stuffing contest. The guy in last place is probably puffed up like the Stay Puft Marshmallow Man.

"You're shooting a deer, an animal slightly smaller than a horse. You need a bigger gun."

I eye a pretty silver pistol in his belt. It has engravings of flowers and vines and a polished wood handle.

"What about that?" I say, pointing to the ornate weapon.

"This is for squirrel," he says.

Was each gun designed to be used for a specific animal? If so, I could understand hunting as man's attempt to accessorize.

He pulls out the silver pistol to show me and, sure enough, the things I thought were vines are tiny squirrels dancing along the barrel. He taps the big shotgun and says, "This is just about perfect."

I figure if I can shoot targets in the field and vampires on a video game, I'll be okay on the firing part. It's the actual killing that worries me—video games don't have any of that in 3-D.

"What happens if I hit something?"

"I'll be proud of you," Jackson says.

Jackson explains that I'll be in a blind with him, which is either a hole in the ground or one of those tree-house-looking things I've seen.

"So, this is sort of a blind blind date?" I joke.

Jackson smiles and kisses me on the cheek in a very chaste way. He grabs my hand. I try to avoid the gesture by becoming very interested in the ammo. He only holds my hand for a little bit. He gets too interested in my attire. He gives it a long analytical look.

"You mind getting blood on those?" he asks about my pants.

Before I have a chance to think about the implications of his question, Baylor walks up. I wonder if he saw the kiss.

"Those are some ugly sneakers," he says.

Men understand nothing about fashion. Sometimes ugly is ironic and cool. But I don't exactly blend with my environment or my hunting companions. Unless the wild game I've yet to see have Burberry plaid coats.

Baylor smiles at my discomfort.

"You'll do fine," he says. "I hear you're an excellent shot."

We walk toward the Jeeps together. In the manner of a polite cattle dog, Jackson separates us, herding Baylor with a group of more experienced hunters.

"Bill has been dying to talk to you, Baylor. Thought it'd be nice if y'all had some time to catch up," Jackson says to close any discussion about the three of us going off together.

"Besides, we'd just slow you down," he adds.

Texas manners prompt what men here call "cock-blocking." Meaning, it would have been rude for Baylor to argue with Jackson about his hunting preferences but it would've been much better for Baylor if he did. This is a quandary that's easily solved for the Texas male—manners trump territorial dating behavior every time.

Baylor's not happy about the situation, but Texas manners dictate that he must comply. Men never let another man see them seethe in a woman situation.

Baylor jumps into the back of a Jeep and gets his back slapped a lot. He sits down and stares at Jackson and me. If he had his druthers today, I think he'd hunt Jackson. The Jeep pulls away, stirring up so much dust as it goes that I can't see Baylor's gaze after a few seconds.

It's just me and Jackson and a whole lot of guns. We jump into the Jeep, drive about a quarter of a mile, and walk the same distance into the brush. He wrangles my hand into a firm hold for the Jeep ride. During the walk, I manage to pry free from his grip and wipe the sweat on my pants. I'm not a hand-holder by nature and the lack of clarity in our relationship makes the gesture feel wrong.

A big hole, about five feet deep, sits just behind a bunch of cedar. It has a couple of chairs and a cooler in it. We climb in. I feel like we're embarking on an adult version of cowboys and Indians.

"So now what?" I ask in a normal voice.

Bad move. Big faux pas.

"We sit as quietly as possible and wait," Jackson says in a barely audible whisper.

"I thought you wanted to talk," I say, perturbed that I woke up early to sit in a big hole and say nothing.

"Later," he whispers and motions for me to be quiet.

"What are we waiting for?" I whisper back this time.

"Mainly deer, and some exotic antelope that Rance imported from Africa."

Exotic antelope Rance imported from Africa. Try saying that ten times fast.

A couple of hours pass and Jackson seems to be in a cryogenic state. I see that he means business. This is going to be one long, dull day. I decide that hunting isn't a very good date activity, unless one of your criteria in a man is his ability to play dead for long periods of time.

I take out my magazine and flip through it. Jackson firmly places his hand on my wrist and shakes his head no. Page-turning is too loud.

I'm bored. I open up the cooler. It's freshly stocked with all kinds of beer and ice. I hand a can of Mexico's best to Jackson.

"You won't shoot straight if you drink it," he whispers.

"I won't ever shoot completely straight."

"Now, don't say that. You have natural talent."

A little fawn prances over to our brush and lies down. I hope we're not going to shoot her. I look at Jackson for guidance. He whispers to me that I should inch toward the fawn, stick my finger in her mouth to make sure it's warm and moist, and check her butt to see if she's well cleaned. If her mouth is warm and moist that means she's healthy. If her butt is clean that means her mother hasn't abandoned her, which means her mother is nearby.

"Why am I doing this?"

"'Cause you have a more gentle touch. You won't scare her."

"Yeah, but if the mother smells my scent on her, won't she abandon her?"

"That's birds."

"You're not going to shoot her mother, are you?"

"No, I won't shoot her."

I crawl with my belly on the ground, toward the fawn. She's so tiny, no bigger than a Jack Russell terrier, and the white markings on her back are as bright as white chalk. I pet her on the head. She doesn't stir. It's when I stick my finger in her mouth that she becomes contentious. She bucks and flays. I want to tell her I'm one of the good guys, not a hunter, but I still have to check her butt and, besides, is a fawn really going to listen? Her mouth is moist. Her butt's clean. The mother deer must be close by.

She is. She walks within ten feet of us. Jackson doesn't shoot. He's looking for bigger deer, I guess.

"Bambi killer," I mutter under my breath.

He hears me and raises his voice to a normal level to explain to me how important hunting is in balancing the ecosystem.

"Hunting restores the natural order. Do you know what happens when deer overpopulate? They starve to death," he says and waves the mother and fawn off.

Jackson has abruptly stopped talking and is staring into space. I don't think he's doing his normal quiet hunting stance. He could be having a seizure. I wave my hand in front of his face. He doesn't respond.

"Hello," I say quietly and then a bit louder and again louder. I am now talking in my normal voice.

I wave my hand in front of his face again. This time he grips my wrist.

"Jenny, I've held off saying this to you but I can't anymore. It's important," he says.

"What?" I ask.

"I need you to accept Jesus into your heart. I care about you and it's important," he says.

"Jesus was Jewish," I counter.

"That's a good start but I need to know that you understand that Jesus is our savior."

"He may be yours and I'm fine with that, but I'm not sold on him being mine," I say diplomatically.

"Of course, I understand." Jackson smiles at me and jumps out of the blind. He crouches down to my level.

"I'll give you some time to think," he says and walks away from me.

I am alone in a big hole in the woods. My options right now consist of trying to flag down someone for a ride, which would mean possibly walking into areas of the wilderness where men are shooting guns at random. I hoist myself up from the hole. I'm not carrying the Winchester back. Jackson can get his gun himself. I gingerly walk a few feet from our hole and listen for gun blasts or beer cans being opened. I don't hear any. I take a few more steps and listen again. I do this for a half mile until I make it to the road. It takes me an hour at least. Once I get to the road my walking speed increases to a near run. I'm fueled by anger and a desire to scream at Jackson.

It's afternoon by the time I get back to the house. I'm hot, sweaty, and very thirsty. I smell like I've rolled in something dead. I collapse on a chaise outside and ask a servant for a liter of cold water.

Jackson walks onto the deck and sits down next to me. I don't bother to move or acknowledge his presence.

"I probably owe you an apology," he says.

"Oh, that wasn't normal hunting protocol to leave your partner stranded?" I quip.

"I . . . I have a very personal relationship with God and he was telling me to get out of there," he says.

"Why? Why was he telling you that?" I ask as I take a large glass of water from a servant and gulp half of it down in one try. Normally, I'd be self-conscious about how I look or smell at this point, but now I'm flaunting my bad odor. I turn on my side, fully leaning on my sweaty armpit.

"Because I was corrupting myself." He looks down, already ashamed of what he's going to say next. "I can't be with a woman who doesn't believe in Jesus the way I do."

"I see," I say, not really seeing but not caring to understand.

"You do?" he asks, brightening up into his typical earnest mode.

"Yeah, we Jews don't like you Christians all that much, either," I say sarcastically.

"It's not that I don't like you. . . ." He trails off. "If you could convert to Baptist and swear to never practice any Jewish holidays, that would be a great start."

"It's okay. I get it," I say, cutting off any other awkward attempts he's about to make to explain his religious views. "I don't feel like talking about Jesus right now but I'll think about what you're offering. You still have some time to get hunting in," I say as I pat him on the arm conspiratorially.

He nods and walks off.

"Think about it. I think this could work given some religious readjustment," he calls back.

Thank God he's so easily swayed by hunting inducements. I don't want another religious discussion that doesn't go anywhere and never ends unless I promise to be dunked fully clothed in water.

I need a nap. I'm halfway across the deck when I observe someone tucked into a chaise lounge in the shade. It's Aimee again. There are a Coke and French fries on the table. She's nursing a beauty of a hangover.

I walk over to her.

"Did you hear any of that?" I ask.

"Enough. Well, how strongly against Jesus are you?" she asks.

"I think Jesus is okay. I don't think a guy who leaves a girl in a hunting blind is okay. He's not very Christian," I say as I finish off my water.

"He didn't."

"He did. You can tell Natalie she's not the only girl Jackson screwed over. How's Rance?" I say.

"It's getting better. Last night we had this huge fight about him touching me."

"How was he touching you?"

"Not how, just the fact that he was," she says. "I yelled at him for an hour. I ranted and ranted until there was nothing left and then he said, 'I don't want any more of those fucking potatoes,' and I laughed so hard. He can make me laugh," she says.

Translation: Those fucking potatoes is a punch line for an old joke about the time the preacher comes to dinner at a family's house. The husband complains about the preacher before he comes, says he always eats all the good food, especially all the fucking potatoes. The little kid takes it all in. When the preacher comes, the little kid asks if his father would pass the fucking potatoes. His father swats him on the head and asks him, "What is it you would like?" The son says, "I don't want any more of those fucking potatoes."

"He made you laugh on purpose or by accident?"

"On purpose. After that, I didn't mind it so much when he touched me. I let him give me a foot massage."

"That's pretty major. Were you on drugs?"

"I wasn't. Isn't that amazing? I mean, I think I'll still need them for sex but not for hanging out with him."

"So you had fun with him the rest of the night?" I ask, shocked by the turn of events.

"After I yelled at him, he told me all these horrible stories about high school, how the kids tortured him, threw him in lockers. It made me feel bad for him."

"That's called empathy," I say. "So someday you might be able to have sex with him without being drugged?"

"I could see that happening in a few months. Maybe by the wedding. And after a little bit of plastic surgery if I can convince him. Not now of course."

"That'd be a nice gift. Enjoyable sex on your wedding night. Where's Natalie?" I ask.

"It's only one o'clock. I doubt she's even woken up yet," Aimee says.

I walk into the house and up to my room. I need a shower and the sleep I missed out on to watch a Christian freak out and strand me in the woods. I sink into the down comforter and sigh so my whole body shakes.

I don't wake up until I feel bouncing on my bed, on either side of me.

"Stay still," I command.

"She did it. She did it!" Aimee screeches.

"I'm officially engaged," Natalie says with awe.

I grab her left hand and look at it. "There's no ring. You're not engaged until you have a ring," I point out.

"She'll have a ring by tomorrow," Cindy says in the distance. She must be sitting on the couch.

I sit up and rub the sleep from my eyes. I demand details.

Natalie walks to the center of the room and holds court. She tells us how as last night went on, Bradford became more and more friendly with the pregnant woman. At one point, he even massaged her stomach in the living room before he caught himself and pretended to be reaching for something across the coffee table. Natalie tracked them from a safe distance the whole evening. She wasn't spotted once. She might consider a career in husband-hunting for other women—meaning hunting their significant others' whereabouts once they're married. It'd be a useful service.

Natalie waited until Bradford went upstairs to the pregnant woman's room. She followed them and stood outside the door, staring at her watch for ten minutes. Then she burst into the room. She caught Bradford and preggers naked and fondling each other on the bed.

"It looked like a whale and a minnow copulating. It didn't seem right. She had these angry red stretch marks all over her stomach and he was licking them," she says.

"At least you know that he'll love you when your breasts sag and you get varicose veins," Cindy says.

So, Natalie continues, she gasps when she walks in the room and starts to cry. She falls to the ground and breaks into the lung-racking sobs that make you sore the next day. She's a method husband-hunter. Bradford freaks out. He tries to cover himself up with the sheet toga-style, leaving the pregnant woman completely exposed. He falls to the floor with her and tells Natalie it's all a mistake. When she says, "Oh please," he comes clean. He confesses everything. He leans into Natalie and starts sobbing. His tears fall into her hair and his snot drips onto her shirt. Natalie doesn't care. She consoles him as she shows the pregnant woman out of her own room.

"Who was this pregnant woman anyway? And where did she go?" I ask. I'm shocked I didn't hear anything about a naked pregnant woman walking the halls last night.

"I met her on Craigslist. She's a man-hater in need of cash. I paid her five thousand dollars plus travel expenses for the weekend. Anyway, I told her she could go to my room before the whole scene. I even ran a bath for her in advance," Natalie says.

"Is there a category on Craigslist that's called Man-Hater?" I ask.

"Something like that, darling," she says.

After a half hour of bonding in the pregnant woman's room, Natalie holds Bradford against her breast and runs her fingers through his hair. She rocks and soothes him like a baby, which he's also sort of into. When his sobs die down, she tells Bradford that she thinks it's best for him if he settles down because it will help him keep his fetish under wraps. Bradford looks up at her with the eyes of a confused and shamed man. "Okay?"

"Honey, people have already started to talk to me about how you're acting with this pregnant woman. It's only a matter of time before people figure out the extent of your sickness. I can give you cover," she says.

Bradford nods in agreement.

"Good, I'm gonna start telling people tomorrow that we're engaged. This is so exciting," she says and hugs him.

"You played that far, wide, and handsome," Cindy says.

"We're going to the jeweler the second we get back," Natalie squeals.

"Oh, darling, I'm so happy for you. We're both gonna be newlyweds at the same time. We should call Lizzy and tell her the good news. We could triple-date," Aimee says, and hugs Natalie.

Through the ups and downs of Aimee's drug haze this weekend, she did manage to keep an eye on Hoss and stay in constant contact with Lizzy. Rance paired Hoss, or J.T., with a hunting guide at the ranch who was with Hoss the moment he woke up in the morning to the moment he went back up to his room alone.

This is great, I think. They could do their divorces at the same time, too. Sorry, that's really cynical, but you have to remember that there's no shame in divorce in Dallas. Look at Cindy. She's been married twice and is still considered a newbie to marriage.

Thinking of Cindy, I turn to her. "Hey, what were you and Meg talking about last night?" I ask her.

"There's something real big going on with her and Byron. I think he might be filing against her soon. I can't figure out the circumstances, though. Is there a correspondent or not?"

"What's that mean?" I ask.

"Is he cheating on her? Is he upgrading to another model? I had her cornered for a while last night but she's a solid little liar."

Great, if she's single with a vengeance, I need to watch my back more than ever.

Chapter Twenty

Never Judge a Trophy Wife by Her Divorce Settlement

We get back to Dallas unscathed. Jackson hugged me and pressed a crucifix on a necklace into my palm when we said good-bye. "This is gonna be the start of something beautiful," he said.

Apparently the look of horror on my face didn't register. He's still on the three-kids-in-Waco track—that is, if I can change my religious ways. What's he going to give me next? A cookie with a picture of Jesus on it? It's funny: If converting wasn't such a big deal I probably would convert or raise my kids Christian, but since I'm being pressured into choosing one religion or the other, I'm not inclined to give up either.

Bradford and Natalie are on their way to buy some serious jewelry. I heard Natalie outlining acceptable parameters for a ring with Bradford as they boarded his plane. It can't be smaller than three carats and must be platinum, either round or square cut. Bradford nodded yes to everything Natalie requested. He seemed relieved. Having a socially unacceptable fetish was a huge burden for him. Natalie glowed with the satisfaction. She doesn't have to

move to Houston or Atlanta to date. She's finally sealed the deal.
Once she gets married her old nickname, Eight Ball, will fade.
Those men who passed her up the first time will give her another
look because as a married woman she's proven that she's desirable.
Who knows, they may be options for her second marriage.

As we board our plane, Rance and Aimee act somewhat like a
couple. She's completely off the drugs. There are no twenty-four-
hour pharmacies in remote Texas. Aimee laughs at Rance's jokes.
They have a few pieces of private couple's humor—a sign of intimacy. Aimee even takes Rance's hand unprompted. When we're
on the plane I get Aimee alone for a few minutes and whisper to
her, "What's going on? You actually seem to like him."

"I don't know. Maybe it's how generous he is, or how patient.
He's a good guy," she says, as confused as I am.

"Sex?" I ask.

"Oh, I still have to be on the verge of being passed out," she says.

On the plane, Cindy is calling all her sources to ferret out more
information about Meg. I don't quite get why she's so obsessed. I
ask her about it and she tells me she is doing me a favor, protecting me from Meg.

"Information is power," Cindy says.

"I think you like the power," I say back.

"That's horrible. I care about you," she says.

Baylor and I are in a weird limbo. He saw Jackson hug me and
he winked at me and handed me a note. The note said, "Looking
forward to seeing you in Dallas."

What does that mean? It's so nothing. He could've written it to
a friend, to Jackson. Why even write it? I have no idea what our
night together meant to him or what he thought when he saw
Jackson and me together. I don't think he's an anti-Semite anymore, just somebody with a family who's made some mistakes;
though I still think he is a womanizer or something. The way he
treated Meg was brutal. I can understand why she's so screwed up,
if other guys did similar things. I'm not sure I want to see him
again after hearing what he did to her. But then I think of his hands
on my back and his definition of what he wants, and my heart
starts to melt.

Drew acquitted himself well at the hunt. He killed Bambi or Bambi's dad. I mean he bagged a really big deer. The other hunters were saying his name with reverence. His reputation as a manly man is intact for another few months. He moans on the plane all the way back home. He makes us bring him drinks and food and whenever anyone complains he hikes up his pants and reveals his calf. The sight of it makes everyone, including me, shudder and scurry to get whatever he wants. I will never play around with a rattlesnake.

Once he gets home, he plans to stay in bed for a week to recuperate. He's hoping to get a nice male nurse to help him get back to top health.

I start back at work bright and early Tuesday morning, but not early enough. Work is frantic all of a sudden. I get in at eight a.m. and the office is already hopping. A half-dozen reporters are in the full throes of interviews and writing. It's earnings season. It comes four times a year, every quarter. To us, it's like Christmas rush on steroids.

I write about missed earnings targets, accounting irregularities, and hostile bids. It's like the business community is a volcano erupting. In three days I write two stories. I write a total of seven stories this week. That's more than I write some months for the whole month. I'm at work until nine every night. It feels good to be so productive. Carol is so busy most nights, she approves of my pieces with very little editing and I notice they go in the paper virtually untouched.

This week she doesn't even snap her gum aggressively at me when she walks by. She doesn't give me an evil-eye stare. Thursday I lean over Skip's cubicle and say, "I haven't been yelled at yet this week. That's a record."

"Good for you," he says.

"I liked your follow-up twisty cat story," I say. Skip went in after me and wrote a poetic story about the freaky twisty cat cult of people who despise regular cats. This is a huge exaggeration of the actual circumstance but no one complained. I guess a story is true if no one asks for a correction.

"Yeah, Carol loved it," Skip says and smiles.

"What's up?" I ask.

"There's a position open in New York and after the twisty cat story Carol said they're considering me for it." He practically bounces in his chair.

"That's great," I say, and mean it. A few months ago I would have been bitterly jealous since it was my fondest wish to be sent back to New York to work for the *Journal*. Something has happened over the last few weeks, though. Chalk it up to Carol's cruelty rubbing away any enthusiasm I had for reporting maybe, or just a natural growing up. Reporting isn't the glamour world I thought it was and I've realized it may not be the fulfilling destiny I had hoped for. I haven't figured out what is yet. I know it's out there, though.

Tonight, I have a late dinner with Cindy. She invites me to the restaurant at the Adolphus Hotel, an old-school glamour place. The chairs are heavy carved wood with thick cushions made of crushed peach velvet and the tables are layered with lace cloths.

This is husband-hunting territory for the advanced.

Cindy glances at a couple of men with big bank accounts and there are no women in sight. But that's all, no flirty line or eye flutter. She doesn't have to do much more. They know who she is because she's already been involved in high-profile society for a few years and she knows them. By glancing at them she has signaled she's available. If they're interested they might stop by the table later or get her phone number from a mutual friend. At this level, a woman doesn't have to work that hard. She has already proven she is comfortable with the type of people a wealthy man mingles with and she knows how to dress for the occasions he must attend. She has the companion seal of approval.

Her elevated husband-hunting stature agrees with her. I think she may have started eating regularly. She's not as skeletal in her silver Armani silk top as she usually appears.

"What's going on with you?"

"I need a new hobby," she says.

"Rich men don't do it for you anymore?"

"I don't need them anymore," she says as she checks out the major jewelry on her wrists and fingers, "though I don't mind them, either."

She checks out an attractive man with silver hair and an impeccably tailored suit.

"What do you need?" I ask. I finally realize Cindy is going through a transformation that's bigger than husbands and hair color. I think she's becoming a person rather than the cardboard cutout of the society snake she used to represent.

"Honey, look at this," she says as she pulls a photo album from her purse. "Open it."

I do. It's filled with pictures of her and different men. I recognize some of them. One is her first ex-husband. Another is her second ex-husband. I notice, too, due to the miracles of modern science, Cindy looks more attractive as she gets older in the pictures.

"These are a lot of the men I used to husband-hunt," Cindy says. "It's sad, isn't it, that these are my memories."

"I don't know. Most of my albums are filled with ex-boyfriends."

"Yeah, but you cared about them."

"You cared a little."

"Sure, a little, but that's not enough, darling."

Cindy launches into a doctoral thesis of husband-hunting. She explains the pitfalls and the positives. She's proud of the intellectual challenges she's conquered to be successful, that is, working around signing a prenup and getting to the altar.

She's happy she took the quick route to wealth and, as a result of two well-placed marriages, never has to work or wed again. She views herself as a tough-minded entrepreneur. That, she says, is the key to surviving these relationships: You must think of them as business transactions, never let emotion get in the way. You have to keep your mind on the goal and do whatever it takes to get it, she says.

This is why she shakes her head in dismay over Aimee; she's let her own emotions get in the way of the goal. She's mistaken her relationship as real, which makes her miserable because she'd never want to be with Rance in a real relationship. That's why she lashed out at Rance publicly this weekend. Very bad form in Cindy's book. A husband-hunter doesn't embarrass her prey by saying "Get your hands off me" when he's surrounded by his friends. She doesn't have that luxury.

"Aimee miscalculated how Rance feels, too," Cindy says.

Rance knows this is a business transaction. While he enjoys the business, he can very easily end the deal.

"Aimee thinks she's something special and she's not," Cindy says. "She has to make sure Rance feels loved and adored. She can't do that if she's trying to make herself emotionally satisfied."

"You're just bitter."

"Darling, I've played this game longer than all of y'all combined. I know the deal," she says.

Cindy runs through the informal husband-hunter commandments that include: Never embarrass your potential husband, always show interest in sex, and love everything he loves.

"Aimee's trying to have a real relationship with a target," Cindy says.

"I think she's trying to make the next two years of her life more meaningful than your businesslike marriages. Can't you understand her wanting to like Rance?" I ask.

"Maybe the irony is that I don't like men," Cindy says.

"At all?"

"I don't think so."

I laugh, think about what she just said, and laugh more. After all the work she's had done, the countless hours she's spent under the knife, recuperating, working out, and trying to be as attractive as possible to men, it turns out she doesn't want them or need them anyway. She can read my incredulity.

"No more marriage?" I ask.

"No," she says. "Either way, you get your dog back."

Translation: It's like the small-town veterinarian who doubles as a taxidermist. Either way you get your dog back. It's a way to describe those circumstances where no matter what you do, you get a variation of the same outcome and it ain't pretty. No matter who Cindy marries or dates, he still comes packaged with a penis and an attitude.

"What about dating?" I ask.

"Well, of course, honey. I'm not dead," she says as she surveys the room, "but I'll only date someone I'm attracted to."

"That's good. It opens up the playing field," I say.

"What?" she asks, jolted from her scan by my comment.

"I mean if you're only dating, you don't have to date rich," I say as I notice a group of men checking out our table.

"Oh no, whoever I date has to be rich. If he wasn't, I couldn't be sure he really likes me," she says.

So the expert husband-hunters don't like to be hunted themselves. I guess we all harbor some double standards.

When our waiter comes to our table for our last-call request, I realize what time it is. The unemployed or idle don't typically understand such things as long workdays and having to get up at six a.m. the next morning. I mention that I need to get going but Cindy orders another bottle of wine so we can continue to talk strategy and philosophy of husband-hunting. Even if Cindy is giving it up, she's happy to help me.

"What do you think about my chances with Baylor?" I finally ask her. This is the thing I'm dying to know but am afraid to ask anyone, lest I get laughed at for being a major goober since everyone has told me in no uncertain terms to stay far away from him.

"I'd never say this about Baylor. I've never said this about Baylor before, but I think he'd be good for you and you'd be great for him. You'd kick his butt mentally. I think he's the kind of guy who needs that. Maybe that will make the two of you stick," she says.

"So the Jewish thing? The Meg thing? They aren't big deals?" I ask.

"Meg's already done her worst to Baylor. She led him on during the first year of her marriage and he tore her up when he broke up with her. The Jewish thing—we warned you about that before. I'd just tell you to be careful."

"So you think it's okay?" I ask for clarification and confirmation.

"I think you're going to do it anyway. I'd just tell you that Baylor isn't as sweet and gentlemanly as he appears to be. If you want to keep your heart intact, the safe money is to erase his number from your phone," she says as she downs the contents of her wineglass.

I shouldn't have asked the follow-up question. I would have been a lot happier with her first answer. Her continued condemnation of Baylor gives me pause, well, more pause. I've already been given lots of reasons to have pause. I'm the only one who thinks getting together with him is a good idea.

I've resisted calling him all week or answering his calls because I thought I needed to clear my head. I also was a little afraid that the blocked caller ID numbers could be Jackson, and I absolutely didn't want to have another conversation about religion, Waco, and children. Jackson did courier over a copy of the New Testament earlier in the week and he sent flowers, but he hasn't gotten more aggressive than leaving a couple of phone messages a day. Baylor has left a couple of messages the whole week. On both he sounds casual. He has mastered the "Call me when you can" carefree attitude that I have never been able to achieve. I haven't called him back but I know I'll see him at Lizzy's wedding this weekend.

In full disclosure, I saved his messages and play them again and again.

Chapter Twenty-one

Sometimes Love and Money Mingle,
But Not a Lot

By Friday night, I am feeling the toll that working at full speed for a week takes on your mind and body. I slowly gather my things as I wait for the okay from Carol to leave the office. All the other reporters left hours ago. I'm waiting for her to approve my story. My stomach is so empty, I think it's eating my other organs as a survival mechanism. Luckily, I have no plans tonight. I'm going home, slathering on lotion, and going to bed early. I want to look my best for Lizzy's wedding tomorrow.

I peer over my cubicle wall at the den of evil that is Carol's office. Her feet are on her desk. She's on the phone and she's laughing. Hello, how about my story? Did you forget about me?

I slink back down in my seat and pull a pack of gum out of my desk drawer. I chew each piece like it's a meal. I surf the Internet. I straighten my desk. I read the millions of press releases that are piled next to my computer.

An hour later Carol walks out of her office, turns off the lights, and walks toward the door.

I pop up.

"Hi," I say.

"I didn't know you were still here," Carol says, surprised.

What does she mean?

"I was waiting for you to edit my story," I say.

"I sent it," she says as we walk out the door together.

"I wish you had told me," I say, trying to control my rage.

She shrugs. She says nothing else.

We ride the elevator in silence. We walk to the parking garage matching steps in silence. She is the most socially awkward woman I have ever met. I have to say something.

"Carol, why didn't you tell me I could go home?" I ask before she opens her car door.

"It's not my responsibility to tell you when to go home," she says.

"You would've been pissed if I left," I counter.

"I would've called you on your cell phone," she says as she opens her car door.

"I don't think you're very considerate," I say.

"It's not my job to be considerate."

"What is your job? To humiliate me on a daily basis? Since I started working for you, you've done your best to make me feel incompetent," I say.

"Has it made you a better reporter?" she asks.

"Maybe. I know it's made me hate reporting," I say.

"Maybe you're not cut out to be a reporter," she says and gets in her car. I want to pound on her window and tell her she's not cut out to be a boss. I want to throw a rock through the rear window. I need a new job. I'm going to quit next week and make myself figure out what it is I want to do when I grow up. I craft and recraft how I'm going to tell Carol that I quit, as I drive home. There are plenty of other jobs out there. I can work for another paper or freelance or go back to school. The thing I finally realize is that working at the *Journal* isn't the be-all and end-all. There's life after working at one of the best papers in America, especially when I don't even know if I want to be a reporter anymore. The thought is freeing. I don't have to be miserable at work.

I'm so glad to get home and slip into bed.

The next morning I wake up early, shower, and eat before Aimee returns from Rance's. I chug my fifth bottled water of the day. I hear that if you drink enough water you won't get wrinkles as quickly. What's enough? I wonder as I go to the bathroom for the fourth time in an hour. I'm peeing clear.

Aimee struts into the house encased in a Badgley Mischka beaded burgundy dress. It's floor length with spaghetti straps and a plunging neckline, which dives so low that if she were a man you'd know what religion she practiced. I bet it cost twenty thousand dollars.

"This one or this one?" Aimee asks as she holds up an Ungaro white silk chiffon ruffled dress with a lot more décolleté than the Mischka, if that's possible. That costs thirty thousand dollars, I'm sure.

"The Mischka. This is a wedding, not a Miami nightclub."

I couldn't fail to notice the rest of Aimee's accessories when she walked in. She's decked out in several carats of diamonds. Her neck is loaded down with a diamond-studded choker. Her earlobes drip with diamond chandelier earrings, which have two-carat stones anchoring them. Even her big toes have little diamonds placed in the nail polish. She's carrying three Judith Leiber bags, shaped as fruit, on her arm. She is a picture of conspicuous consumption. The cost of her accoutrements could feed a small nation.

"Looks like you have a new best friend," I say, motioning to all the diamonds. "How much did all that set Rance back?"

She slows for a second and catches the reference. "I have no idea. I keep charging things on Rance's American Express and he doesn't say squat."

"Things going better?"

"I'm appreciating the perks," she says with a smile.

"Looks like you're draped in them."

I grab my red Marc Jacobs dress with the fishtail—we're talking updated sixties. We head out.

Even though neither of us is in Lizzy's wedding, we're getting our hair, makeup, fingers, and toes professionally done because that's what Texas women do for any important occasion.

At the salon, Aimee convinces me to go all-out retro. The stylists set my hair in big Brigitte Bardot curls, tie them up in a high ponytail, and add extensions. They put fake eyelashes on me and draw black liquid eyeliner on my upper lids. Then they paint red lipstick on me. I look like I'm going to a costume party. Aimee assures me that Dallas women go all out for weddings and I'll fit right in.

"You'll see lots of hats, drawn-on eyebrows, and gold lamé."

"I don't want to be one of those women everyone talks about after the wedding," I say.

"Trust me, you'll blend. Picture a hundred Elizabeth Taylors and you'll get an idea of the guests."

It sounds like Sunset Boulevard come to life. And it is. When I step out of the limo I see that Lizzy's wedding planner has set up a wedding equivalent to a red carpet.

A white carpet leads from the limo drop-off to the backyard. The women filing in work it. They wave, air-kiss, or do a two-hand squeeze. No hugging allowed. It would mess up the dresses.

I spot couture Chanel, Dior, and Saint Laurent.

Up close each garment looks like a piece of art. It is hand-stitched from fabrics that don't appear in most clothing stores. These are more lush, supple, vibrant. And the fit. The dresses look as if they were sewn onto the women who wear them. They meticulously follow each curve, disguise every bulge, and accentuate the attractive parts of the woman. It's a best friend made out of fabric.

Seeing these women walk by me and stand next to me, I feel inferior in my off-the-rack creation. I find myself smoothing the creases that have formed in the front of my dress during the car ride, trying to make my outfit equal. But it can't—it doesn't have the pedigree.

"Don't worry. You look gorgeous," Aimee says as she walks past to find Rance.

"Not that gorgeous," I say under my breath as a woman walks by with a dress made of silk ribbons woven together like a basket. I spot Cindy. She looks sublime in a dress of pink marabou feathers.

The hats range from the wide-brimmed film noir types with an assortment of flowers, veils, and fur covering them to pillboxes made of leather, suede, or the traditional linen. I can't carry off anything outside of a baseball cap. But these women know how to wear hats. They walk around with such confidence and authority that I wish I was wearing one.

I'm glad I went all-out sixties. Aimee was right. I'd be underdressed otherwise. I wave to Tommy Sue and her fiancé, Chase. Her body is so skinny it seems like it could break if Chase wasn't there to hold her. Poor girl, still killing herself to be the ideal woman for a man who doesn't notice the effort. He'd be just as happy with a woman who could give him a good lap dance.

I spot a well-muscled chest moving in the distance. It must be Baylor.

I watch him shake hands and do the single-cheek kiss to women. He can't take a step without greeting someone. The man is a high-society slut.

He notices me watching his slow-motion approach and gives me the eye roll that says "Sorry about this" and blows me a kiss. My toes tingle and I wonder if anyone can see me blushing under my makeup. He glances back over to me again and again.

I can't take my eyes off him. I'm sweating. I can feel him watching me watch him. I feel like I'm posing for my high school yearbook picture. My smile is forced and I have no idea what to do with my hands. At first, they're resting on either side of me at my hips, but that feels too androidlike. I cover my chest and grab my elbows but I think that says I'm defensive. I clasp my hands behind my back. That works for now.

White-gloved waiters mix into the crowd with crystal glasses on silver trays. Baylor grabs two. He is magnificent in a white tuxedo with a pink tie. He walks toward me with the grace of Cary Grant. He hands me a glass.

"I missed you," he says.

"Me, too. It was earnings week at work so I was doing fifteen-hour days," I say as I feel lust surge up from my belly. I'm sweating even more. Why didn't I call him? That's right—I can't think when I'm near his voice or body, and everyone I'm on speaking terms with in Dallas has told me to avoid him.

"And I thought you were playing hard to get. I left you dozens of messages," he says as he escorts me behind the house. "I even thought of driving by your house."

"Thought of driving by or did it?" I ask.

"I think silence is the best answer," he says. I wonder how many times he drove by. I hope my blinds were down.

The wedding is in Lizzy's backyard, which is ten acres of manicured grounds in the heart of Highland Park. Paper lanterns and candles hang on every branch. White peonies wrap around tree trunks, spring up from the ground, and float on the ceiling of the tent, which covers a hundred tables and a wooden dance floor. It looks like a fairy land; everything is soft, floaty, and white. This is the wedding Lizzy's been fantasizing about since she was seven. It's a Barbie dream wedding come to life.

In a back corner of the tent is a nod to Hoss's personality: The bar is made of ice and in the shape of a longhorn, the University of Texas mascot. The bartender will shave off any part of the bull you request to create a frozen margarita. Too many drunken frat alum requested shaved balls; the bull is now neutered.

Next to the bar is the groom's table, which consists of a cake carcass. I guess the drunken frat boys got hungry. The cake used to resemble a longhorn, too. Now it looks like roadkill. Burnt orange frosting bleeds onto the white tablecloth and the chocolate-raspberry innards spill onto the floor.

"The man loved his college years," Baylor says.

"What?"

"Burnt orange is UT's color."

"I guess I knew that."

"Hook 'em horns," Baylor, says flashing the UT hand symbol.

"You know, in other cultures that means 'cuckold.' "

Baylor laughs. "That's what I love about you. You never let me get away with anything."

"At least he's not wearing an orange bow tie," Aimee says, referring to Hoss, as she comes up behind me.

"Was he going to?"

"Oh, they fought about it."

"I don't understand this desire to hold on to your college years to such an extent that your wedding becomes a frat party," I say.

"You're not a Greek," Aimee says dismissively.

I'm surprised that Aimee willingly approached Baylor and me. I wonder if this is a silent approval of him as my new prey. She knows he knows about my Jewish thing and that he isn't freaked out by it. She also knows how attracted I am to him from the mere fact that I've asked her a million questions about Baylor in the last few weeks. I tried to be subtle but the sheer quantity of questions gave me away.

She looks back and forth between Baylor and me, trying to ferret out just where we are in our relationship. Her eyes are much more awake than normal.

I know that in the last week, she's made a concerted effort to cut down on the Vicodin. She told me she only takes one pill at a time when she's with Rance, which makes it easier for her to walk unassisted and talk without slurring as well as speak complete thoughts.

She wraps her arm around Rance's as he joins us and says, "What do y'all think of a December wedding in St. Barth's?"

"We haven't gotten that far yet," Baylor says.

"Oh, not for you, for us," the ever-earnest Rance responds.

Leave it to the socially naïve to salvage a potentially awkward situation.

"That sounds beautiful," I say to Aimee, but she's absorbed in Rance. If I didn't know better, I'd say she's looking at him adoringly. Maybe it could be love or an intense fascination with wobbly chin skin.

They glide off. I see her look back at us out of the corner of my eye. She looks pretty sober.

"Here's to weddings," Baylor says and clinks glasses with me.

Bells chime and white-gloved help usher us to our seats.

Hoss waits at the altar. He bites his fingernails and bounces on the pads of his feet. He is so good-looking that he makes you doubt whether he's attractive or not. I think the best way to describe him is clean. His hair is so sharply cut, it looks like it's drawn on. His face is so symmetrical and his features are so inoffensively perfect that he gives the impression that all humans could look the way he does if they put some effort into it. His tuxedo is creaseless.

Two white poodles walk down the aisle, wearing little tuxedos. The wedding rings are strapped onto pillows on their heads. The dogs obediently trundle to the altar and sit down next to Hoss. The trainer stands close by, intently staring at the dogs, making sure they stay. He even has a little remote control electric device to shock the canines into obedience. I see him press the button manically when one of the dogs tries to lick his balls.

Lizzy's sorority sisters prance down the aisle next in matching Luca Luca fifties-inspired strapless lemon dresses with full skirts. They have on white gloves. Their hair is slicked back into tight buns. Lizzy's not close to them anymore but it's like a rush rule that you have to have your sorority sisters in your wedding.

Lizzy walks down the aisle with her father. He looks like an older model of Hoss. Tall and clean with a glimmer of intelligence in his eyes, he makes good arm candy.

Lizzy's face is peaceful to the point of beautiful. All the surgery, exercise, and hours of rehabilitation have transformed her into a size 4. Her dress, made by a small French design house, is layer upon layer of handmade lace. Her veil trails ten feet behind her. She looks old-fashioned in a classic sort of way.

The guests all hold glasses of champagne in their hands, which the waiters continually refill. In Dallas, it's very in vogue to drink before, during, and after the wedding. A couple of waiters are assigned the extra task of bouncer/babysitter for rowdy guests. The misbehaving guests are hunted, trapped, and escorted inside the house. They are held there until they calm down, their spouses retrieve them, or the service is completed. It's an adult time-out. I see one woman in a large feather-covered pink hat swearing like a professional athlete as two waiters grip either arm and drag her away from the wedding.

"Goddammit, you motherfuckers, let go of my arms and I promise I won't yank your little balls off and stuff 'em down your throats." Others try not to stare. They glance discreetly, shake their heads, and grin. The list of people who wouldn't mind one of their peers stumbling off the pedestal is long.

"She's not coming back," Baylor says.

"How do you know?"

"That's Meg. She doesn't cool down easy."

"Meg? I didn't recognize her. Why is she so mad?"

Baylor looks at me. "You really don't know? I thought you'd figure it out."

"Well, I didn't," I say as I shake my head no. He takes my hand and pulls me out of the row to a spot behind a giant rose plant. He whispers the story.

When I told him I knew Rafe, he thought I'd done some serious reporting to get to him. Apparently Meg never passed on the fact that I used to date Rafe. For months, Byron has been in active pursuit of a divorce from Meg so he can hook up with a more fertile womb. Meg has indeed gotten pregnant (thanks to Rafe) and is trying to stave off the proceeding until Byron can be convinced that the baby might be his, or at least that people would believe that he's the father. Byron has already found a replacement and is eager to divorce her before the five-year mark.

Per their prenuptial agreement, if they're still married after five years, Meg gets fifteen million dollars rather than the two million she's entitled to before that time mark. She's pushing the five-year mark now.

"Byron wants to either change the agreement and wait and see about the baby or leave Meg now," Baylor says. "He says, 'What's the worst she can do, have my baby without me?' "

True, for a man who doesn't calculate love into the marriage.

"He's a ruthless son of a bitch. Treats his marriage like a business deal," Baylor says, shaking his head.

"What about the fact that it isn't even his baby?" I ask.

"Deep down he knows that. He knows he can't have kids and he knows that this is his only respectable shot at an heir and a kid just about everyone thinks is his. In his family, adoption isn't an option," Baylor says.

"But he's still trying to hook up with a younger, more fertile woman?" I ask.

"That's all guy pride. Smoke and mirrors. He knows in his core that if he ever did that and that new young wife didn't get pregnant, the fault would be all his."

"So then, what's the problem? Why isn't he agreeing to stay with Meg?" I ask.

"Byron has more guy pride than common sense. Meg has to blackmail him and manipulate him into it," Baylor explains.

"No way. No guy can be that dumb," I say.

"He married Meg in the first place, didn't he?" Baylor says.

All the pressure is getting to Meg. I'm sure being at a wedding hammered home her situation. To make matters worse, Baylor tells me, Byron's new talent, the one ready to fill Meg's position, is here at the wedding.

Is all this driving Meg back into Baylor's arms? Baylor senses my discomfort. I must have physically recoiled at the thought of Meg being single again.

"Don't worry, I don't befriend women, I represent them," he says and pats my arm.

That's not much consolation considering Meg's ruthless techniques in nabbing men. I see Byron out of the corner of my eye standing with a young blond who's definitely in the prime of her childbearing years. The man is attractive and has good manners, but he has no soul. He doesn't seem to care that his wife has been carted away by security.

"I think she should get a new lawyer," I say a little too loudly, as the wedding has progressed to the silent moment when people can voice their objections. I hope people don't think I'm talking about Lizzy. A couple of women look back at me and nod their heads in agreement. Yep, they think I'm talking about Lizzy.

Luckily the minister didn't hear and the nuptials continue to "You may now kiss the bride." Hoss takes Lizzy into his arms and arcs her back almost to the floor. I hope her bruises are healed. He plants a long, full kiss on her, as if to prove that there's more to this union than money.

Several people stand up and applaud the display. I do, too. That's the thing about weddings—you have to put all your misgivings about the relationship on hold and hope it's gonna last. Even Drew beams for the new bride. He half stands, half leans on his chair. I can tell his calf is still enormously swollen. I don't think he'll be dancing later.

Baylor and I chuck large tapioca grains at the bride and groom. Doves and peacocks are released but they don't fly anywhere. They walk around the yard picking at the tapioca.

Note to anyone marrying: Never have peacocks at your wedding. They may be pretty, but they squawk loud and often. They sound like very large cats in heat.

Four waiters carry the wedding cake to a table next to the band. The cake's icing is tortured into the shapes of violets, lilies, roses, peonies, and daisies cascading down its five tiers. It looks like a garden. We wander over to our tables and waiters appear from nowhere. They serve foie gras; an apple, pear, and walnut salad; quail and other game. I stop counting after the third course. With each course, they serve a different and delicious glass of wine and keep refilling it. There must be six different glasses of wine in front of me. I can't eat or drink anymore. I would like to take a nap.

The band plays softly as we eat. An older woman, who's a renowned jazz and blues performer, sings. It feels like a nightclub in New York without the smoke and crowds. I heard Lyle Lovett is playing later and can't even guess what that cost Lizzy and Hoss. Scalpers get four to five hundred dollars a ticket when he plays anywhere in Texas.

Lizzy and Hoss skate onto the dance floor and execute an elaborate number, which looks professionally choreographed. They even work in the pretzel, something every Texas man tries to twist a girl into while dancing. It involves several turns with changing hand positions that resemble a pretzel. Unfortunately you're the one doing most of the twisting.

Others float onto the floor. Waiters pass out cashmere wraps to women whose nipples become the biggest accessory on their bodies.

A couple behind us argues over how much this event cost. The final consensus is in the range of a couple million. It's much less than it could have been because Lizzy's parents already owned the diamond tiara she's wearing.

Baylor pulls me onto the dance floor. I've never been much good with my feet, I hate to admit. I've been avoiding this moment. Baylor, like all Southern men, attended cotillion dance lessons, and dancing to him is about as natural as shooting a rifle.

"Relax. Let me move for you," he says.

He expertly guides us through the crowd and keeps his feet out of my way. I even let him dip me and I don't fall over.

I'm lost in the magic of feeling Baylor's body brushing mine until I hear screams coming from the house. Meg, never one to shrink from the limelight, is making sure her presence is known. Baylor mutters, "Damn," and sprints toward the house. I race after him.

In the kitchen, Meg is throwing glasses and plates, and screams, "Do you know who I am?" The bodyguards/waiters duck and weave as they try to move close and restrain her.

Baylor strides into the kitchen, past the help, grips her wrists hard, and forces her arms down. He's two inches away from her face and enunciates his words very clearly. I can tell he's giving her a dressing-down that's worse than anything I've ever heard him say.

I move closer to the door.

"You're being selfish and ugly. This is Lizzy's wedding, not Meg's tantrum day. I'm getting your driver to take you home," he says.

Meg's body sinks but she still has some defiance in her.

"No, I don't want to leave my husband with that goddamn cat in heat," she says.

"You're not helping your case. You need to clean up, eat, and get healthy. Listen to me, Meg. You have to calm down."

Baylor leads Meg out of the house toward the car with his hand firmly on her elbow. She looks at me standing by the door, twists her face, and says, "What the hell are you doing here? I thought Baylor dumped your ass."

She makes it so easy to hate her. There she is spewing complete nonsense, ruining what was one of the most perfect moments of my life. Of course, the psycho part of my brain immediately starts spinning—how can Baylor break up with me when we've just gotten started? He seemed so happy when we were dancing. If Baylor heard her, he didn't say anything.

They're halfway to the limo when Meg performs a wrestling countermove worthy of the pro circuit. She breaks free. She sprints directly for the wedding and Byron. Oh, this is bad.

Fortunately, Texans forgive bad behavior more readily than people in other parts of the country, since at any given ceremony or public event they are just as likely to have acted like a drunk horse's ass themselves. They seem to treasure misdeeds and rebellion as signs of the state's character. More than once I've witnessed a drunken acquaintance hold center stage when he was too incapacitated to form sentences. The day after the inebriated performance attendees simply brush it off as "too drunk to fish."

Translation: The phrase is one of several ways to describe the inner bubba in all of us. In this context, it has the dual purpose of suggesting that the speaker has some redneck ancestry while conveying a level of alcohol consumption that compromises even the simplest motor skills.

Meg grabs Byron by the shoulder, smiles, and punches the other woman by her right ear. The cat in heat stumbles backward but doesn't go down. Meg winds up again and lands another punch between the girl's eyes, even as Byron and Baylor both try to grab her. Meg's rings alone are enough to do major damage. This time the cat in heat goes down, collapsing into a group of society matrons and, honey, there isn't a lot of padding on these bony broads to cushion the cat's fall. Blood streams out of her nose and onto the silk and feathers she landed on.

About twenty people crowd around the finished fight. The music's too loud for the rest of the party to be alerted to Meg's meltdown. Baylor, ever the lawyer, moves in fast. He organizes five beefy waiters to help him: Two carry the bleeding woman into the house and lift up the crumpled mavens. Three escort Meg and Byron to their limo. Meg hangs on to Baylor as he accompanies. He turns around, scans for me, and our eyes meet. *Not this time,* I think, and run after him. I catch up with him in the final few yards to the limo where he carries Meg. We all slip inside.

Meg and Byron sit at opposite ends of the limo. Baylor and I form a human wall between them. They don't talk for the entire ride back to their house. When we drive up to their Versailles-inspired home, Meg climbs out of the limo with her chin held high, posture stick straight, and the gait of a supermodel. She is a study in decorum. We all follow her inside. She promptly disappears down a long hallway.

We walk into the living room. No sign of her there. Baylor walks into the dining room and stops.

"Oh, no. Get down from there," he says.

"No!" she screams as Byron and I walk into the room.

She squats on top of a very expensive mahogany inlaid Biedermeier table. I don't think she's wearing underwear.

"No, no. What are you doing? Get down from there and let's talk," Byron pleads. He's an antiques nut in the first degree.

Meg smiles and pees right on the shiny wood.

"You shouldn't shit where you eat," she says.

Byron, in pure panic, throws his hairpiece on the urine in an effort to protect the wood.

"Why don't you take everything from me, you witch? Damn it, Trudy, get out here with towels!" he yells and a maid comes running. Baylor throws a silk damask pillow on top of the mess in an attempt to help.

Meg, with the elegance of a ballerina, descends from the table. She reapplies her lipstick.

I look on in shock. I had no idea Byron was packing a falsie. It must be made out of real human hair that's washed and styled daily. Man, those are common in the South. Ohh, this is too much.

Meg walks straight toward Byron. He takes a couple of steps back, obviously terrified.

"I love you, Meg. You're the love of my life," he says.

"No matter who else you sleep with," she says.

"No matter," he says.

She punches him in the face. He falls like a great redwood onto the plush Oriental carpet. The girl has a good right hook.

I bend down. Byron appears to be temporarily unconscious. After a few seconds he slowly shakes it off. I help him sit up.

"Do you want him, too? Or just Baylor?" Meg asks me as she rubs her right hand. I hope she doesn't try to clock me.

"That's enough. Meg, you have no reason to be angry with Jenny. You and Byron need to talk this out," Baylor says as he lifts up Byron and firmly grabs Meg's arm. He leads them to the living room and puts them on the couch.

"Neither one of you is getting up until this prenup and pregnancy thing is resolved!" Baylor yells.

"That's blackmail!" Byron yells back.

"It's better than getting punched in the face again," Baylor replies.

Byron is silent.

"Do you love Meg?" Baylor asks Byron.

"Yes."

I'm not sure if he's answering from true love or true fear.

"Do you love Byron?" Baylor asks Meg.

"I suppose."

"Do you want to raise this child together?" Baylor asks.

"Yes," Byron says.

"Then, why are you fighting over it?" he asks Byron.

"She's damaged goods," he says.

"You're saying that the woman you love is damaged goods because she had trouble conceiving a child?"

"I guess," Byron says.

"You guess? You guess? This is ridiculous. She's having a child, one that she went to a lot of trouble to conceive for you. You should be overjoyed, not fighting," Baylor says, and pulls a piece of paper out of his jacket pocket.

Byron eyes the paper but stays still.

"Do you want to have an affair with some little bitch, get caught, have Meg beat the crap out of you, and go through a messy divorce? This is a revised prenup. It says lots of things about you giving Meg a more equal share of the estate. I advise you to sign it, then be happy that you are being given the gift of a child and celebrate."

Byron picks up the pen and pauses. Meg cracks her knuckles. He signs the paper.

"There. Prenup changed. Meg now gets fifteen million no matter what. Now you can focus on your other issues. We're leaving," Baylor says as he scoops up the piece of paper and grabs my arm. He leads me upstairs.

"Where are we going?" I ask.

"Not a lot of fun being a lawyer," Baylor says as he loosens his tie, not answering me.

"Why did you do this? It's so far away from your duties as an attorney."

"You know what my momma taught me? When someone betrays you, go out of your way to do something nice for them. They'll always feel like hell for treating you bad."

"So now Meg regrets dumping you?"

"No, she regrets treating me like a piece of trash and forcing me to dump her," he says as he tucks the paper back into his pocket.

He leads me to a bedroom.

"We're not staying here," I declare.

"Nope," he says and opens a drawer in the nightstand. He takes out a gun and puts it in the waist of his pants.

"Just in case," he says.

"Wait a second," I say as I walk over to the other nightstand and remove another gun.

"Smart." He smiles, and kisses me as we walk out of their house fully armed.

We drive back to my place and collapse into bed.

Chapter Twenty-two

Mating Ain't Easy Even with a Contract

That night, Baylor and I sleep like we did at Rance's place, touching each other throughout the night. I'm upset when someone insistently knocks at my front door at eight a.m., disrupting what was the most relaxed I'd been since I moved to Texas. I grab a robe and head toward the front door. I peer out the window and see Rafe's Honda in the driveway.

Is this about Mr. Tatters?

I open the door. Rafe stands with his shoulders caved in, sobbing. I immediately usher him inside and plop him on the sofa. I sit next to him.

"What's wrong? What happened?" I ask. I'd rather not have Baylor wake up and walk in on another man crying. It's a little awkward to have your old boyfriend and your new you-don't-know-what meet so early in the morning and so early in the relationship.

Rafe can barely get words to come out. He chokes out syllables for ten minutes before I get that this is something about Meg.

"What happened with Meg?" I ask.

"She's pregnant and she doesn't want anything to do with me anymore. She gave me a five-thousand-dollar bonus and good-bye sex," he says.

I'm wishing Mr. Tatters had had the chance to give Meg a good-bye present as well, hopefully in an expensive pair of shoes.

"Well, that's not such a bad deal," I say, trying to cheerlead him. "I mean, come on, you don't want to be a dad. You don't want to deal with such a high-maintenance woman for the rest of your life. Meg would run you. You'd be her servant twenty-four hours a day."

Rafe sniffles and considers what I'm saying. He must be running images of waiting on Meg hand and foot, as well as changing diapers, in his head. He stops crying altogether for a few seconds, wipes his eyes and nose with his sleeve, and then starts up again. He must have remembered the sex.

"I want her. She won't even take my calls anymore. She says our agreement precludes us from having any more contact," he says as he pulls out his cell phone to triple-check that he hasn't received any calls from her.

"When did you sign an agreement?" I ask.

"At the beginning of the whole thing, when I didn't care about any of this," he says as he picks at his jeans.

"Honey, I'm sorry, but you agreed to this. You have to accept the consequences," I say. I hate to admit this, but Meg is right here. She paid him, he signed a contract, and he fulfilled his part of the agreement, as she did. Situation over. He should curse his high sperm count.

"It can't end like this," he insists. "I'm not done."

"What else can you do? You signed away your parental rights. I think this is a case of you wanting something you can't have. At some point, you have to get over the whole teenage-me stage," I say, getting upset with Rafe myself. Haven't I been telling him the same thing for years? Why didn't he ever listen to me?

"You never understood me," Rafe says as he tries to kiss me.

"I never understood you and yet you want to have sex with me? Rafe, I think you need to leave," I say, and get up off the sofa. Rafe follows my lead. He follows me to the front door. He tries to kiss me again. It's a halfhearted attempt at best. I push him off easily. I open the front door and push him out.

"I'm disappointed in you," Rafe says as he walks away.

"You need to grow up," I say as he opens the door to his Honda.

"I need to grow up? I'm the one who is acting like an adult with you and with Meg. It doesn't matter. You won't be seeing me anymore," Rafe says.

"Why?" I ask.

"Meg got me a job at the *New York Times*. I'm leaving in a couple of weeks," Rafe says.

"Good luck. It sounds like you got a good bonus out of the contract," I say.

"I totally deserve it," he says with all the subtlety of a five-year-old explaining why he should be allowed to eat the whole tub of ice cream. He slams his car door and tries to peel out of my driveway. Instead his little fuel-efficient car sounds like an angry sewing machine.

I close the door and sigh. I'm glad that was a short-lived temper tantrum. It could have been much worse.

"What a jerk," Baylor says over my shoulder. I turn around and see him dressed in nothing but his boxer shorts, white with green polka dots.

"Why do you think so?" I ask, turning completely toward him.

"Because he's only thinking about himself. Meg, the child, Byron, and about a dozen other people are involved in this situation. He's only thinking about how he can continue to have illicit sex and get paid for it," Baylor says as he walks toward me.

"If he was smart, he'd be pushing Meg for a second child," I say.

"Now you're thinking like a lawyer. But he'd have to wait at least a year to have sex again," he says and comes over and kisses me. I kiss him back. I don't feel like holding anything back now.

"Well, it sounds like she's worth it," I say.

"Not as much as other women," he says as he takes my hand, pulling me back toward the bedroom.

"Sure you're okay with dating a Jewish girl?" I ask, stopping his movement.